THE
MISSIONARY

THE MISSIONARY

WILLIAM CARMICHAEL
AND
DAVID LAMBERT

Revised Version © 2024 by
WILLIAM CARMICHAEL AND DAVID LAMBERT

All rights reserved. No part of this book may be reproduced in any form without permission in writing from the publisher, except in the case of brief quotations embodied in critical articles or reviews. Original version of this book published by Moody Press, 2009.

Editor: Elizabeth Newenhuyse
Interior Design: Amit Dey
Cover Design: Robin Black

1.Missionaries-Fiction. 2. Americans-Venezuela-Fiction. 3. Revolutionaries-Fiction. 4. Homeless-Fiction. 5. Mystery-Fiction. 6. Thriller-Fiction. 7. Political-Fiction. 8. Venezuela-Fiction.

ISBN: 9781632696090
Library of Congress Control Number: 2024948052

We hope you enjoy this book from Deep River Books. Our goal is to provide high-quality, thought-provoking books and products that connect truth to your real needs and challenges. For more information on other books and products written and produced, go to www.deepriverbooks.com or write to:

Deep River Books
1610 W. Williamson Ave
Sisters, OR 97759

1 3 5 7 9 10 8 6 4 2

Printed in the United States of America

DEDICATION

To Nancie and Cindy

"The tragedy of the world is that men have given first class loyalty to second class causes and these causes have betrayed them."

Lynn Harold Hugh

ACKNOWLEDGMENTS

Thanks to Gary, Greg, Mary, and Jose for being such great hosts and being so helpful with the research for this book while in Venezuela. And thank you also for your tireless work in the barrios. You are the true heroes.

Thanks also to Dr. Robert Hakala and Dr. Walt Larimore for your assistance in medical issues. Without your help, I'm sure our handling of wounds, illnesses, and their treatment would have made any medical professional cringe. Thanks also to Paul Walerczak, a seasoned professional pilot with 6,000 hours of flight time in a variety of aircraft flown all over the world, for checking out our flight and aircraft data.

Gracias to Roberto Miller for correcting our Spanish.

And thank you, Heather Kopp, for your editorial help and encouragement with an early draft of this manuscript.

Life turns on small choices.

A last-minute decision to take a shortcut over a snowy pass.

A shrugging dismissal of the odd-looking man in the long coat standing off to one side.

A decision to postpone a physical exam till a less busy time.

A word spoken with the best intentions.

Looking back, after the lives are destroyed, the blood spilt, the families shattered, and even the courses of nations changed forever, the mistakes that started the doomsday clock ticking down often seem minor, even innocent—even virtuous. So easy to make.

David Eller would give anything—no, everything—to go back and undo those mistakes. But life does not give us that chance. Like everyone else, he has no choice but to dangle from the hands of that clock, trying in vain to pull them backward as they tick inexorably toward zero.

CHAPTER ONE

The tall man guided his new Mercedes out of Avenue Casanova traffic and pulled in behind a battered Volkswagen at the gutter; he had just seen the Ford van several cars ahead of him pull over and stop, its emergency flashers on. He leaned to the side, straining for a clear view around the cars and trucks honking, jockeying for position, crowding the avenue. It was late—10:34, he affirmed with a glance at his Rolex—and the glare of so many lights on the rain-washed streets made him squint. He watched the van's driver get out, wait for a break in the traffic, and then jog across the street toward some sort of commotion. There were children running—one was on the ground, a small boy. A heavyset man in a dirty white apron was yelling at the fallen boy, kicking him, and the boy curled into a ball. A girl threw herself between the fallen boy and the man; the man pushed her down. The van's driver arrived and held up a hand, yelling at the man in the apron, who yelled back.

There was nothing unusual about the scene. It was played out scores of times on this and many other Caracas streets every night: hungry, homeless children scrabbling for a living, treated as nothing more than human refuse by the adults annoyed by them or who sought them for other purposes. One needed no more excuse to kick—or exploit, in any of dozens of unsavory ways—a street urchin than one did a stray dog.

The tall man had seen the driver of the van, a missionary, make several such stops over the past few days, usually at night, chatting with groups of these children, teasing them, making them laugh, talking to them as long as the children were willing to stay. Twice the tall man had managed to get close enough to overhear the missionary asking kids where they lived, whether they had enough to eat, whether any of them were sick or knew other children who were sick, whether there were other homeless children nearby.

The name on the side of the van was *Espere la Aldea*. Hope Village. The tall man knew exactly where it was; he had driven past it, slowly. It was a mission—a place that took in young homeless ones.

The missionary stepped between the angry man and the two children on the ground. The girl was talking to the fallen boy. She looked worried. The man in the apron pushed past the missionary and grabbed something from the young girl's hand, then brandished it at the missionary—evidence, no doubt, that the children had stolen from him. The missionary pointed toward the children, spoke to the man, and then reached into his pocket and offered the man something, most likely money to pay for what the children had stolen. The man grabbed it from his hand and stalked away, still yelling back over his shoulder.

Three or four other children wandered back as the aproned man disappeared. If these children had a home with a bed, they would undoubtedly have been in it by this time of night.

A group of young men walked by, their clothes and voices loud, one or two of them taking swigs from their bottles of beer. The avenue was crowded with those seeking thrills, as well as the homeless. From across the street, a prostitute caught the tall man's eye and waved. He ignored her. Peering around a passing truck, he watched as the missionary knelt and placed his hand on the forehead of the young boy the man in the apron had kicked.

This was a good thing that the missionary was doing. The tall man admired him for it. Yes, it was time to meet him face to face. Maybe he was the right man for the job. Maybe not.

The rain had stopped, at least for now.

"*¿Es relacionado cualquiera a este chico?*" David asked. He removed his hand from the child's forehead. The boy was burning with fever, gasping desperately for breath; his chest rattled.

"*Sí.*"

David glanced up at the girl who had tried to protect the boy; she could not have been more than ten.

"He is my little brother. He started coughing five days ago," she said. "And after he runs, he cannot breathe."

"What's his name?"

"Ricardo. My name is Angela."

David smiled and touched her arm. "Angela, where are your parents?"

Angela shrugged. David saw this response often. It meant that the girl's parents were drug addicts, or that they were dead, or that she had no idea where they were and probably hadn't seen them in some time.

He brushed Ricardo's lank hair from his forehead. For five years now David had patrolled the *barrios* of Caracas, witnessing the misery of an endless supply of impoverished and sickly and homeless children. Was there no end to the suffering here?

Swarms of Latinos hurried by in the warm, humid night, seemingly unaware. Salsa music blared from one of the bars down the street. Honking cars, trucks, and buses jammed Avenue Casanova. The stink of urine rose from the gutter, a bitter note blending with the fragrance of fresh *arapas*, frying chiles, refried beans, and beer. "*Vamonos, arribe!*" someone yelled from down the street.

Ricardo stared at David with sunken, panicked eyes, his back rising off the broken sidewalk in his effort to pull air into his lungs.

"How old is your brother?" David asked Angela.

"*Siete.*"

There was no point calling an ambulance. They refused to pick up the homeless. David pulled out his cell and called his wife. "Christie, call Doctor Vargas and see if he can meet us at the clinic in forty-five minutes. Tell him I have a seven-year-old boy I think is in the acute stages of pneumonia. He can barely breathe."

4   The Missionary

There was a pause. "Is he wheezing?" she asked.

"Big time."

"Okay. Get him here quick."

When David clicked off his phone and reached behind the boy to lift him, large olive-skinned hands reached down to help. David looked up to see a tall, well-dressed man.

"Can I please help you lift the child?" The stranger spoke in English. "We can put him in my car just down the street if you need transportation to the hospital."

"Thank you," David said, "but my van's right here." He gestured toward the white nine-passenger Ford van he used as both bus and ambulance. It was double parked, emergency flashers blinking, *Espere la Aldea* painted in bright red letters on the side. "I'm taking this child to my clinic."

Before David could object, the tall man lifted Ricardo's thin little body into his arms and headed for the van. David grabbed Angela's hand and, weaving through honking, halting traffic, hurried ahead to open the back doors. Inside lay a mattress neatly wrapped with clean white sheets. The man gently laid Ricardo on the mattress.

David motioned for Angela to climb into the back of the van with Ricardo. She hesitated. "What about my friends? Two of them are also coughing."

David looked back across the street, where seven children stood watching. He glanced at the well-dressed man, who shrugged.

"We don't have room," David said. "I'm sorry. Right now, I can only take your brother and you. And for your brother's sake, we must hurry."

"Then take Maria instead of me. She has been coughing for three days," Angela replied.

David looked at the stranger, then across the street again. "Jesus!" he whispered, then asked, "Which one is Maria?"

Angela yelled, "*¡Maria, viene!*" motioning Maria forward.

A girl David guessed to be about the same age as Angela wove her way through traffic toward them. Without asking, Angela quickly shoved Maria up into the back of the van next to her brother.

Always choices, David thought, *and most of them are bad. How can it be the will of God to simply choose among the least bad alternatives?*

He put his hand on Angela's shoulder, urging her into the van with Ricardo and Maria. As she scrambled in, she smiled. *Already a skilled negotiator,* David thought.

David shook the stranger's hand and hurried to the driver's door. "Thank you for your help." He grabbed a business card from the dash and handed it to the man, then cranked the engine and slammed the door. "Why don't you visit us?" he hollered through the open window, over the engine noise.

"I would like to. Perhaps soon."

David barely heard him. He waved over his shoulder and inched out into traffic, his headlights reflecting on slick, wet streets. Ricardo hacked a loud, wracking cough.

David took a sharp right, leaving the business district and entering a darker, less congested area, a faster way home. Big raindrops began again, slowly at first, then pounding hard and fast against the windshield while the wipers beat like rapid rubber drumsticks. And there was another sound. At first David thought that the windshield wipers were broken—the motor giving out, wheezing…and then he realized that the sound was coming from the back of the van. It stopped. David glanced in the rearview mirror. The boy's sister hovered over Ricardo. "Angela, how's your brother back there?" David asked. "Everything okay?"

Angela's little face tilted up, her eyes frightened. "Senor!" she said. "He cannot breathe! He is choking!"

CHAPTER TWO

On a remote beach several miles south of La Guaira, they slipped ashore an hour before midnight, undetected except by the small pod of dolphins that followed their ten-foot inflatable to within a hundred yards of the beach. Their GPS took them within fifteen feet of the location they'd targeted. They pulled their craft onto the beach and crouched next to it for a few minutes, listening, watching shadows. Then the leader of the four men gestured, and the man to his left ran in a crouch across the deserted beach to the rocky slope behind it. In the light from his tiny waterproof flashlight, he found the package exactly where they'd been told it would be. He signaled with his flashlight to the men waiting by the inflatable, who pulled the craft the rest of the way across the beach into the shadows.

The leader of the four Israeli mercenaries took the package, wrapped in plastic to protect it from the rain, and carefully opened it. Code-named Hawkeye, he was not a big man by Western standards. At 5' 10" and 180 pounds, he wouldn't have looked out of place dressed in casual clothes and walking down the streets of any city in the Western hemisphere. He'd just turned forty-one. His skin was a sun-darkened bronze. He had black, short-cropped hair. There was a small scar on his right cheek, just under his eye, from an earlier wound. It had damaged a facial nerve, which made his right eye twitch when things got tense. With the body of a decathlete and a razor-sharp mind, he had excelled in every aspect of his training. Never impatient, never over-confident, and always alert to his surroundings, Hawkeye was, in all aspects, a killing machine.

8   The Missionary

The package, as he had expected, contained fake ID's, room keys, and directions to the resort hotel where they would stay, along with the equivalent in Venezuelan cash to twenty-five thousand U.S. dollars and the key to a waiting vehicle.

No stranger to this kind of work, Hawkeye hired out all over the world. Although earlier he'd done it for love of country, now he did it for money. Big money. His last assignment had been for the CIA in Uganda, Africa, secretly exterminating the thugs who were terrorizing the country.

"Drop!" came a nearly inaudible voice, and all four men dropped, disappearing into the shadows. Each immediately saw why the command had been given: wandering down the beach from the north came a solitary figure. A man. He seemed in no hurry. There was something in his hand. If it was a weapon, he was a dead man. Hawkeye flipped down his night-vision goggles, then shook his head. It was a bottle. The man was walking slowly because he walked clumsily, unsteadily. Just a drunk.

But the drunk nearly stumbled in the slight rut made by the inflatable where the mercenaries had pulled it across the beach. When he regained his balance, he gazed down, then turned to follow the furrow with his eyes down into the waves—and turned again, craning his neck forward as if to try to follow the furrow up the beach in the pale light.

Hawkeye felt the man on his right tense, and he put out his hand and touched him. Not yet.

A long moment passed. No one moved. Then the drunk lifted his bottle, tilted it straight up as if draining it, tossed it away into the waves, and continued down the beach.

The four commandos remained motionless until he was out of sight, another minute for good measure, and then at Hawkeye's signal began gathering their equipment. One opened the valves on the inflatable and sat on it to speed its deflation. Another used a branch to obliterate the trail their boat had left across the sand.

They bedded down across the highway, hidden among palm trees and tall grasses, relieving each other on watch every two hours.

CHAPTER THREE

David skidded the van to a stop on the muddy gravel beside the road, threw open his door, and slid through the mud to the back of the van, pelted by warm rain. As he opened the back doors, rain poured in, and he motioned Angela and Maria back away from the opening. He grabbed a blanket and handed it to Angela. "Try to hold this over him to protect him from the rain," he said.

Ricardo's chest was heaving, his eyes were no longer listless but now bright with panic, the cords of his neck strained taut, and most ominous of all, no sound of breathing came from his open mouth. *A fish out of water*, David thought. He pulled the boy toward him, felt his chest, his neck, looked into his mouth—and realized that he had absolutely no idea what to do. He grabbed his cell phone from his belt and hit Christie's speed-dial button.

"He can't breathe!" he yelled when her voice came on the line. "Nothing! No wheezing, no air at all. What do I do?"

A slight pause. "You said he was wheezing when you first picked him up. Was his skin dusky, slightly grayish or bluish?"

"I don't know! I mean, the light wasn't good, and now we're out alongside the road—"

"Okay. You said it looked like pneumonia, right?"

"He's burning with fever, he couldn't breathe—"

"Was he running or exerting himself before you found him? Do you know?"

"He—the kids had stolen some food, and the vendor was chasing them. Ricardo fell down."

"Okay, I think we may be dealing with two different things here. Look in the emergency medical bag. Pull out the epi pen."

"The what?"

"Dump out the bag."

David hit the speaker button on the phone, put it beside Ricardo, and then dumped the contents of the medical bag. "What am I looking for?"

"A plastic ziplock bag. Inside there's a tube about the size of a cigar. Orange cap."

David rummaged frantically. "Okay. I have it. Now what?"

"Take it out of the bag and out of the tube. You'll have a pen-sized syringe in your hand with a black rubbery tip at one end. Got it?"

"Yeah. What now? He looks bad—like he's about to lose consciousness."

"Jam the black rubber end of the tube against the fattest part of his thigh. Not too hard! You're not pounding a nail—you're giving a shot."

"What about his pants?"

"Forget about them—go right through them." She paused. "Okay—have you done it? How's he responding?"

"I haven't—"

"Do it! Right now! Don't think about it!"

David slammed the pen against Ricardo's thigh, felt something give. *Too hard!* he thought. *I broke something.*

"Done?" Christie asked.

"I—yeah."

"Okay, now watch him."

Fifteen seconds passed. Twenty.

"Any change?" she asked.

"Nothing. Not yet."

"Get ready. You might have to do CPR."

David pulled the boy toward him, wiped mucus from Ricardo's nose and mouth, and positioned the barely conscious boy's head toward the left. He tilted Ricardo's jaw upward—and suddenly Ricardo gasped, arched his back, then doubled forward, gulping air.

"Okay, something's—he's gasping," David said. "He's getting air."

"The pen's working. The epinephrine is opening his airways."

"He's—he's smiling."

"They usually do. From the relief."

"He's okay."

"He's *not* okay. He's still in danger. Check the rest of the bag—is there another epi pen?"

David sorted through the pile of medical supplies. "No. That's it."

"The effects of the injection will wear off in twenty minutes, maybe less—maybe only fifteen. How far are you from the clinic?"

"In this rain—maybe twenty minutes."

"Put the pedal to the metal, hon. Get that boy here now."

David had seen Christie watching through the window as he pulled the van up behind the clinic, and she pulled the rear door open as he jogged in with the weakly gasping Ricardo in his arms, Angela and Maria trailing closely behind. He lowered Ricardo onto the nearest bed. "The relief lasted pretty well for about ten minutes or so," he said, "and then he began to labor a bit, and for the past few minutes it's been almost as bad as before."

Christie appeared at his side and without hesitation or wasted motion slapped another epi pen against the boy's leg. As before, twenty or thirty seconds passed before Ricardo's airway suddenly opened and his lungs expanded fully. After several gasps, he coughed heavily, and Christie handed the boy a Kleenex to spit into. His features relaxed; panic eased from his face.

David stepped back and wiped his sweating face with both hands. "So..." he said.

"Not sure. Maybe exercise-induced asthma, or even something he ate," Christie said. "You said he'd been running before you found him?"

"Chased by a vendor," David said. "The kids had, uh, helped themselves to some food. Ricardo couldn't keep up. The vendor got in a couple of good kicks before I could get there, so you might find some bruises, too. Or worse."

Christie shook her head as she positioned her stethoscope to listen to Ricardo's chest. She listened with full concentration for several seconds, her brows slowly knitting, glanced up at David with eyes full of concern, then shifted the stethoscope's position and listened again. She would say nothing within hearing of the children about the congestion in Ricardo's lungs, David knew, lest she frighten them, but her look had already told him that she was alarmed.

"It's always more than just one thing," she said. "The conditions these kids live in... Well, I need to get him intubated and set up a portable humidifier. Why don't you get these girls some snacks out of the cupboard?" She inclined her head toward the far side of the room and cocked an eyebrow. Clear message: *Keep them occupied.*

It was only a few minutes later, though, that Christie joined them, giving her attention first to Maria. She placed her hand on the girl's head and smiled. "*Como se llama usted?*" she asked.

"Maria," the girl answered with a shy smile.

"Me llama Señora Eller," Christie said. "Would you sit here on the bed, please?" Christie pointed to an empty bed. When the girl was seated, looking nervous, Christie held up her stethoscope. "Now, Maria—have you ever seen one of these? I use it to listen to your heart. Want to try it?"

The girl nodded, eyes large.

Christie placed the earpieces of the stethoscope in Maria's ears and the other end over her own heart. Maria's mouth popped open in surprise. "Hear it?" Christie asked. Maria nodded. "Now listen to your own." Christie placed the stethoscope over the girl's heart. Maria gasped, and Christie let her listen for several seconds. "Now I need to listen to your lungs," she said.

David always enjoyed watching Christie work with the children. She had a true gift for it, a gift that he knew he didn't have in equal measure, try as he might. Christie, like Cecil and Martha Duncan, founders of Hope Village, seemed never too busy to spend an unhurried moment with a child. And maybe *that*, David thought wryly, is why so many of the tasks of running this place landed on his shoulders.

A minute later, she turned to David. "I think she just has a cold. I don't hear any rattle in her chest." She gave Maria some cough medicine and Tylenol, then sent her up to the orphanage with one of the volunteers who acted as an assistant nurse.

Christie turned to Angela and smiled. "Come sit with me and tell me about your brother," she said, putting her arm around the girl's shoulders and guiding her toward a low bench against the wall. "What kind of boy is he? What does he like to do?"

David leaned against the wall near them, watching his wife speak in soothing tones to Angela, stroking her soiled hair. There were reasons, of course, that Christie had a greater and more tender affinity for these orphans than David had—reasons David remembered each time he saw, as he did now, the long pink scar that reached above her neckline and ended on the side of her left cheek, the skin uneven and furrowed.

At times, David felt that her past made Christie too protective of their son Davy, born a year after their arrival in Caracas. He was now four. But over the past year, the realization had grown in them that Davy was unusually active, and with a surprisingly short attention span. Only a few months before, he had been diagnosed as ADHD—a diagnosis that, to David's chagrin, had made Christie even more protective and defensive. Once, in a moment of frustration, David had remarked that Davy acted like a hummingbird on steroids. He'd had to spend the next hour trying to convince an angry Christie, her arms crossed and eyes flashing, that he thought hummingbirds were cute, steroids or not.

David looked at his watch. Where was Dr. Vargas?

CHAPTER FOUR

It was a little before midnight when Juan "Durango" Diez parked his car and entered the lobby of the hotel. Two men sat in plush leather chairs around a small table, sipping rum and smoking cigars. These two belonged, Durango was sure, to one or more of the men he was about to meet. The men stopped talking and watched him as he handed two briefcases to the front desk clerk, then held up a couple of folded bills between two fingers, enough money to cause the clerk to raise his eyebrows. "My associate will come for these bags in about a half-hour," Durango said. The clerk watched the money, not Durango's face. "Keep them safe." The clerk nodded, and Durango handed him the bills.

He smiled at the two goons as he walked to the elevator. They were undoubtedly armed and he was not. But that would not matter. For one thing, Durango knew many ways to kill a man with his bare hands. And for another, if his subterfuge failed in the next half-hour, he was a dead man anyway.

When the elevator doors opened, Durango placed his coded key in the slot and punched floor number four. Two provocatively dressed women hurried toward the elevator just as the door began to close. Durango held it for them.

"*Gracias, señor,*" one of them said with a smile as the other punched floor number three. Another night, he might have responded. But tonight was for business only, and Durango kept his eyes to himself and his thoughts focused.

15

16   The Missionary

It had taken nearly eighteen months to gain the confidence of the members of *La Fraternidad*—the Fraternity—the secret name of the drug cartel Durango would meet with in a few moments. It was a dangerous game he played. Each of the drug lords mistakenly believed two things: that he knew Durango's true identity, and that he was closer to Durango than the others who would sit around tonight's table.

There were three of them -- Emilio Antonio Tecero, Julio DiMartino, and Rafael Lopez, each with a powerful organization and each interdependent on the others. One could hardly call this group a "team." But they were of necessity linked together. Tecero produced cocaine in Columbia and brought it to the border high in the Andes. DiMartino was a master at moving it from the Andes through Venezuela and out of the country, where most of it was smuggled into America. And Lopez kept everybody happy by laundering their money and seeing to it they all got very rich.

One false move, one careless word, could cause Durango to fall into disfavor with them—three of the most powerful and vicious men in Latin America.

It had actually been easier for Durango to lure *La Fraternidad* into his plan than he had anticipated. As much as they distrusted each other, they had in common a hatred of Venezuelan President Armando Guzman. For several years, Guzman had been wreaking havoc on their cocaine smuggling. But what had really angered the drug cartel, finally tipping the scale to incline them to agree to this drastic action, had been Guzman's recent move to restrict the transfer of Venezuelan assets into other currencies.

Durango was a man of many talents, many skills, most of them deadly. As a young man in his native Argentina, he had been trained by and worked side by side with U.S. Special Forces, who were developing a highly skilled unit—the *Grupo Especial de Operaciones Federales*—to deal with criminal gangs and terrorism in his country. He had worked with GEOF for six years, combating drug trafficking. That was not, however, what he was doing now.

When the elevator doors opened on floor four, he was greeted by another muscle goon, with two more behind him. "Sorry, amigo," the first one said. "But our boss asked us to pat you down for weapons."

This was why Durango had left his weapon in the locked glove box of his car. He smiled and lifted his arms as one man quickly patted him down, then waved him on toward the large conference room at the end of the hall. The goons had not, of course, found the tiny chip and microphone, sewn into his suit jacket, that would record every word spoken at tonight's meeting. Nor had they noticed his tie pin, a video "eye" wirelessly connected to the digital image recorder in the trunk of his car.

As Durango walked down the long, thick-carpeted hallway, it occurred to him that this would probably be the last time these men would ever meet together. But would it be them—or him—who would die first?

When Dr. Vargas arrived shortly after midnight, David was already feeling the pull of drowsiness. Angela was napping in the chair beside her fitfully sleeping brother; she had been unwilling to leave his side. David and Christie watched Dr. Vargas's stethoscope probe Ricardo's chest.

Slowly and gravely, Vargas folded his stethoscope and placed it in his shirt pocket, then nodded at David. "Among other things that may be going on, this child has pneumonia." Vargas wiped the perspiration from his forehead and paused, looking at David as if reluctant to say what came next. "There's a particularly stubborn bacterial form of necrotizing pneumonia known as MRSA working its way through Caracas's children. I suspect that's what we're seeing here. It can be fatal in seventy-two hours or less. I can't be sure until we take a sputum culture, but I'm not going to wait to start him on medication. He may also have strep throat. Were there other children out on the street exposed to him?"

"There were seven or eight kids where I picked him up, including his sister"-- David nodded toward Angela—"and one other girl I brought here tonight."

Glancing at Angela, Vargas said, "And the other girl? Where is she now?"

"Up at the orphanage. Christie checked her first and thought she just had a cold," David said.

Dr. Vargas shook his head, clearly displeased. "Bring her back here and let me check her. Give this boy oral Bactrim and start him on an IV of Clindamycin. Continue the respiratory humidifier, and someone will need to monitor his breathing through the night. Take a sputum sample for me now. I'll take it to the hospital lab to confirm my diagnosis, and check him again tomorrow morning."

Christie buzzed the night staff at the orphanage on the intercom—"Juana? I need you to bring Maria back to the clinic. Yes, the new girl. No, right now, por favor. Gracias." Then she headed for the supply room to retrieve the drugs and supplies needed to carry out Dr. Vargas's instructions.

When Juana brought Maria back into the clinic, Angela awoke, rubbed her eyes, and looked around. After a moment, she asked David, "Will my brother be all right?"

"We hope so, Angela. But he is very sick. We need to pray that his body can fight this infection," David said, pulling her close.

Dr. Vargas was instructing Juana when Christie returned and gave Ricardo a Bactrim tablet. She skillfully inserted a needle into the vein of his arm, took a sample of his blood, and connected the needle to the IV bag containing Clindamycin, all while Dr. Vargas finished checking both girls.

When Christie was finished and Dr. Vargas had left, she joined David, Maria, and Angela on the bench. David and Christie each took one of Angela's hands. "Tonight you and Maria can sleep in the back room of the clinic, close to your brother," David said. "But first, let's pray for Ricardo. Then I'll have some food brought down for you."

Afterward, David and Christie strolled hand in hand through the night, up the path past the soccer field toward the orphanage kitchen. Mia, one of the orphanage "mothers," was seated near the kitchen when they walked in. Davy, often left in Mia's care while David and Christie were at work, was asleep on the sofa nearby. David scooped him up onto his shoulder and asked Mia to warm up some food for Angela and Maria. Then he and Christie started up the hill toward their house. David felt so tired, so overwhelmed. "What we do here at Hope Village is like spitting in the ocean," he mumbled.

Christie stroked his arm. "Not to those few we're able to help. To them, it means everything. We're doing the best we can, David."

"Tell that to the kids I left out there on the street tonight."

CHAPTER FIVE

When Durango walked into the room, the three drug lords were already seated in leather chairs around a rosewood coffee table on which sat a pitcher of ice water and several glasses. Three bodyguards, one for each lord, stood directly behind their bosses. Strapped to their bodies and hidden, Durango knew, was weaponry more than sufficient to slice and blast a roomful of men into little pieces.

Durango smiled as he extended his hand to the man on his immediate right. Julio DiMartino came from a wealthy Venezuelan family that had maintained strong political ties for generations. Like many of his circle, he loved gold chains and wore too much cologne.

"I see you're still working out, my friend. You look good!" Durango said.

On DiMartino's left sat Rafael Lopez. As Lopez's delicate, ivory-colored fingers reached out to clasp Durango's hand, he looked almost fearful, as if his hand might be broken in the exchange.

"Have any good investment tips for me today, my friend?" Durango quipped.

"Any I give will cost you a percentage," Lopez replied with a smile. The overstuffed chair he sat in looked three sizes too big. But what Lopez lacked in physique, he made up with brains. Harvard-educated, he was without question the most intelligent of the three men—and the most cowardly.

Durango turned to Lopez's left and met the cold brown eyes of the third man, undoubtedly the most powerful drug lord on the planet:

Emilio Antonio Tecero. Outside Tecero's presence, Durango jokingly referred to him as EAT, based on his initials. It was an appropriate nickname. The buttons on Tecero's white dress shirt strained to keep all of his two-hundred-ninety pounds inside his six-foot frame without ripping loose.

Tecero still lived in his native Colombia most of the year, controlling much of that country's cocaine production. Thousands of people were on his payroll, from simple farmers to Colombian government officials. He'd also gained control of the paramilitary group in Columbia known as FARC. It had been estimated that his organization had taken in over four billion dollars in the past couple of years alone. Tecero had some of the most sophisticated communications equipment and weaponry found anywhere in the world. Osama bin Laden would have been envious.

Tecero had topped the Colombian government's most wanted list for the past three years. But unlike his captured or dead predecessors, he was not into flaunting his wealth. No lavish parties, few women. Frequent quiet moves kept him elusive. He was the prototype for a new generation of drug lords who kept a low profile. *Permanezca bajo, vive mucho tiempo* was their motto: stay low, live long.

Tecero was meticulous. No detail was too small to merit his attention. Short-tempered and ruthless, he had little tolerance for mistakes. And Durango knew that it made Tecero nervous to be in meetings like this. He'd landed less than an hour before at Simon Bolivar International in one of his private jets and would depart from there again tonight on another of his jets, just to be safe.

With Emilio Tecero, there was no small talk. He gripped Durango's extended hand and said, "Let's get down to business."

It had been Tecero whom Durango had first approached with the idea of a coup, knowing that Tecero would be the key to its success. With his vast transport and communications resources, he had agreed to provide the means to get the commandos in and out of Venezuela. And, as Durango had suspected, Tecero had insisted on being the primary contact.

Durango seated himself in a leather chair. He carried no notes or papers. Every detail was in his head.

"I want to make this as brief as possible so we can all be on our way," Durango began. "First, the commandos, or *asesinos* as Mr. Tecero prefers to call them, have arrived undetected. There are four of them, well-trained mercenaries from Israel. Their leader comes with high recommendations and incredible experience. He has removed people from positions of power before. His success ratio is excellent. He is one of only two or three men in the world who could be trusted with this difficult assignment."

Reaching for a crystal glass of ice water, he paused, enjoying the adrenaline-spiked command he felt over these powerful and dangerous men. He did not tell them that he knew the commando leader personally, having trained with him years before at the Delta Force base in North Carolina, and had even carried out other missions with him. That would have caused suspicions that Durango had no intention of raising.

For the next twenty minutes, he talked through the details of the coup, discussed three site possibilities for the proposed action, and gave a rationale for his preferred site. His presentation was so thorough that there were few questions.

Durango turned to Tecero. "As you know, we have already delivered a two-million-dollar down payment to the commandos."

"Of course I know," the Colombian growled. "It was all my money!"

"And now that the commandos have landed, we need to deliver another two million," continued Durango, "and the final two million when the job is done. I have left two empty briefcases with the front desk clerk of the hotel. They are for the remaining amounts, in unmarked U.S. one-hundred-dollar bills, as the commandos have requested."

Tecero gave a barely perceptible nod—he was not the type to appear as if he were accepting instructions from an underling—and then waved one hand toward one of his goons, who picked up a decanter of some kind of liquor from a sideboard, along with four shot glasses. He set them on the coffee table and filled each shot glass.

24   The Missionary

Durango turned toward Lopez and DiMartino. "Are our information sources in place?"

DiMartino nodded. "We will know when and where Guzman will be vacationing. Until the last moment, Guzman does not let even his inner circle know his travel plans. But I assure you that we will know, and with adequate lead time. Of this I am certain."

"Good," replied Durango. "And what about our JAM assistants?" he asked Lopez.

In Lopez's organization were people with strong ties to JAM, a group of underground freedom fighters who had named their group in honor of Juan Antonio Macado, killed years before during former president Perez's regime. JAM was now intent on seeing Guzman removed from power by any means.

"A few of Guzman's staff, as well as several on the staff at the expected resorts—drivers, cooks, gardeners—are secret members of JAM," said Lopez. "Each of the three expected locations has been infiltrated, so there is a high likelihood that we can cover most eventualities," said Lopez.

"A 'high likelihood'...'most eventualities'?" bellowed Tecero. "We cannot afford chances—we need certainties! I will not tolerate a screw-up on this!"

Lopez's ivory-pale face turned red. He was about to speak when Durango disarmed the looming confrontation by saying, "We will not proceed unless we know for certain that all of the players are in place. If we are patient, we will find the right opportunity to guarantee success. I will need daily contact with each of you as we proceed."

Durango picked up his drink and offered a toast. "Gentlemen, by the time we meet again, we will have neutralized Armando Guzman, and your assets will be flowing freely to their desired destinations!" All four men drank.

Handing the safe deposit box key and pin number to Tecero, Durango said, "Please have someone deliver the briefcases of cash to this safe deposit box at Banco Provincial near Avenida Urdaneta in the Federal District tomorrow."

Tecero nodded. "Someone besides you will act as our courier pigeon, correct? I want no chance that this can be traced back to us."

"Yes, of course. He will know nothing of you."

Alone in the elevator on the way down, Durango smiled. How ironic that he was using Emilio Tecero's money to pull this off—and putting a large chunk of it into his own pocket.

Before dawn, Hawkeye and the three other Israeli commandos crept to the white Ford Explorer parked a hundred yards north, hidden among the trees beside the highway. Inside, they found tourist clothing in all the right sizes. They changed their clothes, packed their raft and other equipment under a tarp in the back, and drove to an old warehouse near Simon Bolivar International Airport, where a gray van was waiting, filled with the additional equipment they'd requisitioned. They stowed the gear they'd brought in the van and left it parked in the warehouse, where they could retrieve it when the time came.

After a short drive along the coast, they arrived at the Macuto Hotel, small and quiet, just across the road from Macuto Beach and not far from the port town of La Guaira. The front of the hotel provided a sweeping view of the Caribbean, and the lush backdrop of the Avila Mountains rose behind. Caracas was just beyond the mountains—about forty minutes away. It was an ideal place to wait.

Sleep had been fitful out near the beach, and the team fell into their beds as soon as they reached the hotel.

Hawkeye lay awake. This would be his last mission. He had agreed to it only after exacting the highest price he'd ever asked. After this, he would have more than enough money to do whatever he wanted for the rest of his life.

He had survived in his chosen, and very dangerous, profession longer than most. From the beginning, joining and training with Delta Force in the U.S., he had known that this was the only life for which he was suited—but suited for it he was, perfectly. He was no Rambo—but then, Rambo, the emotional, out-of-control killing machine, was a Hollywood myth. The men of Special Forces were the most disciplined and self-controlled in all the military. And Hawkeye was the most disciplined of all.

Still, he had left Delta Force several years before and moved to Israel to join Sayeret Matkal, the elite Israeli commando unit reputed to be the best in the world. It had been Sayeret Matkal that, decades before, had rescued 106 Jewish hostages from the Entebbe Airport in Uganda, probably the most famous hostage rescue success ever. He had made the change partly because he was of Jewish descent and wanted to help Israel, and partly because he'd craved action. Delta Force troops sometimes sat for months without action—rehearsing, role-playing, rehearsing again. Hawkeye had grown restless.

Sayeret Matkal had been different. In Sayeret Matkal, Hawkeye and his fellow soldiers had been in live combat situations nearly every week.

But no one could play this game forever. Yes, this was his final mission. And he had no illusions that it would be as easy as the one he had just completed in Uganda.

Assassinating the president of a country was something he had never attempted before.

CHAPTER SIX

At 6:30 AM, David made himself a cup of coffee, trying not to awaken Christie or Davy Jr. Cup in hand, he walked from his house down the gravel path to the clinic; Dr. Vargas's aging Jeep Cherokee was already parked in the little lot behind. David was grateful that the man seemed to never sleep. He heard the familiar rooster crows from the chicken coop, where Hope Village chickens laid some two hundred eggs a day, many of them used to feed the children, and many more sold at a local market to help pay the expenses of Hope Village.

The look on Dr. Vargas's face as he shook his head told David everything he needed to know. "I won't have the lab results for at least another twenty-four hours. But it may not make much difference by then." Waving a tired hand toward Ricardo, Dr. Vargas said, "See for yourself. He's racked with chills and running a fever of 105. Lack of oxygen has made his lips and fingernails turn blue. His heart is racing and he's semi-comatose."

David looked down at the pale, gray-skinned child, wishing he could simply turn off Dr. Vargas's grim diagnosis.

The doctor continued. "When this strain of bacteria penetrates the body's defenses, it colonizes the lung tissue, then quickly spreads through the bloodstream to the entire body. We probably found this one too late."

Turning to Lupe, the volunteer nurse on duty, Dr. Vargas said, "Keep him on the Clindamycin IV and the oral Bactrim. There's really nothing else we can do.

"There is some good news, though," he added, turning to David. "I examined the two girls. No signs of anything but a common cold. I released them to join the others, and one of the nurses took them. I hope that's all right."\

It was more than all right; it was excellent. David nodded, then tipped his head toward Ricardo. "I'll call the hospitals to see if one will take him, but I doubt that they will." He felt, not for the first time, a sudden sense of kinship with this man with whom he had so little else in common except for their common love for the homeless children of Caracas.

Looking tired and defeated, Dr. Vargas held up his hand in a knowing gesture as he moved toward the doorway—a man with many more patients to see and no time to rest. "I do not give this boy much chance to make it another forty-eight hours, so transferring him from your clinic to a hospital at this point would probably make little difference. You're a praying man, David. This child needs much more than a hospital…he needs a miracle." He pulled the door closed behind him.

Christie was scrambling eggs when David got back to their house.

"I've called three hospitals," he said. "None will agree to take Ricardo."

Christie looked up at him, studied his face, and her shoulders slumped. "Oh, David," she said, "I'm sorry. You care so much for these kids." She stepped close and kissed his cheek. "That's just one of the many of things I love about you."

David wrapped his arms around her waist and they held each other for a moment. "Sit here by the window while I get you some breakfast," Christie whispered.

As he did many mornings, David sat at the small table looking out his kitchen window over the Venezuelan hillside, enjoying the moments of quiet before Davy, Jr., woke up. Years before, Cecil Duncan, the founder of Hope Village, had terraced the hillside and planted a garden and orchard, his pride and joy. Besides being a missionary, Cecil was a first-rate horticulturalist, having owned and run a nursery in Texas before his missionary days.

Cecil had harnessed a spring-fed stream to meet the garden's needs. The water gathered in a small pool at the end of each terrace, then cascaded over rocks and on downhill to the next.

The green mountains stretched out and up for mile after hazy mile, framing the bronze sunrise that David loved to watch as he wrote in his journal in the early mornings, before Christie awoke. It would have been a storybook setting, were it not for the daily reality of death and sickness in the barrios.

Christie reached over David's shoulder and placed in front of him a plate of eggs and some oven-warm banana bread she'd made. Putting her arms around him from behind, she kissed him on the back of the neck. "When are we going to get some time alone, just the two of us?"

David smiled, digging his fork into the eggs. "Maybe this afternoon, hon. We can have Mia watch Davy. How about I take you on a lunch date?"

"Okay, but take me somewhere off campus."

"I know just the place."

After Christie left for the clinic, David parked Davy in front of a "Dora the Explorer" video and took his time showering and getting dressed, even singing in the shower. It felt good just to be rested and putting on clean clothes.

Amazing, he thought, how some tender loving care from Christie could put his world back in order. Like all couples, they had their differences. Christie was fearful of conflict, while David preferred to take it head-on. Christie was, David was perfectly willing to admit, much more thoughtful and emotionally in control than he was. Her Swedish ancestry, coupled with her tragic past, made her more introverted than David's Irish blood. While she wasn't easily provoked, when called to medical emergency action, Christie shifted into another gear---focused, fearless, in control, as she had been trained by her Coast Guard Reserve service. She had gone to school on a ROTC scholarship and received her nursing degree. After her training as a combat medical specialist, she served a six-month term in Iraq on a rescue chopper, right after they were married. She had notified her Reserve Officer of their taking a mission assignment in Venezuela, but she also knew she could still be recalled into active duty if needed.

David stepped out of his house with Davy and drank in the morning sun. Walking Davy toward the school, he realized the sky was cloudless. Would this be the first day it wouldn't rain in the afternoon? The wet season—since the temperature stays about the same year round in Venezuela, seasons are determined by rainfall—was nearly over, and about time, too. It was late this year.

David and Davy reached the school building, the largest building on campus, where David's office also was. David kissed his son on the cheek and handed him to Mia. "Could you keep an eye on him till mid-afternoon?" he asked.

"Sure," she said.

"I'll see you tonight, son," David called. "We'll read Winnie the Pooh again, okay?"

Little Davy was already running back toward the playground, with Mia chasing behind. David shook his head. She would have her hands full. Davy seldom stopped—either moving or talking.

"Senor Eller?"

It was Estella, David's secretary. "Someone is here to see you," she said. "*Un hombre.*"

"One of the local officials?" David asked, looking up from his office desk. Occasionally someone from the local government would show up to ask questions or inspect the facilities.

Estella shook her head. "I do not think so. I have not seen him before."

But David had. As he stepped into the outer office, a tall man turned from the artwork he'd been examining on the wall and smiled. "Buenas dias, Senor Eller," he said. "I hope this is not a bad time. I am Carlos Edwards. We met last night when you rescued the boy on the street."

"Yes, of course," David said. "I didn't expect to see you so soon." He laughed. "If ever. People who express a casual interest in Hope Village seldom follow up. They're glad we're doing what we're doing, but beyond that, well…"

Mr. Edwards shrugged. "I am sure that is true. As for showing up today, it so happened that I had a meeting canceled, leaving me with a morning free. *Espere la Aldea* was on my mind after last night, so I thought, if it isn't too much trouble for you, perhaps this would be a good time to stop by and make a contribution toward your work."

"An excellent time," David said, wondering how large a contribution this expensively dressed man might make. *Part German,* David guessed. His hair was reddish brown, his forehead high and broad. Sharp brown eyes accompanied striking features David thought unusual for a Venezuelan; he looked as much northern European as Latin. About six feet tall, forty or forty-five and in very good shape. Taupe suit, crisp white shirt, deep blue tie, silver cufflinks peeking out from the sleeves. Well-polished shoes.

"How is the boy?" the man asked. "The one you rescued last night."

David bowed his head, then raised it again. "Not good, I'm afraid. The doctor believes we may have gotten to him too late."

"You are not a doctor yourself?"

David grinned. "Hardly. My wife is the head nurse here, but my own position is mostly administrative. We use a local doctor. Thank you, by the way, for your help with the boy. Ricardo."

"We can only hope and pray that he will improve. It is in God's hands. And the two little girls? Are they still here?"

"Yes," David smiled. "Probably in class." He swept an arm toward the door. "May I show you around the compound?"

32   The Missionary

David led Edwards down a hallway and opened the door to one of the classrooms. The teacher immediately stopped talking, and the children turned to see who was entering.

"*Los niños, esto es Sr. Carlos Eduardo. ¿Puede decir usted buenos días?*" David said.

"*Buenos días!*" thirty-nine children replied in unison. [**can we do an upside-down exclamation point?**]

David scanned the class. "Angela and Maria, do you remember Mr. Edwards? Please come say hello," David said.

A bit shy, the two girls stood and moved toward Edwards, who reached down and shook their hand.

" *¿Cómo hace usted?*" he asked.

" *Bueno,*" they both chimed in unison.

Edwards smiled as the two girls returned to their seats.

"My wife and Martha Duncan split their time between the school and the health clinic," David said. "We also have several volunteer teachers' aides."

The day was still glorious as they stepped outside, the air fresh and rain-washed, the concrete-block buildings that made up Hope Village gleaming in the sun. David pointed out the large covered patio area where daily meals were prepared and served to up to a hundred children. "Besides those who live here, many more come during the day to attend school or have a warm meal."

The school and the dormitory were both nestled into the hillside south of the garden and painted banana yellow with sky-blue metal roofs. "There are five bedrooms here," David said, leading Edwards down the hallway in the orphanage dorm. The place had the pronounced locker-room smell of active, sweaty bodies, plus a faint fragrance of corn tortillas. "It's the first time many of these children have had a bed, much less a bed to themselves. Of course, if we had more room we could house more children. Already we have bunks out on the porch."

They walked out the front door of the dorm onto a huge lawn where several of the children were playing soccer. David led Edwards up the gravel drive toward the north and pointed up the hill, "That's where my wife and I live, and our four-year-old, Davy."

The Eller house was a modest bungalow with a brown metal roof and stained wood siding. Incongruously, the wooden door was large and hand carved, something David had rescued a few years back from a hotel fire and refinished.

David hadn't expected Christie to be home, but as he and Edwards passed the house, she opened the front door and came down the walk, smiling curiously. When David introduced them, Edwards took the hand Christie offered and held it in both of his. There was something so gallant in his manner as he bent slightly over her hand that David half-expected him to kiss it. "I am very glad to meet you," he said. "Thank you for your work here."

Christie smiled. "And thank you for your interest. I was just headed back to the clinic, but would you like some coffee?"

"Go check on your patients first while we finish our tour, then we'll have coffee," David said.

As she hurried on, David pointed toward a small, teal-blue concrete-block house across the creek. "That's where the founders of *Espere la Aldea* live. Cecil and Martha Duncan. The most remarkable people I know."

"Yes, I have heard of them," Edwards said. "There is great respect for them here in Caracas."

They strolled down the hill past the three acres of garden, fruit trees, and coffee trees. Cecil was working in the garden, dressed in a pair of soiled coveralls, sweat dripping from his brow. Several children were working with him. He didn't look up, and David decided not to introduce him to Edwards. David had noticed it before—yes, people had heard of Cecil Duncan, but when they met the man who looked like an impoverished gardener, dripping sweat, clothes in tatters, hands encrusted with dirt, they were confused—was this some mistake? No, he would skip that introduction.

The noise level increased dramatically when they stepped into the clinic, the building closest to the road. The small waiting room was filled with mothers and children. A volunteer receptionist tried to keep everyone happy and in order, but the overall effect was barely controlled chaos—sick children were crying out their discomfort, and harried mothers tried their best to comfort them.

David opened a door set into a flimsy divider and gestured toward the three small treatment areas divided by curtains. "Some of the local doctors volunteer a day now and then—we're grateful for that," said David. "Either Martha or Christie is here whenever the clinic is open."

On cue, a diminutive gray-haired woman came slowly out of a treatment room.

"Martha, this is Carlos Edwards. He came to see Hope Village."

As always, David was struck by the radiant smile of this woman who offered both her hands, twisted by the arthritis that had half-crippled her. "God bless you, Mr. Edwards," she said. "Isn't it wonderful what God has provided here at *Espere la Aldea?*" She beamed at David. "Oh, David, did you take him to the school to see the children?"

David nodded. She turned back to Carlos. "Aren't they wonderful? Such beautiful, precious children. Everything we do here is for them. Such gifts of God!"

David watched as Edwards studied first Martha's face, then the gnarled hands holding his. Edwards appeared deeply moved. "You have worked so hard for so many years, Señora Duncan. I am deeply grateful for your work."

"Oh, but Mr. Edwards, this is not work. This is just the joyful way we love these children. They do more for me than I could ever do for them! Jesus loves us all, but He especially loved children. 'Let the little children come to me,' he said, and at *Espere la Aldea*, we make a place for them to come, and then try in our poor way to care for them as he would."

Christie promised Martha that she would return quickly, and then the three of them made their way back up the hill toward the Ellers' house. "Believe it or not, Hope Village actually runs pretty smoothly," David said. "Obviously, more could be done with more resources, but we make do with what we have. It's never enough. The need is great."

"Yes," Edwards sighed. "And growing greater every day."

David and Edwards sat at the kitchen table while Christie prepared and poured them each a cup of fresh-ground coffee, along with slices of the banana bread she'd baked that morning.

"The coffee comes from beans grown here in the garden. The bananas in the bread are from our orchard," David said.

"Both are delicious," Edwards said. "Mrs. Eller, I thank you for your hospitality. Your home is lovely, and even though I am a stranger to you, you have made me feel very welcome. I am honored and moved. Before I forget—" he pulled a checkbook from his inner jacket pocket— "everything I have seen here today has only strengthened my resolve to support this institution, and I will write a bigger check than I had intended to write." He wrote in silence, then tore the check out of his checkbook and handed it to David, who, as always when someone handed him a check, placed it in his pocket without looking at the amount.

"Thank you. I only hope we're worthy of your support."

"Of that I have no doubt. And please, call me Carlos, both of you. I feel that we have become friends." He smiled, then his facial expression shifted. "I must confess, David, that when I saw you in your office this morning I realized why you looked familiar to me last night. I recognize you—and now you too, Mrs. Eller—from a television special on Venevision some weeks ago on which you were both interviewed about this ministry. It lodged in my memory partly because of my admiration for what you are doing here, and partly because I also admired your courage in speaking out for the poor in Venezuela. Believe me, they need champions."

Christie's head turned sharply. She stared at David. He pretended not to notice.

David's comments on that television special had been a source of contention between them ever since, and he regretted that Edwards had brought it up. Not that he regretted what he had said. The segment on Hope Village had been only ten minutes or so of a longer feature on organizations serving the poor in Caracas, and the Duncans had asked the Ellers, younger and more articulate, to take the lead. All had gone smoothly until the interviewer had asked them about the scope of the problem, and whether they saw any answers for the future. Five years of frustration—five years of being able to rescue and serve only a small fraction of the ever-growing numbers of homeless and exploited children of Caracas—had bubbled out of David into a fifteen-second sound bite that Christie had said she would give anything to take back.

"The answer is already here," David had said with passion. "Underground. Venezuela sits on one of the largest oil reserves in the world. The revenue from that oil is more than sufficient to solve the problems of the poor—*if* the Venezuelan government will honor its promises to do so. What we need is for Armando Guzman to meet the needs of his own people before subsidizing countries like Cuba."

Christie had been livid afterward, although when other missionaries had criticized David for his politicization of the issue, Christie had defended him. Had David let his anger get the best of him? Yes. But he was glad he had said it. It needed to be said.

For a moment they sat in silence, sipping their coffee. David felt Christie's eyes still on him but refused to meet them. "I'm afraid," David said at last, "that there is much evidence to support the view of those who say that Guzman's formula for success is to discourage foreign investments, suppress opposition, and continue to offer rhetoric but little substance in helping the poor. More evidence every day, in fact. Forgive me if I offend you."

"Not at all," Edwards was quick to assure him. "Not at all. I feel as you do. Half our population must make do with poor wages, few medical clinics, no clean water, few educational opportunities, and horrible living conditions while Guzman's generals live in palatial accommodations!" He glanced at his watch. "I would love to see Venezuela become a democracy again," he said. "The United States is laughing at us."

"I think maybe, instead, they are crying with us," David said.

Edwards stood. "I hope you are right." He shook David's hand, then took Christie's and with a small bow said, "Thank you for your kindness to a stranger."

"Thank you so much for your contribution, Mr. Edwards," she said.

"We'll put it to good use," David added.

As Christie hurried back to the clinic, David walked Edwards to his Mercedes. "Maybe we could have lunch soon," Edwards said. "I'd like to discuss how we together might find a way to help the poor of our country. Also, I have friends who might want to contribute something to your work here."

"I would like that very much," David said.

"As it happens, I have a lunch scheduled tomorrow with friends who would, I am sure, be very interested in hearing about your ministry and perhaps contributing to it. Will you join us?"

More contributions? By all means. "Yes. I can meet for lunch tomorrow."

"Good. Meet me at the Punta Grill at 12:30."

On his way back up the path to his house, David unfolded the check Edwards had given him. Two million Bolivar.

He heard the back door to the clinic open and close. Christie was walking toward him, her eyes steady and serious. He knew she would want to talk about what he'd said to Edwards, and he would just as soon not. He tried to deflect it by holding up the check. "About a thousand bucks, hon. Do you realize what we can do with that? And he says he has many friends who might want to help us too."

Christie glanced at the check, and then back at David. "I have a strange feeling about that man."

"Why?"

"I'm not sure," she said. "I didn't like the way he baited you."

"Baited me? Honey, he's just concerned about the plight of the poor. He was willing to say so. How can you call that 'baiting' me?"

"Because that's what he did, David! You were being played. And by someone who definitely knew what he was doing. He's a pro. Call it woman's intuition if you want, but there's something not quite right about Carlos Edwards. And *you!*" She slapped his arm, and her expression was not playful. "It's bad enough you had to say those things on TV, to a national audience, but now you say them again to someone you've barely met! How do you know he's not working for Guzman?"

"What did I say? Nothing you can't hear on the street any day of the week. I just said things have to change, that the government has to—"

"No, you *can't* hear that on the street. People are afraid to say it because they never know who'll be listening! People can disappear for saying things like that! Oh, David, please be careful what you say, and who you say it to. And *especially* be careful of Carlos Edwards." She pecked him on the cheek and hurried back toward the clinic.

One thing David had learned in marriage was not to let an argument end this way. "Honey!" he called. She turned. "Don't forget we have a lunch date in about twenty minutes! We'll talk about it some more. I do care what you think about all this."

She smiled weakly, nodded, and disappeared through the door.

David read the check again, smiled, and rushed to tell Cecil.

CHAPTER SEVEN

Hawkeye awoke midmorning, took a shower, and made coffee. He spread the maps he'd been given on the kitchen table and, sipping his coffee, studied them, his eyes moving slowly and systematically. Finally, he nodded.

"Hey, Danny!" he yelled, "Haul your carcass out of bed! We're taking a ride."

Danny—Daniel Benjamin—was the youngest of the group. He possessed one of those no-beard babyfaces and looked as if he could still be in high school. Hawkeye had met him on the streets of Jerusalem. After joining Sayeret Matkal, Hawkeye had begun volunteering as a coach at a local athletic club when not on duty. Danny, one of his players, had come to admire Hawkeye so much that he'd decided to enlist, hoping to move up through the ranks to become a commando. But after four years of hard work, having made it to the last stage, he was cut from the program. Hawkeye had by that time decided to become a soldier for hire, so he took Danny in as part of his group and continued to train him himself.

He heard Danny flush the toilet.

"Tell Aaron and Zach to be ready in fifteen minutes," Hawkeye called.

Like Hawkeye, Aaron and Zachariah were former Sayeret Matkal commandos, both in their early thirties. Aaron was a steady, seasoned soldier, with a wife and son at home. He needed the big payoff this job would bring. He had told Hawkeye he was planning to buy a new house and start his own security business when this assignment was done.

40   The Missionary

Zach was the one on the edge. He lived for the fight. Unlike Aaron, who had typical military short hair and played by the book, Zach's hair was longer, pulled back in a tiny knot; he wore a double earring in his left ear. He sported numerous tattoos. His appearance was deceptive. He was lethal, using stealth with minimal collateral damage. He owned his own set of weapons, to which he'd given affectionate names.

Hawkeye resumed his study of the maps.

Like previous Venezuelan heads of state, Guzman liked the good life, and that included leisure time at the coast. But unlike his predecessors, Guzman did not have just one get-away location. Since an attempted coup several years before, he preferred to keep his enemies guessing by staying in different places, sometimes at the resort homes of formerly wealthy Venezuelans who'd gone into exile. Guzman had confiscated many of these homes and spent hundreds of thousands of the government's money in refurbishing them for his own use.

JAM had moles on Guzman's staff who had reported that Guzman was most likely to go to one of three places in the next two weeks. One was the estate formerly owned by Tony Gervachi, an Italian transplant, who had been one of the largest real estate developers in Venezuela until he fled when Guzman accused him of conspiring to kill him. The estate included a fabulous four-story, 15,000-square-foot mansion nicknamed the Palace, in the midst of the gambling casinos of Isla Margarita. While it was known that Guzman liked more quiet and remote places than the Palace, it was still considered a possibility because his wife had a passion for the tables in the casinos.

The housecleaner and the pool lifeguard at the Palace, Hawkeye had been told, were both members of JAM.

Another place high on the list of possibilities was an exotic estate near Puerto la Cruz formerly owned by Venezuelan billionaire Jorge Lyon Aguirre. Aguirre owned vast holdings in Venezuela, including television and cable companies, a rum factory, and even a professional baseball team. This home was on a rocky outcrop overlooking the ocean, with beautiful sandy beaches on either side. It was called the Vina Estate because Jorge Aguirre, a connoisseur of fine wines, had collected in his wine cellar thousands of bottles of exotic and expensive wines from around the globe. The wine collection had been left behind when Aguirre fled the country in the middle of the night after it was discovered that he had participated in the coup attempt. Aguirre was now an exile in the United States, active in the anti-Guzman movement.

Hawkeye traced his finger up the map to the last location on the target list: the Olas Resort near Rio Chico, over a hundred miles from the Macuto Hotel where Hawkeye and his men were staying. Today would be a good day to drive to the Olas Resort and take a look.

The highway between Macuto and Rio Chico was a narrow two-lane road packed with buses and trucks spewing thick grey smoke from their diesel engines. Tall trees lined the highway, their branches converging over it like a canopy. Makeshift fruit and produce stands with thatched roofs were scattered along the roadside. Many of them had stalks of bananas hanging from the rafters.

Zach and Danny were asleep in the back seat.

The most frustrating part of these missions for Hawkeye was the waiting. While his men were happy to live the good life, posing as tourists near good food, warm Caribbean waters, and miles of sugar-white sand, Hawkeye knew from experience that it could soften them, dull their senses. That could get him or one of them killed. Glancing at the two comatose team members in the back seat, he decided to conduct some exercises over the next few days to keep his men razor sharp.

Hawkeye had one rule about the jobs he accepted. He would fight only "bad guys." In his mind, Guzman fit that profile. Durango, who had hired him and his team for the job, was an old acquaintance. But beyond that, Hawkeye did not know, nor did he want to know, who was behind the coup. As long as he got his payments on schedule and he was hunting a bad guy, he was satisfied.

But he was not satisfied with the intel on the Olas Resort. If that intel was correct, the resort would present Hawkeye and his team with multiple problems. Maybe they would be fortunate, and Guzman would choose somewhere else.

"David, wait," Christie said, interrupting him. David realized that he'd been growing gradually more excited and enthusiastic; his hands were up and waving in front of him when Christie spoke. "You're starting to scare me. What Gutierrez was talking about in his book may be fine, but it's not what we're about at Hope Village."

They were sitting in the open-air section of Los Tiburones, a small thatched-roof restaurant about a mile east of the fishing docks, behind the local McDonald's franchise. David often ate lunch here on the days he came down to the docks to buy fish for the orphanage. He loved the quaint and inviting atmosphere, especially in the covered open-air seating near the walkway, and the restaurant also served fabulous seafood, using an open brick oven to bake the fish. Served with a fresh tomato salsa with green chilies and for less than three American dollars, it was certainly better than the Big Macs they served next door, which cost closer to four dollars.

Rita, the waitress, recognized him and brought two cups of the "Americano" coffee he usually ordered. She had a constant shy and embarrassed smile and what David considered the typical "Indian" look: sturdy, thick body, short neck, very dark skin, twin braids that hung long down her back. She was also quick and attentive and seldom spoke. She wore the yellow dress that constituted the waitstaff uniform at Los Tiburones.

"*Gracias*" David smiled. "*Tendré el pargo asado a la parrilla, por favor.*" He almost always ordered the red snapper.

"I'll have the same," Christie said.

Sipping his coffee, David regretted bringing up Gutierrez. *A Theology of Liberation* by Gustavo Gutierrez, a well-known Catholic priest from Peru who had popularized "liberation theology," had been an eye-opener for David in seminary, despite the fact that his professors had considered it borderline heresy. While David's theological views differed from Gutierrez's, he had been greatly impressed by Gutierrez's criticism that the Church tended to spiritualize some passages in the Bible, rendering them meaningless—especially scriptures about poverty. David believed that in ministering to the poor, as in all things, those who claimed to be followers of Jesus should take the words of Jesus literally and seriously. But now, just when he'd gotten Christie halfway reassured that she was worrying needlessly about Edwards, he'd stirred the pot again.

"Believe me," he said, "I don't want to change our emphasis at Hope Village. We're doing the right thing. But maybe we're in more agreement with Gutierrez than you think. Who was it who said that the only thing necessary for evil to triumph is for good men to do nothing? And that's all Gutierrez is saying—that actions speak louder than words." He nodded in what he hoped was a reassuring manner; then smiled at Rita as she slipped their steaming plates in front of them. He took a bite, savoring the moist and beautifully seasoned fish.

What was wrong with confronting a government that oppresses its people? Wasn't that what Jesus would do? Look how He lashed out at the scribes and Pharisees, and how He turned over the money tables in the temple! He didn't passively sit back and accept the status quo. When He saw evil in the power structure, He confronted it. He spoke truth to power. Not for His own sake, but on behalf of those who were oppressed by it, and whom He loved.

Christie smiled. "I can see the wheels turning, David. I know you wouldn't do or say anything, knowingly, that would jeopardize our mission here. But please remember this: We are not citizens of this country, and we are here to be ministers, not militants. We are here to *serve*, David."

He sipped his coffee. "My dear, we are in complete agreement." And they were—sort of.

Christie studied her husband's face, seemed satisfied by what she saw there, and returned to her fish. "I guess I'm just on edge because things are getting worse here. More and more people are ending up on Guzman's enemy list—and we've seen what's happened to some of the people on that list."

It was true; some of Guzman's perceived enemies were simply missing without a trace. It was widely believed that these "dissidents" were being imprisoned and even eliminated. Recently, Guzman's government had made it a crime even to use insulting language about the president, and in a speech just a week or two before, Guzman had referred to dissenting journalists as "dangerous." On their way to the restaurant just a half hour before, as they'd passed Metropolitan University, several military trucks full of armed soldiers had passed them as college students carrying placards shouted angrily from the edge of the highway. They had reminded him of himself in high school and college. Growing up in central California, and with many Hispanic friends, David's issue had been the rights of immigrants, legal or otherwise, and of the poor. He had shouted angrily during more than one demonstration himself, had waved placards, marched, even taken the podium a time or two, much to his attorney father's disgust. Christie would probably say that he was still too much the firebrand.

Still—how many of those students they'd seen today, pushed to some intemperate action by their youthful rage and sense of justice, not so different from David's own at that age, would someday end up "missing"?

And, for David, that was just the point. How could Christians *not* speak out against such injustice? Fear of man's corrupt government had no place in a Christian's life. Was Jesus afraid of the corrupt Roman government?

Did he try to change it? a quiet voice inside him asked.

They paid their bill and left. On the way back to Hope Village, Christie said, "Autopista Francisco Fajardo will be more crowded this time of day—why aren't you taking the long way? Don't you usually?"

David nodded. "That group of students we saw on our way—I just wanted to swing close enough to see whether it's going to blow up into something."

Christie reached for his arm. "David, that's even more reason to take another way home. We don't want to attract the attention of Guzman's army." She waited. "Are you listening? Tell me you're listening."

"I'm listening. I'll be careful. But the army might be less likely to use violence if they see our Hope Village van. The last thing they want is international witnesses to military excesses."

"David—there won't *be* any witnesses if they put us in prison and throw away the key. Please, David—turn right up ahead and let's take another way home."

"Christie, nothing's going to happen. Look, there's a group of students up ahead. They're just milling around. Nobody's throwing stones, nobody's—"

As he spoke, a larger group of students, thirty or more, emerged from a side street, running pell-mell, overwhelming and gathering up the smaller group, shouting, obviously frightened and angry. When they found something to throw, they stopped just long enough to turn and throw it back down the street behind them, back where David couldn't see, then turned and ran on, some peeling off from the larger group to turn up Autopista Francisco Fajardo. David saw blood on some of them; some wiped their eyes as if weeping and in pain.

"David, pull over now! Pull over!"

"Wait—I can't see what's—"

The first of the soldiers appeared, following the students, just as David heard the first gunshots. He saw two of the students go down. A metal canister about the size of a beer can skittered down the street, bounced off a parked car, and erupted into pale smoke.

"David, *pull over!*"

He jerked the van onto a side street, putting one tire up on the sidewalk, leaving the engine on. "Get down!" he said, pushing Christie's head between her knees. "All the way down! On the floor!" She did. He threw his body over her.

More gunshots. Screams. Breaking glass. David raised his head just high enough to see one of the military trucks rush past, engine whining, soldiers with automatic weapons hanging from the outside. Even apart from their high-tech weapons, the very appearance of the soldiers was terrifying, and no doubt intentionally so: body armor, including vests that bulked them up, helmets with visors that concealed their faces, some with gas masks, heavy boots. They appeared inhuman, alien.

A student limped along the far sidewalk, trying to run on what appeared to be a broken leg. David saw one olive-gray soldier leap from the truck and smash the butt of his weapon into the back of the student's head. He went down. David ducked his head back down to Christie's shoulder. "Stay still," he whispered.

Something struck the rear of the van. Unsure whether it had been a bullet or a rock, David pressed Christie lower in front of the seat. She was holding his hands so tightly he could feel her fingernails digging in.

Time flowed strangely; everything seemed to be happening at once, and yet it all seemed to take forever. The sensations of the fight combined in a strange collage: grinding gears, the deep-throated roar of military vehicles, shouting voices, one woman wailing loudly nearby, the rapid fire of automatic weapons, and the acrid tang of tear gas, weakened by the time it had made its way into the van but still enough to make David's eyes smart. By the time the noise level in the street began to decrease, David felt as if they'd been frozen in their cramped positions for hours, and yet it had undoubtedly been only a minute or two at most. He heard a gunshot or two still, but from further away. He waited a ten-count, then lifted his head high enough to peer out the window with one eye. He waited. He could hear cries for help, he could hear weeping. No gunshots, except one or two echoing faintly back down the city streets from what sounded like blocks away.

"I think it's over," he whispered.

Her head jerked up sharply, almost flattening his nose as he covered her. He winced. "People are calling for help," she said. "Listen."

He lifted his head a bit more. The student across the street who'd been struck in the head by the soldier lay still. David watched a few seconds longer and thought he saw the young man's jacket rising and subsiding. Still breathing.

"David, let me up!" Christie said, struggling against him. "Don't you hear them?"

He waited silently for a moment. Finally: "Yes, I hear," he said, "and yes, we need to help them. But let me go first." He turned the door latch and slowly pushed it open. He stepped outside. Nothing moved except one or two injured students in the street. There were no bystanders, no one else on the street at all. Ghost town. Everyone had disappeared inside. His eyes immediately began to sting worse, and he wiped them.

The door on the other side of the van opened, and he turned to see Christie race to the back of the van and throw it open. He felt a surge of irritation, then shrugged it off. There was no stopping her when people were hurting. It was one of the reasons he loved her. Her military triage training kicked as she grabbed the medical bag and raced into action.

She was jogging toward the nearest injured student—a young woman in the street, leaning against a parked car, who appeared to have been shot through the thigh. The young woman called to them weakly, "Please help me!"

They knelt by her. The wound was bleeding, but the blood was seeping rather than spurting, so David assumed there'd been no artery damage. Christie unpacked a gauze pad from the kit and held it against the wound. "Is this the only place you were injured?" she asked.

The woman lifted her arm to show some deep abrasions. "From when I fell."

"They'll clean those at the hospital. Right now let's just get this bleeding stopped." Christie pulled a pair of scissors from the kit and started to cut away the woman's jeans from around the gunshot wound in a wide X. The wound looked clean, and smaller than David had expected; smaller than a dime.

48   The Missionary

David leaned close to Christie's ear and murmured, "I thought they were supposed to use rubber bullets for riot suppression."

"They never use rubber bullets," the young woman gasped, wincing. "They only say they do. In the last demonstration, over fifty died. That was not from rubber bullets."

"I'll finish with her," Christie said. "Go see who else needs help."

David stood, then looked in all directions and listened carefully. The occasional gunshots still sounded distant—in fact, other than the gunshots and the faint shouts and screams from the conflict blocks away and the few moans and calls from the injured closer by, there was still no sound at all, nor any movement. Everyone had disappeared, hiding either indoors or in their cars. Normally, this part of downtown would be a zoo, with heavy, aggressive traffic, honking horns, a cacophony of loud voices, music seeping out from cantinas... But now there was nothing, not even the music. The carts of vendors were overturned, and most of their contents—fruit such as bananas and mangoes, now smashed and spoiled, leather belts, flip-flops, T-shirts, packs of Chiclets—spilled out into the street, along with the abandoned backpacks, jackets, and caps of students. Although he sensed many eyes watching him, he saw no one but the injured, no movement. A brisk breeze blew leaflets down the sidewalk toward him, printed on marigold-yellow paper, their message bold in thick black letters.

He crunched through broken glass crossing the street. The young man who'd been bludgeoned by the soldier was apparently still unconscious, but now he seemed completely, deathly still. David hurried closer. The back of the student's head, covered in a sickening ooze, seemed oddly misshapen. David knelt and felt the young man's neck for a pulse. Nothing.

Forcing himself past the shock, David stood, looked around, and moved on toward the corner where the students had first appeared, where he could see another student in a Phoenix Suns T-shirt lying in a pool of blood. He looked hardly old enough to be in college. His leg moved slightly.

"Christie," David called. "Here's another." He pushed broken glass away with his shoe before he knelt beside the boy; even so, he winced as he felt a piece cut into his knee. He turned the boy's face toward him. "Can you hear me?" No response. But the boy's chest rose and fell with his breathing. Now that David could see him more closely, there was no way this boy was in college. Mid-teens, at most.

There was some bleeding from the left side of his forehead, but David probed the wound gently with his fingers, and the skull didn't feel compromised. He might have been struck been a soldier's gun butt, or he might have hit his head when he fell. Either way, it might account for his unconsciousness—David wasn't sure. Not for the first time, David regretted his lack of medical knowledge beyond basic first aid. But he knew enough to know that the most serious problem was the gunshot wounds and the bleeding from them.

Christie knelt beside him.

"I think he was hit three times," David said.

"Oh, he's so young," she said.

"I see five wounds, but I think two are exit wounds. He was hit here, just below his shoulder, and here, just above the hip bone—"

"And here," Christie said, "in the upper arm. I don't see an exit wound for the bullet that hit his shoulder, so it may still be in there."

"Look at all the blood!" David said. "He's lost too much." Even as he spoke, he was aware that sound was beginning to return to the street. He noticed approaching sirens at first, possibly ambulances, possibly the police. Also, other voices—he looked up to see a few of the locals venturing out, some of them trying to help the injured, some of them simply standing in small groups, looking angry, gesturing. Some appeared to be looting the overturned carts. "We have to get the bleeding stopped and then get him to the clinic. We have to—"

"David," Christie said, in the take-charge tone of voice he'd often heard her use in the clinic, when she was in her element saving lives. "We do have to get the bleeding stopped, first thing." Even as she spoke, she pulled supplies from the bag, ripping open packages of gauze and

50   The Missionary

antibiotics. "But he needs more than we can do at the clinic. For these wounds, David, he needs surgery. If we leave him, the soldiers will let him lie right here for hours. He'll die. We have to get him to an emergency room. And—" she nodded her head down the street, where soldiers had now reappeared several blocks away, just beyond a traffic circle with a fountain in the middle, carrying transparent riot shields, their voices over bullhorns telling everyone to stay inside— "we need to do it now. Right now."

"This is Venezuela. Emergency rooms here won't take—"

"The Catholic hospital in the Bello Monte district. We'll take him there," she said impatiently. "Get the van. Hurry!"

Jogging back toward the van, he sorted through what he'd seen on Christie's face. Anger. Frustration. Concentration. And, as he had known he would see, the anguish of leaving so many on the street—injured, in pain, untreated. David felt that anguish too. But he felt one thing even more strongly: the need to get his wife, the mother of his child, safely out of here before the return of the soldiers, getting steadily nearer and marching in a solid line, shields raised.

The situation was changing second by second now. The noise was increasing as the crowd, rediscovering their courage in numbers and in their outrage over the violence so clear before them, poured back onto the street, shouting, throwing stones and bottles at the advancing line of soldiers. The frequency of gunshots increased, and a bullet struck the brick façade of the building nearest David as he ran, bits of brick raining down on him. The commands of the soldiers blared through bullhorns.

He ran through a cloud of acrid, lung-burning smoke and looked up—there was an overturned vehicle on the next corner, half on the sidewalk, tires burning. He pulled his shirt up over his nose and mouth for the last several yards, trying to protect his lungs from the smoke. He jumped into the van, then fumbled for the keys, forgetting which pocket he'd put them in. Found them. The engine roared, and the tires bumped off the curb and into the street. As he approached the corner where Christie knelt over the wounded boy, a local man motioned frantically for him to pull close to the curb; Christie had apparently recruited helpers.

A crowd of people ran by him, away from the soldiers, and David knew that the guards would be not far behind, in pursuit.

Before David had even brought the van to a complete stop, the man who'd been signaling to him was opening the rear door. Christie was directing three other men, who helped her lift the boy and carry him toward the van. A guard ran up to the passenger door.

"Move this van, senor! Andale! You cannot move any of these students. They are being arrested!"

"This boy is no student—he's just a child!" David shouted. "He's badly wounded, and I'm taking him to the hospital!" Even with the armed and clearly hostile guard confronting him, David found his anger at this senseless violence against the innocent boiling over. "If you want to arrest someone, go arrest that student you murdered down the street!"

But the guard didn't look at the body of the dead student; he lifted his automatic weapon until David was staring down the barrel, then shouted to the men at the back of the van, who were continuing to load the body of the wounded boy. Another guard jogged up. "Stop or you will all be arrested!" he shouted.

David stared at the guard; the guard stared back. Two seconds. Four. No one moved.

And then there was a tremendous explosion, followed by a shock wave that rocked the van. David ducked, thinking that someone had fired a missile or grenade at them—but when he lifted his head, looked behind him, and saw the huge fireball, he realized that the gas tank of the burning car had exploded. The two guards had crouched to the pavement at the explosion; one had dropped his weapon and covered his head. Now they jumped to their feet and ran toward the burning vehicle; David could see a number of soldiers on the ground near it, a couple of them rolling on the pavement, their clothes on fire.

Christie jumped into the back of the van with the wounded boy. Her helpers slammed the van doors behind her. David punched the gas pedal and squealed around the corner. He would worry in a minute which direction the hospital lay in; for now, he whipped around corner after corner, putting as much distance and as many buildings as possible between them and the insanity of violence behind them.

An hour and a half later, with the badly injured teenager dropped off at the Catholic hospital's emergency room—the nurses and doctors there had already been frantically preparing for the influx of new patients they knew they'd receive after the riot—David walked Christie to the door of the Hope Village clinic, then just stood and held her for a moment before releasing her to her work. She leaned into his shoulder. "I'm sorry," he whispered. "I should have listened to you. I put you in harm's way." He shuddered, remembering the jagged feel of the edge of the bullet hole in the rear of the van as he'd run his finger over it just moments before. "Thank God for your training in Iraq… you saved a life today."

She pulled back slightly and looked up at him, shaking her head. "If either of us was listening to God today, David, I think it was you. I was thinking of our own safety. You were thinking of others. And because of that, we may have saved at least one life today."

"Because of that, you could have been hit by a stray bullet, and Davy might have had to grow up without a mother. I'll remember that next time I'm tempted to—"

She laughed lightly, a sound he loved, a sound like music, then reached up on tiptoes and kissed him. "No, you won't. You'll charge in again like John Wayne. But I love you that way, David Eller. Even if it's sometimes infuriating."

Taking the roundabout route back to his office, David wandered past the garden, where Cecil Duncan was busy pulling weeds among the tomatoes, assisted by three of the children. Years ago, the children had started calling him "Papa Cecil." The name had endured through the generations of orphaned kids who had passed through Hope Village.

Papa Cecil was leading them in a crazy song as they worked.

"¡McDonald viejo tuvo una granja, EIEIO!"

The children begin to giggle.

Cecil was a large man even with the slight stoop of age, at least three inches taller than David's 5' 10" and weighing at least two hundred pounds. He wore striped coveralls; a big straw Western-style hat covered the bald patch that stretched from his forehead across the top of his head. Shocks of thick gray hair ringing the bald spot stuck out around the edges of his hat. His large hands clapped as the children danced around him. *Always* he was surrounded by adoring children, and always it was just as clear that he adored them as well, with all his heart. Cecil, Martha, and Christie—David was surrounded by coworkers who had great and tender hearts of love for these children. David's love for them, he knew, was of a somewhat different type—he worked hard on their behalf. He agonized over their plight. But for Cecil, Martha, and Christie, their love extended always to *this* child, at *this* moment, and they wanted to lift that child onto their lap, gaze into her smiling face, touch her cheek…

David's love was expressed less in touches than in hard work, and his commitment was less to *this* child in *this* place than it was to the vast numbers of homeless children in Caracas.

And though he had long since concluded that he was the poorer for it, he also didn't think he could change. His job, his calling, he knew, was to save even more kids from this awful plight he found in the barrios of Caracas.

As Cecil and the children returned to pulling weeds, David walked down a row between the broccoli and tomatoes. Cecil stood upright and smiled a warm hello. The children continued to work.

"Looks like another ample crop," David said.

"Like every year, David. We plant, and God gives us—well, let's not talk about that. I bet that, after the afternoon you've had, our garden isn't the first thing on your mind. My land, son—you and Christie must've been terrified!"

54   The Missionary

David lifted his hand, checking it for tremors. "Still shaking."

"I don't blame you. I would be. And think of the families whose lives are changed forever by what happened on those streets today—sons and daughters lost, parents' hopes for their children destroyed. Let's have a prayer service tonight, with all the children. We'll pray for those families, and for the soldiers too. I'm sure there were plenty who hated what they were ordered to do today."

David snorted. "I was there. It didn't look to me like they hated it."

Cecil studied him. "We don't know, David. Some of those soldiers may have had brothers or sisters at the university. Can you imagine their pain, not knowing whether the bullets they fired might have injured or killed their own sibling?"

"Then they could have laid down their weapons."

Cecil put an arm over David's shoulder and squeezed. "I'm so glad you're safe. It's selfish, I know, but I'm glad the prayer service we'll have is to support someone else in *their* grief, rather than to deal with our own."

David allowed himself to enjoy Cecil's fatherly affection for a moment, then said, "Speaking of grief—the new boy I brought in last night, Ricardo. You've heard that Dr. Vargas isn't optimistic about his chances?"

"I heard. I've prayed all day for God's comfort for his sister." Cecil fanned his face with his hat.

"You've been doing this for over forty years, Cecil. Ricardo isn't the first child you've seen near death. And it's such a waste."

Cecil reached down to pull another weed. "I know, David, I know. But can you name a time when that wasn't true? Wasn't it so in Jesus' time? Isn't it so in most countries around the world even now? We can't change all that. We're not called to change all that. We're called to love these children and provide for them. That's our charter. That's what Martha and I have spent our lives at. I believe we've made a difference."

For a moment there was silence between them. David reached down and yanked out a weed. "Of course you've made a difference. A huge difference. That's why Christie and I came. But I admit it, Cecil—I get frustrated at the thought that I could rescue children from the streets of Caracas every night of my life, and there would still be just as many of them, or more, when I die. The supply is never ending."

Cecil stood up. Eyeing David, he stretched his back and rubbed his shoulder. Stepping over a row of tomatoes, he sat on one of the large, bench-sized rocks that lined the garden, colorful flowers growing all around them. David joined him. "I just try to live in obedience to Jesus, David." Surveying the garden, Cecil said, "My calling is to do what I find to do, right here, among these children." One of the little girls working in the garden came and reached out her arms toward Cecil. He smiled as he took her in a big hug, squeezing tightly, and lifted her onto his lap. He cupped her face with his hands as her large brown eyes smiled up at him. "Look into the face of this child, David. Do you see the miracle that love has wrought? How can we do less?"

David didn't answer. Avoiding eye contact with Cecil, he watched the girl as she climbed down and moved back out into the tomato vines and began to pull more weeds.

They sat silently for several moments while Cecil fanned his face with his hat. As much as David enjoyed these one-on-one chats with Cecil about life, poverty, theology, suffering, and the work at Hope Village, they had had far fewer of them recently. Just no time.

Cecil rose, patted David's shoulder, walked toward the little girl, and began to pull weeds again.

David walked a few feet down the path, then stopped, turned to watch Cecil for a moment, and said under his breath, "I'm not talking about doing less, Cecil. I'm talking about doing more."

That afternoon, Aaron drove the SUV back along the coast toward the hotel while Hawkeye stared at the ocean, reviewing in his mind their surveillance of the Olas Resort.

Hawkeye didn't consider himself a perfectionist. Perfectionists tended to have a compulsive need to control. Take control out of their hands—as happened at least once on most missions—and perfection-ists froze. Hawkeye did believe in preparation, in skill, and in atten-tion to detail. And he didn't like leaving anything to chance—especially where the success of his mission depended on good intel.

There was much about this mission that made him uneasy. He did not know the members of JAM. Yet he was expected to rely on their information—and they still couldn't tell him, at this late date, even where the op would take place! That uncertainty added complications, dangers.

During Hawkeye's days at Sayeret Matkal, when a mission had been chosen, the men rehearsed for weeks. Often sets were built to duplicate the buildings or other structures the commandos expected to encounter. No detail was too small to rehearse over and over. Every contingency was exhaustively considered. But here, there was no oppor-tunity for rehearsal.

Even if there had been, Hawkeye admitted, every operation held potential for surprise, and few did not live up to that potential. Fortu-nately, he was one of the best at thinking in milliseconds when the unex-pected happened, with his life and the lives of his men on the line. He had proven that time and time again, and that is why he was alive today.

He would need that skill for this job.

CHAPTER EIGHT

David awoke with a start. It seemed late. He picked up his alarm clock and stared at it in surprise: 7:15. He'd slept in, a rarity for him. Normally he was awake by 5:30—but then, besides the exhausting emotional turmoil of the day before, he'd not gotten much sleep for several nights.

Twenty minutes later, showered and in his office, a cup of coffee in hand, he dialed Christie at the clinic. "Hon, I'd better do the shopping, run some errands. Life goes on. Anything you need?" As he talked, he put the Hope Village checkbook into his briefcase, along with some cash, his sunglasses, and his billfold and cell phone.

"Mia made a list."

"Okay. I'll pick it up before I head out. See you this afternoon."

Slight twinge of guilt as he hung up—he hadn't mentioned to her something that, in the confusion of the day before, he'd recalled only just before he'd called her: that he was having lunch today with Carlos Edwards and his friends. Normally David and Christie had no secrets from each other. But if he came back with a fat check…

A little over an hour later, having picked up the items on Mia's list and driven through the tunnels to LaGuaira, he turned the Ford van east down Avenida Principal toward the local fishing docks where commercial fisherman sold their daily catches of shark, tuna, and snapper and where David knew he would find his closest Venezuelan friend, Felix Suturos, an independent commercial fisherman.

On the day David first met Felix, years before, he and Felix had haggled at the dock over the price of a large red snapper. But David's

58   The Missionary

attention had been on the little girl playing nearby on the boat. She appeared to be about four years old and had a severe cleft lip and palate.

"¿Qué es su nombre?" David asked.

"Her name is Blanca," Felix replied, affection showing in his leathery face.

While Felix wrapped the purchased fish in newspaper, David said, "Are you aware that Blanca's cleft palate can be corrected with surgery?"

"I would love to get her this help, señor, but I have no money."

David nodded. "I know of a group of doctors from the United States who come to Central America every year to perform surgeries like this at no charge. I will see if they can help."

And they had. Six months later, David arranged for Blanca and her mother to fly to Guatemala to meet with Medical Teams International specialists in their mobile surgical units. Doctors performed three separate surgeries over a three-year period on Blanca, who was now nine. Her cleft palate was almost completely corrected; only one more small procedure was needed. After that, Felix and Isabel became a regular part of the orphanage volunteer staff.

Now, Felix waved as David approached his boat.

David loved the colors at the wharf. Dozens of fishing boats, small and large, painted in a variety of bright hues crowded together along the dock, bobbing in unison like a chorus line on the water. Felix's boat was bright green around the water line, with white sides, topped with a teal-blue gunwale. In big black letters, the number "2961" stood out near the bow just below the name, ROSI ANGEL. Old black tires used as docking fenders hung from hemp rope on the sides. A bright orange roof topped green and black housing with white trim and box-like windows. The colors, the slap of waves on the boats' hulls, and wails of gulls, and the gentle movements soothed David's ragged emotions. He felt himself relaxing for the first time since the riot.

How incredible that this place of great peace was so close, in time and space, to the terror and carnage of yesterday afternoon.

David shrugged off the thought. He had to move on. A sudden decision: He would not, as he had planned, discuss the riot with Felix. He forced his mind back to the moment.

Over the past couple of years, Felix's fishing business had grown. This was his smaller boat, often captained by one of the fishermen Felix now employed, while Felix himself fished with his newest pride and joy, the *Bahia Bonita*, a seventy-foot steel-hulled vessel with capacity for thousands of pounds of fish, capable of plying the deeper waters for tuna and shark. But the *Bahia Bonita* was being outfitted for a two-week trip to deeper waters off the coast, and Felix had gone out this morning with the smaller boat.

David dropped the large cooler on the dock. He and Felix embraced in the *abrazo* custom of close friends in Venezuela, hugging while patting each other on the back. Felix had calloused, leathery hands, and deep creases parted his sun-worn cheeks when he smiled. Bare-chested and bare-footed, he wore nothing but bright yellow shorts and a San Francisco Giants baseball cap given to him by David, a life-long fan.

"I need the usual amount of your catch for the orphanage, *por favor*," David said, then sat on the bow, feet dangling over the water, and watched as Felix shoveled crushed ice into the cooler from a large locker. He selected some of the red snapper from a barrel and layered them in the ice. Felix would, David knew, as always, refuse payment for the fish.

David watched a group of gulls swarming the water near another boat nearby, fighting over fish entrails and heads. "I picked up a new boy for the orphanage two nights ago."

Felix looked up and grinned. "When do you not?"

"Yes, but this one I'm worried about," David said.

As concerned as he was about Ricardo, this was actually a roundabout way of approaching what he really wanted to talk to Felix about. Felix had become a kind of sounding board for David—a safe person outside the orphanage staff who always listened with interest.

David told Felix about Ricardo's condition, then about meeting Carlos Edwards, his visit to the orphanage, their conversation, and Carlos's donation.

Felix nodded, then looked long into David's face without speaking. "Desperate times, desperate measures, my friend," he said at last. "We have learned that from our past." Closing the lid on the filled cooler, he straightened and put his hand on David's shoulder. "But if you meet with those who oppose Guzman, be careful. When he retaliates against his enemies, he does not bother to check identification."

The Punta Grill was dark, rustic, and expensive—a place for business lunches and elegant dinners for upper-class couples and groups. The reddish tile floors and heavy wooden tables and chairs gave it an elegant but rugged ambience.

After the waiter showed the two of them to a small table near the back of the restaurant, Carlos began by apologizing: "I'm sorry, my friend, but the two men I had intended to introduce you to both had last-minute emergencies. For them, another time." It was a grave disappointment to David. He didn't expect Carlos to make another contribution just one day after his first, and David had very much hoped to come home with another large check—in part, he realized, to justify to Christie why he'd had lunch with Carlos.

They began with small talk. Carlos had many questions about Hope Village—enough that it was clear to David that he had been thinking about what he had seen during his tour the day before. By the time the waiter brought their steaming plates of food—the Punta Grill was known mainly for its steak, and that's what both of them had ordered—Carlos shook his head and said, "I can't tell you how much I admire what you and the others are doing with the children of Caracas, David. Venezuela needs more men like you."

David looked away. Never at ease with compliments, he tended to shrug them off or deflect them to others, and that is what he attempted to do this time: "It was Cecil and Martha Duncan who founded Hope Village. I'm just following in the footsteps of giants."

Carlos nodded, chewing thoughtfully. "And the institution is well named," he said. "It gives hope to children in need. But let me ask: How many Hope Villages would it take to meet the needs of all of Caracas? Of all of Venezuela?"

David took a sip of water. The answer to Carlos's question would not be quick or easy. "I agree that this country needs more Hope Villages," he said. "But unfortunately, it needs greater change than that, and it doesn't appear that those changes are coming very soon."

"One never knows." Carlos chewed a mouthful, looking thoughtful, then said, "David, you spoke of change. What do you think is the most important next step for the Venezuelan government?"

David looked down at his plate, hesitating, remembering Christie's cautions. But David had been longing for someone with whom he could speak candidly about his frustrations with the Guzman regime. The rest of the staff at Hope Village, as well as most of the other missionaries David knew in Caracas, urged him not to speak of it, lest there be reprisals. To David, saying nothing went against his American upbringing—and his sense of a Christian's place in the world. Maybe Carlos was the person with whom he could share his concern for the poor and oppressed.

At a nearby table sat a young boy and girl, about the age of the older children at the orphanage, sitting at lunch with their parents. Their clothes were clean and stylish, the girl's hair lovingly brushed till it shone—perhaps by a nanny—and held back with shiny barrettes. The family, seeming happy, at ease, comfortable, unworried, discussed something with humor and affection. A lovely family. They were doing nothing wrong. And yet David found himself almost resentful of the fact that those two children would no doubt leave on their plates more food than the entire gang of boys David had noticed roaming down the sidewalk as he drove over—dressed in rags, thin almost to the point that their bones showed through—would have for lunch.

The system was broken.

He looked into Carlos's expectant face.

And for ten nonstop minutes he told Carlos exactly how he felt about Guzman and the plight of the poor in Venezuela—about the misguided use of oil revenue to solidify Guzman's hold on power, rather than to ease the burden of the impoverished millions. He talked about Guzman's oppressive control of the media and the military. He spoke of his and Christie's harrowing experience in the riot the day before. He lamented the frequent disappearance of those who spoke out against the regime—often professors or student leaders, sometimes imprisoned and even shot to death because of trumped-up charges of treason.

"He has declared himself an atheist, like Mao," David said. "Given his desire to remake the entire nation and everyone in it in his own image, he won't be able to resist persecuting those whose beliefs are different. In fact, it may already be happening—I've heard rumors that outspoken Catholic priests, as well as evangelicals like myself, are already being persecuted in remote areas."

"I too have heard these rumors," Carlos said. "I believe them."

"And since he's already nationalized many industries and businesses, what's to stop him from 'nationalizing' ministries like Hope Village run by non-Venezuelans like Cecil and me? We could lose all that we've done." He leaned forward and spoke in a softer tone. "Democracy will never return to Venezuela as long as Guzman is in power. He should step down."

Edwards looked intently at David and was silent for a moment, then said quietly, "He will never step down." He seemed to descend into a funk for a few seconds, then, almost as if shaking himself awake, he roused himself, nodded, and prodded David with more questions: How had David come to his conclusions about the current government? Was he afraid of reprisal? How much of his energy was he willing to give to his ideas for reform?

And with growing ease and confidence, David kept talking.

When lunch was consumed and the plates cleared away, and the two men sat over coffee, Edwards finally seemed to have come to the end of his questions. He sat staring to the side, at nothing, as if thinking. David sipped and waited. Finally Edwards said, "David, can I trust you with something extremely confidential?"

"Absolutely," David said.

"What I am about to say must not be repeated to anyone, not even your wife," Carlos said. "I'm placing my safety, and that of several others, in your hands."

Once again, David heard a faint echo of what Christie had said: *Carlos Edwards is not what he seems. He's playing you.* But now the man's intense seriousness, and the gravity of his words, had taken David's curiosity to a fever pitch. "You can trust me to keep your confidence," David repeated.

Edwards leaned closer across the table and said, "A group already in existence is planning to remove Guzman from power. These are Venezuelan people, important people, with money and influence, who believe the only way to bring democracy and prosperity back to our country is to change the system. They do not believe Guzman will ever step down or declare fair elections without intense pressure. We intend to provide that pressure."

David felt his heart beating faster. Could it be that this was actually going to happen? "You're serious?"

"Very." He paused and studied David's face. "Do you wish me to stop speaking of this?"

David shook his head. "No. I'm intrigued. Please tell me more."

"If you would like. But I warn you that the conversation may become more uncomfortable for you."

David cocked his head. "More uncomfortable? And why is that?"

"Because there may be something you can do to help us."

David found himself caught in an odd and frightening moment. His senses switched to hyper-alert, and he was suddenly aware of

64   The Missionary

everything: the clink of ice in glasses at the bar, the squeak of the wheels of a trolley being pushed by one of the busmen, a quiet conversation being carried on in oddly accented Spanish by two people in the kitchen, behind swinging doors. It felt as if the room had suddenly gone cold. "To help you?" he said, and his voice sounded oddly hoarse to him.

Carlos lifted an eyebrow. "In small ways only."

"Wait, Carlos. You can trust me this far: You haven't asked me to do anything but keep a secret, which I can do. But I won't do anything that I think will jeopardize our ministry here, or put the lives of my family and the rest of our team in danger."

Carlos pointed his finger toward David, shaking it slightly. "That is because you are a man of character and courage. Knowing how you feel, I would be dishonest not offering you this opportunity, even it you must refuse. I'm not speaking of major things. Just small favors that will enable the rest of the team to do our work. I think this too could be a part of God's work."

A bead of sweat dripped from David's neck, and he realized that the tapping sound he'd been hearing was his own tapping of his foot, an old nervous habit. He stilled it, sure that Christie, if she knew of this conversation, would urge him to get up and walk out right now. He remembered what she had said about Carlos. "How does either of us know that the other isn't working for Guzman?" he asked.

Carlos chuckled. "You do not fit the profile. As for me, all I can do is assure you that I despise the man and all he stands for, and I am willing to risk much—my very life—to see justice done."

David wiped a faint layer of perspiration from his forehead with his hand. "Other than moral support, Carlos, I'm not sure what else I can offer. You speak of God's work, but God's work for us here is Hope Village." He smiled wryly. "I've had that conversation twice in the past twenty-four hours, first with Christie and then with Cecil Duncan. And they're right. If I damaged the ministry of Hope Village by getting involved in—"

"And if you do not choose to be involved for that reason, David, I understand. Still, I sensed your passion about the need for change, and

I thought maybe you could help in a very discreet way. I understand that you are not a citizen of this country, so you may not consider this to be your concern after all. Please forgive me if I have offended you."

"I'm not saying that. The plight of the poor concerns us all, and it supersedes national boundaries and questions of citizenship. Otherwise, obviously, I would not be here. It's just that...I have no training or background in this kind of thing. I'm not sure I would be useful."

Carlos leaned closer. "The services I'm speaking of require no particular skill or training. When intricate plans are being made like this in total secrecy, sometimes messages or money need to be passed along. Maybe you would be willing to do that type of thing for us. It would only be two, maybe three times at most we would need you to help in this way. Actually, you would be perfect for this. No one would ever suspect your involvement because of your work here." He smiled. "It would certainly be less risky, and far less public, than your comments on Venevision!"

Perhaps true. But David also remembered Christie's observation that he was being played by a pro. Carlos's references to the interview on television could be a skillfully chosen reminder that David had already taken risks born out of his passion for the poor and oppressed. If so, why not take more, if there was a chance of truly making a difference? "You're a businessman," David said, "and a successful one, it appears. Aren't you risking everything by getting involved in this?"

Carlos reached into his pocket and handed David a business card.

> Carlos Patricio Edwards
>
> El Presidente
>
> El Río Una Inversiones
>
> El Samen Suite 202
>
> Av Venezuela Entre Av Sorocaima
>
> CARACAS (1050) Venezuela
>
> teléfono: (58-212) 762.89.41

President, River One Investments.

"I have a securities business. My clients make investments here and in other Western countries, as I do myself. Yes, I have done well, David. It may sound crazy, but I feel that God has placed me in a position of influence, and I want to help make this world a better place." His countenance darkened. "I have not always been wealthy." He grew quiet and stared into his coffee cup, rubbing the edge with his finger. When he spoke again, his voice had changed, taken on a bitter note. "I grew up on the streets of Buenos Aires, Argentina. Like those children you help at Hope Village, I was homeless. My parents drank themselves to death when I was very small—I have few memories of them, and the few I have I do not care to revisit. I stole and begged and did whatever I could to survive, David—you can imagine. When I was old enough to convince a recruiter I was of age to join the army, I did, and I swore I would never be hungry again. But I have not forgotten the feel of poverty. Frankly, it is partly for that reason that I admire you for what you do."

David opened his mouth to respond—and realized that he had no idea what to say. Carlos's story gave David an entirely new perspective on this man across the table in silver cufflinks with a Rolex peeking out of his sleeve, a perspective David could not have imagined just seconds before. Carlos knew what it meant to move from sleeping on the street to warm food and a bed, to a chance at a future.

But how could he agree to help Carlos and his friends, in the face of Christie's direct cautions and Cecil's more subtle ones? He wanted to help—and wanted to run. His reaction was powerful and contradictory: He wished Carlos had not brought it up—and wished at the same time to help Carlos and his team succeed. What a strange and unexpected twist this conversation had taken!

Carlos lifted a hand, as if waving away what David were about to say. "Take some time this afternoon to think about this. Tell no one, of course—we cannot count on their discretion. If you decide you want to discuss this further, call me by five o'clock this evening. If I do not hear from you by five o'clock, I will assume you feel you cannot help, and I will not contact you again...as long as you keep what I have said in complete confidence."

Was that a veiled threat? David wondered. He almost asked Carlos what he had meant, but decided he would be wiser to take some time alone to think. And he certainly intended to keep his mouth shut anyway.

Carlos pulled out his wallet and dropped enough cash on the table to more than cover the meal, then stood, but leaned toward David to speak confidentially. "I also know that, if you should choose to help us, there are many people, including some of my wealthiest clients, who would want to make substantial contributions to Hope Village."

When they reached the parking lot, Carlos opened his car door, then turned, took another business card from his pocket, and scribbled a number on the back. "Please call me on my private cell by five this evening. Plans are moving quickly. If I do not hear from you by then, I will not bother you again."

"I have a lot to think about," David managed to say.

A lot to think about—that was an understatement. Back at Hope Village, David wandered up the path toward the school.

It would be insane to get involved with Carlos Edwards in—in whatever it was he was trying to rope David into. Wouldn't it? Christie was right. They didn't know anything about Carlos except that he seemed to have a lot of money and a business card, but even the card could be part of his cover if he was some kind of political operative, some opposition activist. CIA.

And why not? Why couldn't he be CIA? Think about it. He was coming to David for help. Why would a Venezuelan operative do that? Wouldn't it make more sense for the CIA to trust another American than it would—

"David."

David jumped and his heart flopped like a mackerel on the pier. "Cecil. Oh, man. Don't do that."

Cecil chuckled, coming down the path the other way. "Sorry to make you jump. I saw you were deep in thought, so I hollered to make

68   The Missionary

sure you didn't run me over like an armadillo on the road. Are you—are you okay? You look white as a sheet."

"No, I'm fine, really. It's just...I'm fine."

Cecil studied him quietly for a moment, looking deep in his usual fashion. "Well, I'm glad I ran into you. We didn't finish our conversation in the garden yesterday. In fact, I think I did all the talking. But I don't need you to bare your soul for me to know you've been under a heavy weight lately. What you saw happen yesterday in that riot would be traumatic for anybody. Not to mention being shot at." Cecil swept his long arm in invitation. "Take a walk with me out to the garden."

David was in no mood for a chat, his mind still vibrating with a combination of excitement and fear. But this was Cecil.

On a grassy knoll nearby, a bench looked out over the garden, past the orchard, and up into the mountains. David often saw Cecil sitting here, by himself, with his Bible. Many times, the two of them had talked here. This time, Cecil seemed in no hurry after they sat; he gazed out at the view and sighed contentedly. "Tell me what's bothering you, David," Cecil said at last. "I bet it's more than yesterday's brouhaha, traumatic as that was. Whenever you're ready."

David looked at the ground, surprised at how much he wanted to do just that—to blurt out to this good and trustworthy man everything that happened at lunch. *But I can't*, he thought. *I've already given Carlos my word to tell no one. Not Christie. Not Cecil.* And there was another reason he would keep quiet. He already knew what Cecil's response would be.

After a few moments of silence, Cecil said, "I ever tell you what it was like when I first came here?"

David shook his head—not because he hadn't heard parts of this story before. He had, many times. But he sensed that Cecil was working toward some point, and wanted to give him the freedom to approach it in his own way.

"Course, Hope Village wasn't here yet. We bought the land with a small donation from a church, combined with our personal savings account—which wasn't much, believe me. We bought a tent. Cooked our meals outside on a camp stove."

He chuckled, pointing. "I dug an outhouse right up there, not far from where the orphanage sits now. It was fun at first. We pretended we were camping. Other than that, we had no idea what we were supposed to do. We had no grand vision. But eventually three orphan kids came to sleep in the tent with us. That was when I realized we needed to start an orphanage.

"So I sent letters home to churches and friends, pleading for money. I asked the city fathers here in Caracas for help. I approached businesses for donations. Didn't help that I wasn't Catholic, in a country where ninety percent are. I felt some of the same stress you're feeling now. We were moving too slow—*way* too slow. Nothing worked. And I got sick of living in a tent.

"Felt sorry for myself at first. Then angry. Angry at the government and churches who ignored my pleas for help, even angry at God for bringing Martha and me out here. I was ready to give up."

Cecil picked up a twig and rolled it between his fingers. "This went on for two-and-a-half years. Seemed like eternity. By then, Martha was worried about my health. I was still a young man, but my blood pressure went up and I was having headaches all the time.

"One day, by God's grace, I walked past Our Lady Catholic Church. Father Amada was out in the churchyard. He waved. I hadn't met him, so I decided to introduce myself. Next thing you know, he invited me in for coffee."

Cecil chuckled again. "We found out we actually liked each other. From then on, every week, I'd stop in for coffee and we'd have a chat. Sometimes for a couple hours. Then one day we prayed together. It was like a revelation to me, David. I discovered a brother in Christ in the last place I expected to find one. We never spoke much about theology. We just talked about Jesus, and about the children in poverty we both felt called to love.

"I never thought of it as a way to get something. I just enjoyed the fellowship. But believe it or not, our first pile of concrete blocks and

70   The Missionary

metal roofing was donated by the members of Our Lady! Several of their members came—Father Amada twisted some arms, I'd bet—to help us build that first wing of the orphanage. Right there where the walls and floor are a bit crooked."

David let Cecil talk, wondering where he was headed.

"That's when I had what you might call an epiphany. I realized that I needed to do the Lord's work in the Lord's way…that all my flailing, anger, and manipulation were not of God, but of me."

Elbows on his knees, Cecil looked down at the grass. "God spoke to me then about my true calling. Not in an audible voice—just that silent little whisper you get in your mind and heart that tells you God's on the line. He said, 'Cecil, just love the little ones I give to you and Martha, and let me take care of the rest.'"

He looked at David. "Love sees the need, David—not the cause."

David sat silent for a few moments, resisting the urge to argue with this man he admired so much, but finally the tension was too great. *Love sees the need, not the cause—that's a bumper-sticker slogan, not theology.* He shook his head. "Cecil, no matter how much the local Catholics and short-term missionaries from the U.S. helped build this place, it wouldn't have happened without your blood, sweat, and tears. Someone had a vision and made it happen, and that person was you—you and Martha. You didn't sit around waiting for a miracle. You acted.

"I see your point, and I respect your moment of revelation. But if helping kids is the bottom line, and I think it is, I also think we could save hundreds more than we are. I mean, how can we just dismiss all the little Ricardos out there on the street right now?"

"I don't," Cecil said. "But think: There are kids dying on the streets of Rio de Janeiro, Manila, Hong Kong. There are starving, homeless kids in Calcutta and Bogotá. How will you save *them*? Is it just that these kids are five miles away and some of the others, five thousand? Does God love the kids more here than he does the ones in Calcutta because we're here, you and me? We can't save the whole world. We just have to be obedient to do today what God *gives* us to do today. I don't want to get out ahead of God."

David picked up a small rock and tossed it toward the garden. "Frankly, I'm more worried about getting too far *behind* God."

Cecil pulled off his hat and ran his hand through his sparse hair. "There are children in need world-wide. I don't have an answer to that. But there are two things I want you to think about. First one is, that story I just told you took place long before Armando Guzman came to power. I worried about the needs of homeless kids in Caracas—and there was plenty to worry about—when Guzman was just a private in the army wondering when he'd get his next leave to see his girlfriend. So don't get the idea Guzman invented all this. And second, life has taught me that the best we can do is to help each other muddle through the hurts of this life, one person at a time. Imagine what could happen if every Christian in the world loved and cared for just one more child." A slight smile creased his face. "That may not sound earth-changing. But that's how Martha and I have found a piece of heaven right here with these children."

"I wish I saw more heaven, Cecil. What I see out on the streets and in the barrios seems more like hell." David stood. "What you say sounds like wisdom, Cecil. And maybe it is. Still, while the work never changes, sometimes the methods do. Call it my impetuous youth if you want, but I want the satisfaction of doing something significant, and frankly I'm just not content to sit back and assume that the way things are is the way they have to remain."

Cecil stood and put his hand on David's shoulder. "Be careful." He took a few shuffling steps down the path toward the clinic, then stopped and turned back. "I miss him, you know," he said. "Father Amada. He died a few years before you came—lived to be over ninety. Tough old cob." Cecil laughed. "He could surprise you. He surely could. I wonder…" His eyes twinkled. "Which one of us would he have agreed with today?"

72 The Missionary

Gustavo, the head chef at the Vina Estate, studied the faxed requisition on government stationery: an order for five bottles of Macallan Scotch whiskey, rumored to be Guzman's favorite and very hard to find. To Gustavo, this suggested four things. First, there was a high likelihood that the Vina Estate had been chosen as the site of Guzman's vacation—unless, of course, a similar order had been sent to the rest of the resorts and estates he might choose to visit, to keep from revealing his true destination. Second, if the liquor *was* for Guzman, the event was at least twenty-four hours away, since Guzman's staff would know how difficult it was to acquire the vintage Scotch and have it overnighted. Third, if it was Guzman, Gustavo would soon get another fax with a dinner menu. It would probably feature abalone, Guzman's favorite dish, flown in fresh from Chile. Fourth, ordering twenty bottles meant that *whoever* was coming had a fairly large dinner party planned—or intended to get totally smashed for several days.

Things were moving fast. Gustavo immediately headed down to a local bar to make a telephone call.

CHAPTER NINE

After he left Cecil, David checked on Davy and then trudged back to his office and locked the door. He sat at his desk, head down, trying to think and pray.

What would his older brother, Stephen, do? David had always been proud of Stephen, who'd played tight end on their high school's football team and, at 6' 3" and 230 pounds, had broken several school and league records. He'd been awarded a full-ride scholarship to play for the University of California Bears.

David and his father had gone to almost every Cal home game. Eventually, Stephen had gone on to Stanford Law School and was now working in the Attorney General's office in Washington D.C.

In high school, David would have loved to hear his father talk about him the way he bragged about Stephen's accomplishments on the football field. But at 5' 10" and 145 pounds soaking wet, David had been— he felt—too small to matter to his father. Michael Eller was, after all, a man made for big things. A Senator's son, Harvard-educated, a powerful attorney, David's father had been without question the most dominant figure in David's childhood. His mother, a quiet woman of faith, a loving mother, had always deferred to her husband. In everything.

And perhaps the complexity of those family relationships explained why, even though David thought now about calling Stephen for counsel, he was reluctant. He had no desire to continue being "the little brother." Stephen and his father would respect him more—and he would respect himself more—if he handled this on his own.

A cacophony of voices and opinions began to play in David's mind.

The first, as usual, was that of his father, Michael: *This is your chance to amount to something, David. There are two ways to look at this. First, Guzman's a communist. He's sympathetic to Cuba and to China. He has to be removed. And second, think of the position of influence this will put you in with the new government. Don't chicken out! Finish what you've started.*

He heard Christie's voice: *This is insane, David! Do you realize how risky this is?*

He heard Carlos: *There is risk in any such endeavor, David, but because of the role we envision for you, your risk will be small. Our country needs your help. How many more innocent children will die if we do not act?*

He heard Cecil: *Remember why you're here, David. A cup of love is greater than a pitcher full of ambition.*

Again his father: *David, remember the Junior ROTC code you learned in high school: "I am an Army Junior ROTC Cadet. I am loyal and patriotic. I am the future. I will always practice patriotism. I will seek the mantle of leadership." Be a man, David! What could be more patriotic than removing Communist leaders this near our borders? Reagan would have done it in a minute!*

Christie: *Remember, David—you and I agreed to always make important decisions together. The fact that Carlos asked you not to even tell me about this should say something.*

Carlos: *I can guarantee substantial financial support for Hope Village.*

"Stop!" Startled by his own yell, David snapped his head up off the desk. He rubbed his eyes and glanced at this watch. Four-thirty. He was to call Carlos by five.

Oh, God, help me! I need guidance from you. David glanced at the Bible on his desk. He'd not opened it for several days. Where in the Bible would there be a direct answer for this? *What good are all my years of Bible college if I can't find the answers I need when I need them?* Unsure where to turn, he flipped opened his Bible to the New Testament and read the first verse his eye lit upon. John 1:1: "In the beginning was the Word, and the Word was with God, and the Word was God."

Hmmm. Good stuff, but not exactly a specific answer.

He tried again. Romans 12:1,2: "I beseech you therefore brethren, to present your bodies a living sacrifice, holy, acceptable unto God, which is your reasonable service. And be not conformed to this world, but be transformed by the renewing of your mind that you may prove what is that good and acceptable and perfect will of God."

Better. Sounds a bit like Cecil, but at least it's closer to the mark. I am trying to prove what the will of God is. Still…

He flipped idly toward the Old Testament, trying to think of a passage that might have some relevance. But before he thought of anything specific, his eyes lit upon 1 Chronicles 14:10: "So David asked God, 'Should I go out to fight the Philistines? Will you hand them over to me?' The Lord replied, 'Yes, go ahead. I will give you the victory.'"

There was a knock at his office door. "Yes?" he called, and Lupe, the nurse from the clinic who'd spent the night with Ricardo, opened the door. Immediately, David knew. He did not need to hear the words.

"Señor David, Ricardo murió un hace pocos minutos."

It had happened even quicker than Dr. Vargas had predicted. Now David had to go tell Angela that her little brother was dead. Killed by a deadly infection. And by an even more deadly system that had doomed him, and thousands just like him, to a life of poverty.

"And there's my answer," David whispered.

David took out Carlos's business card with his private phone number scribbled on the back. Without hesitation, afraid that any further argument with himself would only lead to paralysis, he picked up the phone and punched in the numbers.

Hawkeye added the information he'd received on the Scotch order with other intelligence JAM had provided or that he had gathered from other sources. "Olas Resort is scheduled for repainting in the next few days," he told Zach, "so I'm guessing it's out. I think we should do another recon on the Vina location."

Zach considered this. "How many days, do you think, before Guzman's arrival?"

Hawkeye eyed Zach. "Sooner rather than later. We'd better make sure we're prepared."

Christie was reading a storybook to a happily squirming Davy when David walked in the door.

"Hi, hon," he said in as cheery a voice as he could muster. He leaned over and kissed Davy on the forehead, then Christie on the cheek—hoping to not interrupt the story. But immediately Davy leapt off Christie's lap, opened his arms, and jumped up and down, yelling, "Daddy, Daddy!" until David scooped him up.

"Hey, Christie—something came up. I need to go see someone," David said over his son's head. "So don't fix me any dinner. I'll just grab a bite while I'm out."

He hoped he could slip out without further discussion, but after he'd hugged Davy and set him back on the couch—his son's loud protests ringing in the air—Christie followed him into the bathroom. She watched him take off his shirt and begin to shave. "So what's up?"

"What do you mean?"

"Don't mess with me," she said in a rare confrontational tone. Her Swedish-blue eyes had turned steely. "Are you meeting with this Edwards guy? The one who was here yesterday?"

He continued shaving, considering the best way to answer. "He's an important contact, hon. He wants to find out more about Hope Village and discuss how he might get some of his associates involved in contributing to the orphanage." He looked at her reflection in the mirror.

She shook her head. "How can I get you to listen to me? Guzman has people who are just waiting for one slip of the tongue, one time when David forgets he's no longer living in the land of the Bill of Rights. How do we know Carlos isn't one of them?"

David rummaged through the closet until he found a clean dress shirt. "Christie, the guy just cares about disenfranchised kids, same as us, and he wants to help us find resources to do more."

"And he's supposed to be a wealthy businessman, right?"

"Yes," David said. "And I think he's telling the truth."

"Even if he is—aren't you the one who's always saying we shouldn't trust the wealthy, that they became that way by walking on the backs of the poor? A direct quote."

"Carlos Edwards was an orphan. He's a kid from the streets who somehow made it. That makes him different. I think I can trust him."

"And you know this how? Because he told you?"

"Yes."

Christie stood behind him for what seemed to David like several minutes while he buttoned his shirt and put on a tie. Finally she sighed and said, "Okay, David. I just hope you're right and I'm wrong. What time will you be home?"

"I'm not sure," he said, combing his hair, "but don't wait up. If it's late, I'll call and let you know I'm okay."

It was the first time in their marriage he could remember deliberately deceiving Christie. He hated how it made him feel.

CHAPTER TEN

As Carlos had promised, a black Mercedes waited for David in the parking lot of the clinic. The driver standing patiently beside the car opened the back door. "Buenas noches, Señor."

They drove in silence for twenty minutes. *What a difference one day can make,* David thought. *And it's not over.* Unfortunately, the change wasn't all good. David didn't recall ever being this unsure of himself, this uncomfortable and out of place. If this decision was the right one, shouldn't he be feeling a sense of peace?

Rush hour; the streets were gridlocked. When they finally turned down Avenida Principal de las Mercedes, the driver announced, "We are almost at the Radisson. Señor Edwards will meet you here."

Circling the fountain in the middle of the avenue, they stopped in front of the hotel's main entrance. The bellhop sprang to open David's door. The limo driver got out, gave instructions to the valet to park the limo, then gestured to David to precede him into the lobby.

The driver pushed a key card into a slot in the elevator and punched the button for the tenth floor, then stepped back. "Go to room number 1020 and knock. Señor Edwards is expecting you."

When Carlos opened the door of 1020, he was smiling. "I hope you like Italian food, David. This hotel has a wonderful Italian chef, and what you see here—" he gestured toward a table set with a variety of Italian antipasti, breads, and pasta dishes—"is only the beginning. I wanted to find a private place for our discussion, to be sure it remains confidential."

80   The Missionary

Odd—even though David had just as much reason as Carlos for keeping their conversation secret, hearing Carlos say so made his pulse rate quicken.

As they sat to eat, Carlos made small talk, asking about David's parents and his brother. Had they been to visit him in Venezuela? After David told Carlos about his brother's job with the U.S. Attorney General's office, Carlos seemed particularly interested in Stephen, asking how long he'd been working there and what exactly he did.

Spreading a scoop of shrimp over a bed of angel-hair pasta, David said, "I have a few questions."

"Ask me anything."

David munched a shrimp, realizing that, for all his forethought, he hadn't an inkling how to begin. He decided to start with Christie's question. "Forgive me, Carlos—I've asked this before. But how do I know you're not just setting me up? How do I know you're not working for Guzman?"

Carlos laughed, setting down his fork. "David, I can assure you I'm *not* working for Guzman. Eventually I can tell you more, but before I do I must be certain that you are willing to help. People's lives could be in danger if our plans are compromised in any way."

David thought for a moment about how to phrase his answer. Finally he said, "And yet you're asking me to endanger my own life, the lives of my wife and son, and at the very least, the freedom of my coworkers, all on reassurances that you're unwilling to back up with details. Trust is required both ways, Carlos. I understand why you're unwilling to say more, but I don't see how I can agree without knowing more."

Carlos nodded thoughtfully, helping himself to a serving of lasagna. Eventually he seemed to come to a decision and leaned forward. "David, what I'm about to tell you is extremely sensitive. Both our lives could be in grave danger if any of this were leaked to the wrong person."

What could possibly be more sensitive than what he's already told me? David wondered. His knowledge of the world of political intrigue was limited to what he'd read in a few spy novels, but unsettling images came to mind, and he felt his pulse quicken.

"I told you I was a Caracas businessman," Carlos continued. "True. But that business is a front for my real work. I am here in Caracas to organize this coup attempt."

But he's surely not acting alone, David thought. "Are you receiving help from connections outside Venezuela?"

"Yes."

David sat silent for several seconds. "Carlos, these people outside Venezuela…would this be another government hoping to help remove Guzman from power?"

Carlos inclined his head thoughtfully and studied David's eyes. "David, you are a perceptive man. But I think it would be unwise to elaborate on what I have already said."

"Is the United States government somehow involved in this?"

"I cannot say more. Surely you understand."

"Carlos, I must know—are you a CIA agent working undercover?"

Carlos smiled and his expression changed. David tried hard to interpret what that change of expression meant—that David had hit the nail on the head? That David had revealed too much of what he was thinking? Surely Carlos was much more skilled and experienced at this type of mental chess game than David was.

"David, the less you know about who I may or may not represent, the safer you will be. But I assure you—if you had the answer to your questions, you would see even more reason to participate."

So, that may mean he's CIA but can't tell me. Or it may mean that he's working for Cuba, for all I know. But to me, he just doesn't feel like some enemy operative. "So…you're saying that my government has agents here that not only help Venezuela, but look out for the interests of America too, right?"

Carlos waved dismissively. "I am sure they do. The United States has agents everywhere. But we have talked enough about that."

"Then let me ask this: Why me? You could have recruited any number of people, I'm sure, with more experience in this than I have—which is none."

82   The Missionary

Carlos shook his head and dabbed his lips with his napkin. "On the contrary, you have the perfect cover. No one will suspect you. For years, you've been seen in your Hope Village van, cruising the street at any hour, looking for children in need. As I told you, what we need is someone who can deliver information and small packages in their normal course of business, without suspicion." Carlos helped himself to a piece of garlic bread and passed the basket to David. He continued. "We have noted that, in your regular routine, you go to the docks near the ferry in La Guaira once a week to purchase fish for Hope Village."

David felt a rush of something—fear? concern? excitement? "You've been following me." *This would certainly freak Christie out,* he thought.

Carlos shrugged. "We can leave nothing to chance. Our mission depends on it, and our lives as well. I'm sure you understand. Now, we would not want you to change your routine. The exchange place would be Los Tiburones restaurant, where you often eat lunch."

David realized his foot was rapidly tapping the floor.

"What, exactly, would I be carrying?"

"Messages or packages to others who need information or resources from time to time. Sometimes money."

David tried to calm his tapping foot and pointed down the hall. "The bathroom is this way? Excuse me."

A moment later, he stood in the men's room, mostly to be alone for a moment, to slow his racing heart, to figure out his next question, his next step.

What would Christie do? No question. She'd tell Carlos that they would be unable to help him, say good-bye, and ask him not to contact them again under any circumstances. Then she would race home and pray that whatever Carlos was doing wouldn't somehow come back to haunt them.

But David was not Christie. There was no denying Christie's courage. David had often, as during the riot the day before, seen her in full warrior mode on behalf of the injured, or the weak. But she was also a wife and mother. Risking her own safety was one thing. Risking Davy's safety...

Isn't that what he would be doing, too? Risking his own son's safety? Despite Carlos's reassurances, there was risk here. Something could go wrong.

Something *could?* Something already was. He saw it on the streets every day.

He washed his hands and leaned against the counter for a moment, staring into the mirror. He saw the man he knew himself to be.

He was about to become someone altogether different.

A moment later, he sat back at the table and studied Carlos. "This will be a peaceful coup? No violence?"

"Of course. Do I look like a violent man? No one, including Guzman, will be harmed."

"How can you know for certain that this coup will succeed? I guess what I'm asking is: How can I know I won't get caught?"

"I would not ask you to participate if I were not certain that we will succeed."

It seemed to David that Carlos was on the verge of confiding even further, of telling David something he had not intended to reveal. Then the subtle openness disappeared, and his face became veiled again.

"I can only tell you," Carlos said, "that those participating with us are professionals of the highest caliber who have participated in operations such as this all over the planet. You cannot find a more professional, more experienced team than we have assembled. If conditions are perfect and I give the green light, we will succeed, and you will face no repercussions."

David wasn't satisfied. "And yet—how do I know for certain that you're telling me the truth?"

Carlos stood, tossing his napkin onto the table, his eyes boring into David's. David sensed anger or frustration. "You don't. You can't. You should be able by now to understand why I cannot tell you more. I have already revealed to you more than I had planned, and I have taken great risk in doing so."

He carried his drink to the impressive river stone fireplace that dominated one wall and stood leaning against the mantelpiece. "David,

84   The Missionary

here is, as you Americans love to say, the bottom line. I've gone to some time and trouble to present this opportunity to you, after seeing your interview on TV. I am impressed with both Hope Village as an institution and with your own commitment to justice and the poor. Nothing that has been said during any of our conversations has caused me to change my mind. I believe you are the man for the job.

"It would be foolish to expect someone else to accept risk for nothing. In an operation such as this, money changes hands. The people I work with have deep pockets. I selected you not only because I think you have the perfect cover for what we need, but also because I knew that by involving you I could provide resources to help Hope Village."

Carlos paused, looking at David. "Come, David. You have the courage and the commitment to principle to do this. Join us, please."

David pushed his plate away; it had long since gone cold. "What do you mean, money going to Hope Village?"

"I will not insult you by suggesting that you would agree to do this for money rather than for the sake of the children you work with. However, if you do agree to assist us, tomorrow morning fifty thousand dollars will be deposited in a new account we have set up in your name. You can use the money to further Hope Village however you wish."

"*Fifty thousand?*" David gasped.

"You can confirm this tomorrow morning by calling Chase Bank headquarters in New York. Before you leave here, if you agree to help us, I will give you the account and PIN numbers."

Fifty thousand dollars. David sat back in his chair, rubbing his chin, barely aware of what he was doing. Fifty thousand dollars? David had never made that much in an entire year before, much less earned it for a few days' work. *Fifty grand. We could build an addition to the orphanage, or we could use it as seed money to raise even more.*

Carlos came back to the table, sat, leaned back in his chair. "Well, David, can we count on you to help? It's time for you to decide, yes or no."

Was David 100 percent convinced he should proceed? No. But then, on the cusp of a new phase in life, how often was one completely confident that he was taking the right step? He recalled a report he'd read in one of Christie's medical journals a few weeks before, reporting on research that, no matter how much we try to convince ourselves that we decide things on the basis of rational consideration of the facts, analysis of brain waves during decision-making reveals that we actually have our minds made up some time before that, based on gut instinct.

So what was David's gut telling him now?

He was aware suddenly of the steadily increasing adrenaline rush— the increased heartbeat and breathing, the nearly uncontrollable desire to move, to act—his foot was tapping like a machine-gun now, and he had no desire to even attempt to stop it. He felt empowered—indestructible, mighty.

It felt good. Better than good.

The face of his father moved through his mind, and his father's voice sounded: *Don't chicken out now—of course you're nervous, and of course you're not sure. That's why we call it* risk. *The ones who have the stomach for it succeed. Those are the ones who make a difference in the world. The rest just pull a paycheck until they retire.*

David took a deep breath, exhaled. "I'm in."

Carlos nodded once, unsurprised. He reached into his breast pocket and pulled out a small card. "Here are the account and pin numbers for the account in New York. The money will be deposited there tomorrow morning."

Fifty grand!

"Any other details I should know?" David asked.

"Yes." Carlos reached behind a chair against the wall and pulled out a large briefcase. He placed it on the floor beside David. "Take this briefcase to your office and put it in a secure place. I noticed when visiting your office that you had a lockable file cabinet. I suggest that you lock this briefcase in it. It will be your first delivery." Carlos pulled an envelope from his pocket and handed it to David. "In this envelope is a safe deposit key, along with a card on which is written the safe deposit box pin number. Put this envelope in the file cabinet for future reference. When the time comes to access the safe deposit box, you will be notified."

The briefcase looked almost exactly like David's own. He again felt the chill of having been watched. "What's in it?" he asked.

Carlos raised his eyebrows. "David, one of the rules in this line of work is, the less you know the better."

David nodded.

"Tomorrow," Carlos said, "I want you to arrive at exactly twelve noon at Los Tiburones restaurant and sit at an open-air table under the thatched roof, as you often do. Take this briefcase with you. Be sure to wear the red San Francisco 49ers cap we have seen you wear."

David nodded again. By now, he figured Carlos knew what brand of underwear he wore.

"Listen carefully. Another man, wearing blue jeans and a yellow T-shirt, will come to the restaurant carrying a briefcase identical to this one. He will go to the bar and order a drink. When he does, get up from your table, take the briefcase with you and go sit next to him. Set your briefcase down right next to his and order a drink. Do not speak to him. Just relax and drink your drink. Be sure to let him leave first. When he leaves, he will take this briefcase and leave the empty one he brought. You pick up his empty briefcase, take it back to your table, and order your lunch."

Carlos gripped David with both hands on his shoulders. "I know I'm belaboring the point, but you must never forget: All of this is of utmost secrecy. Not a word to anyone, including your wife. The people involved in this can be brutal to anyone who betrays them."

"When will I see you again?" David asked.

"Not until all of this is over." Carlos smiled warmly. "Then we will celebrate. I will take you and your wife to one of the finest restaurants in Caracas!" He squeezed David's shoulders, then let go and stepped back. "Don't worry: I have ways of getting further instructions to you."

Carlos picked up his glass and lifted it to eye-level. "David, to the homeless children!" David raised his own glass, then sipped from it, thinking it might be a toast to his greatest victory.

Or a one-way ticket to prison.

The briefcase was surprisingly heavy as he carried it down to the lobby. The limo driver was waiting out front. It was ten-thirty when he climbed into the limo, feeling more excited and frightened than ever before in his life. A hodge-podge of conflicting thoughts and images battled in his mind, but the one that took hold and forced out the others was the image of him sitting someday with his father and his brother Stephen, recounting this adventure and enjoying their approving nods and smiles, their complete attention on him.

CHAPTER ELEVEN

At 1 a.m. that night, lying a hundred yards from the Vina Estate on a grassy knoll, Hawkeye and Zach glassed the house with their night-vision gear. Aaron and Danny waited just behind them. There was no movement within, and all of the bedrooms on the bottom floor, including the master suite, appeared empty. A lone guard patrolled the grounds. This was good. It was also good that the perimeter fence was being upgraded—and the upgrade was not yet finished. There was at least one hole in the fence big enough to drive a truck through. Was the upgrade because the president was about to make a visit here?

Hawkeye sensed that time was becoming critical. This would be a good opportunity, maybe their last, to enter the house and map out exactly how the mission should be carried out, if this turned out to be the place.

The security lights and alarm systems were activated at the main house. Not a problem.

Some night creature rustled quietly in the underbrush off to the right. Hawkeye motioned Aaron and Danny up beside them, and the creature went silent as the two men moved up.

"How does it look?" Danny asked.

"Only one guard, but he's good," Hawkeye said. "He varies his route and his timing. One of us could avoid him easily enough, but it'll be harder for the four of us."

"I could take him out," Danny said.

90   The Missionary

A snort of derision came from Zach, and Hawkeye reached over and rapped Danny on the head with a knuckle. "If you take him out, you moron, they'll know something is up and cancel Guzman's trip, and the whole operation will be off. We get in and out without a trace, or we don't go in at all."

Moving closer through the trees and through one of the gaps in the unfinished fence, stopping frequently to listen and look, Hawkeye and his men approached the staff quarters. For several minutes they crouched under cover and watched. The night watchman passed. Hawkeye pulled Danny's sleeve to draw him closer, then spoke softly into his ear: "Follow him. Stay back and completely out of sight. Tell us every minute or so where he is, or more often if he's coming close. Don't let him see you."

Danny slipped quietly away.

When the guard had disappeared around the corner of the house, Danny a shadow behind him, Hawkeye and Zach picked the lock to the door of the staff quarters. They wandered through it, getting a feel for the layout.

Aaron went to work on his specialty—disarming the sophisticated alarm system in the main house.

"He's moving away from the back of the house, out into the trees behind," came Danny's whispered voice in their earpieces.

Ten minutes later, after the guard had passed the front of the house again and wandered down the long drive toward the front of the property, Hawkeye and Zach crossed the yard to find Aaron standing in the main entry, smiling, the front door wide open. Zach stayed outside, across the yard with a good view of the house. Room by room, Hawkeye and Aaron surveyed the entire house, taking plenty of high-speed digital photographs, no flash, careful to disturb nothing and leave no trace of their presence.

"Coming back up the drive, approaching the house," Danny's voice whispered.

Only seconds later, Hawkeye and Aaron were finished inside the house and approaching the door again when they heard Zach say, "Danny's in trouble."

"What is it?" Hawkeye said. He carefully pulled a curtain aside and peered out. "I'm looking at the drive."

"You see the guard, taking a cigarette break on a bench alongside the driveway, about fifty yards down?"

Hawkeye saw the glow of the guard's cigarette. "Yes."

"Flip down your night-vision goggles."

Hawkeye did. In the greenish image, he could see Danny crouched immediately behind the bench. Hawkeye swore. If the guard so much as lowered his arm, which was propped on the back of the bench, his hand would land on Danny's head. Danny was too close to risk breathing, much less moving. No way could Danny last through the guard's cigarette without giving himself away.

"Zach, make a noise. Draw the guard away."

From inside the house, Hawkeye could hear nothing. But he saw the guard's head jerk up at something, look up toward the house, take one last long drag on his cigarette and then flip it away into the bushes, a glowing arc. The man stood and moved toward the house—not on alert, as if he truly expected danger, but doing his job, investigating something he fully expected to be routine. Zach had done his job well.

After a few moments, Danny slipped out from behind the bench and continued to shadow the guard.

Hawkeye and Aaron slipped out of the house as soon as it was safe. Guided by Danny's updates on the guard's whereabouts, they mapped all of the roads, paths, and entrances of the property and its surroundings.

It was nearly 4 a.m. when they left the property and returned to the grassy knoll. Hawkeye felt a definite lessening of uneasiness about the mission. His instincts told him that this was the right location, and now he knew the layout. "We'll stake this place out from right here, starting tonight," he said. "Zach, you take the first watch. Aaron will relieve you in a few hours. Danny, start digging a foxhole just below. In the morning we'll start rotating back to the hotel to get some sleep."

Hawkeye and Aaron found a reasonably comfortable place in the tall grass, with the mound around some long-abandoned animal den as a pillow. Although his body rested, Hawkeye's mind went over and over what they'd seen in the estate below. His main concern now was that the president might be planning a large dinner party, if the size of the liquor order was any indication. Would the hit have to take place during the party itself? Would the guests be staying overnight? Was there a way to use the guests to his advantage? A plan began to take shape in his mind. He mentally listed the contacts he'd have to make in the morning to arrange for all they would need.

They lay in silence, looking at the stars, Hawkeye aware of Aaron's watchful alertness beside him. As was his custom, he began to visualize, step by step, a successful outcome for their mission.

There were, of course, other possible outcomes.

David didn't sleep well. He was up at five, pulled on the handiest clothes, and went straight to his office and opened the file cabinet. The briefcase was still there. It looked larger this morning than it had last night. He locked the cabinet again and walked back to his house.

When he'd finished showering and shaving, Christie was making coffee. Davy, awake earlier than normal, came out of his bedroom in his pj's, singing at the top of his lungs "just can't wait to be king" from some Disney video. David sat his son on his lap at the kitchen table while Christie gave him a sippy cup full of orange juice and poured him a bowl of cereal—Apple Jacks (compliments of Grandma Eller back in the states). As Davy greedily plunged his spoon into the cereal, David silently thanked God that kids can't eat and sing at the same time.

"Where'd you go so early?" Christie asked.

"Just took some papers back to the office," he lied.

She looked at him thoughtfully—or was it skeptically? "How did your meeting go with Carlos last night?"

"Good, good. I think he really wants to help the orphanage."

"What did you two talk about for so long?"

What is this, a courtroom? "Well, he wanted to know all about my family, about the orphanage, about the kids here. He's a businessman, stocks and securities, and he told me about his business."

Christie smiled. "Did he try to sell you some stocks?"

David laughed, glad for the relief from the tension. "As if. No. I think he just wants to be a friend of Hope Village."

"Did he give you another donation?"

Probably a whole briefcase full of cash. "No, but I think he and his friends will do something substantial very soon." And the first chance he got, David would call New York to confirm the existence of the account Carlos had said would be created for him.

Hawkeye's surveillance of the Vina Estate paid off. About mid-morning on their first day, Hawkeye himself was watching as a military personnel carrier pulled onto the long drive toward the estate, stopped, and disgorged its load of Venezuelan National Guard troops. Four of them walked beside the slowly advancing vehicle, two on each side. The others spread out across the grass and through the undergrowth on either side, taking their time, stopping frequently to check culverts and other objects where enemies might hide. One soldier took pictures, another wrote on a clipboard.

By the time the Guards had finished, they had walked every connecting road or path, no matter how small. They had taken numerous photographs. They were good. Thorough. Hawkeye assumed that their assignment was to report to Security with a map of the entire area. Another unit would come soon to secure the entire compound.

It was convincing evidence that the Vina Estate was the place Guzman would visit. Hawkeye had spent the past few hours making sketches and notes of his own, and the plan he and his men would carry out when Guzman came was mostly clear in his mind.

Hawkeye's gut told him that it would not be much longer. Fortunately, his plan was nearly complete. As three trucks full of workmen arrived to finish the perimeter fencing, Hawkeye pulled out his encrypted cell and sent a text message to Durango.

Among other things, they would need two limo drivers.

David fidgeted in his office for an hour, looking at his watch every five or ten minutes, unable to concentrate. He'd been putting off calling Chase Bank in New York, half afraid of what he would find. But he could put if off no longer. He picked up the phone.

"Yes—I'm David Eller, and I'm inquiring about my account balance?"

"Of course, Mr. Eller. What is the account number?"

"The account number is 159626378493."

"Thank you, Mr. Eller. For security purposes, would you please give me your social security number?"

David hesitated. He hadn't expected this question. Could this be used against him in some way—identifying him clearly as a participant in the coup? And another question: If Carlos had had to supply David's social security number to set up the account, how had he gotten it? Was this more evidence that Carlos was really CIA? "Uh, social security number…" He was so rattled he had to think frantically for a moment before he could remember it.

"Thank you. And the pin number for your account?"

"1984."

"Thank you, Mr. Eller. Your balance is exactly fifty thousand dollars. Is there anything else I can assist you with?"

"No, that's it." David heard the broad grin in his voice before he actually felt it stretching across his face. "Thank you."

David lost himself so thoroughly in a collage of worries, dreams, and schemes that he was amazed after what seemed like a few moments to glance at his watch and discover that it was ten AM. He buzzed Christie. "I need to run some errands. I'll be back this afternoon."

"I thought you ran errands yesterday."

"I did. But I need to pick up that new external hard drive I ordered for my computer. Customs called and said it was in."

"Well, while you're there, check to see if those medical supplies have come in from the States."

Pulling on his red 49ers cap, he retrieved the briefcase from the file cabinet and headed for the van.

Hawkeye was back at the hotel for the first time since his team's surveillance of the Vina Estate had begun—it was Aaron's shift on the knoll. Just as Hawkeye was collapsing onto the couch for a few hours of sleep, his cell phone beeped. A return text message from Durango. He read it and deleted it. "Danny, I want you to go meet the pigeon at noon. He's got our payday. Los Tiburones restaurant, just off the main drag near the fishing docks. Look for a 49ers cap—you know who the 49ers are?"

"Yeah. I saw them in a Super Bowl when I was a kid. Back when they were a good team."

The closer he got to La Guaira, the more nervous David got, rehearsing again and again in his mind what he was supposed to do—and how many things might go wrong. His biggest worry was that someone might see the swap and yell out that David's contact was taking the wrong briefcase, making a scene.

He parked the van, took a few deep breaths, and carried the briefcase into the thatched-roof patio area at the front of the restaurant. There were only a few other customers there, talking and eating. He sat at a table that gave him a good view of anyone coming in or out, carefully placing the briefcase under the table next to his chair.

The restaurant owner, a short balding man with a soiled tan apron, rushed to David's table. "¡Hola, Señor David! ¿Cómo anda hoy, mi amigo?"

96   The Missionary

David nodded hello. "Muy bueno. ¿Y cómo usted es?"

"Soy bien. Bienvenida," the owner replied. "I am glad to see you come twice in one week! It can only mean you love our food."

Rita brought him his cup of Americano and was taking his order for red snapper when a young man crossed the street toward the restaurant. Blue jeans. Yellow T-shirt. Carrying a briefcase that looked just like David's. David felt an instant adrenaline rush, quickening his pulse and senses.

As Rita walked away, the young man entered the restaurant, looked right into David's eyes, walked past his table, and sat down at the bar several feet away, placing the briefcase on the floor next to his stool.

David's mind flooded with questions: How long should I wait? Is anyone watching? How can I scan the room to see if anyone's watching without looking like that's what I'm doing? What if Rita comes back with a question and sees that I've moved?

He waited about a minute, gave the room a cursory (and, he hoped, innocent-looking) scan, then gripped his briefcase, stood, and walked to the bar. His hands were shaking so badly he wondered if the briefcase was vibrating noticeably. *Be cool*, he told himself. *Just sit down next to the guy and order a diet Coke.*

David sat, carefully placing his briefcase next to the one already there. "Querría una Coca Cola de la dieta, por favor," he said to the bartender. He surprised himself—his voice actually sounded normal, and although he still quivered inside, his hands seemed to have stopped shaking.

The young man turned to David and smiled, not saying a word, taking large gulps of his Maltin Polar, a local Venezuelan beer.

By the time David's Coke arrived, the young man's beer glass was empty. Setting his glass down on the bar, he dropped a ten thousand Bolivar note next to it, twisted on his stool toward David and said, "Adiós, amigo." He picked up the briefcase as he stood.

Only as the young man was walking away did David realize how quickly and smoothly the transfer had gone. He picked up his Coke and started back to his table, glancing around the restaurant. The few patrons were busy talking and eating. No sign that anyone had noticed the swap. Confidently, David sat back at his table. *Piece of cake!* he thought. *The easiest fifty grand I'll ever see.*

A sudden rush of fear—a man still seated at the bar had turned, looked at David, and called out. Had he seen the exchange? Was he an undercover policeman? Then David heard what the man was saying—as he pointed to the floor near the stool where David had been sitting: "Oye, amigo—you forgot your briefcase."

Oops, David thought. *So much for being a good spy.*

Later that afternoon, in his office, David received a phone call from Carlos. "You did a good job this morning. Tomorrow morning I want you to go to the Banco Provincial in the Federal District and get the other briefcase. Do you know where this bank is?"

"Yes."

"Remember to take the lock box key and pin number with you. Put the briefcase in your file, as before. I will call you with the time and place of the next delivery." The phone went dead before David could respond.

Hawkeye watched as the heavyset man labored up the trail through the woods, breathing heavily and sweating, each step looking as if it might be his last. He had little patience with people who allowed themselves to get so far out of shape. When the man was only a few steps away, Hawkeye stepped onto the trail. Apparently neither surprised nor bothered, the man wiped the sweat from his face and said in English, "You're Hawkeye?"

"If I'm not, you're in deep trouble, Chef Gustavo." He was glad Gustavo was speaking English; Hawkeye's Spanish was poor at best, and he did not want to motion Zach down to translate.

The man simply nodded and, as he collapsed onto a nearby rock, fanning his face with his soft cap, said, "Well, if you're an agent of the government, just shoot me now and put me out of my misery. Why could we not have met in a café in town?"

Was this the caliber of spy he was forced to rely on? "My men are watching every possible approach to this site; we can speak in complete isolation here. Durango said you had new information for me."

Gustavo nodded, still panting, and held up a hand to gain more time. He pulled out a handkerchief and wiped his face, took a deep breath or two, then said, "I received a fax this afternoon—a menu for twenty for tomorrow night. It included deep fried oysters, abalone steaks, creamed asparagus, and mango sorbet, among other things. Abalone, as you know, is Guzman's favorite. The chief butler also received a fax. I did not see it, but later I overheard him tell the maid to order some of Mrs. Guzman's favorite roses for her room and have them in place by tomorrow afternoon."

Hawkeye nodded. He scanned the forest on both sides. "Durango said you had been a marine in the Venezuelan navy. You don't look like a marine."

Gustavo chuckled, the deep, wheezy laugh of a fat man. "Ten years ago I looked like a marine. Now I look like a chef." He coughed into his handkerchief and put his hat back on his head. "So. From all of this I think we can assume that Guzman and his family and several guests will arrive sometime tomorrow afternoon for an evening dinner party. Durango has other sources who confirm that the dinner guests will not stay the night. Only Guzman and his family—apparently just his wife and granddaughter—will stay. In the morning, they plan to wander the beach so that his granddaughter can find sea shells."

Perfect. No collateral damage.

"You know the grounds and buildings, Mr. Former Marine Turned Chef," Hawkeye said. "Let me go over our plan with you. I want you to listen for any possible problem, anything that might go wrong." As he spoke, Hawkeye smoothed the dust of the trail in front of them and began to sketch out the buildings and grounds of the estate. "Tell me anything I don't know about the property, the security system—anything you can think of. I want to leave nothing to chance."

Gustavo nodded. "And let us not forget," he said, "that all of this must be done under the watchful eye of Guzman's usual heavy contingent of bodyguards."

CHAPTER TWELVE

Danny had been on surveillance duty at the Vina Estate most of the night. As first light was graying the eastern horizon, he heard footsteps approaching and shrank silently back into the undergrowth.

"It's me," Aaron's voice said softly.

"Hope you brought something to eat," Danny replied, and almost immediately a backpack landed heavily beside him.

"Half of that's mine," Aaron said.

Danny unzipped the pack, rummaged, and brought out some kind of plastic-wrapped sweet roll. As he tore into it, Aaron said, "You stay here. I'll move down a little closer and off to the left, near the rocks. Hawk wants us to check in with him hourly." Aaron pulled a couple of bananas out of the pack and faded away.

At 8 a.m., government security arrived at the estate. They brought dogs to sniff for explosives; they brought airport security-type x-ray machines and metal detectors, presumably to check the dinner guests. By mid-morning, it appeared to Danny that the house and grounds had been secured.

Of course, what the government security team had not checked, he thought, smiling, were the four personal limousines, not yet on the property, that would be bringing the guests that evening for dinner.

102 The Missionary

The Banco Provincial, like every bank in Venezuela, did not open until 10:00 a.m. At about 10:30, David parked his car in a fenced parking lot across the street from the bank and stepped out, wearing the suit and tie he'd chosen to appear as businesslike as possible. As he waited to cross the street, traffic was the usual bumper-to-bumper. Vendors had set up their wares along the street and under the overpass to the north.

Unwelcome thoughts flooded his mind, as they had all morning— and much of the night, as he'd lain awake. It was still possible that this was some kind of trap to have him arrested by Guzman, just as Christie had feared all along—or, even if not a trap set up by the government, perhaps the government had penetrated Carlos's team and learned that David was cooperating with them. *What if I'm arrested with the briefcase when I leave the bank, thrown into prison for espionage, then left there to rot for years? What if—*

No, not these thoughts. Not now. He needed his wits about him. Instead, he tried to think about how he would use the fifty thousand for Hope Village. *We could have a huge direct-mail campaign, soliciting donors from all over America. If we can tap into some matching funds, we could produce a documentary to play on Christian TV stations, or build more housing for orphans. Maybe we could use it after the coup to lobby the new Venezuelan government to give us land and money to build another Hope Village campus in another barrio!* For that matter, why should they spend that precious money to buy the land? The new government, knowing that David had helped them come into power, would perhaps just give them new land.

He jogged across the street. Four or five young toughs eyed him sullenly from the street corner. This was a rough neighborhood. The thought crossed his mind that someone—maybe those same young men who'd watched him just now—could steal the briefcase as he left the bank. He suddenly wished he'd worn something more casual. His mouth was dry. He gripped the lockbox key in his damp palm. As he reached to pull open the huge glass door, a bank guard pushed it open for him, nodding as David entered. To his left stood a long row of teller booths, covered with heavy glass except for the small cut-out just above the marble counter. A long double row of blue upholstered chairs occupied the center of the room, where at least a dozen customers waited for their number to be called by one of the tellers. On a desk against the wall on the right stood a placard with the word *Información*. A middle-aged, dark-haired woman in a starched blouse and scarf and more-than-ample make-up sat behind the desk.

"Buenos días," David said, showing her the key in his hand. "I'm here to access my lockbox account."

The woman pointed toward the back of the bank, telling him to turn left there and approach the "Bank Services" window.

David felt as if everyone were watching as he walked. *Why do I feel like a criminal?* And then came the answer: Because the current Venezuelan government would consider what you are doing a crime punishable by death. He had a sudden impulse to bolt, but by willpower kept himself moving at a controlled pace toward the back wall, where he turned left and saw a young Venezuelan woman in a dark blue business suit and white blouse.

"Buenos días," he said with as much confidence as he could muster, and slid the key across the marble counter separating them.

The solemn young woman took the key, checked the number on it, then stood without a word and walked several feet behind her where a young man sat behind a large desk, apparently some kind of supervisor. The man peered around the woman and studied David.

David felt a trickle of sweat under his shirt collar. The man stood, picked up his phone, and punched in a number, staring at David as he spoke quietly into the receiver.

David turned, trying to appear nonchalant, and picked up an informational brochure off the countertop. *If I run, they'll shoot me before I can reach the front door. Stay calm.* He shook his head. He wasn't cut out for this life. How had he allowed himself to be sucked into it?

The man hung up the phone and approached David. It was an incredible relief to see him politely smile. "Buenos días, señor." He

104   The Missionary

gestured toward a door on the right and said, "Venga por favor por esta puerta."

David followed. Walking down a long hallway, they passed several more desks. The man stopped in front of a tripod on which a large camera was mounted. He motioned David to stand against the wall, where there were outlines of a pair of footprints on the floor.

"¿Qué es eso?" David asked.

"It is our policy to photograph all those who access the bank's vault," the man replied.

David felt his anxiety blossom into fear. A photograph? How many ways could that be used against him? *Jesus, protect me*, he prayed as the camera flashed.

The young man motioned for David to follow him through the huge open door to the bank's vault; the guard stationed there observed them both impassively. Just inside, to the right, was a plain metal door; the man took a key hooked to a chain on his waist and unlocked it. David followed him into a large room where several rows of large brushed stainless-steel safe deposit boxes lined every wall. The doors of the boxes in the two bottom rows appeared to be about two feet square. Those in the rows above were only about half that size.

The man turned to David. "The number of your lock box is on your key. After I leave, place your key in the lock. Punch your pin into the number panel. Turn the key and it will open. I will wait right outside this room. There is a buzzer here by the door. Push it when you are finished and I will let you out."

The man handed David his key and left the room, closing the door behind him. David stood thinking. *Obviously, this guy knows I've never been here before, or he wouldn't have felt it necessary to give me such detailed instructions*—an idea that made David even more nervous.

He searched the wall for number 01125, the number on his key. The thought hit him as he followed the numbers down a row of lockboxes: *Putting a missionary in a room with, no doubt, millions and millions of dollars is like parking a pig in a palace. What would Christie think if she could see me now?* He remembered the movies in which a group of sophisticated bank robbers drilled their way through the floor in the middle of the night to pull off the robbery of the century.

Lockbox number 01125 was second from the bottom in the fourth column on the south wall. He placed his key in the keyhole. It wouldn't turn.

Enter your pin number, dummy!

Just below the keyhole was a panel of black buttons with gold numbers and letters. He pulled out the card on which he'd written the pin. He punched in A214T555W18BC. It would have been a good idea to bring gloves to avoid leaving fingerprints, he thought. He heard a tiny click. This time, when he turned the key, the lockbox opened. Inside was a brown briefcase, identical to the first one. He pulled it out. This one seemed just as heavy as the one he'd delivered the day before. He used the sleeve of his coat to try to wipe down the lock box door and panel of numbers. As he did, he remembered that it probably didn't make much difference—they'd just taken his photo. And then it occurred to him that he might be under video surveillance at that moment—and the camera had just caught him trying to wipe off his fingerprints. For the first time in his life, he felt like a thief.

He raised his hand toward the buzzer, then hesitated. He imagined the manager on the other side, surrounded now by police and security guards, just waiting for David to press the buzzer.

No choice now. There was only one way out of the room. He gently pressed the buzzer.

Within seconds, the door opened. Standing alone with the same polite smile was the man who'd ushered him into the room a few minutes earlier.

David followed the man back through the long hallway and out to the open foyer of the bank. The man turned and reached out to shake David's hand. "Gracias, señor. Is there anything else I can assist you with?"

"No. Gracias," David replied. Switching the briefcase to his left hand, David offered his right. The man bowed slightly as their hands clasped. David quickly headed for the front door, walking past the staring eyes seated in the blue chairs scattered across the middle of the room. Again the guard pushed the large glass door open for him as he left the bank.

Now the biggest challenge: getting back to my car without being mugged. He descended the steps of the bank and stepped off the curb. Winding his way through the crawling, bumper-to-bumper traffic as he crossed the street, he hurried through the cyclone fencing and back to his car.

Driving out of the parking lot, he felt the tension in his muscles beginning to ease. "That was easy!" he said out loud, then laughed at himself, knowing it had felt like anything but.

And a nagging sense of foreboding told him that things wouldn't get any easier.

It was six o'clock when the limos began to roll. Hawkeye had already been lying under the back seat of one for thirty minutes, and it would be at least another forty-five minutes before he would be able to drop the panel to the trunk and slip out. Gustavo's planned diversion would give him only about forty-five seconds to exit the trunk undetected. It was risky, but he and Zach had rehearsed their quick exit from the limos at least a dozen times. Even though they were dressed in uniforms identical to those of Guzman's guards, that would fool no one if someone saw them popping out of a limo's trunk. But it was this kind of risk that fed Hawkeye's adrenaline addiction—and that he would miss most after this final mission.

The Vina Estate was designed so that entering vehicles had to come up a hill in full view of the house, past the servants' quarters, past the six-car garage to the north side of the house near the kitchen, then around to the covered drive and front entrance where guests were greeted and guest cars parked.

"I have your limo in sight," Hawkeye heard Aaron whisper through the tiny receiver in his ear. The limo slowed to a stop. "Security check," he heard Aaron whisper. "Opening trunk, hold your breath."

Hawkeye gripped his pistol tighter; he heard the lock click, then the nearly silent movement of well-oiled, quality hinges. He felt his eyelid begin to twitch from that long-ago wound. Just an eighth-inch-thick panel now separated him from the guard's eyes. They'd made sure the trunk was completely empty—nothing to draw the guard's eyes, or induce him to rummage around for even an extra second. Hawkeye let out a breath when he heard the trunk lid slam shut.

"Forty-five seconds till arrival. Good luck, boss," he heard Aaron whisper. Hawkeye clicked his mike once to let Aaron know he'd copied.

Aaron was Hawkeye's "eyes" on the ground. They'd spent a long time deciding where he would be best positioned to see all Hawkeye would need him to see, and had finally decided that the best vantage point was the foxhole Danny had dug on the slope of the grassy knoll, outside the compound, viewing the action through powerful binoculars. The most sensitive time for Aaron would come shortly: he would have to sneak into the compound while it was heavily guarded, and for that reason he alone of the four commandos was dressed in camo and disguised with blackface make-up.

"The oil for the oysters is the correct temperature?" Gustavo asked. "Yes? Leave it as it is, then. I will handle the oysters and abalone myself—the president is very particular about his abalone. You may finish the appetizers."

Gustavo bustled around the kitchen, busy preparing the meal with his staff of two at the same time he nervously watched the clock—and not just to be sure the meal would be ready on time. President Guzman preferred his oysters deep-fried in hot oil and his abalone pan-seared in butter and cognac, but it was not just because of the president's finicky tastes that Gustavo had insisted on being the one to prepare the seafood.

Guzman, along with his wife and granddaughter, had arrived at the estate two hours earlier. Now Guzman sat with his granddaughter playing a game of cards while his wife hurried about overseeing last-minute details for the dinner. Maids and servants scurried back and forth as Guzman's staff of mostly Cuban bodyguards stood watching from their assigned stations.

Gustavo watched out the window as the four limousines stopped, allowed their guests to exit, then continued about twenty-five feet past the entrance and parked in a row.

Moments later, he could hear Guzman and his wife in the main foyer, greeting their guests. Gustavo glanced at his watch, wiped the sweat from his forehead, and turned back to the immense stainless-steel industrial range. "Do not interrupt me now," he muttered to his assistants. "I must concentrate on the seafood."

And concentrate he did—so that it was exactly ten minutes after the limos parked that Gustavo's two assistants burst out of the kitchen screaming, "El fuego, el fuego! Fire!"

The rangetop was engulfed, and the flames were spreading—Gustavo's oil, somehow heated to the point of combustion, had ignited.

On instinct, Guzman's entire security force went into action. Some rushed toward the kitchen, trying to slap at the flames with a rag; some searched for an extinguisher; four of them ushered Guzman and his guests to the viewing room away from the kitchen. There was temporary pandemonium.

Hawkeye heard Aaron signal: "Fire's on...GO!" He had already released the eighth-inch panel and rolled into the trunk; he'd been waiting, his hand on the trunk's interior safety release, for a minute, waiting for this signal. Now he pulled the release, opened the trunk lid just far enough to allow him to roll out onto the drive, and then closed it again as he crouched behind the limo. He raised his head far enough to see Zach similarly crouched behind the limo that followed his and to make sure that all the security guards on this side of the building were gone—he saw the last of them racing around the front of the house, toward the kitchen. He signaled Zach, and together they raced in a crouch toward the south side of the house, sticking close to the wall. They pushed open the small basement window that their plans had instructed someone on the inside, another JAM member, to unlock. Zach pulled it closed behind them.

Within three minutes, the fire was out with little or no damage to the kitchen. Chef Gustavo apologized profusely for his stupidity. Everyone had a good laugh. There was no damage, aside from a bit of smoke stain on the stove hood. "Fortunately," said the chef, "I had not started cooking the oysters or abalone yet. I will have a wonderful meal for you soon—a delay of ten minutes, at most."

From the small basement closet where he and Zach were hiding, Hawkeye heard the laughter of the guests above—clearly, they had no idea anything was amiss. He hoped none of the guards had noticed anything.

Soon, Aaron's low voice came over the mike, "Installing the diversion." At this point, while the dinner party was loudly carrying on, Danny's assignment was to crawl up the road using a ditch that ran along the driveway as cover and plant a charge of C4 under the Humvee.

After about ten minutes, Hawkeye whispered into the mike. "How's it going?"

Aaron replied, "Danny's about twenty feet from the vehicle. Guzman's guards are standing behind the Humvee smoking cigars. Telling dirty jokes, from the sounds of their laughter."

Hawkeye smiled. He was glad to have Aaron on his team—except that Aaron was the only one who that had a wife and kid back home, which is why Hawkeye tended to give Aaron the safer assignments. As if there were anything "safe" about their missions.

Aaron continued, in whispers, to inform Hawkeye as Danny slipped under the Humvee and attached the explosive device under the engine. Detonating it would turn the Humvee into a roadblock for any vehicle trying to get in or out as the commandos made their escape.

Ten minutes later, Aaron's voice again whispered into Hawkeye's ear, "Big man's car bomb aborted. There's a guard on top of it." Hawkeye clicked acknowledgment.

They'd planned to attach a C4 explosive to Guzman's Mercedes as well. No way to do that now. But if the car were armor-plated on the bottom, as Hawkeye suspected, the explosive might have done minimal damage anyway.

Leaving behind his binoculars and anything else he wouldn't need, Aaron slipped out of his foxhole and down the hill, careful to stay hidden by the thick brush. Just a couple of minutes later, he tucked himself behind some type of low-growing palms a few feet from the compound's fence.

For Aaron, this was one of the most sensitive parts of the operation. From this point on, he would be needed inside. And that meant he would have to cross into the compound, and do so while the compound was heavily patrolled. Entering the compound wouldn't be difficult. Danny had already come in this way, in fact, cutting an opening in the fence that all of them would later use as their point of exit. The trick would be entering without being detected. He'd been watching the guard patrols for the past hour, and they were random. No predictable periods when Aaron was confident no guards would happen by.

So he simply waited until a pair of them crossed in front of him, murmuring to each other in Spanish. Then he slipped soundlessly up to the fence, pushed through the opening Danny had cut—it took a moment for him to find it, Danny had done such a good job of hiding the breach by cutting out a yard-wide square in the fence and then hanging it back in place with wire clips at the top—and rolled into hiding behind a bit of brick landscaping wall.

He lay breathing deeply but slowly. The two guards came back nearby in less than a minute, in the opposite direction. If Aaron had delayed, he might have been seen.

Soon, Hawkeye heard double-clicks in his receiver, the signal that Aaron and Danny had made their way to the buildings undetected and were now crouched under cover of thick shrubbery behind the garage, waiting.

Hawkeye checked his weapons. He and his team were armed with Heckler & Koch 9 mm MP5 SC3's with collapsing stocks and sound suppressors, the perfect weapon for the job. The first stage of the silencer system would absorb the gases, and the second stage would absorb the muzzle blast and flame. A buffer made of rubber would absorb the bolt noise. With their subsonic ammo, shots from this weapon could not be heard more than ten feet away. And if Guzman proved to be a sound sleeper, Hawkeye's U.S. Marine kabar—still his favorite combat knife, a memento of his days training with Delta Force—would be the preferred choice, making no sound at all.

If everything went as they'd carefully rehearsed, a couple of bodyguards and Guzman would be the only ones to die tonight. Neither Hawkeye nor Durango liked collateral damage.

Now, all they needed to do was wait.

CHAPTER THIRTEEN

Despite Gustavo's kitchen oil fire, the dinner party continued without problems. The limos departed soon after midnight with the guests, most of whom had drunk far too much and should have been grateful for drivers to take them home.

At 3 a.m., Hawkeye could envision Guzman's security, based on the briefing he'd received from both Durango and Chef Gustavo of information they'd received from JAM sources inside Guzman's organization: two of Guzman's bodyguards, armed with AK-47's, would be in the living room. Another would be standing by the front door, and another, Guzman's emergency driver, at the back of the house, by the General's bulletproof Mercedes. Aaron had confirmed, from his vantage point near the garage, the presence of those two, as he had the four in the Humvee at the bottom of the road—unaware, hopefully, that that car could now be detonated at the push of a button. Aaron had also confirmed that, as they had expected, fifty or so National Guard troops were stationed on the road below the Humvee, blocking the only vehicular entrance to the estate. Three pairs of guards patrolled the estate, and if the JAM intel was accurate, two choppers sat on alert at the beach.

At precisely 3 a.m. the guard outside the front door turned to his left, alerted by a tiny clicking noise. He never found out what it was. Danny gripped the guard's mouth from behind with his left hand while the carbon-steel blade of the CRKT Ultima high-tech fighting knife did its work in his right. At the same instant, with his left, Danny snapped the guard's neck.

He slowly lowered the man's body to the ground behind a large bush. Then, in a uniform identical to the guard's, he assumed the guard's position at the door.

Hawkeye and Zach tiptoed up from the basement. Two bodyguards in the living room were seated across from each other, asleep. Hawkeye made a split-second decision to let them sleep. If they did not wake, they would live. He motioned for Zach to crouch in the corner with his weapon trained on the guards. Then, like a ghost, Hawkeye made his way down the broad hallway to the door of the bedroom where Guzman and his wife were sleeping.

Just as he began turning the knob ever so slowly with a gloved hand, he heard a noise behind him. He turned his head; he could see down the hallway and into the living room where one of the guards, awake, was starting to stand. He heard a quiet *pffft* as Zach's subsonic 9mm bullet zipped through the guard's skull.

If the guard had just fallen back into his chair, all would have been well.

Instead, the dead man's falling body tumbled over the arm of his chair and onto the floor, knocking over a lamp, which woke the other bodyguard. Hawkeye heard another quiet burst of gunfire.

If Guzman had been awakened by the noise... Hawkeye twisted the knob and rushed into the bedroom. He ripped the covers back to make sure of his target—and Mrs. Guzman and her granddaughter sat up in bed and screamed.

Hawkeye swore.

Their screams almost masked the sound of window glass breaking down the hall. Hawkeye raced toward the noise and threw open the door just in time to see a trace of Guzman's head ducking under the sill of the window.

"Out the back! Shoot him!" Hawkeye roared to his men as he leaped toward the window. He flattened himself against the wall beside it, then cautiously peered through, aware that Guzman's guards might have their weapons trained on the window already.

Guzman had disappeared.

Before Aaron and Danny reached the back of the building, they heard a car engine start. Within seconds, Guzman's Mercedes ripped around the back corner and followed the drive down the hill. Aaron and Danny reversed direction and opened fire on the Mercedes—a futile gesture, they knew, since their bullets simply glanced off the car's bulletproof back window as it raced down the driveway. Zach flew out the front door, followed almost immediately by Hawkeye.

Aaron pulled a small remote out of his pocket, flipped a switch, and pushed a button. The explosion blasted the heavy Humvee several feet into the air. Fire shot out of its engine compartment, as well as the passenger compartment. The Humvee landed with the crash of tortured metal on its side, turned crossways to the road and blocking most of it.

Blaring the horn, Guzman's driver swerved to miss the overturned Humvee, catching it on the rear bumper and spinning it smack into one of the guards, who sailed off the road into the ditch. The Mercedes veered back onto the road and exited onto the highway, quickly followed by two military personnel carriers.

President Guzman would live because earlier in the evening, just before going to bed, his granddaughter asked if she could sleep with her grandma tonight.

As previously planned and without speaking, Hawkeye and his men left together on a dead run, heading east up the hill and away from the driveway. They'd rehearsed this route earlier: turn south at the big rock, duck behind the landscaping wall and exit through the hole in the fence Danny had cut, follow the fence north, turn east at the mango grove and run for another quarter mile through the thick grove of palm trees and then into the brush by the small lake they'd found earlier that week, where the van was parked.

Inside the van was their change of clothing. The plan was to drive four miles to where they'd stashed another rental car, drive four miles further, abandon the rental car in a parking lot, and escape back to their hotel forty miles away in their Jeep. If the assassination had been successful, the following morning their payday would have been delivered to the same restaurant as before, and they would be out of the country that night the same way they had entered.

But the plan had gone terribly wrong. Hawkeye cursed again.

Hearing gunshots, two startled soldiers of the Venezuelan special forces stationed in the rocks behind the house poked their heads over the rocks, looking toward the estate buildings. At the same moment, the earbuds attached to their waist radios crackled to life with the shouted words, "¡Alerta roja! ¡Alerta roja!" which meant only one thing—an assassination attempt was taking place.

A movement knifing through the night caught the eye of one of the soldiers. He pulled his night-vision goggles into place and peered through them; he saw four men in a crouching position coming toward him. He tapped his partner's shoulder and pointed. They fixed their scopes on the first two men. When the crouching men got within one hundred yards, the soldiers opened fire; two of the men dropped like puppets whose strings had been cut.

Instinctively, at the sound of the gunshots, Hawkeye and Zach dropped and rolled left and right. They heard Danny groan as he went down. They heard nothing from Aaron.

Zach crawled up to Aaron. Hawkeye, just a couple of feet away from Danny, covered Danny's mouth to dampen his painful moan. Hawkeye watched Zach's face as he checked Aaron's pulse. Zach shook his head. Hawkeye raised his head an inch to see—the bullet had split Aaron's head open. Zach stripped him of his gun and radio and left his body where it lay. There was nothing else they could do if the rest of them expected to live through the night.

Danny's left leg was bleeding badly. Hawkeye ripped a scarf from around his neck and fastened it like a tourniquet around Danny's leg to slow the bleeding. "Come on, Danny, let's move," Hawkeye commanded.

"I think my leg is broken," Danny groaned.

"*Come on!* If we stay here, we're dead."

They pulled themselves across the grass toward cover with hands and elbows, unwilling to raise their heads. When the bullets fired by the soldiers on the hillside above them began to dig divots in the grass nearby, they rolled behind some shrubbery. They'd moved less than thirty yards from where Danny and Aaron had been hit. They heard the soldiers' radio crackle—undoubtedly, they were calling their comrades, which meant things were about to get much worse.

Danny spoke. "Hawk, I can crawl downhill easier than up. I'll take the ditch back down to the garage. These soldiers will follow you up the hill—"

"Forget it. I'm not leaving you here," Zach said.

"Then we'll all be dead. Listen, my only chance to live is if you two run uphill and create a diversion. By morning, this place might be deserted enough for you to come and get me. We'll stay in touch by radio. Go on. Now!"

"They'll find you," Zach said.

"Maybe not," whispered Hawkeye. "The servants' quarters is next to the garage. Earlier, I saw an opening in the foundation into a crawlspace. Danny could hide under the house till we come."

They heard troops making their way up toward them from the buildings—orders were being shouted, and they heard the sound of running feet. Danny sounded desperate. "Zach, I want to live. This is my only chance. Please!"

"Keep your radio on. Let me know when you're safe," Hawkeye said, giving Danny a firm farewell pat on the shoulder.

Occasional shots still came from above them, shredding some of the shrubbery, an apparent attempt to keep them pinned down. The weapons Hawkeye and Zach carried were not designed for long-distance work, and from the sound of the gunshots, the soldiers firing at them were still too far away.

As Danny started his descent, Hawkeye and Zach belly-crawled as fast as they could up the hill. Zach stopped for a moment to peer through his night-vision goggles, finally spotting two men crouching partially behind a rock above them. He tapped Hawkeye, who looked into the distance and nodded. It was still a bit out of range for their weapons, but both men were skilled marksmen. They opened fire. The two soldiers fell.

Hawkeye and Zach jumped to their feet and raced up the hill, following their rehearsed route.

David awoke sitting up in bed, suppressing a cry of alarm. His breath came in gasps; his heart beat at what felt like twice its normal speed. He glanced around the room wildly, looking for the source of his panic, but even as he looked, he knew it was not an intruder. Nor had it been a nightmare—although he had plenty of reason for nightmares.

In the dim moonlight filtering through the window, he watched Christie to make sure he hadn't wakened her. She stirred, but settled again, her breath regular and untroubled.

What had awakened him, David knew, had been the upwelling of panic and fear that had been building all day as he had, consciously and unconsciously, considered all the possible—and terrifying—consequences of what he was doing. Was it worthwhile to try to help bring about a more humane regime in Venezuela? Yes. David had attacked that question from all possible angles before he'd made his decision. No need to revisit it. He was convinced he had decided right.

But was the risk to his family, and to the mission, acceptable? What if the coup failed?

He sat long into the night. And when he lay down again and tried to calm himself into sleep, it was with one prayer filling his mind: *Lord, guide the hands and minds of these people. Help them to succeed. For the sake of Venezuela's poor. And for the sake of my family...*

Danny's left leg felt as if it were on fire. He heard soldiers heading in his direction; he hoped they would continue to chase Hawkeye and Zach so he would have time to reach the garage. A chopper hovered overhead, its spotlight roving. Danny hoped it wasn't equipped with infrared or they would find him within seconds.

He continued to pull himself downhill in the cover of the ditch and tall grass as quietly as he could. A group of soldiers came close, and he froze, listening to their talk and wishing he knew Spanish; he understood only a few words: *aqui, el presidente, hombres...*

He lay motionless for a minute or so after they passed, then continued toward the garage. The pain in his leg was growing worse. Like all military personnel, Danny had been taught techniques for managing pain, and he stopped for a moment to employ some of the mental exercises to contain and manage the pain: Envision the pain, then envision a shape around it. Danny saw his pain in a box. Now imagine the box getting smaller, smaller, gradually smaller, and the pain shrinking with it...

It seemed to help a bit, but not much. Danny scolded himself for not being more disciplined, more experienced, more mentally strong, like Hawkeye, whom he idolized. Well, if they got out of this, they'd have some stories to tell...

The gunfire up the hill had stopped. Danny hoped that that meant Hawkeye and Zach had gotten away. He felt horrible about Aaron—in some ways, he'd been closer to Aaron than to any of the others. But he'd think about Aaron later. The first order of business was survival.

He found that he was almost to the garage now, and near a patch of shrubbery that would cover his approach to the buildings. He peered above the verge of the ditch and listened; it didn't appear that any of the bands of soldiers searching the grounds were near him. Not near enough to spot him if he moved quickly. Nearly groaning with the additional pain the movement caused his leg, he pulled himself over the verge of the ditch and scrambled as quickly as he could for the bushes.

He lay panting for a moment before continuing on. He could see the servants' quarters now, and unless it was just a trick of the poor light, he thought he could see a dark patch in the foundation that might be the hole Hawkeye had told him about. He had to get there quickly. Even with the bushes as cover, he felt exposed here—

The last thing Danny felt was something cracking into the back of his head.

Nicolas Torres, Guzman's head of Special Forces and Senior Commander of the Presidential Guard Regiment, was there within minutes. He was furious when he saw the commando lying unconscious, blood running out of the back of his head. He turned to the guards. "Who hit this man?"

After a moment's hesitation, one guard stepped forward, looking frightened and guilty. Even before the man could speak, Torres slapped him backhanded and hard. "You probably killed him, you idiot!" he screamed. "I wanted this one alive! You don't kill the prisoners until *after* I extract the information I need. Now you'd better hope he wakes up long enough for me to interrogate him, or I will kill you!"

CHAPTER FOURTEEN

David slept fitfully the rest of the night, waking often in the dark, worrying about his next delivery. The first one had gone smoothly—just beginner's luck? So much could go wrong.

He got up at 5:30 a.m.; it was futile and counter-productive to lie any longer tossing and turning. He took a shower and made coffee. He was sitting in the kitchen at 6:30, having his third cup and mentally rehearsing the delivery of the briefcase, when Felix called.

"Are you watching TV? No? Turn it on. Someone tried to assassinate Guzman last night!"

David froze. Surely this wasn't... "Did they kill him?"

"No, he is still alive. That's all they have told us."

"I've got to go."

David flipped on the TV. The reporter was reading a prepared statement. "...approximately three o'clock this morning, while President Guzman and his family slept as guests at an undisclosed location near Puerto La Cruz, several gunmen broke into the compound in an attempted coup. President Guzman and his family survived the attack. Further details will be given as soon as they are known."

What did it mean, Guzman survived the attack? Was he now under house arrest? Was this the first, careful announcement of a successful coup—or did it mean that the coup attempt had failed? And if it had failed—where were Carlos and his co-conspirators?

David became aware of Christie beside him; she had wandered out of the bedroom in her robe and now stood studying the images on TV.

"David, what's wrong, what happened? Who was that on the phone? You look white as a sheet."

"Someone tried to overthrow Guzman last night."

"Oh, my..."

They watched side by side as the announcer repeated the same bulletin over and over.

Christie turned toward David, her hands clutching her mauve, terrycloth robe closed just below her throat. "What do you think's going on? Is this the same group that tried to remove Guzman the last time?"

"I don't know. Probably not. Most of them have fled or been executed. But if you assume Guzman actually is in custody and removed from power, then this has to be a good thing, whoever's behind it."

"How would that affect us?" she asked.

"It would have a positive effect on everybody. How could it not? Guzman's only one step removed from a dictator. To have a true democracy in Venezuela, instead of one in name only..."

"But *has* he been removed from power? I can't tell," Christie said. "Besides, it sounds to me like more than an attempt to overthrow the government and arrest Guzman. It sounds like somebody tried to kill him."

It sounded that way to David, too, but the announcer's few words gave him little to go on. He mentally replayed his conversations with Carlos. Carlos had clearly and emphatically told him that there would be no violence. "Do I look like a violent man?" he'd said. The television report probably sounded the way it did because Carlos and his group didn't have all their pieces in place yet. Once they did, there would be a full announcement of the coup and of Guzman's deposing. Obviously, Guzman *hadn't* been assassinated—he was alive, and probably under some kind of house arrest by the new government.

David's first impulse was to contact Carlos, seeking reassurance that there was nothing to worry about. But he decided to sit tight— today might be the day for the second briefcase drop at the restaurant, now that the coup had taken place. Carlos would surely call him to confirm that the drop was a go. David would ask him then.

Christie reached out and took his hand. He felt her fingers slide against his sweaty palms.

"David, are you all right?"

"Yeah. Sure." He stood and kissed her on the cheek. "Just trying to figure out what this all means. I think I'd better go to the school and talk to the teachers as they arrive this morning. Could you keep the TV on? Buzz me if you hear anything new."

At seven a.m., David locked his office door and dialed Carlos's cell, too nervous to wait.

"Please leave a message," was the sterile reply.

"Carlos, this is David. I've seen the news and I need you to call me." David hung up and waited.

Thirty minutes later, David called again. Again he got the answering device. "Carlos, I need to know what's going on. I'm confused. Please call right away."

Thirty minutes later, still no response from Carlos. *Just sit tight*, David told himself. *You don't know that anything's gone wrong. This might all be according to plan. If Guzman is out of power, this is exactly what you wanted.*

He took a few deep breaths.

The seas were calm when Carlos left the dock at 6 a.m. and headed out to sea, following his GPS system's guidance east/northeast at 72.7 degrees toward the island of Grenada.

As soon as he'd received word, at 4 a.m., from Hawkeye informing him that the mission had been a failure, his first priority had been to get out of Venezuela. He'd driven to his office and destroyed the few incriminating records on his computer. He wasn't worried about Guzman's men—by the time they connected the dots and came after him, he'd be long gone. The drug lords were a different story. While they still knew him only as Durango, they would soon discover not necessarily his true identity but at least the others he'd used in Venezuela, and they would learn where he lived and where his office was. They were far more resourceful and determined than Guzman's men -- and better funded.

By 5:00 a.m. he'd been driving toward Marina Portofino in Vargas, where a Donzi 38 ZR boat with twin Mercury 525 EFI engines was moored and waiting. Donzis were a brand of boat drug runners often used—if they could get their hands on one. Wide open, this model could do more than ninety miles per hour on a flat sea. Carlos's boat had been modified to carry enough fuel to go at least four hundred miles.

If the sea stayed glassy—and if he was lucky enough not to be sighted by the Venezuelan Coast Guard—it would take him six hours or less to speed across the Caribbean sea and quietly enter the harbor at St. George's.

CHAPTER FIFTEEN

At 6 a.m., General Raldo Dukai, the Director of Intelligence and Prevention Services (DISIP) and the senior officer in charge of the assassination investigation, was in uniform and in his office. He had arrived there within thirty minutes after being awakened with news of the assassination attempt. He was seated in his desk chair, looking out the window, a notepad half-filled with cryptic notes on his lap, when his private command phone rang.

"I'm standing over the prisoner right now," Commander Torres said. "He's still only semi-conscious. He received a severe concussion as he was being captured, but the doctor thinks he will regain full consciousness soon. Looks to be in his twenties. Caucasian, about five-eight. I don't think he was the leader. We'll find out who he is and what he knows—and then he will die."

And then he will die. Yes, that was typical of Torres. Secretly, General Dukai hated Torres's attitude, as he hated the rest of the new breed of tough-talking, bloodthirsty men like Torres. They enjoyed the violence and torture that characterized Guzman's treatment of prisoners, including the Venezuelan citizens Guzman considered his political enemies.

In five more years, Dukai could retire on full pension. He could hardly wait.

A career military man now in his late fifties, Dukai had invested himself in Venezuela's army long before Guzman's regime had taken control. He was considered by his colleagues to be quiet, efficient, brilliant in his investigative knowledge and abilities. Even so, it was a minor miracle that he had not only survived Guzman's purge of top-ranking military officers, but actually been promoted to the position he now held. Dukai himself did not fully understand how or why he had been spared the purges. It certainly hadn't been for lack of ambitious men beneath him trying to engineer his military demise so that they could climb the ladder another rung, kicking aside his body on their way up.

It reminded Dukai of the story of Daniel, told to him by the nuns at the Catholic school he'd attended as a child. Daniel too had been targeted for demise by his rivals, then spared, then promoted. And like Daniel, Dukai felt that he had been placed in his current position for a purpose, a purpose that transcended the ambitions of men like Torres.

And perhaps, in the larger historical view, even of men like Guzman.

"It will serve no purpose to kill the prisoner," Dukai told Torres. "He may prove useful to the investigation. Let's not forget that we are a civilized nation that signed the Geneva Convention. We must treat our prisoners humanely."

"General, this man tried to kill our president," Torres said, angry. "Five of my soldiers are dead, and several more wounded. There is nothing humane about that! He deserves to die, and I think our President would agree."

"Of course, after a proper trial, I would agree that his crime is punishable by death. But we will follow the law in this, Commander."

"He is of no value to us if he does not cooperate. And he is of no value once we are certain he has told us all he knows. With all due respect, General, I have been charged with the responsibility of extracting information from this prisoner. I believe the urgency of this duty compels me to do whatever is necessary to get him to talk. I will call you when I have more information."

Torres hung up the phone.

Dukai was tempted to call Torres back and discipline him for insulting a superior officer by hanging up on him. But a battle of wills with Torres was the last thing Dukai wanted right now.

Guzman had allowed and even encouraged this new breed of rogue soldier. How foolish of Guzman not to realize, as history had proven here in Latin America as well as elsewhere, that a rogue military could not be controlled—not even by its makers.

Sitting in his office, waiting for Carlos to call, David kept the radio on. News was slow in developing, but by nine o'clock, it had been announced that Guzman's elite bodyguards had killed one assassin; another had been wounded and captured. Three of Guzman's guards and two National Guard soldiers had been killed.

Six people dead. Not good. Why is Carlos not returning my calls?

David called again, leaving another message. He paced the floor, wavering between growing panic and rationalization: *They're just being cautious. Carlos must be very busy this morning. Obviously, no coup will be announced until they've secured the government, persuaded the military to stand down, gotten all their ducks in a row...*

But why hasn't he called me to make the final delivery?

By 9:15, Carlos Edwards was making good time at 65 mph across a calm Caribbean sea. He turned on his SAT phone again; as a precaution, he'd kept it off while still in Venezuela to avoid high-tech electronic detection systems. There were three calls from Tecero, three from David Eller.

Tecero's messages were nasty and to the point. The first two Carlos had listened to earlier. They demanded to know what had gone wrong and told Carlos to find a way to silence the pigeon and retrieve Tecero's money.

Fortunately for David Eller, neither Tecero nor any of the other drug lords knew the pigeon's identity. But when the government finally identified David—as they surely would—Tecero too would discover

128 The Missionary

who he was, find him, retrieve the two million dollars David carried in his briefcase, and then kill him. That is, if they found him before the Venezuelan military did. Neither option would be a pleasant one for David. Or, more than likely, his family.

Carlos scanned the horizon. He was alone as far as the eye could see.

Tecero's third message was angry, an outright threat. "Call me, Durango! Or I will track you down anywhere in the world. There is nowhere you can hide from me. I will make you wish you were never born. I will find you, you coward!"

Carlos smiled. Emilio Antonio Tecero was a strong, dominant, frightening man, and he had many contacts. But Carlos was confident that he could dodge Tecero forever if he had to. He also knew that he had enough video and taped information to hang Tecero and make him unwelcome anywhere in the world—a potent bargaining chip.

The most recent message from David was like the others: short and increasingly frantic, begging Carlos to call him.

How would this missionary, untrained in espionage or combat or survival in a hostile environment, survive and save his family? Perhaps he had reserves of strength and ingenuity and courage Carlos didn't see. But Carlos doubted it. He saw little chance of David surviving this, unless someone reached in and saved him.

He debated for a moment, tempted to call him.

He regretted having used David. It had been bad judgment. The truth was, he had allowed his admiration for David and the others at Hope Village to get in the way of the nasty business of killing. The fifty thousand he had put in the coffers of Hope Village in return for David's simple task was the kind of mistake Carlos had never allowed himself to make before. If he had not been so confident the coup would succeed, he would never have put the Ellers in harm's way.

It had been a stupid mistake—by a man who had survived in this dangerous game for so many years because he did not make mistakes. That had not been why the assassination plot had failed, of course, or why Carlos was now fleeing across the Caribbean, but it was why a good and innocent man was now facing, in all likelihood, a very unpleasant death.

Carlos looked at his phone. Should he call?

But even Carlos had his orders, and they were to destroy and dispose of the sat phone and activate the backup phone he'd not yet used. If, for any reason, the phone in his hand had been compromised, using it to contact Leprechaun would be a mistake.

The depth sounder indicated a sea depth in excess of a thousand feet. Carlos accessed the phone's call log, memorized David's cell phone number, and then tossed the sat phone into the sea.

The Donzi cut through the warm Caribbean waters toward Grenada.

Danny awoke slowly. He felt drugged. At first he was aware only of a generalized pain that seemed to take in his whole body, and he seemed to be slipping in and out of consciousness. Gradually, though, the periods of consciousness became longer and more vivid, and he became aware that his head was pounding and that each breath hurt.

He tried to open his eyes and discovered that his left eye was swollen so badly he could open it only a slit. He felt bandages around his head. He tried to move his arms and legs—a jabbing pain shot through his left leg, reminding him of his wound. Other than the pain, his attempt to move his limbs accomplished nothing—they didn't move. He lifted his head and tried to see. His hands and feet were tied to the metal posts at each corner of the small cot on which he lay. He was stripped down to his shorts.

The darkened room had no furniture except a small lamp in the corner and a wooden chair. He tried to take a full breath and immediately felt a chestful of sharp pains, as if he had several broken ribs. He groaned.

"¿Como se llama?"

Danny slowly opened his good eye. A bright light shone directly at him now, outlining the silhouette of a man in fatigues. Presumably, a Venezuelan military officer.

The man repeated the question in both Spanish and English.

Danny didn't answer. In his short time in Venezuela, he'd heard enough Spanish to recognize that simple question. And, having been raised in New Jersey before his family moved to Israel when he was sixteen, he understood English perfectly well. And of course he'd picked up Hebrew during his years in Israel, which might come in handy as he stalled for more time.

Several other questions followed, with pauses between: "Who do you work for? Where have you been staying? How did you get into the country? Who is working with you? How many of you were involved in the coup?"

Danny said nothing.

"*Mira*, you can make this easy or difficult. The choice is yours. If necessary, I can add to your pain beyond what you ever imagined. Do you understand what I mean?"

Danny had no doubt that Guzman's people would not hesitate to torture and kill him. After all, he was part of an assassination team. They would use any method to get him to talk, and then they would kill him. He figured he was a dead man already. Since he could not save his own life, his only goal was to try to hold out as long as possible, to give Hawkeye and Zach time to escape.

Abruptly, the man left the room. A few minutes later, a man in a white jacket appeared, syringe in hand. He jammed it into Danny's leg. Within seconds, the room began to blur again. Danny welcomed the sensation. Knowing that they would torture him when he awoke, he prayed that he never would.

CHAPTER SIXTEEN

At 9:45 that morning, David's cell phone buzzed again. He glanced at the incoming number, hoping it was Carlos. No—his mother again, for the second time that morning. And like the first time, he didn't answer. Fifteen minutes earlier, it had been his brother Stephen in D.C. Obviously, his family had seen the news in the States and wanting to be sure he and Christie were okay. But David wasn't ready to speak to them—not yet, not until he knew more. Maybe when they didn't get through to him, they would try Christie on her cell. Her voice would be reassuring; David's, he was sure, would reveal a hint of the danger he now knew he faced.

At ten-thirty, David returned to the quiet house—Christie had gone to the clinic—to watch the news on TV, wanting visual images to go with the words he'd been hearing on the radio. Guzman had given a one-minute press conference earlier, and this had been re-broadcast several times. He had stood before a bank of microphones, a bandage on his left cheek, vowing to capture and punish all involved in the assassination attempt. He had looked furious and taken no questions.

David could no longer hope that things weren't as they appeared to be. Not only had the "peaceful coup" been in reality an assassination attempt, but it had failed. Guzman was still in power.

And Carlos hadn't returned his calls. He was either in hiding, or he'd already fled the country.

The locked briefcase in David's office was probably full of money—money for paid killers—or maybe something even more incriminating,

131

like explosives or sophisticated weaponry. If Guzman's people found him, he would be tried and convicted as a conspirator in the attempted murder of the President of Venezuela.

David clicked off the TV and threw the remote across the room. The plastic cover flew off as the remote hit the wall, the batteries skittering across the floor.

He slammed the door behind him and returned to his office to wait by the phone, pacing, listening to the radio. Two more news reports aired. In one, Venezuelan officials reported that JAM was suspected but had not yet claimed responsibility. Another report suggested that the CIA was involved.

"The conspiracy to assassinate President Guzman was definitely larger than had been thought at first," one reporter said, then added that literally thousands of police and special agents had been assigned to the case and were casting a wide net to catch the perpetrators.

"The Venezuelan military and law-enforcement agencies will do everything possible to bring to justice those responsible for this brutal act against the president and his family."

At noon, David came home found Christie folding clothes in the living room and little Davy working a wooden puzzle on the floor. She glanced up briefly and smiled. It was such a simple scene—domestic, idyllic. And their lives together had been filled with such scenes. Why had he never properly valued them before? Why had he not seen them as something worth protecting?

"Hi, Daddy," Davy said. It was a rare moment of calm for this hyperactive child.

"Hi, punkin," David said, and squatted to kiss his son on the top of his head, then sat on the couch across the room from Christie, aware even as he did so that he was choosing the point of greatest physical distance from her, afraid of how she might react.

"You know, hon—I've been listening to the news all morning, and I'm getting worried. There seems to be a massive manhunt underway for anyone involved in this coup attempt. I mean, knowing this government, who knows where they might look next?"

Christie looked up and studied his face more carefully. "You do look worried. You look like you haven't slept. But why would they look here? We both know what you said on TV, but you haven't done anything other than that. Even if they question you, they won't find anything."

If you only knew, he thought, but said, "Think of who you're talking about, though. If they decide to question me, they might want to question you, too. And do we really trust their methods of interrogation? Besides, if some of our friends break down and mention that I've said I thought Guzman should step down—well—I'm wondering if this wouldn't be a good time for us to take a vacation. Go home to the states for a few weeks. Visit some churches to raise some support. When this all blows over, we can head back." *IF it blows over,* David added in his head. But when would that be, exactly? If the Ellers escaped, David could never come back as long as Guzman was in power, whether Carlos was ever captured or not. He looked around the cramped but homey room. How many more times would he see it?

Christie was folding David's *What would Jesus do?* T-shirt. "David— are you sure? There's never a good time, but right now I feel like I'd be leaving Martha to handle so much on her own." She sighed. "I don't want to put the others here at Hope Village in danger. If we take off now, won't that create more suspicion than if we just stick to our work here?"

"There won't *be* work here for us if I get arrested—and probably not for anyone else, either. And I won't leave you here alone. I don't trust this government. Too many people have just disappeared—and that was before this coup attempt."

Christie shot a sharp glance at David. "Just a few days ago you told me they wouldn't harm a U.S. citizen. Now you're telling me the opposite!"

Davy looked up first at his dad, then his mom. "Are you mad, Mommy?"

She looked down at the clothes again, clearly trying to calm herself. "It's okay, honey. Maybe we should go visit Nana and Papa, like Daddy said." She held out her arms for Davy, and he climbed into her lap. "Would you like that?"

Davy nodded, hugging his mom's neck.

"If you think we should leave for awhile, David," she said, "I'll go. But what about Cecil and Martha?"

"They'll be fine. They've always been careful about what they say. I'll see if I can get us a flight for later tonight. And I'll tell Cecil and Martha that we're planning to leave for a few days."

David returned to his office without eating. Before he logged on to the Internet to try to find a flight back to the states, he tried to call Carlos one more time.

Somewhere beneath the Caribbean, the cell phone David was calling sank slowly deeper and deeper, its innards gradually filling with saltwater.

Danny awoke slowly, hearing muffled voices. When he opened his eyes, the same officer was standing over him.

"I am Commander Nicolas Torres, Senior Commander of President Guzman's Special Forces," the man said. "You and at least three other men tried to assassinate the president. We sedated you so that you would be fully rested for this interrogation."

Danny lifted his head and looked down at his body. There were electrodes adhering to his skin in several places; wires led from them in the general direction of Torres. Danny's heart began to pound, and he felt adrenaline spike him fully awake.

"If you resist my questioning, I will do whatever is necessary to extract this information from you."

Danny knew that Torres would do just that. In a near-dictatorship like Venezuela, failure to extract information from a prisoner would be construed as the kind of failure that could doom a military career, and Torres would be ruthless in making sure that his own career didn't hit such a roadblock; he would subject Danny to whatever pain was necessary to extract what he knew.

Danny knew from his training that he had been injected with some drug intended as a "truth serum," probably some form of sodium pentothal. While this drug had put him to sleep and would continue to relax him and make him more talkative, it could not force him to tell the truth.

Commander Torres repeated the questions he had asked the day before.

Danny remained silent. He closed his eyes. *Be brave,* he told himself. *You can't save yourself—but you can save Hawk and Zach.*

Torres moved his arm.

Danny's screams rattled the walls.

Two hours later, Commander Torres sat in an impersonal, utilitarian office in building number two on El Burro Island, Guzman's newly refurbished torture center and holding facility for political enemies. He stared at the walls.

A courier, a private who looked as if he were quaking in his boots, brought in a leather pouch, set it in front of Torres, then stood back at attention, waiting for further orders. He was followed, before Torres could even open the pouch, by another private, an orderly carrying a tray with a carafe of coffee. The orderly poured some into a mug, placed it within Torres's reach, and then retreated. Torres took a sip of the coffee and examined the papers in the pouch. He looked at his watch. "What time is it, private?"

The courier looked confused, then looked at his watch. "It's two twenty-six in the afternoon, Commander."

Torres nodded. "Yes, that's what my watch says too. So why—" he held up the papers—"am I just now seeing communiqués that are very plainly time-stamped twelve fifty-three?"

136   The Missionary

The courier froze. "I—I just received them at—"

Torres's mug of steaming hot coffee bounced off the private's chest, splattering across his shoulders and face. Torres jumped to his feet. "I don't want excuses, private! I want important communiqués to be delivered on time. That is your responsibility, and if you fail in it, there are no excuses I will accept." He threw first the leather pouch, then the offending papers, at the courier's head. "Go and explain this to those bumbling fools in the general's office. Now!"

The courier saluted, coffee dripping from his face and spreading in a dark stain down the front of his uniform, and fled the office, the pouch and papers clenched under his arm.

Incompetent idiots! Why was he expected to put up with such mediocrity? Was this the future of the Venezuelan army?

He knew, of course, why he was so angry. He had so far been able to get nothing from his prisoner. Oh, the man had talked—not at first, but after a half-hour or so of electrical shock, judiciously timed and placed. But who knew what he had said? He was speaking a language of some kind, but nothing Torres or the language specialist he'd called in had been able to identify. Certainly not any form of Spanish or English, or anything else spoken commonly in South America. Gibberish.

He felt like slitting the prisoner's throat. But if he failed to extract the information they needed from this prisoner—and especially over something as trivial as a language problem—that would be considered a failure, and in the Venezuelan army, failure had a way of terminating careers. Or worse.

But he would not fail. This prisoner knew what Torres wanted to find out, And this prisoner would speak. With the infliction of enough pain, this prisoner would speak in Spanish, or Chinese, or Zulu if he had to, to get the pain to stop.

Torres would see to it.

◆   ◆   ◆

Christie finally found the other battery for the remote under the couch. She'd thought at first that Davy must have dropped the remote or stepped on it, and she'd even scolded him mildly for it, but she'd been able to tell from the confusion on his face that he hadn't been responsible. Besides, the remote had been hurled with enough force to crack the plastic casing pretty severely. Davy hadn't done that. She hadn't done it. That left David.

She pieced it back together and tried it. It still worked, but she'd have to hold it together with scotch tape.

What had angered him so severely that he'd thrown the remote against the wall? When they'd first heard about the coup attempt, David had seemed hopeful, not angry, thinking that perhaps Guzman had been deposed. But as the day had progressed, as he'd wandered back and forth between his office and the house, glued to the TV news when he was home, his frustration and uneasiness had grown. She couldn't remember seeing him so uptight--ever. She'd seen him twice that day simply walking around the compound, hands in his pockets, lost in thought, occasionally shaking his head.

And now he was convinced they needed to flee the country. All because of a few intemperate words spoken weeks before in a television interview.

No, that wasn't what was bothering him.

It didn't take her long to figure it out. What had changed in their lives just before the assassination attempt and now this nearly inexplicable paranoia David was experiencing?

Carlos Edwards had come into their lives.

Who was Carlos Edwards?

By 3:00 p.m., Carlos Edwards was sitting on a barstool at the Mourne Rouge Beach Bar in Grenada. He was not accustomed to failure. He tore his eyes from the emerald-blue water lapping the sand, raised a hand to attract the bartender, and ordered another Corona.

138 The Missionary

David Eller. Eller had been the only nonprofessional in the operation. And now, besides Carlos's sense of guilt for leaving an innocent man behind, Eller was also the only man who could link Carlos to the coup attempt—other than Hawkeye, and Carlos was confident that Hawkeye and whoever remained of his team was even now on their way to Grenada.

Not that Carlos was worried about his own safety. He was safely out of Venezuela, and he would simply take back up one of his other identities for a while. Only Hawkeye knew about the one-million-dollar kickback Hawkeye had agreed to pay Carlos as a "commission" out of Tecero's payments to Hawkeye and his team. That money was already sitting in Carlos's private Cayman Island account, and along with similar amounts Carlos had secreted in other safe places, he already had more than enough for retirement, when he tired of the game. He could go into hiding and never be found.

Taking a drink of foamy beer, he tried to dismiss Eller from his mind.

Collateral damage. A dead pigeon. Forget it and move on. It's happened before.

His mind wouldn't cooperate. The truth was, it *hadn't* happened before, not like this. Carlos had used people shamelessly on many occasions, but this had been different. He'd enlisted David Eller in the effort precisely because he admired the man and what he was doing, and the organization he worked with, and wanted to help them.

Carlos deliberately gave little thought to his own childhood. It was a habit he'd adopted as a young man simply to escape the horror, but as he grew older, he found it useful to simply set aside those experiences as unhelpful to the image of the man he'd chosen to become. The implications he'd spun out for David Eller—*I grew up on the streets of Buenos Aires, Argentina…I was homeless. My parents drank themselves to death…I stole and begged*—were all lies, of course. Except for having grown up in Buenos Aires. Carlos never told anyone the truth about his childhood, and never would. But one attitude that Carlos cherished from those early years was his respect and admiration for people like

David and Christie who lived their lives in service to the downtrodden, the oppressed, the helpless—those who could not help themselves.

And now Carlos had ruined all of that, and put their lives in danger. Not simply the man David Eller himself, but all that he valued and held dear.

Including a wife and young son.

Eller was no spy, no mercenary, no soldier. He was helpless in the face of Guzman's battle-hardened soldiers. He would be captured, tortured, and most likely killed.

Carlos thought of the two orphaned girls he had met, Angela and Maria. What would happen to them and hundreds like them because of what Carlos had done? Of course, Carlos had been trying to remove a dictator from power, which would have helped them. But he had failed.

Why was he so concerned about one missionary? He had seen many men die for a cause and had risked his own life countless times.

But David's cause had been the Venezuelan children, not the assassination attempt. Carlos looked deep into himself. Was he, in fact, envious of David—of the simplicity of his life, of his family, his mission, the immediacy with which he was able to see the results of his efforts, his unshakeable faith in God, his certainty that he was serving a cause worth giving his life to and for? Carlos had, in fact, none of those things. Yes, Carlos believed in what he was doing. But in recent years, it had become a way to feather his own nest as much as a way to make the world a better place.

Had his motives *ever* been as simple as trying to make the world a better place? Hadn't they always been more about Carlos himself than about the world?

A brief image from his childhood flashed across his mind, then another, and another in swift succession, along with a decades-old memory of pain so sharp he arched his back and grimaced, and he shook his head to clear it. *I have that right,* he thought. *If anyone has the right to remake my life however I choose, that person is me.*

He motioned the bartender to bring him another Corona.

His phone rang. Only one person had the number to this new phone.

"Do you have an update since we last talked?" It was a voice Carlos knew well.

"Not yet," Carlos said. "The operatives are on their way here now. I'll debrief them as soon as they arrive."

"Call as soon as you have more information. Our intelligence tells us that the situation in Venezuela is deteriorating fast. The noose is tightening."

The phone went dead.

People at a higher pay grade than Carlos were beginning to panic.

He shook his head. What had gone wrong with this mission?

Carlos came to a sudden and unpleasant realization: He disliked his life.

He had disliked it for years. That was why he'd felt increasing pressure in recent campaigns to create the financial cushion he needed to make his escape. His life thus far had been about manipulating governments, exterminating people, and fighting for what others considered just causes. That life had cost him his marriage. He had no children, no family. Only a series of false names and secrets, a montage of deception and brutality. And now, because of him, a man more noble than he would probably die.

By now, Hawkeye and Zach were no doubt on their way here to Grenada. But there had never been an escape plan for David Eller. If left much longer in Venezuela, he would die, he and his family—if they were not dead already.

For the first time in his life, Carlos Edwards felt like a coward.

CHAPTER SEVENTEEN

The break came shortly after 4:00 PM, and instead of encouraging Commander Torres, it enraged him even further. He had just finished inflicting a lengthy period of electrical shock on the prisoner, during which the prisoner had screamed in a most gratifying manner. Torres was about to light a cigarette when the prisoner leaned to the side, vomited bile, and then yelled—in English!—"My name is Daniel Benjamin! I don't work for any government, and I don't know the names of anyone else involved! My name is Daniel Benjamin! I don't—" He stopped to vomit again, and then continued, repeating the same thing over and over.

The unlit cigarette fell from Torres's mouth.

English! This man spoke English! After all the time wasted trying to decipher what he'd been saying in whatever imbecilic language he'd been speaking, all the frustration and rage Torres had been feeling…

He motioned for Corporal Ortega, who'd been standing near the wall—a trusted man, and good at extracting information. "Continue the electrical shocks, and see how much you can learn from him now that we've got him softened up. If within thirty minutes you haven't learned the names of all of his confederates, bring in a branding iron. Heat it to red-hot right beside his cot, where he can see it and even feel the heat."

"And if he tells us everything before I use it on him?" Ortega asked.

Torres sneered. "Burn him anyway. This man mocked me."

By 5:15, Danny Benjamin, a brave, tough, highly trained and agile young mercenary commando, was feeling pain such as he had never imagined possible and doing something he'd told himself a hundred times he would never do under any circumstances. He was spilling his guts.

And among the first things he told them was that he had met a man at Los Tiburones Restaurant to exchange briefcases.

At 5:33, Commander Torres telephoned General Raldo Dukai.

At 6:00 p.m., David and Christie sat silently on the couch, watching the news. A nationwide hunt was on for those responsible for the assassination attempt. Grainy footage of the captured assassin made David flinch. Even though the prisoner's face was grotesquely swollen, David had no trouble recognizing him as the man who'd come to Los Tiburones Restaurant to exchange briefcases.

He rushed to the kitchen, turned on the cold water, and splashed some on his perspiring face. His stomach churned.

David had no clue how many people might be involved in this plot, or how many of them knew about him. But one thing was certain: the captured commando could describe him. He splashed more cold water on his face, but it wasn't enough to quench the burn that ran through his soul.

Rita the waitress thought her heart would burst through her ribcage.

Just moments before, a dozen uniformed men had strode into Los Tiburones, dismissed all diners—who hadn't waited to be told twice—and instructed all employees to line up along the bar. Rita had had a sudden fear that, for whatever reason, they were going to be machine-gunned as they stood. But instead, the leader of the soldiers had taken Senor Ramirez, the owner of the restaurant, aside and spoken to him quietly.

Then Senor Ramirez, wiping the sweat from his face with a white towel and appearing to be in great distress, had faced those lined up in front of the bar and said, "Mis amigos, these soldiers are here to ask us about one of our patrons. Please—you *must* answer all of their questions, fully and accurately and without delay. If you do not, it will not go well for us." He mopped his face again, glanced quickly back over his shoulder at the stern uniformed man who had given him his orders, and said, "The country, as you know, is in turmoil because of the attempt on the life of our beloved president. Now all loyal Venezuelans must band together in support of our government. Please." He gave them all an imploring look, then turned to the soldiers and said, "They will do as you say."

Three soldiers stepped forward, selected the first three employees in line—poor Julietta burst into tears, so frightened she was—and took them to separate corners of the dining room.

Rita would be in the next group.

She closed her eyes and tried to breathe deeply and calmly, tried to slow her heart. But she could not help it; she was terrified of men in uniform, terrified of the Venezuelan army in particular. And with good reason.

Now they would ask her questions, and she would have to answer. She hadn't needed Senor Ramirez's urging to tell them the truth. She knew better than to conceal information from these men.

But what brought her such sorrow was that she felt she already knew which patron they were seeking information about. She had been worried about him since she had seen him with that other man, the man in the yellow shirt. He had been trouble, that one.

She was not brave. She would tell them what they wanted to know from the first, before they decided to force her to tell.

General Dukai stood gazing out the window of his downtown Federal District office. Even though he looked toward the green mountains that rose picturesquely in the distance, vividly outlined in the late afternoon light, his thoughts were about the investigation and where all of this would ultimately lead. His team had already made significant progress.

In the fifteen hours since the coup attempt, a captured commando was talking, the secret compartments in two limos had been discovered and the drivers arrested, the owner of a restaurant where a drop had taken place, along with his staff, were being questioned, and the terrified servants at Vina Estate had explained about the kitchen fire. The chef had been detained for questioning.

Dukai sensed that it would be a productive evening. Leads were pouring in faster than he'd anticipated.

Per standard procedure in situations like this, local and national police as well as all branches of the military were being kept apprised of the details of the investigation—or at least, in this secretive administration where knowledge was power, of those details concerning which they might be expected to provide help. Over a thousand police and military were investigating every lead Dukai's team had provided them.

But Dukai was troubled.

Dukai had more than one goal in this operation. There was, of course, his official goal.

And there were other goals, not so official.

Investigations such as this one tended to expand rapidly, as this one already was. If Dukai was not both shrewd and forceful, it could easily slip out of his control. If that happened, he would be in danger of not achieving all of his goals.

In fact, if that happened, he would be in danger, period.

David had just hung up the phone when it rang again. He was feeling the first hint of relief he'd felt all day—he'd just reserved tickets for himself, Christie, and Davy to fly out on a red-eye from Caracas to Seattle late that night. Now he had much to do—explaining to Cecil and Martha that they needed to leave on short notice, pack—and very little time to do it in if they were to get to the airport on time. He didn't have time for a phone call.

On the other hand, it could be Carlos. He glanced at the number. It was Felix. David answered.

"Hola, mi amigo," Felix said. "I called because I was worried about you."

David hesitated. "Worried? Why?"

"Well, I was thinking over our conversations about the government, and some of the things you have said." He chuckled. "I said to you myself, just two days ago: 'Desperate times, desperate measures.' And since then, ay! The times in Venezuela have gotten even more desperate. How are you doing, my friend?"

David exhaled sharply. "This is a timely call, Felix. The Ellers are not doing very well, to tell you the truth. Like you, I'm afraid of how Guzman's people might interpret the things I've said. The time may have come for us to leave Venezuela. Just for a while."

There was a pause. Then Felix asked, "You are planning to fly?"

"Yes."

"Something you should know," Felix said. "Tonight I am talking to my neighbor, who is a policeman."

David froze. Would Felix have felt compelled to tell the police about their conversations?

"My neighbor tells me that the airport is almost shut down," Felix continued. "A few flights are going out, yes, but security is very tight. Anyone suspected, even remotely, of having information about the assassination plot is being detained. I do not think it is a good idea for you and your family to try to get through airport security. Surely, after the events of last night, you are on some kind of list. And if you tried to leave the country, my good friend—well, that would not look good to the authorities. They would see that as a sign of guilt."

David's heart sank. Just when he thought he'd figured out a way to get his family safely out of the country. He almost asked Felix's advice—and then realized belatedly that he had no way to know whether

Guzman's forces had already tapped into his phone line. They could be listening right now—in which case they would know about the flight reservations he'd just made. Best to say as little as possible.

He thanked Felix and hung up. Time to make one more call, but he would use his cell—and make it from outside, not only so Christie wouldn't hear, but also just in case they'd already bugged their house and his office. He was in big trouble, and his enemies were a lot bigger, stronger, and more experienced in this kind of thing than he was.

Which was why he was going to make this call.

It was seven p.m. and nearly dark when Hawkeye and Zach slowly guided their powerful Donzi speedboat, its twin engines rumbling, out of the harbor at Rio Chico and set their heading for Grenada. Tonight, there would be a full moon to help them see—but it would also provide more vision for those who would be hunting for them. Both men kept a close watch for any signs of the Coast Guard as Hawkeye accelerated the engines on what, for now, was smooth water.

The past eighteen hours had been hellish for the two men. After they had left the body of Aaron and their wounded comrade, Danny, on the hillside, and shot the two soldiers who'd been firing on them from above, they'd continued on a dead run to their van without further resistance.

They knew of Danny's capture. Danny's microphone had been on, so Hawkeye had heard the crack of the rifle butt on Danny's head, and then an officer cursing and berating his soldiers. Hawkeye believed that Danny would not live another forty-eight hours, if he wasn't dead already. The Guzman regime wasn't known for humane treatment of political prisoners.

They had returned to their hotel as planned, gathered everything from clothes to weapons, wiped down the rooms for fingerprints, and packed the car. Then they had sat at the table and looked at each other.

"They will torture Danny if he is still alive," Zach had said.

Hawkeye nodded.

"We don't leave a man behind," Zach persisted.

"Zach—we knew—we *all* knew—this might happen. Danny too. We discussed it in training. We—"

"Then, it was just talk," Zach said. "Now it's a man's life, a man we trained with. What if it was you—or me?"

"If it was me," Hawkeye said, "I would be fervently praying that you would all leave me and escape. Coming after me would only get the rest of you killed. It wouldn't help me. Besides—if he *is* still alive, which is doubtful, we don't have a clue where they've taken him. Where would we go?"

The two men had driven the back roads, first along the coast and then through the mountains, to Rio Chico where the Donzi awaited them at the marina. Arriving shortly after noon, they had decided to wait until dark to leave, since traveling in a fast boat in broad daylight might attract the attention of the Venezuelan Coast Guard. They'd parked behind a large dry-docked vessel and waited, occasionally listening to the radio. They knew little Spanish, but enough to allow them to understand that Guzman's forces were intent on finding them.

Their boat was nearing fifty-five knots, less than a mile after leaving the harbor, when Zach spotted a larger vessel on the horizon off the starboard bow. Hawkeye thought, from its size and shape, that it was probably a Coast Guard vessel. Zach removed any doubt when he viewed it through the binoculars and reported the fifty-caliber machine gun on its bow.

They were still at least ten miles away from international waters, but even that nebulous border wouldn't help if the Coast Guard spotted them and suspected their identity.

Hawkeye slowed their boat to a crawl, hoping they wouldn't be seen, but the Coast Guard vessel was angling in a northeasterly direction that would take it only a few hundred yards in front of the Donzi. Hawkeye began a slow turn in the opposite direction, hoping the other vessel hadn't yet spotted them.

Zach kept his binoculars trained on the Coast Guard vessel. "They're turning directly toward us," he said with apparent calm.

Hawkeye considered their options. If the Coast Guard vessel got within four hundred yards, the Donzi would be easily within range of the bow-mounted fifty-caliber. For now, Hawkeye suspected that the other vessel just wanted to check them out, which meant that the advantage of surprise still rested with him. But they were closing fast, nearly within range.

The larger vessel's powerful spotlights came on. *Time to see if this boat can actually hit ninety miles an hour,* Hawkeye thought. "Hang on, Zach!" Hawkeye pushed the two engine accelerator knobs full forward, and the boat shot out of the water on an instant plane; a huge spray of salt water gushed behind them from under the props. Swinging first in a vast circle in an attempt to keep their distance from the Coast Guard cutter, Hawkeye then gradually resumed his heading toward Grenada.

The cutter, more cumbersome and slower, tried to turn with them. Suddenly, there were small pelts of spray landing to the side and rear of their boat. The fifty-caliber had opened fire. Hawkeye felt the boat lurch in a way that had nothing to do with its speed or the chop of the water, and bits of fiberglass flew past his head.

"Keep your head down!" Zach screamed over the roar of the engines. Both men ducked. The Donzi continued to accelerate…sixty, seventy, seventy-five.

"How bad are we hit?" Hawkeye yelled.

Zach looked back. "Not bad, I don't think. Good thing it didn't take out an engine; we'd be dead."

Now the bullets were hitting the water well behind them. The cutter would never catch them. At eighty miles an hour, Hawkeye and Zach were steadily and rapidly pulling away. Hawkeye still had concerns: Were there any other military boats farther out that could intercept them? Or even worse, would the Coast Guard call in armed aircraft to shoot them out of the water?

It all depended on who the Coast Guard suspected they were.

⬦ ⬦ ⬦

David strode quickly down by the fruit trees and dialed a number in Virginia he knew by heart. He had talked to his brother, Stephen, just over a month ago—but it seemed like a lifetime.

David admired his older brother, which made this phone call even harder to make. Stephen had graduated near the top of his law school class at Stanford. For two years he'd worked as a law clerk at the Supreme Court; then he'd been recruited by the Attorney General's office. In their last call, Stephen had told David that he'd just been re-assigned to a division dubbed "Nutcracker"—the Narcotics Unit Tracking Team.

"Hey, man. How's it going with your new assignment?"

David heard his brother breathe heavily into the phone, as if he'd suddenly drawn the mouthpiece closer. "David! Are you and Christie okay?" His voice was anxious.

"Yeah. At least for now."

"My phone's been ringing off the hook! Mom and Dad are frantic. I've tried to call about a dozen times but couldn't get through—and frankly, it may be just as well I didn't. I don't know how closely international calls are being monitored."

"That's why I didn't use our land line. I'm on my cell."

"You sure you're okay? I've been following the news, and it doesn't sound like any picnic down there. NSI has been watching everything closely. The one commandant, Torres, who was credited with the capture of the commando—they've had their eye on him for a long time. He's a bad one. Ruthless."

"Wait—what's NSI?"

"National Security Investigations. Part of the same division I work with. After 9/11, the Justice Department started a review of every part of our operations, including how we gather and share intelligence information. That's what I'm still doing. So how is it on the ground?"

David hesitated. "Well, let's just say a lot has happened since we last spoke. I may be in some hot water here…I'm not sure."

Stephen's voice took on a decidedly big-brother tone. "You want to explain that?"

150   The Missionary

"You won't believe it." But with sudden assurance, David realized that Stephen *would* believe it—would think this was just what David would do. But now David had no choice. He told Stephen about Carlos, about his interest in David's feelings about Guzman's regime.

"Oh, man," Stephen said. "Tell me this isn't going where it sounds like it's going."

"Stephen—I'm telling you, I think this guy is CIA. He never came out and said it, but he implied it. Pretty strongly."

"If he *had* been CIA, David, he never would have even implied it."

"Come on. You weren't there." David gritted his teeth as he heard old patterns of conversation creeping in, old tones and attitudes. The long-ago voices of two boys rang in his ears. "Anyway, he said they needed me for a couple of short-term assignments. Nothing dangerous, just run an errand or two."

Stephen sighed. "Tell me you turned him down."

"Well—no. Not exactly."

"David—"

"Just an errand or two, Stephen. Just pass along a briefcase—I think it had money in it—to the guys who were supposed to bring on what I thought—what they *told* me—would be a peaceful coup. He said he'd help the orphanage. The new government was supposed to help the poor here...all that stuff."

Stephen swore. "David! I can't believe this. Tell me you're joking!"

"It's no joke, Stephen."

"Do you still have the briefcase?"

"One of them."

"Wait—'one of them'?"

"One briefcase I already delivered. The other's here in my file cabinet. And now Carlos isn't answering his cell phone. I'm worried, Stephen. The guy I delivered the briefcase to is the one commando who got captured."

A pause. "He saw your face?" Stephen asked at last, in dark tones.

"Yes."

"David. David. We've got to get you out of there. Does Christie know any of this?"

"She met Carlos. Doesn't like him or trust him. If she knew the rest, she'd go ballistic."

"Tell me about Carlos."

David told all he knew, which wasn't much.

When he finished, Stephen spent several seconds just making the candy-sucking sound he made when he was concentrating. But when he spoke, it was only: "CIA or not, Dave, it was stupid for you to get involved."

David felt the sting of his brother's words. "Can we skip the finger-pointing? I don't know what to do here, bro! That's why I called you."

"Okay, okay. Calm down. You said Carlos had an office number. Have you tried calling that number instead of his cell?"

Duh. "No, bro. See? Your head's a lot clearer than mine is right now."

"Give me both numbers," Stephen said. David did. Then Stephen said, "Have you checked this address out or talked to anyone else who knows this Edwards guy?"

"He swore me to secrecy, even with Christie."

"Yeah, right. This guy swears you to secrecy and then stops answering his phone. Leaves you high and dry when it all hits the fan. Sounds like a setup to me."

Neither spoke for a few seconds.

"David, before you got involved, did you even stop to think about how this might compromise Hope Village or put your family in danger?"

"Of *course* I did, Stephen. I'm not an idiot. I just wanted to do something more! Besides, he offered a big payment to Hope Village."

"Wait—you mean you've accepted money for this?"

"Not yet. Well, sort of. See, they promised to make a fifty thousand-dollar donation to the orphanage after the coup. They opened a bank account in New York."

"In your name?"

"Yeah."

152 The Missionary

"So now you're a paid mercenary yourself. Or at least that's how it'll look to the Venezuelan authorities. Not to mention the fact that whoever was behind the assassination attempt—and I don't for a minute think it was the CIA—is going to be ticked that they paid good money for something that failed. Look, I'll snoop around with some of my Washington contacts and see what I can find out. But you, Christie, and Davy should get out of Venezuela and back here as soon as possible. Get the next plane out."

"Well—that's a problem. I've got reservations for the three of us for tonight. But the airport is crawling with security. Flights are being cancelled, they're checking everyone—remember, they may already have a description of me."

"Get to the American Embassy. Go now."

"And if they find out I really did participate in this thing—"

"Tell 'em you were coerced. Tell 'em you were lied to. Tell 'em about Carlos—but insist that you're an American deserving of protection who was caught up in—"

"That all sounds great, Stephen—except that I have absolutely no assurance, once I walk into the place, that they won't decide that the politically expedient thing is to turn me over to Guzman. The commandos who tried to assassinate Guzman weren't Venezuelan, Stephen. At least the captured one wasn't. It's starting to feel like an international incident. Would the embassy be able to keep us safe under those conditions? Tell me their decision wouldn't be made on political grounds—and not on the basis of our safety."

Stephen was quiet. "Well, at the very least you'd be detained at the embassy." Before David could respond, Stephen continued, "Okay, listen, I've got to make some calls. I'll try to find a way for you and Christie to get out of there. But don't count on me. Find a way from your end to either leave or go into hiding. You're in danger, David. Ultimately, you're not who they want—they want Carlos. And they'll torture you to find him."

"I don't know any more about him than I've—"

"They won't believe that! So get someplace safe for now, whatever you have to do."

"All right. I'm leaving now. I'll have my cell. If you find out anything, let me know."

"No, bad idea. Cell phones aren't secure. Somebody could be listening to us right now. Besides, how are you going to keep it charged if you're on the run? No, before you leave the compound, I want you to set up a new email account. Remember the name of your first girlfriend, the one I caught you kissing when you were ten? Don't say it—someone could be listening. Set up an email account at yahoo.com using her first and last name and my birth year. If I need to contact you, I'll do it via that email address. I already have a private email account at Yahoo using the pirate name I had when we were kids playing pirate ships in our treehouse. It's my pirate name at yahoo dot com. You remember the name?"

"Of course."

"Email me there. And don't sign your real name to any emails you send. All right. Think before you act. Keep your head straight. Don't trust anyone. I'll try to figure something out."

When David hung up, it was dark. He headed for his office to set up a new email account—and to get the one remaining briefcase out of his file cabinet.

Stephen looked at his watch—7:45 p.m. He thought for a moment, then dialed a number.

"Hey, Roger. Stephen Eller here. Sorry to call you off hours."

"S'okay, man. What's up?"

Roger Garlock, one of Stephen's fellow employees in the Attorney General's office, served as their liaison to the CIA. As Stephen sketched the outline of what David had told him, he could almost hear Roger's head shaking over the phone lines.

"No way, man. There is no way this is a CIA operation."

"Are you sure? To your personal knowledge? We know from classified briefings that Guzman has come up as a subject in more than one NSC meeting in the past year. And after the last attempted coup against Guzman, he claimed it had CIA backing. Office gossip said it was true."

"The U.S. denied it. And even if the CIA was involved before, I doubt they would make that blunder twice."

"This is my brother, Roger. So could you check Carlos Edwards out for me? See if he's CIA?"

"You realize what you're asking? Most agents work undercover. Some are known only to one or two CIA contacts. Besides, they never use real names while working under cover. And neither you nor I have high enough security clearance to get CIA operative names anyway. Don't forget the whole Valerie Plame deal."

"Either this guy was working for the CIA or he wasn't. If he was, then the CIA needs to take some responsibility for my brother's safety and get him out. If not, then David's in double trouble and I need to warn him."

Roger sighed. "Okay, I'll see what I can find out. First thing tomorrow morning. One thing's for sure: the CIA's never going on record about this, even if they *were* involved. In the meantime, tell your brother to get out of the country."

The phone was on its second ring when Felix picked it up. It was David's voice: "Hey, amigo. We need to talk, but not by phone."

"I will be over as soon as I can."

When Felix hung up, he looked up to see his wife, Isabel, watching him. "That was David?" she asked.

Felix nodded.

"I have been worried about him, too," Isabel said. "When I was with Christie last week, she said she wished she could find a way to convince David to be less vocal about his opposition to Guzman. And this was before the assassination attempt." She looked into the kitchen, where their daughter Blanca sat over her bedtime snack. Felix saw the love in her eyes—and also the gratitude. Every day, Isabel prayed prayers of thanksgiving for what David and the doctors had done for Blanca. "*Did* he help with the coup attempt?" she asked, still watching Blanca.

"I do not know. He may have."

Isabel nodded, then looked back up at him, her expression firm, her voice resolute. "What can we do?"

"David wants to talk to me. We need to go to Hope Village right now. Maybe we can get them out on the *Bahia Bonita.*"

Isabel hurriedly threw clothes for her family into two plastic bags. Five minutes after Felix's phone call with David, he was helping Blanca into their old Ford van. After he buckled her in, he looked up and saw Isabel standing motionless in the doorway of their home, looking back in. He cleared his throat. She remained for a moment more, then turned out the lights and locked the door.

CHAPTER EIGHTEEN

The house was quiet when David stepped back inside. Both Christie and Davy were gone. For a moment David panicked. Had Guzman's goons shown up already and taken his family? He looked out the window, scanning the compound for signs of danger he might have missed walking back from his office—and saw instead that everything was quiet and peaceful. No lights on at the clinic, but the windows at the Duncans' house were lit. He glanced at his watch. Almost 8 p.m. He hurried down the hill.

Already in his pajamas and robe, Cecil opened the door. Christie and Davy were on the worn, floral-print sofa with Martha, who looked sleepy in her robe. Davy sat on Martha's lap.

"Come in, David," Cecil said. "Christie was just talking to us about your concerns."

Christie's eyes were red from crying. David's heart sank. Clearly, she'd already guessed that things were far worse than he had told her. "Uh, yeah," he said. He followed Cecil into the room and found a chair across from Christie. "I think I may have spouted off about my anti-Guzman position once too often. Now that somebody tried to kill Guzman, they may consider me a suspect."

He looked across at Christie. Should he tell them all, right now, the truth? He hated the idea of admitting to them all how foolish he'd been, how he'd put them all in danger.

And, frankly, the more he thought about it, the less wise it seemed to tell them. *I haven't even told Christie the truth yet. And the*

158   The Missionary

less the Duncans know, the better for all of us, in case the authorities come asking about me.

Davy yawned, up past his bedtime. So innocent, so vulnerable—and now so much at risk, because of David's actions.

"David," Martha said, "I don't think you have anything to worry about. I think the authorities know that you're just trying to help the children here."

"Maybe, Martha. But we can't trust the Guzman administration. I think we need to leave Hope Village for a little while, just to be safe. And I'm concerned that my involvement here might endanger you and Cecil. Are you sure you'll be safe staying here?"

"Of course we're safe here," Martha said. "This is our home. Proverbs says, 'The name of the Lord is a strong tower, the righteous run to it and are safe.'"

Cecil had come to stand beside David's chair; he put his hand on David's shoulder. "We understand your need to get your family out safely. Our prayers will go with you, David."

Without jostling Davy, who had now fallen asleep, his head back against her shoulder, Martha reached out her hand and said softly, "I think we ought to pray right now."

The others knelt before her, making a small circle.

"Lord, you are a strong fortress, and in you we put our trust," she said. "We pray for safety and courage for David and his family. Give them your protection, and give David wisdom about what he should do. You alone have the answers, Lord, and in times of crisis we depend on you. You have promised to make the crooked ways straight before us, and the darkness light. We ask you to do so now. Amen."

Rather than feeling calmed and reassured by the prayer, David felt a sense of delay, as if someone were holding onto him, pulling him back, when what he needed to do was act. Time was short—whatever he was going to do, he needed to do it now. "Amen," he said, and stood abruptly. He took Martha's hand—she gripped him powerfully and clung to his hand for a moment—and then embraced Cecil. The thought came to him: Would this be the last time he ever saw them? "Cecil, I feel so stupid. I just wanted to do more for these kids, and now…"

"I know, David. You have a compassionate heart." Cecil put his hands on David's shoulders and held him at arm's length. "There's much you're not telling me, I know," he said quietly, "but that's all right—it's between you and God. And God will help you in this crisis. Just trust Him."

As he and Christie made their way back toward their house, Christie silently wiped tears from her cheeks. How David wished he could take back his decision to help Carlos! He had only wanted to help. Now Davy might grow up without a father. David had been called to mission work—but things had gotten so confused. Had he done the wrong thing? Or just the right thing in the wrong way?

And the most painful question of all: How would he tell Christie the real and awful truth?

God, forgive me for making this mess.

David hugged Davy's limp body against his chest as if he thought he might drop his son. In a way, he thought bitterly, he already had.

A vehicle, headlights shining, pulled into the clinic's parking lot before David, Christie, and Davy reached their house. David felt a surge of panic—was this the police coming for him? But that wasn't likely—they'd have sent a whole fleet of vehicles that looked and sounded more menacing than this one. The vehicle turned—it was Felix's old Ford van. He handed Davy off to Christie and sent her up to the house to pack.

David put his arm around Felix's shoulder as they walked, drawing him close to speak softly. "Thanks for the warning about the airport, amigo. You were right. I have get my family out of here. If the airport is closed, what are my options? I can't trust the embassy." They entered the house, and Isabel scurried off to help Christie.

"I can get you to Grenada on my boat. From there, you can get safe passage back to the U.S."

"Is it safe? I mean—on the open sea?"

"The *Bahia Bonita* is seventy feet long. It is designed to easily handle such a voyage. In fact, I have fished those waters many times. I have already filled the boat with diesel for a trip I was planning to make after tuna early next week. It holds plenty of fuel for the trip. The weather forecast is good—I can get you there within three days at most."

"Aren't the police checking the docks?"

Felix nodded. "But I can find a way to get you and your family on my boat without being seen."

David turned to Christie, who had begun wrestling Davy into his jammies. "What do you think, hon?"

Christie seemed to have regained control over her emotions, but she still seemed distant. She looked up at him only briefly, but David had learned to read her eloquent looks, and this one clearly told him that she had figured out at least some of what he was not telling her. "If it means you'll be able to come with us," she said in a flat tone, "I think we should give it a try."

Eighteen hours after the failed assassination, Hawkeye was seated along with Zach in the Mourne Rouge Beach Bar in Grenada, across the table from Hawkeye's mission contact and old friend, Carlos Edwards.

"Okay, give me the abbreviated version, Hawk. What happened?" Carlos said, speaking English, the birth language of neither of them, but the only language mutually comfortable for both.

"A tiny piece of information missing," Hawk said, swirling the drink in his mug. "One thing not rehearsed."

"Specifically."

Hawkeye sighed. So soon after a mission, he preferred to replay it in his own mind several times first, to make sure he understood what had happened. He didn't have that confidence yet. "First, the guard woke. He knocked over a lamp when Zach shot him. Second, we weren't smart enough to guess Guzman's granddaughter would ask to sleep with her grandma. I blame myself. I should have had Zach cover the other bedrooms."

"There were seven bedrooms besides the guest suite where Guzman was supposed to be sleeping," Carlos said. "How could Zach have covered them all? And if Zach was down the hall with you, who would have taken care of the waking guards?"

"I should have slit the guards' throats while they slept. Then Zach and I could have surveyed all the bedrooms to verify the target before anyone was awake." He shifted in his chair. "Guzman would have been removed and Danny and Aaron would still be alive."

"Someone failed us," Carlos said. "Who could have told us that the granddaughter and grandmother would be the only ones in the master suite that night?

"Perhaps we failed ourselves. Perhaps our plan was faulty. Even if one of our JAM informants found out about the change in sleeping arrangements, how would they have gotten word to us?"

Carlos stared across the room for a few moments, saying nothing. "No word about David Eller?" he asked at last.

"Who?"

"The pigeon."

Hawk shook his head. He'd never seen his friend looking so old, so tired. Carlos stood. "I have to call Leprechaun," he said. "Have another drink."

Carlos waited until he was on the beach near the water, his deck shoes sinking only slightly in the damp sand, before he punched in the number. He gave Leprechaun Hawkeye's account of the botched assassination, and Leprechaun responded, "We're worried about your missionary spilling his guts if he's caught by Guzman."

"Anyone caught by Guzman will spill his guts eventually," Carlos replied.

"Given what you've told us about Eller, he's a liability."

"Two days ago he was an asset."

"Two days ago we needed him. Now we don't."

"He knows nothing. And how do we know he's not in Guzman's hands already?"

"If he was, knowing Guzman, he couldn't resist telling the world. Eller's an American citizen. That in itself would have major international implications. We can't let that happen."

"What are you saying?" Carlos asked.

"We've decided your missionary needs to be removed. One way or another. I want you and your operatives to figure out a way. Come up with a plan. By yesterday."

"We just escaped from there and you want us to go back? We don't even know where Eller is."

Carlos heard the tension in Leprechaun's voice. "Then find him. If our intel people hear anything, I'll let you know. If you need more resources, we'll provide them. Just get it done."

Hawkeye fiddled with a matchbook as he waited for Carlos to come back. He'd been gone for nearly a half-hour. It didn't take this long to tell Leprechaun Hawkeye had blown it.

He'd ordered another Corona by the time Carlos returned. Hawkeye, trained to notice things, noticed immediately that Carlos seemed less old, less tired. There was a light of determination in his eyes. So Hawkeye waited for him to say something after he'd come back to the table. But Carlos said nothing—just looked at Hawkeye quietly, not smiling, but with a strength of life in his face that hadn't been there before.

So Hawkeye spoke first. "I lost half my team. Aaron had a wife and a kid. And Danny…" Hawkeye paused. "He's only twenty-four, Carlos. They'll eventually break him. I can only imagine what he's going through—if he's still alive."

Carlos leaned closer to the table. "Maybe we can find some redemption in this yet."

CHAPTER NINETEEN

For almost an hour, David, Christie, and Davy Jr., along with Felix, Isabel, and their daughter, Blanca, rode in Felix's rusty 1977 Ford Econoline van toward the docks near La Guaira where Felix kept his boat. Davy Jr. and Blanca were asleep. The only sounds were the laboring engine and multiple noises of the ancient van as it rattled along the highway leading to La Guaira.

David had seen Christie glance at him a few times during the drive. He couldn't tell if her expression was rage or fear. She'd said nothing to David since they'd hurriedly left Hope Village. They'd had little time to pack. The only luggage the Ellers carried were two medium-sized duffels stuffed with clothing and their U.S. passports, along with a couple of boxes of food Isabel and Christie had thrown together from the Hope Village kitchen.

David also carried the briefcase. Maybe he could at least use it as leverage with Carlos to get some help in getting out of the country, if Felix's plan didn't work out. At any rate, David hadn't wanted to leave it behind as evidence, in case the authorities decided to search the compound. He still didn't know what it contained, but whatever it was, he didn't want his mistakes creating any additional problem for the Duncans or for Hope Village.

Felix had suggested that, after boarding the *Bahia Bonita*, they travel only as far as Isla Margarita, twenty-five miles off the Venezuelan coast. It was a popular destination for American tourists. They would

166 The Missionary

spend the rest of the night there, monitoring the news on Felix's radio, then decide in the morning whether to continue on to Grenada.

As badly as David wanted to get out of Venezuela, the journey by boat across the open Caribbean sea loomed large and menacingly in his mind. It wasn't just the risk of storms or rough seas—a much greater risk was their vulnerability. If the Venezuelan Coast Guard was looking for them, a large boat on a open expanse of water seemed like such an obvious place to look. There was no place to hide. Felix felt confident that, if David and his family stayed out of sight, they would not be stopped. But if they were, and if the boat was searched...

David didn't think of himself as a control freak—he'd never have become a missionary if he did. Still, it angered and frightened him that, through his own foolish decisions, he'd been forced onto this journey he could no longer control.

Time to try to break the ice. David turned to Christie, speaking over the head of Davy Jr., who nestled in his arms. "We'll be safe on the boat." he said, trying to express a peace he did not feel. "When we get back to the States, we'll keep in touch with Martha and Cecil, and when things blow over, we'll come back and pick up where we left off."

This, he knew, was a lie. He'd been growing increasingly convinced in the past few hours that they would never set foot on Venezuelan soil again. But that sad truth would be too much for her to handle right now. He leaned closer. "I love you, Christie," he murmured. "I'll explain more of this later, when I know we're safe. I am so sorry. I never thought it would turn out this way."

She flashed her eyes toward him for one burning moment, all the anguish and confusion and anger she was feeling so evident in those eyes that never seemed able to hide—or interested in hiding—what went on behind them. Then her face crumpled, and she covered it with her hands. Her body began to shake, and the muffled sounds of her weeping filled the van. Davy Jr. awoke, raised his head sleepily and stared at his mother, and then shot a glance of concern toward his father.

"It'll be okay, son," David said. "Remember, we'll soon be at Nana and Papa's house in Seattle. Just try to go back to sleep."

As Davy settled against his shoulder again, David desperately hoped his words were true.

After a few moments, when all was quiet again, David tapped Felix on the shoulder. "I need to find an Internet café or someplace to email my family and let them know we're safe. I don't want them to worry. Can you stop somewhere that has Internet access?"

"I know a good place not far from the boat," Felix said. "Silvia's Cocina de Sopa."

David glanced at his watch. "Almost eleven," he said. "Would it still be open?"

"I have known Silvia for many years," Felix said, smiling. "She lives above her restaurant. She will not mind too much being bothered after closing hours." He looked at David in the rearview mirror. "I also know that she hates Guzman."

Felix lightly knocked on a door at the rear of the restaurant, which was dark except for the neon sign in the window: "Silvia's Cocina de Sopa." After a minute, he knocked again, harder.

"¡Es paciente, vengo!" a gruff voice yelled from inside, and a moment later the door swung open. "Felix! What are you doing out in the middle of the night? Isabel kick you out?" exclaimed the woman David assumed was Silvia. She was indeed a large woman by Venezuelan standards. Overweight, but more thick than fat, she looked about 5'9" with a physique that would enable her to hold her own with any man who gave her trouble. "Come in, and bring your friend," she said.

Carrying the briefcase, David followed Felix up a narrow, enclosed stairway and into the tiny apartment. A small kitchen sat to the left of the living room; on the opposite side, an open door led to what David assumed was her bedroom.

168   The Missionary

When Felix introduced David, Silvia smiled and stuck out her thick-fingered hand. "Is this the man who arranged for Blanca's surgeries?"

"Yes. He is also a champion for the poor here in Venezuela." Felix leaned toward Silvia conspiratorially. "And no friend of Guzman."

Silvia gripped David's hand tighter and lowered her voice to a raspy stage whisper: "I wish whoever tried to kill the son of a goat last night had been successful! You are welcome here, Señor Eller. Let me know how I can help you. I have heard many times of your effort on behalf of the oppressed."

"It is best if he and his family leave Venezuela until the current unrest blows over," Felix said. "We left the orphanage in a hurry, and now Señor Eller needs to use the Internet to make contact with his family in the U.S. May we use your computer for this purpose?"

"Of course," Silvia said, gesturing expansively. "I am happy to help." She grabbed a ring of keys from a bowl on the table and handed them to Felix. "Felix, you know where the computer is." She turned to David and smiled. "Like the other fishermen, Felix uses my computer to get weather reports. Just lock the door and drop the keys through the mail slot when you are done." She reached out again and took David's hand in both of her own. "If I can be of any further assistance, I am happy to help."

A few moments later, they were seated in a small, cluttered office in the back of the restaurant, next to the kitchen. "First I will get the latest weather report for our trip, and then you can email," Felix said.

David nodded, then stood and nervously wandered out into the dining area, where there was room for perhaps fifty people at old, mismatched tables. The air smelled like fish and cooking oil. At several places in the restaurant, there were corkboards on the wall with photos pinned to them—mostly, photos of fishermen standing in front of their simple wooden fishing boats. Others, coffee mug in hand, sat in Silvia's restaurant. Clearly, she had built a clientele among the close-knit community of small-time local commercial fishermen. In several of the photos was another woman who looked like Silvia but shorter and broader, wearing an apron—probably a sister who worked with her in the restaurant.

David glanced out the front window. The van still sat in the dark, quiet and apparently undisturbed. They had left the two women there to watch over the sleeping children. His mind supplied an unwanted image: government military trucks swarming into the tiny unpaved parking lot, soldiers jumping out with automatic weapons all around the van…

He jumped when Felix touched his arm, holding up the printout of the weather report in his other hand. He gave the keys to David. "I will wait in the van. Do not be long."

When the barmaid had brought each of the three men in the Mourne Rouge Beach Bar another drink, Carlos left his untouched in front of him. Unblinking, he locked eyes with Hawkeye. After a pause, Hawk said, "You'll have to give us more than that, Carlos. I don't see any way to redeem a mission that failed in its purpose and cost me two men."

Carlos looked off toward the ocean. He would have to play this exactly right—strike exactly the right tone. He said, "Look—Danny wasn't the only one we left behind. There's also David Eller, the guy who gave Danny your briefcase full of money. That's two million dollars you wouldn't have except for the risks he ran. He's probably on the run by now, if he hasn't been captured. I've had no contact with him since before the attempt. If he's still alive, he has the other briefcase with your two million."

Hawkeye shook his head. "It's not mine. I didn't finish the job."

Carlos smiled without humor. "I know. I'm sure Tecero agrees with you. But if we're going back into harm's way in Venezuela, I see two reasons. One is a briefcase with two million dollars in it. The other is to extract David Eller. Along with his wife and child."

Hawkeye and Zach looked at each other for a long moment, then Hawkeye shook his head. "We left Danny there, Carlos. Now you're asking us to go back in for a guy we've never met, who wasn't part of the team, who never put his life on the line—"

"Wait—he *did* put his life on the line. He just didn't know it. Danny came here knowing he might die. So did Aaron. They signed on for the mission, and they knew what their job was: take out one very bad guy, and earn a bundle of cash for it. Eller only knew he was helping a group of people who wanted to bring about regime change. I told him it would be a peaceful coup. I told him he and his family would be in no danger."

"Then you lied to him," Hawkeye said. "But that's your problem."

Carlos snorted. "If that was the only lie I told on this mission… But the point is, I left an innocent man behind. Someone who's not equipped to deal with Guzman's military, someone who'll be captured and tortured until he tells them all he knows, and then killed." Carlos leaned closer to the table. "I've been given orders to remove him. One way or another. The risk of what he might reveal under torture is too great."

Hawkeye shrugged and shook his head. "They give orders to you, Carlos. Nobody gives orders to me. I take the risks I choose to take, when I choose to take them."

Carlos felt a surge of anger, but he stifled it quickly. "I know you didn't want to leave Danny behind. But Danny had been captured. There wasn't anything you could do about that. David may well still be free. We can find him, extract him—and you earn back the two million. You'd have even more money to share with Aaron's wife and kid."

"Minus your cut."

Carlos shook his head. "I don't claim any of it. You and Zach split it."

A pause. Then: "You want me and Zach to return to Caracas," Hawkeye said, "in the middle of what will undoubtedly be a massive manhunt. Drive up to this guy's orphanage, load up him and his lovely little family and their luggage and deliver them to the airport? You want us to wave as their plane takes off? Buy them some snacks for the flight?"

Zach had been quiet but growing increasingly agitated. Now, his knee bouncing, he said, "Ten to one the guy is already captured or dead."

"And if he's on the run, not a snowball's chance we could find him," Hawk said. "Even if we did, what if he already chucked the briefcase? Why should I risk this not knowing if he still has the cash?"

"If Eller doesn't have the briefcase, you can have the one million you paid me from Tecero's money," Carlos said. "Look, I can see you hate the idea of going back in for Eller after leaving Danny behind. But I haven't given up on Danny. I still have contacts in Venezuela. I will do what I can. I can't tell you more than that."

Next to the computer in the little one-room office of Silvia's Cocina de Sopa was a television. David turned it on, flipping channels until he found CNN Spanish. He listened for thirty seconds—some story on the Middle East. He channel-surfed: a story about gourmet Italian food. He flipped the channel to the government-run station. It was on a commercial break.

Then he logged onto Yahoo and checked the mailbox of his new email account: vonniecox1971@yahoo.com. David grinned as he thought about the time, in the basement of the church, his brother had caught him and Vonnie Cox in a vacant Sunday school room, kissing.

But his smile faded. No email yet. He realized that it had been only a couple of hours since he'd set the account up, but he'd been so hoping that Stephen would have found something helpful by now.

He checked his regular email address, deller@juno.com. He knew that this address might be monitored, since it was on his business card and his letterhead. There were four messages—two from his parents and two from Stephen, both of them from before their telephone conversation.

The government TV station launched into the local weather report.

He hit "reply" to his parents' first message and wrote, "*We are all okay. Hope to be home soon.*"

How much to say, he wondered. If this account *was* being monitored, which seemed likely, then the less he said, the better. Unless, of course, he said something that would lead them in the wrong direction. For instance...

"*Flying from Caracas via Miami,*" he wrote. "*More later when we get to the States.*"

172 The Missionary

He nodded, pleased with himself. Guzman's people were undoubt-edly going to discover that he'd booked plane tickets for that night. By confirming that here, he might throw them off his trail—even though it would rattle his mother when they didn't show up. He would explain from Grenada later.

He hit "send," then noticed that the news had resumed on TV. The announcer was talking about the coup attempt.

And then there it was. He felt as if his body and mind were slipping into an alternative reality. In his world, this kind of thing couldn't happen.

David's picture was being shown on TV.

"The Venezuelan government is looking for this man for question-ing," the announcer said. "He is an American missionary named David Eller. If you have any information about his whereabouts, please con-tact your local police headquarters."

At first David couldn't imagine where the photograph had been taken—and then he recognized the background: the Banco Provincial.

So they must know he had the briefcase.

Did they know what was in it?

If so, they knew more than he did. He was only guessing that it contained money; it could just as easily be explosives or weapons or anti-Guzman leaflets.

The reporter added, "It is believed that David Eller may have infor-mation that could be of help tracking down the perpetrators of the attempted coup."

David was halfway to the door before he realized that he hadn't yet shut down the computer, still open to his personal mailbox. Foolish. He rushed back to the computer and logged off, then powered down. He jogged back across the restaurant, toward the door. Halfway there, he tripped over a chair in the murky light. There was a sharp pain in his shin, and he sprawled onto the floor.

Pulling himself up onto a nearby chair, he took a few deep breaths while checking his bleeding shin.

He had to get his family out of Venezuela. Right now. But he wasn't going to manage it this way. His emotions were out of control.

He stood and peered out the window. Felix was quiet and still in the front seat of the van, his head back—probably too keyed up to sleep, but resting.

Think, David!

He sat back down at Silvia's desk. So they knew he'd been to the bank. They knew he had the briefcase, and the mercenary he'd handed the first one off to had probably given them his description and reported that the handoff had been at Los Tiburones. The restaurant manager and Rita the waitress knew his name and knew he was from Hope Village. It was all so obvious.

If these briefcases were working against him, it was time he tried to make them work for him. What was in this one?

He opened the top drawer of Silvia's old desk. Rummaging, he found a pair of scissors, but when he tried slipping the end under the briefcase latch, it was too fat. He rummaged further: an ancient screwdriver. He slipped the screwdriver under the latch, carefully prying upward, digging the end into the leather—one instant praying fervently that this was no bomb, the next thinking if it was a bomb, it may be his easiest way out.

With increasing pressure, the latch bent a little, bent further—David pressed as hard as he could, and it popped open. Breaking the other latch took only seconds. He opened the lid and stared inside: stacks of one-hundred dollar bills, neatly wrapped in small bundles. He lifted out several and laid them on Silvia's desk. Then he dug toward the bottom of the case, searching for notes, letters, or other clues. Nothing but more money.

David picked up one of the wrapped stacks and counted. Fifty one-hundred-dollar bills...that was five thousand dollars in each stack. And there were dozens—no, hundreds!—of stacks. There had to be over a million dollars here!

But there was nothing else. No notes, no names, nothing but U.S. one-hundred-dollar bills. David took two stacks out and put them in his pocket. In case he lost the briefcase, he would have enough cash to negotiate passage home.

He found some duct tape in Silvia's desk and taped the briefcase shut. He reached to turn off the television, hesitated, then flipped to the local Venevisión affiliate. Another late-breaking report about the coup.

"Sources tell us that the Venezuelan government has arrested Cecil and Martha Duncan, the founders of Hope Village, an evangelical ministry to the poor in suburban Caracas, and taken them to police headquarters for questioning. These same sources tell us that the Duncans may have been part of the coup conspiracy, and almost certainly have information regarding David Eller's whereabouts."

David sat stunned. The Duncans arrested. All because of what he, David, had done. He felt as if something were crushing him. It was hard to breathe.

Two of the gentlest and most loving people David had ever known, subjected to who-knew-what indignities and insults. He was ashamed. He was outraged by his own stupidity.

The thought came to him suddenly, unwelcome and frightening: He could not run. He could not leave Venezuela. He had to help Cecil and Martha. They were like parents to him. He wouldn't be able to live with himself if anything happened to them. Would Christie agree? Maybe not. Probably not. But then, when in this entire ugly chain of events had he stopped to think what Christie would agree to?

A new and brave resolve gripped David. *Better to die than to live with the knowledge that Cecil and Martha were tortured or even killed because of me!*

He heard a light tap on the door. His heart stopped. But then the familiar voice on the other side of the door said, "It's me, Felix, amigo. We must go."

"I'll be out soon. A couple more minutes."

He booted the computer again and logged back into the new email account he'd opened to communicate with his brother. Typing in the address, *blackbeard@yahoo.com* and leaving the message line blank, he wrote, "*Cannot leave Venezuela. Hope Village founders Cecil and Martha Duncan arrested. My fault. Sending family out, but I have to stay behind. There are people here who might help me. Will hide until I figure out what to do next. Will try to email again tomorrow. Pray for me. P.S.—Briefcase I was given to deliver is full of money—probably over a million U.S. dollars.*"

After shutting down the computer and locking the door, David marched toward the van, jaw clenched, to tell the whole truth and nothing but the truth.

CHAPTER TWENTY

Christie had a favorite photo of her parents—one of the very few photos of them she possessed. Even though it had been taken in the 1970s, it had the feel of a much earlier era, partly because of their out-of-date, almost stereotypically hick clothes—neither of her parents had had much interest in or time for fashion—and partly because the blue grain truck on whose fender the two-year-old Christie sat had been an antique. Her father wore coveralls, her mother a straw hat. Christie sucked her thumb in the photo and looked with serious intent into the camera; over her head, her parents looked at each other, mouths open in laughter.

A year later, they were dead, killed in the fiery auto crash that left Christie with the burn scars on her cheek and neck, her torso, her leg and hip. Her father had died, in fact, in saving her. There was a reminder of that on her right thigh—the unburned shape of a hand in the midst of the scar tissue. Her father's hand, gripping her, shielding her skin, in that one place, from the inferno the burned the rest of her. The other hand, she'd been told, had been across her face, protecting her lungs from the superheated air that had entered his own lungs and killed him. She had been only three years old, of course, and remembered little of the incident itself, other than a sense of terror. But she remembered the nearly unbearable physical pain of the years of convalescence and recovery.

And she remembered the vast aching void left in her life when the two people on whom she had most depended, and had most trusted, had suddenly and without warning departed, without a second chance, without a further word.

It was something of the same thing she felt now, in Felix's van, Davy still sleeping on the seat next to her, as she dug her hands into her scalp on each side of her head and looked at David through her tears, trying to make sense of what he had just told her.

"David—I don't understand—why did you—"

"Christie, I don't know. It was crazy. I wish I could go back and undo it all, but I can't. And right now we just need to focus on what needs to be done."

David stood beside the van's open sliding door. Christie felt a surge of panic. She reached over Davy and grabbed his shirt and pulled. "David, get in the van! Now! We have to get to the boat! We have to leave Venezuela now!"

He grabbed her hands, gently but firmly, and resisted. "No, hon—I can't. There's more I have to tell you."

More? How could there be more? How could there be anything worse than what he'd already said?

"I can't leave with you. The news also said that Cecil and Martha have been arrested. If anything happened to them—I could never forgive myself. I'm not sure what to do, hon. But I want you to go with Felix and Isabel to Grenada."

"David, they will *kill* you if you go back!" she screamed. "Think of everything you've always told me about Guzman!"

"If I don't go back they might kill Cecil and Martha!"

"Oh, God, this can't be happening!" she wailed. Davy had awakened; he began to cry, and Christie, still weeping, gathered him up.

David slid into the van, pulled the door shut, and said, "I'll go with you to the dock, but after you leave, I have to go back and make all of this right."

"Oh, David—*David!* You can't make it right! Listen to yourself!"

Felix started the van.

"Felix, I'm really sorry to get you into this mess," David said. "If you want to back out now, I understand."

Felix shook his head. "I know your heart, mi amigo. No matter what you have done, I will get your family safely to Grenada. But rather than wait until morning, I think it is best to leave tonight and go straight there."

As they drove, Christie's mind swirled. Did she even know this man sitting beside her? For years she had loved and touched and smelled and kissed and held a man she had adored and trusted. Was he still inside this body, or was he lost to her now? In a flash of rage and fear, she leaned into him and pounded his chest and shoulders with her fists, screaming, "Why, David? How could you do this to us?"

David grabbed her wrists to stop the blows, tightly enough that it hurt. "Christie! Get a grip! I already know it was stupid, but we have to figure out what to do now." He wrapped his arms around her. She buried her head in his chest and wept, hurt by the smell of his skin, that very personal and individualistic smell that was like no one else, and that now she was afraid she'd lost forever. Pressed between them, Davy's cries rose.

"If you're staying, we'll all stay," she said quietly.

"What? No!"

"Yes. We have to stay together, David. I'm just afraid that if we split up now, we'll never be together again."

"Christie, do you think they'll give us a special family cell? If we stay, and if we're captured, we won't be together. Our best bet is for you to get yourself and our son to safety. I'll try to make sure Cecil and Martha are safe. After that—after that, I don't know."

The van sped toward the docks.

David drew his crying son onto his lap; Christie's arms entwined with David's around him. They rocked him together, and he quieted. With one hand, David lifted her face so that she was looking at him. "Christie, listen carefully. I'll open a new email account called *sweetgrass hills girl at yahoo dot com*. Can you remember that?"

She nodded. The Sweetgrass Hills had been a favorite spot of hers growing up in Montana; she had once taken David there on a pilgrimage to her home state.

"I'll use your birth date as the password. When you're safe, check for email. If I can, I'll email you to establish communication."

"How will you email me if you're in jail?" she cried.

"I don't know. Maybe I'll turn myself in to the U.S. Embassy and try to negotiate Cecil and Martha's release from there. But somehow, I'll try to let you know what's happening. I'll leave messages at the new email address as often as I can to let you know I'm still alive. When you get home, open a separate new email account for yourself. We'll use *sweetgrasshillsgirl@yahoo.com* as the receiving box for both of us. When you email me back at that account, don't refer to anything I've told you tonight. And don't use my name."

Christie nodded, her breath still coming in heaves.

As they approached the docks, David glanced out the window. "If you don't hear from me, keep checking the international news sources," he whispered in Christie's ear. "And when you get home, contact the U.S. Embassy. Make sure they know Cecil and Martha had nothing to do with this."

She stared up at him in disbelief. "David, I am so scared," she whispered.

How would she cope as a widow?

By a quarter till midnight, Hawkeye, Zach, and Carlos had taken a break from their argument long enough to order some steaks. Zach had wandered outside for a while, then come back in, and now the three sat again over fresh beers.

"So, how do you plan to rescue this pigeon?" Hawkeye asked.

"By now, he's probably discovered what's in the briefcase, and he sleeps with it under his pillow," said Carlos.

"I'm betting he's either dead or on the run with no pillow in sight," Zach said.

"If Zach and I agree to help you," Hawkeye said, "how do you plan to locate him? How do we know he's even still in the country? Maybe he's already rescued himself."

"Or maybe we go in and find a corpse," said Zach. "And no briefcase."

"I know his cell phone number," Carlos said. "If he's alive and on the run, we could plan to rendezvous with him at some remote beach in the middle of the night."

"And if he doesn't answer?" asked Hawkeye.

"If he's still on the loose, then he's panicked and desperate. He'll answer. If he doesn't return my call in twenty-four hours, or if somebody else answers his phone, then we can assume he's already lost."

Felix parked behind a warehouse three blocks from the dock where his boat was moored. David waited with the others in the van while Felix went to check out the docks. He returned in a few minutes, climbed back into the van, and drove it to his usual parking spot just a couple hundred feet from his boat.

David carried Davy, sleeping again, down the wharf to the *Bahia Bonita*, Felix's seventy-foot trawler that would take David's wife and son out of the harbor, east across a stretch of the Caribbean, and into Grenada. He looked down at Davy, filled with regrets—regrets for not taking more time for Davy, for not putting Davy's welfare, and Christie's, above all else. He remembered how impatient he'd been with his little "hummingbird on steroids" when he couldn't sit still, when he seemed to talk incessantly. How would Christie cope, raising Davy without him?

Felix carried a sleeping Blanca down into the cabin, then turned to take Davy from David. David put his arms around Christie, who was weeping again.

182   The Missionary

Isabel, her arms full of bags, hurried back and forth from the van to the dock, and Felix stowed the bags on the boat.

David took Christie's face between his hands. Her cheeks were wet under his palms, and he felt the cool night air against his own wet cheeks. "I love you so much, Christie. Will you forgive me?" He thought his words sounded hollow, weak, completely unsuitable for what could be the final words of a husband to his wife. But he could think of nothing better to say.

And Christie seemed to have no words left at all, just the tears in her reddened eyes. She looked at him as if she didn't know him. Finally, she reached one tentative arm out and clutched at his waist—and still said nothing.

He tried again. "My love for you is what will keep me going, Christie. You'll always be the joy of my life. If anything happens, please tell Davy his daddy loves him," he whispered. He kissed her forehead and cheek.

Her hand stroked his head. "David, please come with us," she choked out. "I don't think they'll do anything to Cecil and Martha."

"I can't take that chance, Christie."

Her body stiffened. She said nothing else, just turned and stepped across the gunwale and into the small cabin of Felix's boat.

Felix started the engine to warm it up, then came toward David on the dock. "Guillermo, a friend of mine, is ill and will not be fishing this season," Felix said. He pointed down the row of moored boats. "He owns a boat moored there. I know him well. He will not mind if you sleep in the cabin of his boat tonight. No one will bother you. He keeps a cabin key taped to the bottom of a bucket under one of the aft cockpit doors."

David nodded, still in a daze.

"I do not know the boat number, but the name of his boat is *El Delfín azul*. I can take you there before we leave."

"No, Felix, please—just get on your way. I'll find his boat." David reached into his pocket and handed Felix a wrapped stack of fifty one-hundred-dollar bills. "Here's some U.S. currency. After you refuel in Grenada, please give the balance to Christie for her airline tickets."

Without looking at it, Felix dropped the bundle into a tackle box nearby.

"I will not be back for several days," Felix said, coiling the mooring ropes and tossing them onto the bow of his boat. "After I deliver your family to Grenada, I will fish on the way back so I have a full boat and there will be no suspicions."

"I'll probably take a taxi to the U.S. Embassy tomorrow and turn myself in," David said.

"You can use the van," Felix said, holding up the keys.

"No, that would implicate you. I'll get my things from your van and wipe it down for any fingerprints. It will stay where it is until you return."

David stepped over the gunwale and poked his head into the cabin where Christie sat with little Davy asleep on her lap. With a blank look of anguish and despair, she clutched their four-year-old and turned her gaze away.

Hesitating, he turned, climbed back onto the dock and embraced Felix. Felix gripped him hard. "You are a good friend and a great man, Senor David. I will see your family to safety, and I will never forget all you have done."

David watched the *Bahia Bonita* move away, a shadow knifing through the moonlight's reflection on the water. The boat slipped quietly past a giant cargo ship at anchor in the harbor.

He sat in darkness on the dock for several more minutes, gripped by loneliness, even after the tiny glimmer of cabin light from the *Bahia Bonita* had disappeared. He wanted to pray, but he doubted that God wanted to listen.

At Felix's van, he retrieved the briefcase and the duffel with his clothes. He found a rag and tried to wipe down the entire van, inside and out. He locked it, then walked back to the dock and found Felix's friend's boat, *El Delfin azul*.

He found the key, unlocked the door, and climbed down into the dark cabin. It smelled of rotten fish. He felt around the room, finally locating a thin mattress atop a wooden bench. He put his duffel at one end for a pillow and lay down. He stared into pitch darkness—a perfect match for the darkness in his soul.

CHAPTER TWENTY-ONE

Emilio Tecero sat watching the nightly news. At the moment, the photo of David Eller in the Banco Provencial was being shown for the hundredth time, while the anchorman's voice intoned that the Duncans, with whom Eller had worked at *Espere la Aldea*, had been taken into custody. Clearly, this Eller, this missionary, was the pigeon Durango had hired. A *missionary?* What had Durango been thinking, hiring an amateur like this? This may have been the very reason the assassination attempt had failed!

Even so, this amateur had somehow managed, at least so far, to evade Guzman's forces, or else they would not be asking for information about him on TV. And that gave Tecero hope that he might find Eller first—thereby recovering not just some of his money, but also helping him find Durango, whom he still intended to provide with some exquisite agony before his well-deserved death.

He called in one of his lieutenants. "Tape this broadcast and print out copies of this photo they keep showing. Many copies. Get them to all of our people and put out the word. Find this missionary. Keep him alive until he surrenders my money and we have found out all he knows. Find him before Guzman's goons find him. Whatever it takes.

"And start at *Espere la Aldea*. Guzman's people have already been there, but perhaps they missed something. Make sure our people are persuasive."

186   The Missionary

General Dukai watched the couple through the two-way mirror. Cecil and Martha Duncan were seated in a small room—one bare light bulb dangling from a cord above, one small table. They had, he knew, had a rough night for an elderly couple—roused from their beds, ushered to a waiting police car, forced to sit there for over an hour while Dukai's team had combed Hope Village in search of David Eller, then taken downtown to the Federal District police station.

Now that Dukai's people had identified David Eller as a likely contact of the commandos, Dukai's number-one priority was to be the first to find him.

He entered the room and seated himself across the table.

"Señor Duncan, Señora Duncan—my name is General Raldo Dukai. I am in charge of the investigation into the attempted assassination of President Armando Guzman. The Venezuelan government highly respects the work you have been doing at Hope Village. But this man, David Eller, who is your associate—we are quite certain he was an accomplice in the coup, and we need to find him for questioning. Please tell me where he has gone."

Cecil Duncan seemed exhausted but did not show any of the telltale signs of lying or withholding information as he answered in a weak voice. "General Dukai, as I already told your officers, David told us only that he was taking his family back to the United States to visit his parents in Seattle for a couple weeks. We assumed they flew."

"Did you see them leave Hope Village?"

"No. After we prayed with 'em and said goodbye, we went on to bed."

"There are no vehicles missing from your mission. How would they have gone to the airport?"

"I don't know. Maybe they took a taxi. General—I think you're wrong about David. I know he flaps his jaws a little too much, but an assassination attempt? No. That would violate his deeply held moral convictions."

Dukai smiled. "I too was surprised he was involved. But my team of investigators has come up with convincing evidence. We have positive identification from one of the men who tried to murder President Guzman. This man confessed that he took money from

David Eller. We have a waitress from Los Tiburones restaurant where the money exchange took place who identified both the commando and David Eller." Dukai held up the bank photo of David. "Is this David Eller?"

Both Senor and Senora Duncan leaned closer and peered at the photo, and then both seemed to wilt. "Yes," Senor Duncan said weakly. "That's David."

Dukai placed the photo on the table in front of them, where they couldn't help but see it. "This photograph was taken at the Banco Provincial the day after David Eller met the commando at Los Tiburones restaurant. Two witnesses there, workers at the bank, have testified that on the day this photo was taken he visited the bank and took a large briefcase from a lockbox. We believe this was a briefcase full of money to pay off the assassins."

Martha bowed her head. She seemed to be praying.

Dukai watched them both and waited.

After a moment Cecil spoke. "General Dukai, if he was part of this, then I agree he should be brought to justice. But I honestly don't know where he is. Or how he left Hope Village. He told us he was worried that he and his family might be in danger because of what he said on Venevision some weeks ago, but we had no idea he was in any way connected to this coup attempt. For my part, I had encouraged him to be about God's work and to leave politics to the politicians."

"I'm certain that his wife, Christie, knew nothing about any of this," Martha said.

Dukai sat in silence, watching the old couple. Could it be that they were more complex, more devious, than they appeared? Was this a clever lie to cover David's tracks? If so, it was very convincing.

No. This was simply an elderly couple who had been too trusting, assuming everyone was as guileless as them.

He was glad this couple was not being interrogated by Torres. The Commander would not have given up until he had broken them through torture.

"Señor and Señora Duncan, you can go. One of my officers will drive you back to Hope Village, If we need you for anything else, I will telephone you. And if you should happen to hear from David Eller, I expect you to promptly contact me. Remember—a serious crime has been committed. If you hear information about this crime and do not report it, you too will be guilty under the laws of Venezuela. And make no mistake—you *will* be prosecuted. You might ask yourself what would happen to *Espere la Aldea* then. Venezuela does not take lightly crimes against our government."

He paused, establishing eye contact with each of them in turn, then slid his business card across the table, stood, and left the room.

When the Duncans returned to Hope Village, they found the staff in hysterics. Men had invaded the compound and ransacked every building. Mia, the nighttime orphanage supervisor, wept as she explained, "They said they were looking for Senor Eller and threatened to kill some of the children if we did not tell them where he'd gone! I told them *no sabe*, that we did not even know he was gone. I begged them not to shoot. The children were all awake—the poor things were terrified, screaming and crying. It was *muy horrifico*."

Cecil and Martha knelt to hug several of the children still awake, too frightened to return to their beds, faces streaked with tears.

Mia continued. "They made me tell them where David's house and office were. They tore everything apart, but they did not tell me what they were looking for."

"Did these men say who they were?" Cecil asked.

"No."

"Were they in uniform?"

"No, no uniforms."

"Well, thank God they didn't follow through with their threat," Martha said. "All of the children are safe, and we have our Lord to thank for protecting them. Now let's all pray that God will calm our hearts and let us sleep well. We can clean up the mess in the morning."

But before Cecil climbed into bed, he called General Dukai.

"I assure you that these were not my men, Señor Duncan. I will send guards to patrol your compound during the night. In the morning, someone will come to investigate. I think I may know who these people work for. I do not think they will come back tonight. Try to get some sleep."

The weather report said it would be another crisp, sunny day in D.C., with highs in the forties. Roger Garlock had been in his office since before 6 a.m.

He'd had trouble sleeping. His mind kept wandering back to his conversation with Stephen Eller the evening before, when he had insisted that the CIA couldn't have been involved in the attempt to assassinate Guzman. But the thought had nagged at him all evening, and at ten o'clock he'd called Skip Little, a friend with a high security clearance at CIA headquarters, who had promised to check and get back to him.

At 6:30 a.m., the call came. "Hey, Roger. Skip here. I checked up the line, passing the word that a supposed operative on the ground in Venezuela is claiming CIA involvement in this. Our Embassy in Venezuela called late last night and asked the same thing, so apparently the rumor is getting around. But I have it on top authority that there was absolutely no CIA involvement in the attempted coup in Venezuela. In fact, our sources think it was prompted by some of the drug lords who want to get rid of Guzman. There's no way this had any connection to us."

"Okay, sure," answered Garlock. "But we all know the U.S. has mixed feelings about Guzman. So—is this the official line, or is this the truth?"

"God's honest truth, Roger. I've been assured that we had no interest in taking Guzman out. It wasn't us."

190   The Missionary

Confused and alarmed, Stephen read again his brother's words:

Sending family out, but I have to stay behind. There are people here who might help me. Will hide until I figure out what to do next.

David was staying behind, in Venezuela, where his life wasn't worth a nickel? When he had a chance to make it out with his family? And all because some elderly couple had been picked up for questioning? David couldn't even be sure the Duncans were in danger!

The phone rang. Stephen picked up.

"Stephen," Roger said, "we think your brother was working for drug lords instead of the CIA. He may not realize that yet. Any way you can warn him? He probably has two teams after him—Guzman, and the drug kingpins."

In two minutes, Stephen was sending an email to vonniecox1971@yahoo.com:

You are in danger. My sources believe you were not working for the people you thought you were. Instead, very bad guys. Probably powerful drug lords. Which means two separate groups may be competing to see who can find you first, both with bad intentions. Do not communicate with Carlos. He is probably not who he said he was. If you haven't already, get out of Dodge FAST. The Duncans are in much less danger than you are.

He had just hit "send" when the phone rang again.

"Stephen! Oh, thank God!" his mother said. "Have you heard anything from David or Christie? We're worried *sick!* The Venezuelan government seems to think David had something to do with this coup attempt down there—it's all over the news, even with his *picture!* But that couldn't be. Could it? Stephen? Plus we got an email saying they were coming home, flying into Miami, but then nothing..."

Stephen didn't have to think hard about what to say; he didn't want to alarm his parents. "Mom, it's what—3:30 in the morning in Seattle? You need to get some sleep. I got the same message about them flying into Miami, and I'm sure they are trying to get home, but things are hectic and unsettled there. Flights may be backed up."

"Your mother's in a panic," Stephen's dad chimed in. "No point in trying to sleep. Son, tell us what you know. Is David mixed up in this thing somehow?"

"All I can say is I'm trying everything I can to find out the truth. If I hear from them, I'll let you know. In the meantime, just keep praying. We'll hear from them soon."

"Get them out of there, Stephen!" his mother said. "Just get them out! Send in some troops! You're with the U.S. government, for pete's sake."

When he hung up, it hit him: There was a strong chance that he would never see his brother alive again. And he would be the one to break the news to his parents.

CHAPTER TWENTY-TWO

David was awakened by the creaking sound of *El Delfín azul* rubbing against the old sun-hardened tires tied to the dock. Cracks of pale light seeped in around the cabin door, but it was too dark to see his watch, and he had no idea how long he'd slept. He opened the door a few inches; gray light crept into the tiny cramped quarters. Now he could see his watch: 6:35 a.m.

Clouds had rolled in during the night and a light rain was falling.

His first thought was of Christie and Davy. Still safe? He sent up the first quick prayer in a day he suspected would be filled with them.

A few isolated fishermen buzzed around the dock; many of the slips were empty, and David assumed those boats had already headed out for the day's fishing. He slowly and gently closed the door and sat back on the bunk.

He figured he'd been sleeping about four-and-a-half hours since finding his way to *El Delfín azul.* At ten knots, Felix should be about 60 miles out to sea. They would have nearly a full 24-hour day yet to travel, and probably a bit more. Much too long to be so vulnerable.

His next thought was to check his new email account to see if there was a message from his brother.

His stomach growled. He hadn't eaten in almost twenty-four hours. Silvia's restaurant was less than a quarter mile away. There was a route David knew behind several warehouses and fish processing buildings above the waterfront, where he would be unlikely to be seen except by those who worked there. He felt his chin; there was the beginning of a scruffy beard. Between that, his slept-in clothes, and his disheveled hair, he hoped that he did not look like the photo of himself shown on TV, taken in a suit and tie.

He might decide to turn himself in today. But he still wanted to determine for himself the time and place when it would be safest to do so.

He made sure the stack of money was still in his pocket, then left everything else on the boat. He locked the cabin door and set out toward Silvia's in the drizzle.

Art Snell stared bleary-eyed at his alarm clock, wondering who was making his phone ring at 6:47 in the morning. Reaching for the handset, he knocked his watch off the nightstand.

"This better be important," he growled into the receiver. He could still feel in his pounding temples the effects of the half-bottle of tequila he'd consumed the night before. Normally his alarm went off at seven a.m. anyway, but this was his day off, and he'd planned on sleeping off the hangover until at least ten o'clock.

"Art, this is Stephen Eller. Sorry to bother you, but I've got to talk to you right away. Can you meet with me?"

"Stephen! It's my day off!"

"My brother in Venezuela. I told you about him last week at lunch."

"Yeah, yeah, the missionary. But what—"

"He's in some trouble since the coup attempt."

"So tell him to go to the U.S. Embassy. What does this have to do with me or the bureau?"

"Let's do this face to face, Art. Seriously, he's in big trouble. I need your advice. I'll make it easy for you. I'll buy your breakfast at the Royal Cafe out there in Alexandria. Can you meet me in an hour?"

Art heard an edge of panic in Stephen's voice. "Yeah, okay," he groaned. "I'm coming. If my feet can find the floor."

Stephen chose a seat toward the back of the restaurant in one of the red upholstered booths with a black-and-white checkered tablecloth. Twice before, Stephen had met Art for breakfast at the Royal Café, Art's regular breakfast hangout. It was a quirky, eclectic place. Advertised as "the best breakfast in Alexandria," it had once been a fifties-theme restaurant and still displayed, at the front of the restaurant, a jukebox contained in the body of a '57 Chevy. For lunch and dinner it served Greek food.

Five minutes later, wearing navy-blue sweatpants and a yellow Harley Davidson T-shirt, Snell ambled through the front door and headed back toward Stephen's table. For twenty-four years, Snell had been an FBI agent. In the field, he'd been considered an iron horse, physically one of the toughest guys in the bureau. But he'd spent the past ten years behind a desk as a senior agent with the FBI's Intelligence Division. Now, his soft two hundred thirty-five pounds overwhelmed his 5'10" frame. And he looked even less impressive without the rumpled blue suit and un-cinched red tie he wore almost every day to the office.

The usual waitress—Sharon? Shirley? No, Sheila—saw Art come in and said, "Hey, you're early this mornin'." Art slumped into the booth without bothering to answer. He pointed his finger at the empty coffee cup in front of him. Sheila was right behind him, coffee pot in hand, and just laughed as she poured.

It was obvious to Stephen that she knew Art's routine—black coffee, and don't-bring-anything-else-until-at-least-two-cups-have-been-downed.

Stephen leaned forward, elbows on the table. "Thanks for meeting me, Art."

"No problem, I had to wake up to answer the phone anyway," Art grumbled.

Driven by anxiety, Stephen wanted to launch into his questions. But what he needed now was Art's interest and sympathy, and he wasn't going to get that by pushing him at this hour of the morning.

When he was halfway through his first cup, Art sighed and said, "So what's the deal with your brother?"

196 The Missionary

"Here's the story. Take it for what it's worth. He says he was recruited by the CIA to be a courier for whoever was hired to assassinate President Guzman of Venezuela."

A moment of silence. "You're kiddin'."

Stephen shook his head. "I asked Roger Garlock to check with his contacts at the CIA to see if it was true."

"What good'll that do? Those CIA loonies would deny being involved either way. They'd deny eatin' a donut even if they still had powdered sugar all over their face. Congress outlawed using missionaries and journalists as spies, but they do it anyway. No wonder they deny things, the stunts they pull." It was no secret in Washington that CIA and FBI people hated each other. For years, they'd been competing for resources and recognition.

Stephen started to relate what he'd heard from Roger Garlock, but Art snorted. "Yeah, I saw the report on the drug lord story. I think it's a CIA-floated rumor to cover its own behind. Look, the big-shot drug thug is a guy named Emilio Tecero from Colombia. He's been briefly sighted in Venezuela more than once. He's on the top of our most wanted list—been there a long time. A very elusive guy with a ton of resources. We know he's been responsible for killing some Colombian senators, mayors, other local government workers, but it's a stretch to think he would try to assassinate the reigning president of Venezuela. Besides, according to the briefing I got yesterday, some of Guzman's insiders have leaked that an underground group called JAM was somehow involved."

Sheila was back with more coffee. She looked at Stephen. "Know what you want, hon?"

"A poached egg on dry toast and orange juice."

She looked at Art. "You want the usual waffle and sausage, or are you gonna take a lesson from your friend here and eat somethin' healthy for a change?"

"Careful what you say, Sheila. Offend me and I'll quit flirtin' with you, even if you beg for more," Art growled. She grinned and slapped his shoulder as she left.

"I saw the memo about JAM, too, Art," Stephen said. "But I've researched this group. I don't think they're smart enough. I don't think they have the connections. This operation would take some pretty big bucks. If they *were* involved, they had help. Besides, why should we believe what Guzman's people are telling us?"

Art looked at Stephen with exasperation. "Why would Tecero take the risk of trying to assassinate a foreign head of state? That would be like declaring war on the whole darn country!"

"You know more about Tecero than I do. But we do know Guzman has been hell on the drug lords down there. I heard he'd caught and killed one principal drug thug—you hear that too?"

Art nodded, looking as if he were beginning to wake up. "Yeah, that's true."

"Art, it's not rocket science. Tecero must have some pretty well-organized help inside Venezuela to run his drug cartel. Your security clearance is higher than mine, but the reports I've seen point toward people fairly high up in the Venezuelan government having some connection with the drug trade. Guzman must be pulling his hair out trying to find out who. Maybe those people participated in the coup attempt as well—someone on the inside," Stephen said.

Art was intrigued. "Maybe I should recommend you for a job with FBI's Foreign Intelligence Division."

Stephen smiled. "Forget it. I wouldn't make it through the training. Don't you guys have to learn to walk on water and catch bullets in your teeth?"

Sheila was back with an armload of steaming plates. "I'll be back with more coffee in a second, boys."

Slathering butter on his waffle, Art said, "Well, okay, it's certainly possible Tecero was involved. But God help him if we could actually link him to this. That would give the Venezuelan government reason to send their entire military after him and chase that sucker all over Latin America." He smiled. "Their rotten relations with Colombia would get a heck of a lot worse." He was wide-awake now, clearly entertained by the prospect of two of his least-favorite Latin American nations preoccupied by disputes with each other.

Sheila came back with the coffee, but one look at their faces and she poured and left without a word.

"I emailed my brother and told him to watch his back, that he might have more than just Guzman chasing him. Here's the deal—he still has a briefcase full of money he hasn't delivered. Whoever gave it to him will want it back. David said it contains over a million in U.S. currency."

Art looked up, wiping butter from his chin, "Geez, Stephen, the plot thickens every time you open your mouth. So tell me—as fascinating as all of this is, how does it relate to me? You haven't yet explained the urgent need to wake me before seven on my day off." Art took another big bite, almost halfway done already with the waffle and sausage on his plate.

Stephen tried to bore into Art with his eyes. "I need to get my brother out of there. Today. I think he's safe for now—his last email said some people were helping him hide. But if I don't get him out within a matter of hours, I'm afraid he'll be caught by Guzman or whoever hired him."

"In the first place, you're too optimistic. Your brother's no trained agent, Stephen. He's in over his head. How do you know these, quote, people who are helping him aren't working for the bad guys? And in the second place, I'm too darned old and arthritic to go rescue your brother. So get to the point—what do you need me for?" Art took another gulp of coffee. He was almost finished eating, while Stephen had hardly touched his breakfast.

"My brother's convinced a CIA guy named Carlos Edwards recruited him for this nasty little job and promised to pay Hope Village fifty grand in exchange."

Art wiped his face with a balled-up napkin. "You haven't convinced me yet that the CIA is behind this."

"Whether CIA operatives were actually involved makes no difference in terms of the political fall out. If my brother is caught, and if he *says* he's working for the CIA, Guzman will trumpet his capture and confession far and wide. It'll be a big embarrassment to the State Department. It might give Guzman a reason to sell even more of his oil to China." Stephen leaned forward. "Listen, I can guarantee this—if they catch my brother, he will eventually tell them what he believes to be true: that he thought he was working for the CIA."

"I see your point," Art said wryly.

Sheila was back, pouring more coffee. She picked up Art's empty plate. "Why didn't you lick the plate clean?"

"What? So you wouldn't have to wash it for the next customer?" he said.

She bopped him on the cheek with her elbow as she left.

Stephen continued. "It's in the interest of the CIA and the State Department to rescue my brother before he falls into the hands of Guzman. It could save them a lot of embarrassment. Especially considering that they *may* have been the ones who put all this in motion."

Art stared at him for a moment. "So you still haven't told me why you came all the way out here to buy my breakfast."

"Art, I need you to contact the higher-ups at the CIA and sell my idea. Then I need them to get my brother out of Venezuela."

"What about your brother's wife and kid?"

"They may have already made it out. David said in an email that he'd already sent them away. He didn't say how."

"Then why didn't he go with them?"

"He didn't say much. Just that the Duncans—the elderly missionary couple there—had been taken in for questioning. I think he felt responsible for their safety. He hasn't made very good decisions lately, so this may be another bad one."

While Stephen dug into his lukewarm egg-on-toast, Art sat quietly watching him. Then he spoke up. "The guy we need to convince is Dennis Vansant. He's about the only guy over there who has his head screwed on straight. Vansant is the CIA Deputy Director for Operations. His primary responsibility is the clandestine collection of foreign intelligence, and if anyone knows whether this Carlos Edwards guy is connected to CIA, it would be Dennis. Not that he would ever admit it to me or to anyone else, mind you, but he would know. I speak to him often because our jobs frequently dovetail with regard to drug traffic intelligence. The one other person I would like to talk to is Rosa Lopez, the Assistant Secretary of the Bureau of Western Hemisphere Affairs at the State Department. Sharp woman. She would be very interested in a plan for damage control if she were aware of the potential embarrassment this could cause her and her boss."

"Can we get them to a meeting where I could share the information I have?"

"Let me make some phone calls."

CHAPTER TWENTY-THREE

David stopped behind a rusting Ford flatbed truck in an alleyway and surveyed the area around Silvia's Cocina de Sopa. Already the open-air fruit and produce stands out front—made of wood planks stacked on plastic milk boxes and each covered with a large umbrella—were being loaded with bananas, potatoes, onions, green beans, carrots, and squash. Today the umbrellas were providing limited shelter from the light rain.

David saw no evidence of the military or police vehicles he had half-expected, and feared, to see. Pulling his 49ers cap lower over his eyes, he hustled past the fruit stands and entered the restaurant, already bustling with customers. Silvia, near the door, looked at him with surprise and motioned for him to follow. She led him into the back room he'd used the night before.

"What are you doing here? I thought Felix was taking you out of the country," she said in a hoarse whisper.

David explained about the Duncans.

"Yes, but the news this morning said they were questioned and released last night! They are no longer being held."

David's first emotion was great relief, and he offered a quick prayer of thanks. The thought that hit him a second later made him sick. *I could have left with Christie and Davy.*

Silvia sighed. "We need to hide you until Felix gets back and can take you to be with your *familia*. Or maybe one of the other *pescadores* can take you. I could ask—"

202   The Missionary

"No, don't ask anyone else. I don't want to put anyone else in jeopardy. I was planning to go to the U.S. Embassy this morning, but now I'm not sure what to do. I have to think. I need to use your computer to see if my family has tried to contact me."

"Of course," replied Silvia. "Sit here. Are you hungry? I will get you some breakfast."

David turned on the computer and logged on to his new yahoo account. The screen blinked. Up popped an email from Stephen: *You are in danger. My sources believe...*

By the time he'd finished reading the email, David was shaking. He read the message again, then again. *This can't be! Carlos* had *to be CIA. No way was I working for drug lords!*

But...

What if it were true? Then the drug lords and their goons would be looking for an American toting a large briefcase. And they'd seen his picture. Anyplace he might be likely to go—the embassy, Hope Village—they would probably already have someone stationed to grab him as soon as he showed up. They had no shortage of money or manpower. And no scruples about doing whatever it took to get their money back—and perhaps to shut him up. Another good reason not to go to the Embassy.

Silvia returned with a plate of *arepas* filled with cheese, some scrambled eggs, and a steaming cup of coffee.

He hit "reply" between mouthfuls and began to type:

Still here in jeopardy. Thanks for the warning. I can't believe the agency was not involved. I am an idiot, probably a dead one soon. Christie and Davy are already on their way. I thought staying here was the right thing. Instead, just one more rotten decision. Some friends are helping for now. If you think of something, let me know. But no telling whether I'll have email access again. I always thought someday I could make a difference in the world, as you have. I'm sorry, Stephen. You have been a great brother. Tell all the ones I love I'm thinking of them.

He hit the "send" button, then created the new account for Christie, *sweetgrasshillsgirl@yahoo.com*.

My Dear Sweet Christie,

First, the good news: Cecil and Martha have been released. They were questioned, but this morning the news broadcast said they were not charged and were taken back to Hope Village. Hallelujah!

Now the hard part:

Watching you and Davy drift away from me last night was one of the most difficult and painful things I have ever experienced, made even worse by the fact that you were so angry, as I had given you every reason to be.

I wouldn't blame you if my actions have destroyed all hope of your ever loving or trusting me again, even in memory.

As I review in my mind my reasons—my excuses—for doing what I've done without consulting you first, without seeking your wisdom, I realize that I deserve whatever is coming to me.

If you can, please set aside for a moment the anger, however justified, and try to forget how foolish I've been. Please just listen to the words of a man who loves you more than his own life and who fears he may never hold you in his arms again.

Christie, I don't know what tomorrow holds, or even the rest of today, but this I do know: I have known a love few men are fortunate to have. You have been an incredible wife, a worthy model for all wives, and I am grateful. If I don't make it back, I want you to find someone else, someone better than me. Someone who will listen, and love you as you deserve to be loved. I wish I could have been that man. I wanted to be. I thought I was.

Please tell Davy I love him beyond words. Tell him happy stories about his daddy.

Pray not only for my safety, but for wisdom for this one who has shown so little.

My love forever,
David

204   The Missionary

He was finishing his breakfast when Silvia reappeared, coffeepot in hand. Filling his cup, she said, "I called a friend who owns a small hotel on Isla Margarita. He agreed to let you stay there. And I just asked one of the fishermen out in the restaurant if he would take you. He has a fast boat."

David said, "Silvia, I appreciate your help, but if any of you are caught helping me, Guzman's people will imprison—"

"You must understand," she said fervently. "We *know* the risk, but we *want* to take it. It is our way of showing our appreciation. Most people down here in the fishing district know what you did for Felix's little girl, and they know about the work of Hope Village. Felix talks about it all the time. We insist on helping you."

David's choices were limited. He could continue to sleep in the tiny cabin of *El Delfín azul*, but the risk of his being found there increased every hour. Once the Venezuelan authorities determined that Felix had helped David escape, and when Felix's van was found near the docks, they would, no doubt, search every boat in the marina. If the drug lords looking for their money figured it out first, they would do the same.

"I accept. Thank you. But I can pay those who help me."

"No, Reverend, we do not want pay. This is our way of helping."

"Felix let me sleep on *El Delfín azul* last night. Do you know this boat?"

"Si, si! Guillermo's boat. He is a sick man right now. But he would be proud to know you were able to use his boat to hide last night."

"I need to return to Guillermo's boat to get my things. When and where should I meet the man who is taking me to Isla Margarita?"

Silvia walked to the small office's open doorway. "Francisco! Oye, Francisco!" She motioned.

A smiling man appeared in the doorway. He was younger than David but already had the leathery look of a fisherman.

"Francisco will take you to Isla Margarita on *La Dama Subió*. Go back to *El Delfín azul*, gather your things, and wait out of sight."

David nodded. "How long will it take us to get to Margarita?"

"My boat has a 200-horse outboard motor and can move very fast if the sea is calm. We can make it there in less than four hours if God is with us." Francisco gave the Catholic sign of the cross over his chest as he spoke. "I have to fuel up. I will come get you in about a half-hour."

David wanted badly to give Silvia and Francisco money for the help they were providing him—and the substantial risks they were taking—but he also knew that the pride of the Venezuelan people was great. Silvia had already said no, and she would be offended if he offered again. Still, he pulled the stack of bills from his back pocket, peeled off a one-hundred dollar bill, extended it to Francisco, and said, "Here is money for gasoline."

Silvia grabbed it before Francisco could. "That is more money than a *year's* worth of gasoline!" she exclaimed as she handed it back to David. "*You* know gas here in Venezuela is cheap!" Reaching into the pocket of her apron, she handed Francisco 5,000 bolivars—about four dollars in U.S. money. "Here's money for gas," she said to Francisco. Francisco nodded. He and Silvia left.

David sat back at the desk. Sending a second message to his brother, he typed:

> *Friends have just made new plans for me. Tonight I will be staying at Hotel le Flamboyant on Margarita Island. It's across the street from a beach called Playa El Agua. If I move, I'll try to let you know where.*
>
> *One other thing. Check this out:*
>
> *Chase Bank*
>
> *Ph. 212.447.3400*
>
> *Hope Village Account 1596263784931*
>
> *Pin 1947*
>
> *Use my name and SS#*
>
> *I trust you to figure out what to do with this if I do not make it back.*

Jose Montoya, sitting in the corner of Silvia's Cocina de Sopa, had looked up from his breakfast when the white man walked in. He had thought that the gringo's face looked familiar. He had been intrigued, too, by Silvia's behavior, quickly ushering the man to the back room. *Where have I seen that face before?* He looked something like the guy whose picture was on the news late last night, the one wanted for questioning in connection with the Guzman assassination attempt. *What was the guy's name...David something.*

Jose watched Silvia take food to the back room, then beckon Francisco. It did not take a genius to figure out that they were helping this David something, the one wanted by the police.

But Jose may have been the only one in the restaurant who knew that it was not only the police who were looking for Senor David something. In fact, he'd gotten word directly from his boss first thing that morning that a two-million-Bolivar reward had been announced for a tip leading to this man's capture. Montoya's boss, Tomas Fernandez, was a self-described "lieutenant" of Venezuelan drug lord Julio DiMartino. "If you hear anything, if you see anything, call me immediately," Fernandez had said.

Jose waited. When he saw David emerge from the back room, Jose came to the front of the restaurant to pay his bill. Then he studied the man's face carefully, from just a few feet away. Yes, that was the guy. Jose needed to call the boss. He had to try hard to keep from smiling. He was going to earn some big money! Maybe Fernandez would be so grateful he would make Jose one of his top men.

Jose hurried past the open market and around the corner to the back alley, where no one could hear him. Using his cell phone, he called Fernandez. There was no answer, so Jose left a message explaining what he'd seen. He hung up and he scurried back to the open-air market and surveyed the area in front of the restaurant. And again. And again.

But David something was gone.

CHAPTER TWENTY-FOUR

David made his way back toward the docks, following the route he'd taken earlier and walking stooped, head down, with a shambling, uneven gait. The rain had stopped, and the sun was trying to break through the thinning clouds. It already felt humid.

By now, there were many more people and vehicles bustling everywhere around the dock area and the warehouses behind which David walked. He hoped his unshaven face and wrinkled clothing helped him blend in. David had always bemoaned the fact that Latin America attracted so many drunken and wasted white Americans and Europeans, men in tatters, filthy, eyes unfocused, hands shaking. Now he was just thankful that he looked like one of them.

Not only was this an area where commercial fishermen docked and unloaded their catches, it was also a loading area for large ships. Bright orange forty-foot metal shipping containers were stacked three and four high on what seemed to be acres of asphalt and dirt. Semi-trucks and trailers carrying loaded containers moved back and forth through the area. In the distance to the south, huge cranes loaded and unloaded ships. Trucks waited in line while their drivers stood in small groups, chatting and gesturing.

Pulling his cap low, David made his way down a narrow drive that ran between two large warehouses. He had walked only a couple of hundred yards when he heard a vehicle approaching from behind. He turned—and stared into the windshield of a white Jeep Cherokee with emergency lights mounted on the top. A police car. His heart lurched.

He moved close to the warehouse to allow the vehicle to pass. As it did, he looked down and tried to make himself small. It passed not three feet from his side; he could have reached out and touched the "Policía" written in large black letters on the vehicle door. Even looking away, David could feel the intense gaze of the officer nearest him. He felt his face flame red. He turned and began walking back the way he had come.

Tires screeched. He heard the car doors open. "¡Parada!" the officer yelled. "Halt!"

David ran.

"¡Parada! ¡Parada!" the man yelled again.

Afraid they would shoot, David ducked into the open door of a warehouse. He could see light coming from a doorway at the far end of the building, but the officers were close behind; he would never make it that far. Twenty feet in, he leaped to the side and squatted behind some large gray plastic bins that smelled of fish. Peeking through a crack between them, he saw the two officers enter the building and run past, guns drawn.

When the officers neared the far end of the warehouse, David slipped out from behind the crates and ran back toward the door he had entered. Too soon. They must have heard him. "¡Parada! Or we will shoot!" they yelled as he ran back into the sunlight.

He would not be able to outrun the policemen. Fifty yards down the road sat the police Jeep with the driver-side door open. He raced toward it.

At 9:03 a.m., Venezuelan Coast Guard vessel GC-403 was patrolling the waters off the north coast. One hundred sixty feet long, its hull painted gray with a bright white angular stripe, it moved slowly through the water at seven to ten knots. The rain had vanished, the sea was calm, and visibility was excellent. Raul Valdez, a nineteen-year-old

ensign, was on morning watch. It was normal for the Coast Guard to ply these waters, usually in search of drug and customs violations. But this morning they were on heightened alert because of the attempted assassination of President Guzman. Their orders were to search any vessel, large or small, that looked suspicious. Four ensigns in all slowly swung their powerful binoculars along the horizon.

Ensign Valdez was looking toward Grenada when he spotted a Venezuelan fishing vessel. Routine, no doubt, but on this particular morning, his orders were to report everything and let the captain decide what bore further investigation.

And the captain gave orders to follow the fishing trawler apace.

The vessel was moving at about ten knots—probably full speed for a vessel of this type—at about 72 degrees north by northeast, the exact heading to Grenada. It was obvious that the vessel was not fishing at the moment; there was no gear in the water. The Coast Guard captain decided to move in closer for a better look. For about five minutes, they followed about eight hundred yards behind the trawler, apparently unnoticed.

Driving the boat from the fly bridge, Felix was feeling gradually less tense as the day progressed without problems. It was a beautiful day for navigation. Clear skies, no wind, calm seas, and good visibility. If this weather held, he would make it to Grenada by sometime tomorrow. Blanca and Davy were sitting out in the open on the aft deck, playing with a wind-up toy. Felix turned to check on them, lifted his eyes to the horizon behind—and immediately spotted the Coast Guard vessel in the distance. "Quick!" he yelled. "Blanca! Davy! Into the cabin! *Andale!*"

Christie flew out of the cabin onto the aft deck. "What's wrong?" she called.

"Get the children and go back into the cabin! There's a vessel following us—it may be the Coast Guard!"

Christie looked toward the stern. Then she herded the two children back into the cabin and closed the door—but not before Felix had seen the terror on her face.

Monterey Castillo-García, captain of Coast Guard GC-403 following *Bahia Bonita*, was glassing the boat with powerful binoculars when he saw a blond woman rush out on the aft deck and take the two children inside.

"Full speed ahead!" he ordered. "I want to search that boat!"

The first bullet whizzed past David's right arm so close it passed through his shirt; it slammed into the open jeep door. He hadn't even had time to process the thought that they were shooting at him when something grabbed him by the left shoulder and hurtled him forward, into the car door headfirst and onto the gritty, broken pavement.

He felt a searing burn in his shoulder.

He felt confusion.

He wanted to stay where he was for a few minutes and clear his head.

But there was another loud report, and grit flew up from the ground near him, and he looked up at the open car door. A wide splatter of blood fanned across it, just beginning to drip down the surface.

His blood.

He'd been shot.

His left arm didn't seem to work, so he pulled himself up with his right and slid into the driver's seat. The engine was still running. The two policemen screamed as they closed in behind: "*¡Pare o dispararemos!*"

David jammed the gearshift into drive and slammed his foot down on the gas, peeling rubber as the Jeep lurched forward. The driver's door slammed shut. Shots rang out again behind him and the windshield cracked in a spiderweb pattern just to the right of his head.

"Jesus, help me!" he screamed.

At the first corner, he whipped the wheel to the right and skidded, almost turning the vehicle over. Regaining control, he sped down the street about five hundred yards toward stacks of bright orange shipping containers. Seeing a narrow alley between two stacks of shipping containers, he again whipped the vehicle to the right and found that the alley was a long one, a hundred yards at least. Near the end of it, he stopped, put the vehicle in park, shut the engine off, and took the keys. He threw open the door and ran awkwardly down a similar narrow passage that tended toward the fishing docks, holding his left shoulder tight with his right hand to try to stop the bleeding, but his shirt was already soaked to the waist.

Two hundred yards later, he saw a container with the door ajar. It was stacked on another container. He grabbed a steel bar hanging from the open door, climbed up the side of the container, slid his body inside, and pulled the door closed until there was just a tiny crack he could see through. The inside of the container was pitch black except for the sliver of light coming in through the slit in the door. He heard what he guessed were rats scrambling at the far end of the container.

It was too dark to assess the damage to his shoulder. He continued to press the wound in front to try to stop the bleeding; he pressed the back of his shoulder against the container's wall. He tried to flex his left hand, then his elbow. Weak and numb, but they worked—at great cost in pain.

Blood oozed through his fingers and dripped on his pants.

In his wildest nightmares, he'd never imagined that being shot stealing a police vehicle might be how he would die.

CHAPTER TWENTY-FIVE.

Felix put the *Bahia Bonita* on autopilot, descended the ladder, and entered the cabin. "They are only one hundred meters behind and gaining quickly," he said. "I think they plan to board us. If they do, we will probably be arrested."

Isabel began to cry.

Felix put his arm around her shoulder. "Let's not upset the children. If we are fortunate, they may just ask a few questions and then pass by. All of you stay in the cabin."

Christie ran her hands through her hair, clearly in emotional anguish. "I'm so sorry to have involved all of you in this mess," she said. "I should tell them who I am, that I hired you to transport me, and that you did not know who I was."

"No," replied Felix. "They would easily find out that was not true. A few telephone calls and they would find out about Blanca's operations, about my supplying fish for Hope Village. To lie would be worse than to simply stick to the story we have both agreed to. No one on this boat has done anything wrong."

Felix walked out onto the aft deck. The Coast Guard vessel, which dwarfed Felix's boat, was now to the starboard, about 100 feet away from *Bahia Bonita*. Three men were out on its deck. Two of them gripped AK 47's and one clutched a bullhorn. "You are hereby ordered to stop your vessel!" the man called.

From the controls at the fishing station on the aft deck, Felix obeyed, putting his engine in neutral. Two inflatable fenders were lowered next

214　The Missionary

to the Coast Guard vessel as it prepared to raft up to Felix's boat. Felix caught a line tossed to him and tied it to a forward cleat; a second line came down, which he tied to a stern cleat.

A rope ladder appeared over the side of the big gray ship. The captain called out, "I am Captain Monterey Castillo-Garcia of the Venezuelan Coast Guard, and I request permission to board your vessel."

This, Felix knew, was only a formality. It was useless to deny the captain permission to board his boat. *"Sí, viene a bordo,"* Felix replied.

Two Coast Guard ensigns descended first and with their weapons took up positions on either side of the rope ladder as Captain Monterey Castillo-García descended, while two other men at the rail of the Coast Guard vessel trained their guns on Felix.

The Captain did not waste time. "I have observed a woman and children on your vessel and I wish to speak to them."

"Yes, of course," Felix said. "I am Felix Suturos. I have on board two women and two children. One woman is my wife, Isabel Suturos, and one child is my daughter, Blanca. The other woman is Christie Eller who is accompanied by her young son, Davy Eller." Felix noticed that the captain's eyes widened slightly at the Eller name. "Everyone on board has valid passports."

"And where are you going with these people?" the captain asked.

"We are taking Señora Christie and her son to St. George's, Grenada, where they plan to vacation."

"Is it a common thing for you to use this fishing vessel as a passenger ship, Señor Suturos?"

"No, sir. These people are our friends, and we are doing this as a favor."

"Is it a common thing for Senora Eller to vacation alone without her husband?"

"He is busy with other matters and could not come with her."

Captain Castillo-Garcia laughed without humor. "Yes, I am sure Senor Eller is very busy. Are you aware that David Eller is being sought for questioning by the Venezuelan authorities?"

So he has not yet been captured, Felix thought. He considered his answer carefully. "Sir, David Eller is not on board with us. I was not aware that his wife and child were being sought by anyone."

"Bring all the passengers up to this deck!" the captain demanded.

Felix opened the cabin door and asked the women to come out. The children clung to their mothers as they came onto the aft deck. Turning to his men, Captain Castillo-Garcia shouted, "Search the boat!" and motioned toward the cabin. One ensign stood ready with his rifle pointed toward the door while the other quickly entered, crouching defensively. Felix watched through the door as the soldiers pulled up the mattresses on the beds and opened all the cupboards. In a few moments, they emerged and reported to the captain that no one was hiding inside.

The captain turned to Christie, bowing slightly. "Señora, may I see your passport please?"

By then, three more armed soldiers had scurried down the rope ladder to join them.

"My passport is in my purse," Christie said, in a voice that Felix was pleased to hear came out calm and firm. "Back inside the cabin."

The captain swept his hand gallantly toward the cabin. "Please," he said, and as Christie re-entered, the captain motioned one of his men to follow her. The other four, guns in hand, fanned out across *Bahia Bonita*.

Christie re-emerged and handed the captain her passport, along with Davy's.

He scanned both documents quickly, then said, "Mrs. Eller, are you aware that your husband is being sought for questioning by the Venezuelan authorities?"

"My husband and I are missionaries who have labored to help the street children who often die in the barrios," she said.

The captain paused, brow wrinkled, then continued: "Is your husband hiding on this vessel?"

"No."

"When was the last time you saw your husband?"

216   The Missionary

"Yesterday."

"And where was this?"

"In Caracas."

"Where in Caracas?"

"I saw him at Hope Village yesterday," she said.

"Do you know where your husband is now?"

"No."

Captain Castillo-Garcia motioned for his men to search again. "Look for any hidden compartments!" he yelled. Felix watched the guards open the fish holds. One climbed down inside. Another searched the engine compartment.

The captain climbed back up the ladder and onto his vessel. Felix glanced at his watch. It was nine-fifteen.

A few minutes later, the captain descended the ladder. "On the authority of the Venezuelan government, I have been instructed to take all of you into custody and impound this vessel," he said. "All of you will need to come aboard our ship. Two of my men will bring your vessel back to the government dock in Caracas."

"We are in international waters," Felix said. "You have no right to arrest us, and no right to impound my vessel."

The captain pursed his lips. "This will go much easier on you and your passengers if you cooperate with my order."

"Please, Felix, let's just do what he says," Christie said. "We have done nothing wrong."

It was true that she had done nothing wrong, Felix thought, but it was also true that, as they all knew, none of that would matter to Guzman. Still, resisting was out of the question.

One of the soldiers held his arms out for Davy, who shrank from him. But the soldier's eyes were gentle. "Por favor, Señora, let me climb the ladder with the child."

Davy began to cry, clinging to Christie. "It's okay, honey," she said, handing him to the soldier. "The man is just going to carry you up the ladder. I'm coming right behind you."

One by one, they began their ascent onto the government vessel. Felix thought that this, most likely, would be the last time he would see *Bahia Bonita*—not only his pride and joy, but also his primary means of livelihood.

His thoughts soon turned to a more pressing question, one that had plagued him since that fateful phone call from David. What would happen to him, his wife, and his child? What might Guzman's soldiers do to try to extract information from them about David—information that they did not possess? Recalling Guzman's history of brutality against political prisoners, Felix felt chilled to the bone.

David had been hiding only a few minutes in the shipping container, the pain and stiffness in his wounded shoulder steadily growing, when he realized that it was foolish. The police would find the car he'd hijacked and know that he'd fled on foot from there. They would check every empty shipping container. In fact, in all likelihood, he'd left a nice clear trail of blood.

He heard more and more sirens. If he was going to make a move, he should make it now, before Francisco was frightened away.

Cautiously, he stuck out his head and checked both ways. He saw no one. He slid open the door as quietly as possible, jumped down from the container—a shock of pain in his shoulder as his feet hit the ground—and slipped through a narrow passage between containers. All was quiet around him. Like the one rabbit in a forest full of foxes, he treated the vast acreage of stacks of shipping containers like a maze, sticking to the narrowest, darkest passages, and making lots of turns. He had no desire to be shot again.

Five minutes later, he was hiding behind the last stack of shipping containers, very near the fishing docks. Immediately in front of him was a road that angled toward the docks. There was little cover between him and Guillermo's boat, about seventy-five yards away. David fervently wished that it were night, rather than a clear and bright morning.

218   The Missionary

Spilling from the open door of a mostly empty container near him was a pile of rags and dirty towels, half-rotted and foul. David sorted through them for the least filthy and tore it into strips. He peeled off his bloody shirt, tossed it into the dark of the empty container, and wiped the blood from his skin as well as he could. He packed his wounds with wads of towel, then tied—using his right hand and his teeth—the strips of towel into some semblance of a bandage. He formed a long strip into a sling.

The sirens were growing louder and more numerous; he could see several police cars scattered throughout the vast commercial area around the docks, but none near him. He couldn't wait any longer.

A large semi pulling a trailer loaded with a container rumbled slowly past his hiding place in the direction of the fishing dock, and on impulse, David sprinted into the road and fell in beside the huge rear wheels, jogging along on a pace with the truck, as close to the huge wheel as he dared. When he reached the point at which the road came nearest to Guillermo's boat, he slipped behind the truck, jogged there for a moment, and then broke for the docks. He was tempted to run as fast as he could to the boat, but knowing that would just draw more attention, he kept to a fast walk, remembering to keep his head down, to slump.

As if anyone with a bloody bandage on his shoulder and his arm in a sling could truly be inconspicuous.

When he neared the boat, he lifted his head—and saw that there was another boat moored next to *El Delfín azul*. And on the deck of that boat stood Francisco, gesturing frantically for him to hurry. David held up a hand—*wait*—and slipped onto *El Delfín azul*. With his good arm he grabbed his duffel bag first, which he slung up to Francisco, then quickly retrieved the briefcase before hopping onto Francisco's boat. He hadn't been aboard ten seconds before Francisco practically shoved him into the cabin.

"Hide in here till we're out of the harbor," Francisco said. "There are cops everywhere!" He closed the cabin door.

The tiny cabin of *La Dama Subió* had no bed, just a small unpadded bench among nets, ropes, shrimp traps, anchors and a variety of other fishing gear. The heavy smell of hemp rope and spoiled fish all these boats seem to have made David retch.

Still, he was, for the moment, safe—and profoundly grateful. And he was experiencing very strange sensations. He knew the human mind has strange ways of coping with extreme anxiety in times of crisis. Now, lying on a hard, rough bench, his heart was racing so hard he thought he could hear it. There was a small, rusty, white box that appeared to be a first-aid kit hanging on the wall, and David knew he should treat his wounds, but he couldn't generate the energy. He noticed for the first time that his pants were wet with sweat and blood. He was shaking and felt short of breath. For a moment, it almost felt as if he were outside his body, or as if he were someone else rather than himself. He added "light-headed" to his list of symptoms, just before he lay back with a sudden urge to sleep.

It was mid-morning when Montoya's boss, Tomas Fernandez, got around to checking the messages on his cell phone. He'd partied all night at the Gran Melia Hotel. His head was still pounding and groggy from all the rum he'd consumed. But when he heard the message from Jose Montoya, the grogginess disappeared in a rush of adrenaline, and he immediately called Montoya back. "I got your message. You sure it was him?"

"Si. I know it was the same face on the TV last night."

"So where did he go when he left the restaurant?"

"Ah…I don't know."

"Did he get in a car? Did you see what kind of vehicle?"

"Umm, no."

"You don't know whether he got into a car or walked away?"

"No, I went down the street to call you."

"¡*Estúpido*! You fool! Why didn't you follow him? If you mess this up…"

"Sorry, boss, I just thought—"

"Shut up! Okay, so you say this woman at the restaurant spoke to a *pescador* named Francisco who you think was somehow helping David Eller?"

"Si, the three of them talked together."

"You see or hear anything else?"

"I…I don't think so. Except that now there are lots of police cars down here, police on the street asking questions…"

"¡Ay! That means you are not the only one who recognized him. But if they are still asking questions, they have not found him yet. We do not have much time. Find out everything you can about this Francisco. Find out where he keeps his boat. Go back and talk to this woman… her name was Silvia?"

"Si."

"Find out everything she knows about David Eller, but don't tell her who's looking for him, and don't threaten her. We may do that later, but not right now, because if she is helping Eller, we may want to follow her. And *keep your eyes open!* If you see Eller again, follow him! You hear me, Montoya? Right now you're worth nothing to me—you mishandled this whole thing. You want to prove your worth? Find David Eller!"

Fernandez hung up and immediately punched in Julio DiMartino's number.

Jose Montoya did not like being called *estupido*, especially by his boss. He spent the rest of the morning wandering around the docks asking about David Eller. He spoke with fishermen, cannery workers, truck drivers, dock workers, and loiterers. He knew if he could tell his boss more about Eller, or maybe even capture Eller himself, the reward money would be his, and his boss would have to eat his words. There were rumors about a shooting. Jose cursed in dismay as the number of police and military in the area increased. If they found Eller before he did, the reward would be lost and his boss would be furious.

It was 12:30 when Jose Montoya returned to Silvia's Cocina de Sopa. He scanned the dining room, full because it was lunchtime. Most of those in the room were people he had already talked to earlier that morning; he had learned nothing more from them. The noisy conversations in the restaurant ceased, and Montoya looked around, startled; everyone was staring back at him, with hostile intent. Silvia stood by the register, eyeing him as if he were something someone had scraped off their shoe onto her floor.

Silvia had watched Montoya enter; now she watched him approach almost as if he were afraid of being attacked. Well, good. Let him be afraid.

Almost in a whisper, Montoya said, "Señorita Silvia, may I speak to you in private?"

He had been in her restaurant a few times before. He was not a regular, and she had assumed from his general manner that he wasn't her typical honest, hard-working patron. But she hadn't guessed until today, when her customers had told her that he'd been asking for information about David Eller, that he was a criminal. After all—who else besides criminals and the police would be looking for David Eller? And Montoya certainly wasn't with the police.

Motioning with her head, she directed him to her little office.

"Señorita," he said, leaning against the office door jamb, "this morning I saw a man come into your restaurant who looked very much like a man on the TV news last night who is wanted in connection with the assassination attempt on President Guzman." His eyes shifted to the computer on Silvia's desk. "It would be a very serious thing if the police discovered that someone might be aiding this man."

Silvia suspected that the last people Montoya wanted to contact were the police. She said nothing and continued to glare at the man, daring him to say more. He shifted his gaze back toward the restaurant where one could still sense the unusual silence.

222   The Missionary

Looking at Silvia again, he said, speaking barely above a whisper, "It could be very profitable to you if you could give me information about this man's whereabouts." He paused, waiting for a response. Silvia said nothing. Montoya continued, "And it could be very bad for you if some people I know thought you helped him escape."

Silvia despised this man. But because she didn't know for sure whom he was working for, she didn't know how much danger she might be in. Should she play it safe? Try to placate him? Finally, she unfolded her arms and smiled. "Yes, I did recognize him this morning. Do you know that he and his wife work at *Espere la Aldea*, helping our poor children who live on the street?" Silvia said.

Montoya shrugged his shoulders.

Silvia began to speak loudly so those in the restaurant could hear. "Did you know that many of the people in this restaurant admire David Eller for his work with the poor? And they also believe he had nothing to do with the attempted assassination of President Guzman?" Her Latin blood pressure was now rising rapidly.

Montoya nervously glanced toward the restaurant's silent audience, motioning for her to speak more quietly.

Silvia did lower her voice, and spoke through clenched teeth. "I told Señor Eller that since he is innocent, he should turn himself in to the authorities and answer their questions to clear his name. He told me when he left that is what he intended to do," she lied. "I assume that he has already notified them and is now in their custody." She had heard the story from many that morning of the hijacked police car, of shots being fired—she had heard them herself—and she silently prayed that that last thing she had said was not true.

Montoya thought for a moment. "What were you saying to Francisco?"

"Oh, Francisco," she scoffed. "That was nothing to do with David Eller. I asked Francisco to bring me some tuna from his catch tomorrow."

She watched Montoya leave the restaurant. He was easy to fool, but Silvia could see that even he doubted her story about the tuna. And he would speak to others who may not be as dumb. She would need to lie low for a few days. She had no regrets about helping David Eller, but she also had no intention of waiting for trouble to come.

The lunch hour rush was almost over when she spoke to her cook. "Lucho, I have decided to take a few days off. I am leaving now and I will be back sometime next week. If anyone comes around asking questions about me, tell them I went to Puerta La Cruz on holiday for a few days. You are in charge. I will call you early next week to see how things are going."

Just before leaving the restaurant, she spoke to a close friend of Francisco's, sitting at the counter eating carne asada. "Has Francisco left yet?"

Jorge nodded excitedly, then swallowed his mouthful of food. "Si, he left early this morning. I saw him leaving the harbor."

She looked around and spoke quietly. "With his passenger?"

"I think so."

It took Silvia only a few minutes to pack her things, lock her apartment, and drive away toward her sister's place in Valencia, several hours in the opposite direction from Puerta La Cruz.

CHAPTER TWENTY-SIX

After the midnight meeting with Durango a week before, Emilio Antonio Tecero had returned to the Colombian jungle where, in the safety of one of his communication bunkers, he had waited for news of the assassination. Enraged when the attempt failed, he had spent the past two days frantically attempting to find Durango. Now, seeing the televised reports about David Eller, he was focusing his attention on the missionary. If he found either Eller or Durango—"Everyone will know that nobody double crosses me and stays alive!" he screamed to his communications assistant.

There was an incoming call. "It's DiMartino," his assistant said. "He says he has new information for you."

Tecero took the telephone, listened briefly, then cursed. "Where have you been? This is old news! We've been monitoring the police scanners. The police think Eller is hiding in one of the shipping containers near the docks. They're searching each container, and if they find him before we do, they'll find my money too. But he may be hiding somewhere else. I sent some of my men down to La Guaira to search the boats. I need you to find this woman Silvia. I want to know everything she knows."

He slammed down the receiver.

The only new information DiMartino had given him was regarding the fisherman named Francisco. Tecero decided to send two of his men to find the fisherman.

226 The Missionary

General Raldo Dukai was at his desk reviewing reports on the search for Eller when his assistant came in with a printout of an email from the Coast Guard.

> This morning at approximately 9:10 a.m. Coast Guard vessel GC-403 under the command of Captain Monterey Castillo-Garcia boarded a fishing vessel named *Bahia Bonita* approximately 100 kilometers off the coast of Venezuela and found Mrs. David Eller aboard with her son. The Bahia Bonita is owned and operated by Felix Suturos, who was also aboard the vessel, along with Mrs. Suturos and daughter, for a total of five on board. Mr. Suturos claims that the boat was headed to Grenada. This boat was thoroughly searched and no other passengers were found.
>
> We have taken all five passengers into custody and we will be docking at the Coast Guard dock at La Guaira at approximately one-twenty-five p.m. today. It is our request to turn these passengers over to you.
>
> We have also seized the *Bahia Bonita*. Coast Guard personnel are bringing her back to our dock. This vessel will remain quarantined and guarded there in the event you wish to search her again.
>
> We request that you have personnel waiting at the dock to receive our passengers.
>
> Admiral Omar Andrés Braulio Contreras-Álvarez
>
> Comando Naval de Operaciones

Dukai was elated. This was very good news. If David Eller were to evade their dragnet, Mrs. Eller might be able to help Dukai lure David out of hiding. He smiled. He would be there at the dock himself to meet Christie Eller and the others.

Things were falling into place. It occurred to Dukai that it was time to put the captured commando someplace safe, out of the hands of that madman Torres. The commando could become an important bargaining chip later.

Christie guessed that the room into which she and the others had been placed on the Coast Guard vessel was a conference room of sorts. But as they'd entered, Christie had seen two guards with AK-47's stationed just outside the door—which had been locked behind them, removing any doubt about whether they were prisoners. They had been given bottled water and stale sandwiches.

Since then, Davy and Blanca had mostly sat on the floor playing; now, they were putting together a simple puzzle that Christie had brought for the trip to Grenada. Felix and Isabel had found a quiet spot on the floor in one corner. Isabel sat with her back against Felix, with his arms wrapped around her while they appeared to nap, although Christie couldn't imagine that they were actually relaxed enough to fall asleep. Christie sat at the other end of the room at a round table anchored to the floor and surrounded by six chairs. She had plenty of time to think.

As a teenager, she had sometimes stood in front of the mirror looking at her scars and thinking that she would never have a boyfriend, let alone marry. And then came David. Like a miracle. They had met in college. At first, he was just one of the students among a group in charge of planning volunteer work with migrant workers. Over time, though, their conversations became more frequent and more personal. They talked about things that mattered to them—God, their dreams, even their doubts. Yet always the words came naturally. And with David, Christie often forgot to use some of the hand gestures with which she hid the scars on her neck, gestures that had simply become second nature. One day, David had come right out and asked her how

228   The Missionary

she'd been burned—something few people dared to do. Oddly, that was when she'd first suspected that she was falling in love.

On their wedding day, David kept saying how absolutely beautiful she looked. Had he known how terrified she was that on their honeymoon he would for the first time see all her scars—including the worst one, on her belly? Despite herself and the fact that she was now a prisoner of a hostile government, she smiled as she remembered how gracious and gentle he had been, how at first he'd asked if he could touch her scars—and had then proceeded to kiss them, making her giggle and forget her insecurity.

But now. Now there were new scars. They seemed to hurt more than the physical scars ever had. Before, she had often imagined what some wives might endure who were married to men less than David— husbands who betrayed their wives by cheating with other women or by their addictions to alcohol or drugs. Or even couch-potato husbands who simply had no vision for life larger than a paycheck. She'd known when she'd married David she would not have to cope with those problems. But now—she wasn't at all sure that she wouldn't trade places with these wives. Given David's betrayal, and where it had led, right now those other kinds of betrayals seemed manageable by comparison.

Fear gripped her—fear that her love for David was slipping away, fear that he might be dead already, and that her child would grow up fatherless, fear of Guzman and what he might do to them, fear that she was losing her mind.

God, I need You... please help us...

The words to a familiar hymn she'd learned as a child and had sung many times since came to her.

Great is thy faithfulness, Oh God my father.

She heard herself softly, almost involuntarily humming the tune.

There is no shadow of turning with thee.

She looked up to see Isabel, eyes closed, smiling and rocking her head gently in time to Christie's humming. Christie began to sing:

All I have needed thy hand hath provided,
Great is thy faithfulness, Lord unto me.

She sang it again, this time in Spanish so Isabel could understand the words:

Gran es Tu fidelidad,
Ah Dios mi Padre.

Soon, Isabel was singing along with her.

Gradually, she felt her anxiety ease. When she ran out of words, she began humming again.

Would they get out of this all right? Would they find David again, and in one piece? She didn't know. She didn't know whether any of them would be alive by this time tomorrow. Yet still she felt that God was faithful, and that He could be trusted. A scene flashed through her mind from what she considered one of the hardest stories of the Bible, and yet one of her favorites: Shadrach, Meshach, and Abednego saying to King Nebuchadnezzar, "Our God whom we serve is able to deliver us from the burning fiery furnace—but if he does not..."

"Mommy, look!" screeched Davy, interrupting her thoughts. He held out the finished puzzle for her inspection. It was a farm scene—with a happy farmer, his wife, two kids, a cow, and a chicken standing before a barn.

"That's great, Davy!" she forced herself to say, her eyes watering. "I'm so proud of you."

"I'm so proud of you, too, Mom!" Davy announced, making her smile. Then he marched back over to Blanca and upended the whole puzzle on the floor again, making a clatter. Christie whispered loudly for him to be quiet, nodding at Felix and Isabel. Then she lay her own head on the table, closed her eyes, and prayed for God to make her brave again.

Rebekah Eller looked around her living room at the friends who had gathered. She reached out her left hand and grasped the hand of her best friend Dee. Rebekah knew she had never been brave, and in times of trouble she relied on the strength of friends and on her rock, her husband Michael.

It was mid-morning in Seattle, Washington. They had issued the invitation by telephone just that morning, to their best circle of friends: Come for lunch, but come by ten o'clock, because first we need to pray for our son and his wife and child, being persecuted in a godforsaken country where there is no bill of rights.

Michael began, as he always did, winding through a long and formal and eloquent prayer that somehow sounded a great deal like his closing arguments in court. When he finished, the others, one by one, as they felt led by God, offered audible prayers for David and Christie. Several asked God for safety for the Ellers. One asked God to hide David from those who might want to harm him.

When the final prayer lapsed into silence, Rebekah felt that a burden had been lifted from her. She began for the first time to feel a sense of hope that David and his family would somehow be safe.

Wouldn't it be nice to close with a song? she thought. *Maybe "It Is Well With My Soul," or*—

Michael clapped his hands loudly and stood. "Now!" he said, grinning widely, his politician's grin. "Where's that food?"

General Dukai had sent several of his own investigators to La Guaira, in addition to the police and National Guard, to search for David Eller. He had been briefed about the stolen police car and about finding a blood trail after shots were fired. Not knowing how badly Eller had been hit, he wondered whether they would find that Eller had bled to death.

Dukai himself was already on his way there to meet the ship bringing in Christie Eller when he received a call from his lead investigator.

"General Dukai, we seem to have company at the docks looking for Eller. Most of the fisherman here say someone else already boarded their boats and searched them, asking about Eller. These men said they were searching on behalf of President Guzman."

"There is no one else investigating for Guzman. This must be the same group that ransacked Hope Village last night."

"The fishermen said there were four or five of them, dressed in suits."

"Drug lord goons. I suspected that drug lords might have been a part of the assassination plot, and now they want to silence Eller. Are they still there?"

"We have not seen them. The fishermen say they were here fifteen or twenty minutes ago."

"If you find any of them, arrest them and call me."

These men who had ransacked *Espere la Aldea* and questioned fishermen at the docks were undoubtedly only the drug lords' hired goons, but Dukai wanted to catch them anyway, if for no other reason than to slow down his enemies' search for Eller, thereby buying himself more time. Besides, some of the goons might talk, especially if he turned them over to Torres.

David awoke to a gentle touch on his shoulder. He opened his eyes to find Francisco, who had apparently already removed David's makeshift bandage, examining the wound. He helped David sit up, which brought on a surge of light-headedness. By the time David's head had cleared, the fisherman had returned with a pan of hot, fresh water and a bar of soap.

"Who is driving the boat?" David asked.

"I have put it in neutral."

David was amazed at how gentle Francisco was as he cleaned the wounds, given how calloused and hard his hands were. But Francisco was also painfully thorough, for which David was grateful, aware of the possibility of infection.

The pain and stiffness made David suspect that the bullet had clipped a bone somewhere, but nothing seemed broken, and the bullet had passed clear through. Francisco's ministrations were not only thorough but efficiently speedy; David thought Christie would have approved.

232 The Missionary

After the boat was underway again, David found himself lying back on the rough bunk, this time awake enough to be aware of his own discomfort. The bench upon which he lay was no bed, and the pile of rope that formed his only cushion was hard and bumpy. Exhaust from the boat's outboard added to the fumes. He needed air. A small metal hatch in the ceiling looked as if it hadn't been opened for years. David fumbled with it until he managed to force it open a crack. The fresh air seeping in was so refreshing he kept his nose pressed against the hatch for a long time.

Sitting back down on the pile of rope, he thought again of Christie, traveling for hours with Davy on Felix's boat in a small cabin—fortunately, one bigger and more comfortable than this. He guessed—hoped—they would be about a third of the way to Grenada by now. *God, be with them,* he breathed. He would not allow himself to consider that they might not be okay.

From Christie, his thoughts turned to Cecil and Martha Duncan. He did not think of himself as a hero, as a warrior—and yet, just a few hours ago, he'd been willing to let his wife leave without him and to subject himself to almost certain death just to save Cecil and Martha. What was it about Cecil and Martha that meant so much to him? In truth, he was sometimes angry at Cecil for what David perceived as inaction—he recalled with embarrassment that he'd chosen not to introduce Cecil to Carlos—and yet despite these things, he'd still made saving them his first priority. And deep down, he knew that he'd do it again if necessary. Not because he was brave. Not because he was self-sacrificing. But simply because he recognized something in them of great value, greater value than he perceived in his own life.

He lay back on the rope and looked at the plywood ceiling just above his head. He remembered once challenging Cecil to get more politically involved. Like many wise people, Cecil had great respect for the wisdom of others who'd come before him, and loved to quote them. On that occasion, pointing toward the Federal District of Caracas, Cecil had said, "Out there I am but one person in the world. But here at Hope Village, I can become the world to one person."

David rocked with the swells as the boat raced up and over, then plunged down again. He recalled a quote he'd memorized and often quoted from C.T. Studd, a pioneer missionary from England who'd gone to China: "*Some wish to live within the sound of a chapel bell; I wish to run a rescue mission within a yard of hell.*" That quote of Studd's had became a sort of mantra for David during college, when he was so full of hope and optimism and energy to work for justice.

Well, I'm certainly within a yard of hell right now.

Praying brought some sense of comfort, so he prayed on—for safety for Christie and Davy, for his own successful escape, for all of those who had helped them and could face persecution if it were discovered, for Hope Village, for wisdom for himself…

And somewhere in this prayer, exhausted by loss of blood, too little sleep, and too much anxiety, David fell asleep.

He awoke to the sound of his own moans, so painful was his shoulder. He also felt a series of sharp pains in his back from sleeping on a pile of rope and a feeling of nausea from breathing the fetid, oily air of the tiny cabin, It was the nausea that sent him quickly up to the grate in the ceiling for a few gulps of fresh air. When his head and stomach had settled down, he looked at his watch. One-twenty-five. They should be arriving at Isla Margarita any moment.

The boat lurched; David nearly lost his footing, and realized another reason for the nausea he'd felt—the seas had risen, and the boat was pitching far more drastically than when they'd left.

He pulled a shirt out of his duffel, shrugged painfully into it, and poked his head out the cabin door. Francisco stood at the wheel, his clothes whipping about him in a strong wind. He looked troubled. "Anything wrong?" David asked.

Francisco gestured toward the ocean ahead of them. "We are making poor time," he said. "There is a strong headwind, and the motor is

234   The Missionary

laboring. It is the carburetor. I should stop and clean it. We will get there sooner if I do. How is your shoulder?"

"Sore," David said, in ludicrous understatement. "Thanks for bandaging it. How far are we?"

"About halfway."

"*Halfway?* I thought we would be there by now."

Francisco shrugged. "Normally, yes, four hours. But today, with this wind, these swells…" He shut the motor down. "I will fix the carburetor. We will make better time."

Within seconds, the boat turned sideways to the wind, and the chop and swells pushed the boat violently side to side, making it difficult to stand.

Grabbing the door jamb, David looked around. Behind them, the high mountains around Caracas still stood menacingly close, it seemed to him. He could not see an island ahead. Could he trust Francisco? Was Francisco actually in Guzman's pay?

David ducked back into the cabin, reached into his duffel, and pulled out his cell phone. He came back out onto the deck and found a place somewhat out of the wind. He sat and, using his feet, braced himself between the cabin wall and the gunwale. Maybe Christie had tried to call.

There was one message. But it wasn't from Christie.

"David, this is Carlos. I am sorry for the delay in contacting you, but it has been very dangerous and hectic since we last spoke. I have a plan to help you, and I need you to call me so we can determine a rendezvous point. I have a new phone number. 58-416-299-8457. Call me immediately when you get this message."

What had Stephen said in his email? "*Your previous contact is not who he said he was…*" Stephen had also said that there might be two hostile groups looking for him. And if Carlos wasn't working for the CIA, he was probably working for the drug cartel, or whoever had set him up.

David played the message again. Funny. He'd been so desperate yesterday to hear back from Carlos. Now, the sound of his voice filled

David with disgust—not just for the man who'd used and deceived him, but also for himself, and for the stupid decisions he'd made. He was briefly tempted to dial the number just to ream Carlos out, but he'd made enough foolish, impulsive decisions. It was time to follow the advice of his brother and stay off the cell phone.

David saved the message so he could give Carlos's new number to his brother next time he emailed him.

There were also two "calls missed" that didn't leave messages—both from the same Caracas number, which he didn't recognize. But the authorities would have his number by now; these two calls were probably from them.

David peered around the cabin to see what Francisco was up to. He sat on the deck, screwdriver in hand, surrounded by greasy carburetor parts. He looked at David and grinned, several teeth missing.

"Is someone meeting me on the island?" David yelled through the wind.

"Si," Francisco said. "I have radioed him already that we will be late."

David nodded. "Aren't we drifting in the wrong direction in this wind?"

Francisco shrugged again, his all-purpose gesture. "Si. And also the current. But I know these waters very well."

David sat back out of the wind. He hadn't been worried about getting lost. He'd been worried about straying into the path of a Coast Guard vessel. Or capsizing in this increasingly choppy water.

David was suddenly amused. He had stared death in the face several times in the past twenty-four hours—fleeing Guzman and the drug lords, being shot and pursued by police... Was it luck or the hand of God that had kept him so far? He realized, to his surprise, that the fear of death had somehow left him. Was this how soldiers felt, caught in a fierce firefight? No longer afraid of dying, he was more afraid of what lay ahead should he live.

CHAPTER TWENTY-SEVEN

When Coast Guard CG-403 was secured at the Coast Guard dock, Captain Castillo-Garcia came to the room below deck where his passengers were being held. "It is time for us to disembark. Come with me, por favor," the captain said. As they stood, a guard approached Felix and motioned for him to turn around. The guard put Felix's hands behind his back and placed him in handcuffs. The children stared. Isabel began to cry.

Christie said, "Captain, he has done nothing wrong. And you're frightening the children. Can't you leave his hands free? He's a fisherman, not a commando."

The captain looked at her haughtily. "It is a matter of procedure, Senora Eller. It is required. If you prefer, we can handcuff you and Senora Suturos as well, so that Senor Suturos is not singled out. No? Then come, we must disembark."

The group made their way up the steps to the main deck. The gunwale door was open, leading to a gangplank descending to the dock below. As they walked down the gangplank, Christie noticed a small man in a neatly pressed uniform waiting on the dock, puffing a cigarette, standing somewhat apart from the soldiers. He was clearly someone of importance. And Christie noticed that his eyes never left her as she descended.

At noon, Stephen Eller received a call from Art Snell: "Hey, man, your brother's generating more interest than I anticipated. Vansant wants to

238 The Missionary

meet with you this afternoon. He's here on Capitol Hill meeting with the Senate Intelligence Committee and wants to meet in my office. I didn't bother to tell him this was my day off, since he was in town already and your situation's urgent. So I'm on my way in—but you *really* owe me one now."

"Wow. Art, what can I—"

"Vansant thought he would be done in time to meet us at two-thirty. I also called Rosa Lopez with the State Department. She'll try to make it."

At two-fifteen, Stephen left his office and walked to the J. Edgar Hoover Building on Pennsylvania Avenue. It was a clear, sunny day, although with the tall buildings the only sky visible was directly overhead. There was a chill in the air. Passing through security, he took the stairs to the fourth floor—the habit of a former athlete, now a desk jockey, who didn't want to get completely out of shape. He turned right out of the stairwell and walked to office 453. The receptionist led him to a small conference room. Art was already there, as was Rosa Lopez, a petite woman with dark red hair. Stephen guessed she was in her forties.

After introductions, Rosa said, "Art was just telling me about your brother's situation. Sounds very serious."

"Younger brothers can be a pain," Art said. "I've got one too. My brother is, or I should say was, into motorcycles. He now has two artificial knees and a deep scar across his face to prove it."

Art seemed set to launch into the whole gory brother-on-a-motorcycle story when Dennis Vansant entered the room. More introductions, then Art said, "Well, since this is supposed to be my day off and all of you have other things to do, let's get right to the point."

Art was looking at Vansant and Rosa. "I've given both of you most of the details of how Stephen's brother, David, got himself into this mess down in Venezuela, so we won't do another history lesson here. The main thing is what, if anything, can or should be done now."

Vansant spoke: "Stephen, Art says you've talked to your brother by phone and email. Tell me again what he says regarding the CIA."

"He first contacted me two days ago," Stephen said. "Before that, I had absolutely no clue my brother was involved in this mess. When he phoned me, he said he thought he might be in some trouble because he'd been recruited by a guy named Carlos Edwards to work for the CIA as some kind of courier. He said he'd been given one briefcase, which he suspected contained money, although it was locked and he didn't open it. He delivered it the day before the coup attempt. Then Carlos Edwards instructed him to pick up another briefcase containing money."

"How does he know the second briefcase contained money?" Vansant asked.

"Because after everything went south, he opened it to see if there were any clues to help him out of this mess. He said it was full of one-hundred dollar bills. Stacks of them."

"Are you aware that there is a ruling issued by the United States Congress prohibiting the CIA from recruiting missionaries without the specific approval of the President?" Vansant said.

"Yes. I'm also aware that the CIA is sometimes accused of coloring outside the lines."

Vansant glared at Stephen, then softened his expression, seemingly as an exercise of will. "The CIA was not involved in any way in this coup attempt. And we don't recruit missionaries or journalists to work for us, plain and simple."

Stephen tried to remain calm. "I know that's the official line, but my brother—"

"Mr. Eller—let's get one thing straight at the outset. We consider your brother to be a fool."

Stephen's hands clenched. If this CIA troll thought he could—

But Vansant continued. "He's a fool, but he's an American fool, and the last thing we want to do—the last thing we *would* do—is leave him in the hands of a rogue nation. I'd like to wring his neck—and I suspect you would too—but I don't want Guzman to do it."

Stephen nodded, only slightly reassured. He still didn't know whether he believed this man. "Thank you."

"But there are some things I need to know," Vansant continued. "Such as: Why is your brother so convinced, if indeed he is, that this is a CIA op?"

Rosa asked, "Did your brother try to verify the identity of this person…this Carlos Edwards…who supposedly recruited him?"

"My brother is at best naïve and at worst dumb about things like this. He said Edwards seemed legit, but he didn't seek any verifiable proof. So whether the CIA was involved or not, my brother is running for his life with a briefcase full of money and the firm belief that he was working for the CIA."

Vansant was impassive. Stephen decided to press the matter. "Look, you can see where this is going. It's immaterial whether my brother *was* working for the CIA. The fact is, he *thinks* he was working for them. And if under duress or torture he tells the Venezuelans he was working for the CIA, the political fallout for our government and the intelligence community will be the same as if it were true."

Rosa looked at Vansant seated next to her. "He's right."

Vansant scratched his head, obviously annoyed. "Art, what's your take on this?"

"It's simple. I think you have to get to Stephen's brother before Guzman's men do."

"Nothing simple about it," Vansant replied. "Besides," he said, turning to Stephen, "our sources think your brother was probably working for the drug cartel. Knowingly or not. If so, he'll probably end up disappearing with no trace in fairly short order."

"In which case—what? End of problem?" Stephen said.

"I didn't say—"

"We let a few South American drug lords knock off an American missionary who just happened to get crossways with them while he was trying to do a good thing, and we're happy about it because it snatches our fat out of the fire?"

"Hey, listen, Eller," Vansant said, getting hot. "Nobody put your brother in harm's way but himself. He created his own problems. Not us."

But Stephen guessed that there might be something else going through Vansant's mind. The CIA could make people disappear without a trace too, and then blame it on someone else. "Mr. Vansant, I realize that the CIA may have more than one option to silence my brother and prevent embarrassment to the U.S. I don't mean to offend you, but anything other than David's rescue is not an option, as far as I'm concerned, and I want to see any other options taken off the table now."

Vansant's face had turned red, but once again he made a visible effort to cool off. "I've already said we want to get your brother out of there safely. We don't go around killing U.S. citizens on foreign soil or anywhere else. So let's put that speculation to bed right now. But you'd better understand just how sensitive this situation is. The reputation of more than just the intelligence community could be severely damaged here. And not just with Venezuela—frankly, who cares about Venezuela—but with the international community. And no offense, Eller, but regardless of the fact that this is your brother we're talking about, the decision as to how that threat will be eliminated will be made at a level a bit above your pay grade."

"Okay, we've talked about the general parameters," Art said. "Let's get practical now and look at some options. Stephen, didn't you tell me you knew where your brother was hiding?"

"I know where he'll be tonight."

The change in Vansant's expression was subtle—just a slight flickering or widening of the eyes—but Stephen knew that he'd just confirmed something of vital interest to Vansant. He could never outplay someone as experienced as Vansant at his own game, he knew, but he also had no intention of giving up any advantage. He said, "But I'm not going to reveal that information until I have Mr. Vansant's word that the CIA will attempt to *rescue* my brother."

Vansant looked at Art and lowered his voice. "Look—I can't commit until I have more information. We don't have any military assets on the ground in Venezuela. And if we were to go in there and be discovered, we would suffer the same public relations problem Eller's brother may cause. But tell me where he is—or where he'll be, and when—and we'll do our best to get him out."

Art looked at Stephen for a response.

Vansant's assurances didn't guarantee a thing. But Stephen also knew that he had little choice. Whether by Guzman, the drug lords, or the CIA, David could die soon. David's only hope was for Stephen to negotiate a rescue. And Stephen's best chance for that was to trust the word of Vansant.

"Okay. Mr. Vansant, I'll take you at your word. I'll give you my brother's location if you'll agree to try to rescue him."

Vansant softened. "I understand the damage your brother could cause our country if he were caught by Guzman. I'll agree to take this back to our situation room and see what we can do. But I can't guarantee he'll be rescued. No one in their right mind could guarantee that. The department may decide they don't have a dog in this fight. In that case, they might do nothing."

"If there's anything our department can do to help you assess the situation," Rosa said to Vansant, "let me know. We do at least have some people on the ground there who could advise you of current conditions in the neighborhood where David might be hiding." Vansant nodded.

Stephen pulled a 3x5 card out of his pocket and slid it across the table to Vansant. "According to his last email, this is where my brother will be hiding as of tonight. I think he'll be staying for a couple of days."

"Can you still communicate with him?" Vansant asked.

Stephen explained the email and cell phone possibilities.

"Give me his cell number, and send him another email telling him to stay put," Vansant said. "But don't say anything about a rescue attempt. I don't want to tip anyone off. Or get your brother's hopes up."

After jotting down David's cell number, Stephen stood and extended his hand. "Mr. Vansant, sorry for raising my voice, but—"

"Hey," Vansant interrupted with a wave of his hand, "no need to apologize. If my brother was in a similar mess, I'd be on edge too."

Walking back into his office a few minutes later, Stephen glanced at his watch. Three-fifteen. He immediately sent another email to David.

I'm working on a plan. I need you to stay put at the place you told me you were going. Don't leave to go anywhere. I need to be able to locate you at any hour. Keep checking email as often as possible.

Three hundred and seventy miles east of Caracas, on the island of Grenada, Carlos Edward's new secure satellite cell phone rang. Only two people knew this phone's number—Carlos's contact and handler, code-named Leprechaun, and David Eller. Or perhaps someone else, if David Eller had been captured. Only one way to find out. Carlos pushed the green button to answer the call.

Tecero pushed his men relentlessly in his search for David Eller. A couple of his men went to Silvia's Cocina de Sopa to talk to the cook. When they learned that Silvia had gone to Puerto La Cruz on holiday, Tecero dispatched more men to Puerto La Cruz, where they questioned every hotel and bed-and-breakfast. By three-thirty p.m., when Tecero was already furious that no one had located the woman named Silvia, he was told that no one had found Francisco's boat, or the fisherman himself. Tecero hit the roof. He ordered that two men be stationed at the dock twenty-four hours a day, to make sure that they did not miss him when he returned.

CHAPTER TWENTY-EIGHT

Christie had been in the tiny room for over an hour by herself.

Their arrival at the police station had been horrible, a parent's nightmare. A woman in uniform had taken Davy, kicking and wailing, his arms reaching out to her as he screamed, "Mommy! Please! I want to stay with you! Mommy, let me stay with you!" The expression on his face showed the absolute terror only a four-year-old can feel. When Christie had tried to move toward him, two armed guards had grabbed her—in full view of her son—and forced her down a dimly lit hall and into this room, where they had shoved her into a chair and then left, locking the door.

She was sitting now on one of three wooden chairs pulled up to a small rectangular wooden table. A single light bulb dangled from the ceiling; the room smelled faintly like sweat or urine mixed with the scent of musty wood. One wall held a large mirror framed like a window; Christie assumed it was a two-way mirror and she was being watched. Dark stains splattered one wall: old dried blood? The air was humid and thick. Looking into the large mirror, she saw that her hair was matted, uneven, and sticking to her face. She looked awful, worse than any early morning pre-shower, pre-coffee time she could remember. Without new makeup, her facial burn scars stood out, especially the more grotesque one on her left cheek, one she often attempted to hide with a hand or a high collar.

She needed a shower, clean clothes, warm food, some sleep. But that could wait. Her mind was focused on Davy. Somewhere, he was screaming for her—she knew this with a mother's certainty, as if she could hear his screams, as if her skin vibrated with them. But she had no idea where they had taken him, or what they might be doing to him. Surely they would not be cruel to him. Surely not.

She sat silent when they'd first brought her to this room, thinking that someone would come soon to speak to her. But after several minutes alone, panic for Davy's welfare had overwhelmed her. She'd pounded on the door, screaming for someone to let her out to see her child. Once, she'd even thrown her shoe at the mirror in hopes of breaking the glass, but it had ricocheted back toward her, bouncing off the table onto the floor.

Crying, she'd put her face up to the mirror and pushed at it with her hands. "I know you're out there and you can see me! Please let me see my child!" she'd wailed.

But it had been futile; no one had answered. Eventually she'd pushed away from the mirror and collapsed into one of the chairs.

Exhausted, for the past fifteen minutes she'd sat quietly with her head on the table, praying. Once again, she felt the cocktail of rage, love, and worry for her husband. One minute she prayed for his safety, the next minute she rehearsed the anger she would unleash at him if she ever saw him again.

Finally, she heard the latch move and looked up to see the door open. It was General Dukai, the round-faced officer who had met them at the dock. He wore the same green uniform decorated with gold stripes and some kind of colorful bars pinned to his shoulders. He was accompanied by two armed policemen.

Before General Dukai could speak, Christie said, "I want to see my son!"

He seated himself across from her in one of the wooden chairs while one guard stood by the door and the other stood behind Christie's chair.

"There will be plenty of time to see your son if you cooperate with us. We need to ask you some questions. If I believe you are telling me the truth, you will see your son soon. But if you do not cooperate, you may not see your son for a long time."

"Where have you taken him? He's a small child! He's *terrified!* All these uniforms, guns…"

Smiling, Dukai simply nodded. "As I mentioned to you at the dock, my name is General Raldo Dukai, and I am in charge of the investigation into the attempted assassination of President Guzman. We believe – correction -- we *know* your husband was involved in the plot, and we need to locate him for questioning."

"Please, General, can I see my son?" Christie said, reaching her hands imploringly across the table. "There is nothing I can tell you that I haven't already told you and the other officers. I do not know where my husband is!" She began to weep.

"Mrs. Eller, there are others besides me and my men who are looking for your husband. I am speaking of individuals who are more brutal than my men. If those individuals find your husband first, he will certainly be tortured and killed."

This was a new thought. Looking at Dukai with bleary eyes, she asked, "Who else besides you and your people would be looking for David?"

"Your husband was hired to pass money to the men who tried to assassinate President Guzman. We think your husband still has some of their money. Did your husband have a briefcase with him when you saw him last?"

"Yes. I thought it was his briefcase. The one he always carries."

"It was a briefcase full of blood money, money paid to those who tried to assassinate our president. The people behind this coup attempt will want the rest of their money back. They will also want to silence your husband, because he can implicate them. This means that your husband is in grave danger."

"Last night," Christie said, "before we left in Felix's boat, my husband told me he was going to turn himself in to the U.S. Embassy."

"Well, that is not what he did, Mrs. Eller. Today your husband stole a police car near the docks and managed to evade several policemen. He is hiding somewhere in the area where he left you, and we intend to find him. If he tries to run, he will be shot. You can help your husband by telling us what you know of his habits, his friends or contacts, and where you think he may be hiding."

She wearily shook her head, staring into her lap. An odd thought: She was no longer shocked by things like stolen police cars or shootings. It was as if she'd been dragged into an action movie but at the same time was still watching from the audience, powerless. Was this what victims of abuse felt…numb, in a fog of hopelessness?

She forced herself to think. What Dukai was telling her might very well be the truth. David was in grave danger—but, she firmly believed, David would also be in grave danger if Dukai got his hands on him. Guzman would eventually bring David to trial and most likely execute him. No, David's best chance was for her to stick to her story. Besides, she was far too tired and emotionally spent to think on her feet.

She and Felix had coordinated their stories as a precaution after leaving the dock the night before, just in case they were apprehended. They'd both agreed that David's connections to Silvia's restaurant and Guillermo's boat were the most vital things not to divulge. And as tired as she was, she was resolute still that she would not reveal these things, even though she guessed that David was no longer at either location.

"Did you have plans to communicate with your husband when you got to Grenada?"

"Of course. I planned to email him."

"What is the email address?" Dukai asked.

"deller@juno.com." she replied.

Dukai wrote this down. "And we have obtained your husband's cell phone number," which Dukai then recited. "Is this the correct number?"

"Yes." It would be pointless to deny it, and she knew that David wouldn't answer a call from an unfamiliar number.

"Have you tried to phone your husband on his cell since leaving him?" Dukai asked.

"No, we agreed not to use the cell, since we knew that you and your people would probably be listening in," she said matter-of-factly.

Dukai smiled. "You and your husband are very clever, aren't you?"

He stood and started to leave the room.

"I want to see my child!" she demanded.

Dukai turned. "When I am sure you have told me everything."

She tried to stand, but the guard pushed her back into the chair. "Wait…" she said.

Dukai paused in the doorway, his hand still on the doorknob, and turned to look at her.

He had asked about David's contacts. Perhaps there was one thing she could tell him that would take some of the pressure off David, send their search in another direction, and even convince Dukai to let her have her son again. She paused a moment, weighing the possible consequences, evaluating whether this could possibly hurt David, then plunged ahead. "There was one man David spent some time with in the past few days. Neither of us knew much about him. But perhaps he knows something about the coup attempt."

Dukai took a step back toward the table. "What makes you think he would know something about the attempt on our president's life?"

Christy shrugged. "I don't know for sure. It's just that I thought he was hiding something. And trying to manipulate David. And the timing—David met him and had lunch with him just before all of this began."

"His name?"

"Carlos Edwards. He claimed to be a financial advisor, or stockbroker, or something like that. He visited Hope Village once and contributed some money."

Dukai smiled wryly. "A briefcase full of it?"

"No. A check."

Dukai waited. "Is there something else you can tell me about Senor Edwards?"

"That's all. Except that I never trusted him. He was not a truthful man."

Dukai nodded. "Thank you, Senora Eller. We will look into this Senor Edwards." He turned to go.

"My son!" Christie yelled. "You said I could have—"

"I said that your son would be returned to you when you have told me everything. Of that, Senora Eller, I am not yet convinced."

Dukai paused in front of the closed doorway to the tiny interrogation room where Felix Suturos sat waiting and, no doubt, trembling. But he was not planning his interrogation of Suturos. He was evaluating what he had just heard from Senora Eller.

So she had identified Carlos Edwards. Dukai had expected the name of Carlos Edwards to arise in his investigation, but he had not expected it quite so soon. Senora Eller had played it like a pro—he had to admire her. Give him the name of Carlos Edwards, and perhaps he would let her have her son back, and also send his men in search of Edwards, thereby taking some of the heat off David Eller and allowing him the opportunity to escape.

But that would not happen. For now, David Eller would remain the primary target of the official investigation. And Carlos Edwards...

Dukai would pretend that he had never heard Christie Eller mention that name.

Commander Nicolas Torres was *muy furioso*. So far this day he had kicked a wastebasket across his office and through a window, given a private such a dressing down that he had reduced him to tears, and then ordered him to clean the toilets with his toothbrush, and fired his driver because he would not drive on the sidewalk to avoid a traffic jam.

Now he paced back and forth alone on the packed dirt of the parade ground, chain-smoking cigarettes and seething, as he obsessed on the reason for his anger: His prisoner had been taken away from him.

And far too soon. It was true that they'd learned nothing new from the commando, Daniel Benjamin, in the past twenty-four hours or so, but Torres was convinced that he knew more. Despite the torture, he was still holding out. And Torres was perfectly willing to continue to torture Benjamin until he told what else he knew, or died resisting.

Either outcome was satisfactory. After all, the Israeli—a national identity he had revealed after the last round of torture—had attempted to kill *el presidente*, and deserved to die for that offense. If he died on the table of interrogation, rather than before a firing squad, it made little difference.

Who was head of Special Forces and Senior Commander of the Presidential Guard Regiment? He himself, Nicolas Torres. Who had been in charge of the president's protection the night of the assassination attempt, and therefore deserved credit for the fact that the president had escaped with his life, and one assassin had been killed and another captured? Again, Nicolas Torres himself. Who had tortured the prisoner within an inch of his life but still kept him alive to spill his guts, providing the information that now fueled the frantic manhunt for the remaining members of the team of plotters? Torres.

And yet his prisoner had been taken away?

And Torres knew who had ordered the interrogation stopped. General Raldo Dukai. Dukai had resisted Torres's interrogation from the beginning. If Dukai had had his way, they'd never have found out about Eller, or Los Tiburones restaurant, or the identities of the rest of the assassins.

Why?

Torres threw a half-smoked cigarette onto the dirt, paced a minute or two more, and then lit another.

Why indeed? Why had Dukai tried to stand between Torres and his rightful prisoner?

There were reasons, of course.

First, Dukai was weak, one of the few surviving holdovers from the old regime. But this was now the army of President Armando Guzman. And there was no place for weakness in Venezuela's new army. If Dukai was squeamish about blood, he should resign and let officers of resolve and unwavering commitment—such as Nicolas Torres—move up the chain of command.

But there had to be more. Was Dukai maneuvering for even greater power and dominance? Of course. As everyone did, Torres included.

But Torres's gut told him that Dukai was up to something more than that. And there was no way Torres would allow himself to be outmaneuvered by a short, scrawny coward like Dukai. He would find out what Dukai was up to and use it against him. Even if he had to make it up.

After two hours, Dukai's interrogation of Felix Suturos had produced nothing. Suturos simply corroborated Mrs. Eller's story. Both claimed they had left David on the La Guaira dock at around 1 a.m. the night before.

But Dukai knew that Suturos had the information he wanted, and he knew that eventually he would get it. Unlike Christie, Suturos could be charged with the crime of aiding a fugitive, since he had transported David as far as the docks.

"There is something I would like you to think about," Dukai said. "In a locker on your boat, we found a wrapped stack of $100 bills. I would like to know where that money came from. Perhaps you received that money from David Eller for helping his family flee Venezuela. Perhaps you are protecting David Eller, and will choose not to answer. But if you do not cooperate, you will be tried for treasonous acts. I think you would be convicted, and if so, you would be sent to prison for life. In that case, you might never see your wife and child again."

He slowly stood and walked out. He returned fifteen minutes later to a perspiring Felix Suturos, who told him that the $5000 in crisp $100 bills had been given to him by David Eller to pay Senora Eller's expenses.

"Expenses?" Dukai smiled. "Senora Eller must have a lot of expenses. Was Senor Eller carrying a briefcase when you last saw him?"

"Si."

"And did the money he gave you for so-called expenses come from this briefcase?"

"Si, I believe so."

Si. Same answer as Mrs. Eller. No assassination, therefore no pay-off, so Eller kept the money. If Dukai could find David Eller, he would also find the briefcase full of money.

Dukai was a skilled interrogator, often able to extract information no one else could—not even Torres, with his electrodes and hot irons. Dukai read people well, intuitively grasping their points of vulnerability. Suturos, for instance, was fairly simple. A strong man, and loyal, not someone who would break quickly. But Dukai had merely to turn the pressure up a notch, wait patiently as this simple fisherman wrestled with the implications, then turn the pressure up a notch more...

In this way, Suturos was soon telling Dukai that Senora Eller was intending to fly back to the United States from Grenada and await her husband, who was also trying to find a way to escape. Suturos also said that David had originally intended to leave with them on his boat, but had had a change of heart when he discovered that the Duncans had been arrested.

Dukai silently cursed himself for not keeping the Duncans in custody. Why had he not considered that Eller might have protective feelings toward the elderly couple? "How did David know the Duncans had been arrested?"

"We heard it on my van radio," Suturos said, then explained how they'd driven to the dock in Suturos's van and left it parked there. He did not know whether David had used the van after that or not. Dukai's men had already found the van, so Dukai did not doubt this part of Suturos's story.

Dukai stepped out into the hallway. He lit a cigarette and stood for a moment, leaning against the faded, discolored wall. He knew that the search of boats at the La Guaira dock had turned up nothing, but he decided to order the Coast Guard to search all fishing boats headed out

254 The Missionary

to sea, especially those headed toward Grenada. Eller carried enough cash to entice some fisherman to take him anywhere he wanted to go. Dukai hoped that the drug lord's goons hadn't found Eller either, but there was no way to know for sure—unless a body turned up. For now, he had no choice but to presume that Eller had somehow managed to escape. With the kind of money he was carrying, it would not surprise Dukai if Eller tried to make it to Grenada on another boat by paying a ridiculous amount to counter the substantial risk.

He opened the door of the other interrogation room but didn't enter.

"Señora Eller, we know from Senor Suturos that you were intending to fly from Grenada back to the United States in hopes of rejoining your husband. We also know that your husband was planning to go with you on Senor Suturos's vessel, but changed his mind at the last minute. This is true, no?"

She nodded her head.

Dukai stood in the doorway, thinking. He sensed the humiliation Senora Eller must be feeling. The thought occurred to him that she too was a victim of sorts. Looking at her unkempt appearance and the obvious scar on her face, he felt a certain sense of sympathy. But not sympathy only. Admiration. This was a strong woman—even a formidable one. A woman of character. And perhaps some of that strength came from whatever had given her those scars. It would be a mistake to underestimate her.

And it would be a pity if, as he suspected, he had to use and manipulate her to accomplish his goals. But if he had to, he would.

He had done all he could, at least for now. Leaving Senora Eller and Senor Suturos in their interrogation rooms, he told his staff to simply monitor them while he was gone. He called for his car and driver.

An hour later, Dukai was sitting alone at the Intercontinental Hotel bar, sipping a martini while pondering his next move. It had been a long and trying day, and his thoughts felt random. He suspected that, like the Duncans, neither Senora Eller nor Senor Suturos had any more information to give, or at least any that would help him. But everything could unravel if he did not find David Eller before the others. If the Duncans were the reason Eller had not attempted to flee with his family, maybe Senora Eller could be of significant use in smoking him out, especially if Eller found out that his family was in custody.

Tired or not, a plan began to emerge in Dukai's mind.

CHAPTER TWENTY-NINE

It was just after six p.m. when Francisco docked *La Dama Subió* at Puerto Balbez, a remote fishing dock on the west side of Isla Margarita near the village of Pampatar. David had spent the second half of the voyage on the deck—partly for the fresh air, and partly to make sure Francisco was doing what he was supposed to be doing. It had taken the fisherman three hours to clean and reassemble the carburetor and make other engine repairs, and the whole time, David had expected to be approached by a Coast Guard vessel full of automatic-weapon-toting thugs while Francisco's boat was dead in the water. In David's imagination, after he was captured and handcuffed, the guardsmen handed Francisco a bundle of cash, and the fisherman gave David his gap-toothed grin.

But it hadn't happened, and David had to admit that after Francisco's repairs, the motor ran like a charm, with a deep, regular growl, and provided plenty of power. The wind that had pushed the sea into high, rolling swells earlier had died, and it was a beautiful evening, the sun making its descent in the west amid sculpted clouds, shading the sky in shell pink and oriole orange. It surprised David that, despite his well-earned sense of failure and guilt, and his concern about those he loved, he could still feel the joy of a majestic late-fall sunset.

And that wasn't all he could feel. His shoulder throbbed, incredibly tender to the touch even a few inches from the wound. He could barely move his left arm. His forehead felt hot to his touch. The infection he'd been dreading seemed to have settled in.

Near the docks sat a red early-'90s nineties VW bus with a man leaning against it. There was no one else in sight except for a young boy poking around for crabs in the rocks nearby, and another fisherman mending his fishing nets on the deck of his moored boat.

Standing on the dock—and feeling guilty for the fantasies of betrayal he had entertained about Francisco, this gentle fisherman who had doctored his wounds—David handed him three U.S. one-hundred dollar bills. Francisco grinned broadly, "Gracias, gracias," he said. David had been certain that, without Silvia to snatch it away, Francisco would take the money. It would take most local fishermen a couple of months even at the peak of the season to realize that much cash. He pointed at Francisco and grinned. "Maybe you should use it to get that motor overhauled." Francisco laughed.

Francisco gestured toward the red VW bus parked at the end of the dock. He grabbed David's briefcase and duffel and started toward the bus.

"Wait," David said, and grabbed the briefcase from him. "I'll take this myself. The latch is broken."

The man leaning against the bus was middle-aged, thin, with reddish-brown hair, nervously smoking a cigarette. He moved to the back and opened the luggage door as they approached.

"Ian O'Leary?" David asked.

"Yes." He smiled briefly and motioned for David to get in, looking uneasily at David's heavily bandaged shoulder, blood seepage showing through his shirt.

David shook Francisco's hand. "Sleeping on the boat tonight? Returning in the morning?"

"No," he said. "I can see the lights of the airport at La Guaira and find my way home." He grinned. "If the motor continues to run, I can be back well before midnight."

David climbed into the van. Ian stood beside the van and looked in all directions one more time, then climbed into the driver's side. He cranked the ignition and spoke for the first time: "Welcome to Margarita Island." He spoke English with a hint of Irish accent.

"Thank you. I just wish it were under better conditions."

"Likewise," Ian said. "That's why I chose this remote dock. Now if I can get us back to the hotel without having an accident, all will be well."

David smiled. "How far?"

"About forty-five minutes. It's on the northeast shore. I'll take the main roads through the tourist sections, where there are lots of cars and people to get lost among. I'm sure you're hungry, but let's not stop, if you don't mind. I asked my cook to save you some food. However, if you don't mind my asking…"

Was he about to ask for more money? "What is it?"

"Are you in need of immediate medical help? My contact said nothing about you being wounded."

David thought about his apparent infection. But… "It's a gunshot wound," he said. "I don't think I can take a chance on a hospital emergency room. Too many questions."

"Indeed not," Ian said. "Bullet still in?"

"Passed clear through."

"Lucky. Bone damage?"

"If so, only minor."

"You're the fortunate one, aren't you? Never fear, then. We can patch you up at the hotel."

They rode in silence for a while, then David asked, "Where are you from, and how long have you been living on Margarita?"

Ian smiled. He added more accent as he spoke, "Originally from Ireland by way of Nova Scotia. Me father was Irish, me mum was Brazilian. They met while working on a cruise ship in the Caribbean, fell in love, and I was born six months after they docked. I bummed around for a few years after going to culinary school, working on commercial fishing boats out of New England, then as a cook on St. Martins. I loved the spirits and the women!" He laughed. "Fifteen years ago I met me wife under Big Ben in London one day and she set me straight. She's from York, had a bit of an inheritance and always wanted the island life. She has a good head for business, my wife, better than mine. Me, I'm a fixer upper...can fix most anything. So ten years ago we bought this hotel and have been here ever since. It's not a bad life, actually. Guzman has made it worse for tourism the last few years, so no one I know would have been sorry to see him go."

They passed several premium hotels on the white sand beaches. They were driving on Avenue Bolivar; David had been on this street once before with Christie. As they passed the Hilton Margarita and Suites, now abandoned, grounds covered with weeds, he recalled the three glorious days of R & R they'd shared together a couple of years before, swimming and sunbathing at the huge pool—Christie, of course, sunbathing in a sun dress to hide her scars—eating in fabulous restaurants, and in general rekindling their romance. It had been like another honeymoon.

Something he was unlikely to ever experience again.

Striding into the room where Christie was being held, Dukai said, "Senora Eller, we have arranged for you to spend the night at a local hotel with your son. You are not under arrest, but you are being detained for the time being for possible further questioning. Two of my men will accompany you to the hotel and stay just outside your door for the night. I hope you find the accommodations comfortable."

He leaned across the small table, getting close so that she would not miss the importance of his words. "It would be foolish for you to attempt to leave the hotel with your child." He paused, staring into her face, then leaned back and smiled. "I will speak with you again tomorrow morning."

"What about Felix and his family?" she asked.

"We have released the wife and daughter. Senor Suturos will be held here at police headquarters tonight for further questioning tomorrow."

Dukai stood and left the room. In the hallway, he stopped next to one of the men he had instructed to convey Mrs. Eller to the hotel and said, "Disengage the TV in the room Senora Eller will be occupying. I do not want her able to watch any news tonight."

A half-hour later, Dukai sat on a stool in the government television station. He straightened his uniform as the countdown to airtime began. When a light appeared below the camera lens, the reporter seated next to Dukai began to speak.

"*Buenos noches*, and *bienvenidos* to late night news. We have with us General Raldo Dukai, head of the coup investigation, who has a late-breaking announcement with regard to the attempted assassination of President Guzman." He turned to Dukai. "General, can you bring us up to date?"

Dukai pushed his shoulders back in an effort to expand his slight, 5' 7" frame. "We are making significant progress in the investigation. We have arrested five JAM members we believe were involved in the assassination attempt, including the chef at the house where the attempt occurred and two limo drivers who brought guests to the house. One of the assassins is dead, and another is wounded and in our custody. We also have detailed physical descriptions of the two assassins we have not yet apprehended. We believe there were a total of four gunmen involved in the coup attempt, with a support group of many more. We will hunt them down. We will bring every one of them to justice."

Turning to look directly into the camera, he said, "Also, today the Venezuelan Coast Guard detained and searched a fishing vessel and found on board the wife and son of David Eller, hiding in the cabin of the vessel. David Eller is wanted for questioning in this matter."

A video clip of Felix Suturos being interrogated began to play, taken from the DVD Dukai had brought with him from police headquarters. He'd purposefully selected those clips in which an anguished-looking Suturos appeared to be spilling his guts.

"This vessel," Dukai continued, "owned and operated by a man named Felix Suturos, whom you see here, was attempting to flee to Grenada. David Eller was not on board.

"Unfortunately, while Senora Eller and her son were being transferred onto the Coast Guard vessel, she slipped off the ladder with her son in her arms and fell about four meters back onto the deck of the smaller vessel. Both Senora Eller and her son were seriously injured. A medical evacuation helicopter transported them to University Hospital here in Caracas. Senora Eller is in critical condition. The boy is in serious but stable condition."

Dukai paused for effect. "At present, we do not know David Eller's whereabouts. It is sad that we cannot get word to him of this most unfortunate and tragic accident. Hopefully he is listening to this broadcast. If he decides to come forward for questioning, we of course promise to take him first to the bedside of his wife and son."

Leaning toward the camera, he said, "If you have information that will help me with this investigation, I ask you to please contact me at this phone number."

A number flashed on the screen.

From his room in Grenada, Carlos watched the interview of General Dukai on the Venezuelan evening news. He knew immediately, when Dukai leaned forward and said, "If you have information that will help me with this investigation …," the words were designed to send a specific message. *I hope Eller isn't seeing this,* Carlos thought.

What Dukai's message confirmed for Carlos was: first, Christie Eller was in Venezuelan custody. Second, David Eller was not in Venezuelan custody. Third, commando Danny Benjamin was still alive. And fourth, General Dukai was getting desperate.

Carlos scribbled down the phone number shown on the screen.

He decided to not yet tell Hawkeye that Danny was, most likely, still alive. After all, Hawkeye still needed some persuading. And Carlos hadn't yet told Hawkeye of all he still wanted Hawk and Zach to accomplish. Best to keep the news about Danny to himself for now, until he'd decided how best to use it.

After another forty minutes, David and Ian arrived at Le Flamboyant Hotel on the northeast corner of Isla Margarita, just across the street from the beach. The small, intimate hotel was already well lit, though it was not yet dusk. Ian drove the van up the circular driveway, hidden from the street by a white stucco wall. The open-air entrance and registration area contained a large seating area for reading and relaxation, decorated with tile floors and white stucco pillars. Typical Venezuelan architecture, with a warm, charming feel. The hotel was small by American standards—two stories high, and David guessed that it had no more than fifty or sixty rooms.

Ian carried David's duffel while David clung to his briefcase. He was relieved to see that there were no other guests in the registration area. Ian pushed through a half-door leading him behind the pink stucco registration counter, where he grabbed a key, then emerged and motioned for David to follow him. Small floodlights illumined the area. Lights from the pool lent a bluish shimmer to everything, like an underwater fairy world. Davy would love it. The grounds were a tropical garden of palms and other shrubs. The walls, ceiling, and area rugs were done in hues of reds, blues, greens, yellows and browns in a variety of patterns, like so many Venezuelan establishments and homes.

"Please, allow me to pay for my room," David said.

"We'll worry about payment later," Ian said. "Right now you can put your things in your room, then let's hurry to the dining room so you can eat."

Ian installed him in room 104—on the bottom floor at the front of the hotel, nearest the street. The air-conditioned room was modest, containing a king-size bed with an orange-patterned bedspread, a

264 The Missionary

couple of nightstands, and a dresser with mirror. Double glass doors led to a small private veranda overlooking the garden and the hotel entrance. There was a small private bath but no television. That meant that he wouldn't be able to watch the news to find out the latest on the hunt for him. But he was grateful that the other guests at the hotel most likely hadn't seen his picture on the screen. He would just have to find another source for news.

Locking the door behind him, David followed Ian to a large, open-air dining area where a couple of waiters were already dismantling the buffet. Ian motioned David toward one of the tables, then spoke to one of the waiters. Then he joined David at his table. Soon a blond in her late thirties appeared with a tray of food. Another, larger woman followed with a second tray of food. There was far more on the two trays than David could possibly eat.

"David, this is my wife, Helen," Ian said, as the blond placed her tray on the table next to the one where they sat.

David stood. "Nice to meet you," he said. "And so much food!"

But Helen's attention was fixed not on David's face, but on his shoulder. She shot a stern look at Ian. "This man is wounded," she said in a heavy English accent. She moved closer and touched David's shoulder as if reading it through her fingertips. "And in pain. Didn't you think that might need some attention first?" Then she smiled at David. "Forgive my husband. He thinks of his appetites before anything. But this food will keep. The first thing you need is a shower, and then you need to let Ian doctor your wounds and give you something for the pain. And the injury is from…" She looked up questioningly.

"Let's just say it's a type of wound I've had some experience with," Ian said.

"Ah." Helen looked into David's face from just inches away. "You've been through the wars, then, haven't you?" She peered into his eyes intently, and touched his face with her hand. Ordinarily, David would have been put off by such intimacy from a stranger, but somehow, with this woman who apparently recognized few boundaries of personal space, it seemed appropriate. "But you're not a soldier. You *are* a fighter." She smiled. "And a man of compassion. Off to your room now. Hot shower first, and then Ian will doctor you up and we'll feed you." She laughed. "If you're still awake."

It had only been, in truth, a couple of days since David's last hot shower, but as the water cascaded over his head and down his chest, it felt as if it had been years. He wished he could have stayed under it until the hot water ran out, but he could already feel himself fading, and he did want some food. He shampooed one-handed—no easy task, he discovered—and soaped up and rinsed, then with great reluctance turned the water off.

A minute later, wrapped in his damp towel, he came into the bedroom where Ian had a healthy assortment of first-aid supplies laid out on the bed. Ian motioned toward a stool. "Sit here, so I can easily get to you front and back," he said. When David was seated, Ian first examined the wound carefully, then used betadine wipes to clean it. "I know you just soaped up, but soap really isn't a disinfectant, so these will—"

"No need to explain," David said. "We run a clinic in Caracas."

"Ah."

David winced as Ian tried to work an antibiotic cream into the wound.

Ian stepped back and looked at the wound critically, almost as if he were about to offer an opinion on art. "I don't think I'm going to stitch those up," he said. "You'll have a nice romantic scar either way, and I suspect they'll heal just as well without. Frankly, they look pretty good. You'll heal."

"You sound like an authority on gunshot wounds."

Ian shrugged and raised an eyebrow. "Let's just say that, wherever I am, I have a hard time keeping myself out of passionate causes. And when I've lived in the U.K., I've tended to hang out in my family's ancestral home. Northern Ireland."

266 The Missionary

David nodded. "Meaning you were—"

"Meaning I learned something about doctoring a variety of wounds. And meaning that the morning I left Ireland, the British military arrived at my flat to say good-bye. They arrived a little too late. Fortunately."

As he spoke, Ian applied gauze pads over the wounds and wrapped the shoulder in gauze to hold the pads in place—by far the most professional treatment David's wounds had received yet. Then he handed David a Hawaiian-type shirt from his duffel. "Just pull this over your shoulders," he said. "Don't even button it. And, I suppose—" he pointed toward David's towel—"you ought to pull on some pants."

After David had pulled on the shorts he planned to sleep in, Ian gave David two shots—one a painkiller, one an antibiotic to fight the infection. "That painkiller will knock you out," he said, "so you've got limited time to eat. Let's get to it."

David followed Ian back down the hall to the dining room, where Helen sat waiting. "*Much* better," she said. "Now I can welcome you properly." She stood on tiptoe to kiss him on both cheeks and then swept her arm toward the chair before which a king's feast sat. "Enjoy while you can; I assume Ian gave you one of his famous knock-out shots."

"I did," Ian said. "A trip to Le Flamboyant wouldn't be complete without it."

"Don't worry. My hunger will keep me awake for awhile," David said.

She winked at him. "So you say."

A variety of fruits, some cheese and cold cuts, and sweets sat on one tray. Another held plates of broiled fish, a large steaming bowl of white rice, and some sliced squash. David heaped his plate. "I just wish my wife could have been here with me," he said.

"She'll be more than welcome another time," Helen said.

"How many other guests do you have?" David asked, shoveling food into his mouth.

"This is the slow season. We have only twenty guests right now," Ian said. "If you would feel more comfortable, we can bring food to your room so you can stay out of sight while you're here. You're welcome to stay as long as you wish, although I'm sure you'll be safer getting back to the states as quickly as possible."

David nodded. "I suppose that means you've seen my face on TV. I noticed that there's no television in my room."

"No, Le Flamboyant prides itself in providing a retreat experience. We don't want our guests distracted by television. A true island get-away."

"Seen any news about the investigation today?"

"Only what I read in the paper. All I know about you is what Silvia has told me. None of us in business here on Margarita trust Guzman. He's ruined the tourist trade."

David nodded. He was finding it harder to stay awake. Hungry as he was, chewing seemed like a lot of work. "He's done worse things than that. Was my picture in the paper?"

"No. For whatever reason, the only photograph was of President Guzman with a bandage on his face. Hello? Still awake?"

David realized that he'd stopped eating. Even the thought of raising his fork seemed too hard. "I need to check my email," he mumbled.

"You're in no shape now to check email," Helen chuckled. "You can check it tomorrow. Ian?"

David felt himself being lifted to his feet and tried to help. Suddenly the hallway loomed in front of him. It appeared much too long, the perspective shifted out of proportion, but then he was sitting on his bed, and Ian was saying, "What do you sleep in?"

"What I've got on," he tried to say in reply, and apparently succeeded, because Ian eased him back down onto the pillow and pulled a sheet over him.

CHAPTER THIRTY

Shortly before eleven p.m., with his running lights glowing off the bow, Francisco returned to his docking space at La Guaira. He'd been thinking all the way back from Isla Margarita how fortunate he was to have taken David Eller there. The three hundred dollars in his pocket would not only pay for the new nets he needed, he would also buy his bride the stove she longed for. He grinned. And yes, maybe he would even take Senor Eller's advice and get the motor overhauled.

Dim lights scattered along the dock left deep shadows. It was almost dark where Francisco was maneuvering his boat.

Tying up to the dock, he heard footsteps behind him. As he began to turn, he was grabbed from behind and picked up off the ground, feet dangling. A forearm choked him. For an instant he thought he was being robbed—how could they possibly have known that, for once in his life, he had money in his pocket? He stretched his legs to try and find the weathered wood of the docks, but soon realized that the person holding him was much too strong to resist. He prayed that they would not find the new wealth hidden in the inner pocket of his weather-beaten raincoat.

He relaxed his muscles, and in return the man holding him slackened, just slightly, his hold around Francisco's neck. "Please, I am a poor fisherman," Francisco managed to choke out. "I have nothing to give you."

The man holding him lowered Francisco just enough that his toes could barely reach the dock. A second man walked slowly around in front of him. "You are Francisco, no?" the second man said, his voice deep.

"Si," he managed. The man had a large round face, with bulging eyes and flat nose.

"And you have transported a man named David Eller somewhere, no?"

Francisco forgot about fearing for his money and began fearing for his life. "Who?" he said, trying to buy time to think what to say next.

The man in front of him motioned to the man behind, and suddenly Francisco's feet left the dock again, and the choke hold was so tight he could not breathe. "Don't mess with me, Francisco!" the deep-voiced man growled.

The man behind took a couple of steps to the edge of the dock, dangling Francisco over the water.

Francisco turned his head to the side, fighting for breath, and choked out, "Please! I can't swim!"

"Well, that's good to know," the man laughed. "A fisherman who can't swim. Do you see that oily, rancid water below you? If you don't tell me where you took David Eller, we'll drop your sorry brown carcass right into it. Adios." He stepped closer so that he was growling into Francisco's right ear, so close Francisco could feel his hot breath on his ear and smell the chili peppers from the man's dinner. "Tell me. Did you take a man named David Eller somewhere tonight?"

Francisco was in no mood to lose his life to save David Eller. "Si, si!" he choked.

The man behind him stepped back and eased his grip so that once again Francisco's feet touched the dock.

Now he was facing the man with bulging eyes again.

"Tell me where you took David Eller."

"Isla Margarita," Francisco gasped, twisting his head again to find more air for his nearly squashed windpipe.

"Margarita. Where on Margarita?"

"The west end, at the fishing dock near Pampatar."

"And who was there to meet him?"

"I don't...some hombre."

"*Who?*"

The man behind took a step toward the water again.

"Some hombre named Ian, I think!" Francisco said rapidly. "I had not seen him before."

"Where was he taking him?"

"I don't know! I think he owns a hotel there."

The man with bulging eyes began to search Francisco's pants pockets. "And you were paid for this service by Eller, no?"

"No!" Francisco lied

Still searching pockets, Bulging Eyes said, "You take fugitives across open waters forty kilometers using your boat and gasoline for free? I don't think so." He found the pocket in Francisco's raincoat and held the stash of money in front of Francisco eyes. "Anything else you lied to us about?"

"No!" Francisco insisted.

Bulging Eyes jerked his head toward the water, and before Francisco could think, he was cascading off the dock and into the murky harbor. His head went under, and panic filled him. He clawed for the surface; his shoes felt like rocks. When his head broke the surface, he gasped for air and choked out, "Help me! I can't swim!"

Desperately he tried flailing his arms toward the dock fifteen feet in front of him. He had seen people swim before. Was this how they did it? His head went under, and he gulped a lungful of putrid, oil-covered, fish-rancid water. He choked; his lungs filled with it. Frantically he tried to claw back toward the top, but it felt as if he were sinking farther. Of course. His clothes, soaked, were pulling him down. He tried to peel off his jacket, but somehow it became entangled, pulling his arms behind him and trapping them there. He could not paddle toward the top. He kicked his feet like a frog.

Think, Francisco! But he couldn't think. His mind felt foggy.

His lungs, filled with water, were cold and painful. He tried to keep his mouth closed, but it seemed to have a mind of its own. It flew open; more water rushed in. He tried to close his mouth, but it remained wide open, gasping again and again, like a fish in air, seeking what it could not find…

Then he felt warmer. His panic lessened. He saw something—what was it? Someone coming to rescue him? He thought of his bride, married only three months. Yes, this was the feeling he got from her…a warm glow…like an angel…

When *La Fraternidad* received the information Francisco had given, it did not take them long to decide where, most likely, David was hiding. Only one hotel on Isla Margarita was owned by someone named Ian: Le Flamboyant Hotel on the northeast corner of the island.

At twelve-forty-five a.m., Tecero picked up his phone and ordered two of his men in Caracas to go to Margarita as quickly as possible. "Bring him to me alive," he demanded. "He has information I need. He also has my money. When I am finished with that little weasel, I will take joy in killing him myself."

"How should we get there?" the voice on the other end of the line asked. "The first commercial flight isn't until 7:45."

Tecero seethed. Must he always be frustrated by such mundane things as transportation? "Go to the marina where DiMartino moors his float plane. I will have his pilot meet you there."

In the dead of night, two men dressed in dark clothing beached their inflatable among some trees on El Agua beach toward the southeastern edge of Isla Margarita, after a half-mile row from the float plane. It did not take long to jog, in a crouch, the three hundred yards north up the beach to Le Flamboyant Hotel.

The two men crouched near the stucco wall, waiting for the lone night watchman to pass. When he walked by, one of the men clicked his stopwatch. He clicked it again when the watchman came by the second time. Seven minutes. This time, as the watchman circled past the entrance and disappeared toward the back of the hotel, the two men quietly made their way into the darkened and deserted open-air lobby. It took one of them only a few seconds to pick the lock on the door to the reception area. While his partner stood guard, the other, mag-lite in mouth, sifted through the registration cards he'd found in a metal box on the desk. There were several names, but Eller's was not one of them. On one card was simply written "Special Guest," with no checkout date. Room 104.

Next, he looked for keys. There was a locked cabinet under the desktop. Within seconds, he'd picked the lock and found a box of keys—actual old-fashioned metal keys, rather than plastic cards. Part of the laid-back Caribbean ambience. "Room 104" was printed on the plastic tab of one of them. *Too easy*, the man thought.

Exiting back out the front of the hotel, and with a glance at their watches to make sure the watchman wasn't about to appear, the men moved around the outside of the first section of hotel rooms where the front doors were numbered. On the first door of the first building was the number 104. *Much too easy*, the man thought again.

They crouched and waited for the watchman's next pass. Then, easing themselves over the small white stucco railing, they moved up to the door and listened. No movement inside. The man with the key slipped it into the door and slowly turned the knob, trying to avoid any sound. Adjusting their night-vision goggles, they entered the room and waited by the door. The only sound was the heavy breathing of the person sleeping in the bed. One of the men crossed the room, compared the face of the man lying on the bed in a deep sleep with his mental image of the photograph he'd studied. David Eller.

He was dreaming about a Thanksgiving dinner at the home of Christie's parents—people he knew only from a few photographs. People long dead. His brother Stephen was there, too—which was strange, especially considering that Stephen was in his Cal Berkeley football uniform. They were all seated at the table with Christie's parents. David's mom was there too. He didn't see his dad. There was a mountain of mashed potatoes near the roast turkey. A large bowl of gravy sat nearby. Everyone was engaged in lively conversation—everyone except for David. When he tried to enter the conversation, no one would listen. He tried to tell Christie how thankful he was for her, but she was busy talking to her mother and ignored him. He asked Stephen why he was wearing his old football uniform, but Stephen looked the other way. He asked his mother where Dad was, but she kept talking to little Davy. That's when he realized that he was invisible to everyone—no one could see him or hear him.

"Hey, everybody—I'm here!" he yelled.

No one reacted.

"Hey, it's really me! I'm home!"

Jumping up from the table, David grabbed a goblet of ice water and was about to splash it on his brother to get his attention when he felt his body being pinned down and tape slapped over his mouth. At first he thought it was part of the stupid dream. Something was being slipped over his head—a pillowcase? Too stiff.

Suddenly he was awake. He could feel his legs being taped. He struggled to sit up, shaking his head violently from side to side in an effort to dislodge the bag over his head. A strong arm quickly pushed him back onto the bed; a forearm painfully pressed his throat. A sharp pain in his thigh—a needle—some kind of injection. He tried to kick, but his legs were held too tightly. Tried to scream through the duct tape and the bag, but he could barely hear himself. Then, dizzy, drowsy, he began to sink.

Fading back into sleep…

◆　◆　◆

It took the two men less than five minutes to tape and sedate Eller. After the night watchman passed again, one of the men, with arms like tree trunks, hoisted the captive onto his shoulder, while the other grabbed the briefcase and duffel next to Eller's bed. The men had been surprised to see that Eller's shoulder was heavily bandaged.

Softly closing the hotel door behind them, they made their way back across the street and down onto the beach.

No one was likely to miss Eller until morning. Maybe no one would miss him for days. It didn't matter. If they could make it back to the float plane, it would be mission accomplished.

CHAPTER THIRTY-ONE

Stephen Eller was still awake at 2:30 a.m. He'd tried to sleep, but had given up, and for several hours he'd surfed the web. He was checking the international news wires when he came across a report out of Venezuela about Christie and Davy being injured and taken into custody. How much of it was true, if any? He suspected that they'd been captured; the accompanying video of Felix Suturos seemed legit, although, again, it could have simply been stock footage of some hapless fisherman who forgot to pay his taxes, taken a year ago. And the injury story might simply be a ploy to get David to surrender. Stephen had no way of knowing for sure.

On the same wire, he found the story about David stealing a police car as he avoided capture near La Guaira. How had his little brother gotten himself into such a mess? *Vintage David*, Stephen thought. *But thank God he escaped, at least that time. Heaven knows they're hot on his trail.*

At 2:45 a.m., Stephen tried to call the U.S. Embassy in Venezuela, but no one answered the phone. A recorded message invited him to call back during normal office hours. He'd try again first thing tomorrow morning, to confirm whether Christie had actually been injured. Either way, he hoped David wouldn't see the report of Christie's and Davy's injuries, knowing that David would throw caution to the wind and fall right into what was undoubtedly Guzman's trap.

He decided to send another email:

Don't believe the rumors and lies you may see on the news. They could be a trap. They'll use every trick in the book to get you to surrender. Don't believe anything, and don't be persuaded to turn yourself in. They wouldn't keep any promise they might make anyway. Stay put unless you hear otherwise from me.

At 2:55 a.m., two of Tecero's top goons—along with Jose Montoya, who could identify David Eller—were standing at the registration desk at Le Flamboyant Hotel, asking a sleepy-eyed Helen O'Leary, whom they'd awakened with the night emergency bell, if she would give them the room number for David Eller. "He's a friend of ours," they said. "It's an emergency."

Helen called her husband, Ian.

"We don't have a David Eller registered here," he said, dry-mouthed and nervous, convincing no one.

The goon with the big round face and flat nose reached inside his coat pocket and pulled out a 9 mm automatic. Grabbing Ian by the front of his shirt and ripping a button off near his throat, he shoved the pistol under Ian's chin. "I think you should tell me which room he is in," the man said slowly in his deep voice, "or this gun will splatter your brain all over the ceiling. You have ten seconds. Ten…nine…"

"Mr. Eller is sleeping in room 104!" Helen cried. "Please, let go of my husband!"

Without moving, the goon said, "Give me a key to his room."

Helen turned to the wooden cubicles behind her where the guests' keys were kept during the day. She grabbed a key for room 104 and handed it to Jose Montoya.

The goon eased his grip. "Where is room 104?"

Helen pointed toward the northeast corner of the building. The three men walked in that direction.

Ian picked up the phone and dialed the local police.

Jose Montoya slid the key into the room lock and slowly turned the handle as the two goons stood to either side of the doorway with guns drawn. Flinging the door open, the three men rushed into the room. The bed sheets were rumpled, the bedspread was on the floor, but the room was empty—except for a pair of deck shoes beside the bed. No briefcase, no luggage, no David Eller.

They stood looking at each other like the Three Stooges.

It had taken less than an hour to fly the rented float plane back to Grenada. Carlos had flown, although Hawkeye was just as experienced a pilot. They'd gotten back to their digs about 3 a.m. and put David Eller, still out cold and likely to stay that way until late morning, in a back bedroom.

The adrenaline rush of the rescue was keeping them awake. Zach flipped on the TV and found *Die Hard Two: Die Harder,* one of his favorite movies. Hawkeye and Carlos heated some old coffee in the microwave and sat down at the kitchen table. For several minutes, they sipped their coffee and said nothing. Then Hawk said, "I'm done after this. Zach, he'll probably stick with it for the rush. How about you?"

Carlos considered carefully how to answer—simply telling the truth didn't come naturally to him—then said. "I sometimes think I'd like to start a life so different that people who knew the new me would never believe me if I told them—" he gestured around him— "all of this."

Hawkeye shrugged. "When I was younger, this was all I ever wanted to do."

Carlos nodded. "Maybe as you get older, you think differently about what's important. I hope so. What good is experience if you don't learn anything?"

Hawk raised an eyebrow. "You getting religion?"

Carlos shook his head. "I had religion when I was a kid. I went to mass, was an altar boy, all that stuff. That's not what I'm looking for."

"Me, I'm going to do the right thing with Danny's parents and Aaron's wife, then disappear. Get my own island somewhere. A beautiful woman."

"I'd like to find someone to share the rest of my life with. But I think what I'm really looking for is meaning. Look at us—we've had some pretty exciting adventures, taken some risks. But what have we really accomplished? I've done other people's dirty work all my life. Now, I want to do something that lasts beyond my lifetime."

"You've gotten rid of dictators, prevented wars. Those things don't last beyond your lifetime?"

Carlos shrugged. "There are always more dictators. More wars. We've tried to be the good guys, but when you've got two teams of people shooting guns at each other for pay, it can be hard to tell the good guys from the bad ones. I want to do something not because I'm paid for it, not because it helps some government, but just because it's the good and right thing to do. Even if I don't get paid."

"Like your missionary boy. Then he decided to stick his neck into politics. And espionage."

"Well, I'm the one who recruited him."

"He made his own choices. Like all of us. How's his wound healing?"

"It looks good. He'll be OK. He got lucky." Carlos poured himself another cup of coffee, punched the buttons on the microwave. Time to chum the waters. "I saw Dukai on the news last night, before we left to rescue Eller. He said some interesting things."

"Like what?"

"He said they had Eller's family in custody. But he also let slip that one of the commandos was still alive."

Hawkeye set his cup down on the table. "He said what?"

"He said they had killed one commando and had one in custody. I take that to mean your boy Danny may still be alive."

"What do you mean he 'let it slip'?"

"I mean I don't know whether releasing the information that Danny was alive was intentional or not."

Hawkeye's eyes bored into Carlos. "You had this information before we went back into Venezuela to rescue Eller—and you didn't tell me?"

"That's right. For the same reason I was hoping David Eller hadn't seen the news report. Both nuggets of information released in that interview—about Mrs. Eller being injured, and about Danny still being alive—could both be traps. Dukai would love to get his hands on David, but he knows David is a low-level player in this drama. The people he'd really love to nab are the three of us. Dukai may be thinking that if you believe Danny is still alive, you might try to rescue him. The truth is, we just don't know—Danny may already be dead. But my gut tells me that they fingered David Eller in large part on information they got from Danny. He was alive then—he may be still. If he's strong enough to talk, there'd be no point in killing him yet."

Zach shut off the TV and came over to the table. "Did they say where they're keeping him?" he asked.

"If they had, we'd have *known* it was a trap. But they didn't. They flashed a photo. His face was swollen and bruised. I'm sure he's under heavy guard. They're probably planning a big trial."

"And no doubt more torture before they fry him," Zach said with disgust.

Hawkeye leaned forward and put his hand over his face—but not before Carlos had noticed the eye twitch that told him Hawk was agitated. "Carlos," Hawk said, "Zach and I agonized over this decision once already. Now you dangle it in front of me again. How can I confirm this intel one way or the other?"

"We got Eller out," Zach said.

"Eller wasn't under armed guard in a fortified prison," Carlos said. "He was asleep in an unguarded hotel room on an island forty miles off the coast. A couple of Girl Scouts could have gotten him out. No offense."

"We don't have a clue where Danny's being held," Hawkeye continued. "Show me a way to get him out, and I'm on it—but as far as I can see, nothing's changed."

Carlos paused, setting the hook. Then: "There may be a way we can find out if he's still alive. And if he is, there may even be a way to get him out."

Hawkeye sat up. "How?"

"So far, I have only part of a plan. I'll know more after I make a phone call to my contact first thing tomorrow morning. But here's what I need to know: Whether my contact approves my plan or not—are you with me?"

"Does your plan include trying to rescue Danny?"

"If I can confirm that he's still alive…yes."

"Then I'm in," Hawkeye replied.

"Try and stop me," Zach said.

CHAPTER THIRTY-TWO

The room was dark when David awoke. He was aware only of that darkness and of the sensations of his body: His head was splitting, his shoulder ached, and his left leg felt sore. Dizzy, he lay still, trying to get his bearings.

His leg. He reached for a spot on his thigh and winced. He remembered then—the needle, strong arms holding him down, the bag over his head. He turned his head to look at the one source of light in this room, a tiny crack of light coming under what appeared to be a door, and realized that this was a different door, a different room.

His mind began to retrace his steps from the last point in time he could clearly remember: *Felix, fishing dock, Christie, Silvia's... Ah, yes. Being shot. Francisco, Le Flamboyant, room 104, Margarita Island...the needle...* He looked up through the dim light at something moving above his head—the leaf-shaped paddles of a ceiling fan, turning slowly. *Where am I? How did I get here?* He tried to open his mouth, but his lips resisted, then popped open. He felt his mouth with his fingers. A sticky residue—no doubt from tape.

Muffled voices filtered in from the other room. He strained to listen. One sounded familiar. His mind cycled through fruitless possibilities: Uncle Simon, Professor Clausen—and then he knew: Carlos Edwards. He froze. *So, if Stephen was right that Carlos worked for the drug lords, then the drug lords have me. What do they plan to do?* Was this just a nightmare? No, the pain he felt was real.

284 The Missionary

"...said they were captured ...injuries?"

Carlos's voice: "Yes, they intercepted a boat headed here and found her on it."

" ...boat was the Bahia Bonita... confiscated."

"She's in custody back in Caracas...little boy too"

Were they talking about Christie and Davy? And about Felix and his family, who all must have been captured if the *Bahia Bonita* had been confiscated? David's heart began to pound. He felt first a bitter disappointment and anxiety for Christie and Davy, and then a surge of adrenaline. He had to do something, had to force himself out of bed, had to get free. He tried to move—then collapsed back onto the pillow. He was sore all over. The room tilted and reeled like a roller coaster— instant nausea. He remembered Ian's "knock-out shot" from the night before. He'd had a double cocktail.

He heard what sounded like a chair sliding back, then footsteps getting nearer. He closed his eyes, heard the door open, someone breathing, footsteps moving closer. His eyes wanted to open, wanted to flinch, but somehow he kept them shut and relaxed. The footsteps retreated; he took a chance and opened his eyes a crack to see the door closing.

"Your missionary's out cold, Carlos. He should stay that way awhile."

"Then let's all get some sleep. It's been a long night," Carlos's voice said.

What now? If the drug cartel had him, then that must mean he was still in Venezuela. Maybe near Caracas. So if Christie and David were being held in Caracas, then David wasn't far from them.

He waited, silently praying, for twenty or thirty minutes—aware that his sense of time might be seriously thrown off by whatever he'd been injected with. And he had no doubt what Carlos and the others would do if they caught him trying to flee. *No doubt these guys plan to silence me...permanently.*

Finally, not sure whether all of his limbs were functioning, David moved. Working through the pain in his shoulder and leg, he maneuvered himself as silently as possible into a sitting position, then lowered his feet to the floor. He felt nauseous. He was still in the shirt and shorts he'd put on before going to bed at Le Flamboyant, but now, for some reason he couldn't fathom, they were wet in spots. And—what was this? He pushed his shirt aside. Someone had replaced the dressings on his bullet wound. Who? And why, if they just intended to kill him?

He sat for a moment to let the wooziness subside, then tried to stand. Both legs held, but his balance was iffy.

Moving slowly, stopping to regain his balance after every step, he quietly moved to the door. The last man through had left it open just a crack. He pulled it another inch and peered through: a dim light came from the hood over a stove in a kitchenette. Just beyond, a man sleeping on a sofa. He heard the man snore.

Moving back toward the bed, David felt for his things. His duffel was at the end of the bed. But the briefcase? He felt all around the bed. No briefcase. Well, why would there be? These men knew exactly what was in it.

By now, David's eyes were adjusting to the limited light seeping in from the crack in the door. His room contained a bed, a small nightstand, a dresser in the corner, his duffel, but no briefcase. And no shoes.

No shoes, but he remembered throwing a pair of sandals into his duffel.

The briefcase of money was what they wanted. Therefore, the briefcase of money was what David needed—his insurance package. Getting it back might give him the only leverage he would have to stay alive long enough to get Christie and Davy freed.

He moved back to the doorway in his bare feet and peered through the crack. There was a holstered pistol on the kitchen table. *More insurance.*

He couldn't wait any longer for his energy and general mental awareness to improve, for more control to return. He pulled the door open a couple of feet and crept out into the other room. He tiptoed to the table, constantly watching the man snoring on the sofa. Slipping the gun from its holster, David stuck it into his pants. It gave him a feeling of control—although, in truth, he had no idea how to fire it and didn't even know how to check whether it was loaded. *Point, shoot, hope for the best.*

286   The Missionary

There was a partially open door. David tiptoed to it and peered through. Moonlight seeped in from the sole window. David was almost certain that was Carlos on the bed—on his back, mouth open, breathing heavily. And there was the briefcase, at the foot of the bed.

Looking back to check the man on the sofa—still snoring—David slowly opened the door wide enough to move inside.

The door squeaked.

David froze.

Carlos stirred, and David pulled his head back out of sight. But soon he heard heavy breathing again.

Methodically, David moved toward the briefcase. One foot at a time—survey floor for obstructions, pick up foot, shift weight, set foot down, pause to establish balance, survey floor… He reached down and gripped the briefcase by the handle. The leather squeaked as he started to lift, and the heavy breathing stopped. Again David froze, this time with his head down, unable to look at Carlos. Hadn't he read someplace that when you're trying to hide, don't look at the one you're hiding from, lest your eyes draw their attention? A few seconds later, heavy breathing began again, and David moved toward the door with one hand gripping the briefcase and the other gripping the handle of the pistol.

Moving back to his room, David slipped into his sandals and rezipped his duffel.

How would he get out of the apartment? And where was the third man whose voice he'd heard? No time for hesitation—he grabbed the handles of the duffel and the briefcase in his right hand and stepped as silently as possible out into the other room.

At the back of the kitchen area was another doorway. He peered into it: a small laundry room—and another door. It might be the door into a bedroom, and if he opened it, he might find the third man, and the third man might put a bullet into David's belly. Or it might be a door to the outside. David walked quietly to the door and put his hand on it. Cooler than the air inside. A door to the outside. As quietly as he could, he opened the door and exited into a yard, walked between some buildings and out onto a street. He could smell the ocean, hear the rhythmic pulse of waves.

There was a slight breeze blowing, ruffling the palms along what appeared to be a main street. Looking left and right, David saw some neon lights a couple hundred yards to his left and started toward them. His legs felt heavy. So did the briefcase and duffel. David realized that, besides the effects of whatever he'd been injected with, which seemed to be wearing off, he was exhausted, physically and mentally—and that wouldn't wear off. Although the cool night air helped a bit. The neon signs, to David's surprise, were in English. Where in Venezuela would the signs be in English? Some expatriate enclave he wasn't aware of? He put it out of his mind—too difficult to deal with in his present state.

Toward the back of the neon-lit building sat a small shed on pilings that raised it several feet off the ground. A porch light illumined the door of the shed. The moon was bright. Moving to the rear of the shed, David got down on one knee and felt the dark ground under the shed. Soft sandy loam sifted through his fingers.

On the walk toward here, he had decided it was time to bury the briefcase. No doubt Carlos, as soon as he discovered David missing, would come after him. The money was David's ticket to stay alive, at least for a while.

Even one-handed, it didn't take long, in this soft soil, to dig a hole deep enough. Removing the duct tape, he reached into the briefcase and pulled out a wrapped stack of bills. He put it in his pocket, then secured the duct tape again and slid the briefcase into the hole; he piled sandy loam on top. Smoothing the sand nearby, he rose to his feet and made his way to the front of the bar. He took the gun from his pants and put it into his duffel, then dropped the zipped bag near the front door and entered the bar.

There were no customers, only a burly, aproned man mopping the floor. The man looked up. "We're closed," he said in English with a strong island accent.

288　The Missionary

More English. David heard a voice he barely recognized as his own--a slurred, hoarse rasp—ask, "What time is it?" His legs felt weak; he put his arm against the bar to steady himself.

The man smiled. "Time for you to go home and sleep it off. I'll call a cab."

"I'm not drunk," David croaked.

"Yes, and I'm the king of England," the man laughed as he picked up the phone.

There was a digital clock on the wall the shape of a beer bottle being poured out with the name Corona on the side. It read 4:12 a.m.

Well, he wasn't drunk—but this wasn't a bad development. The cab could take him where he wanted to go.

A few minutes later, he thanked the aproned man and shuffled toward the cab with his duffel in hand. David rasped, "Necesito para llegar a Caracas."

"What?" the man replied.

"I need to get to Caracas," David repeated in English.

"Caracas! Eh-eh. You will need a sea bath, my friend!" said the cabbie, with a decidedly calypso voice and a big belly laugh.

Two things didn't make sense to David: First, what the cabbie had said, and second, how he had said it. Since when did cabbies—and bartenders, for that matter—in Caracas speak English with a calypso accent. "Where am I?" David asked.

"My friend, you are so tight you do not even know you are on de island of Grenada! Let me take you to your hotel. Which one?"

"No, please—I really do need to get to Caracas. Can you take me to the airport?"

Another big laugh. "It is four o'clock in de morning! De airport is closed. No planes out of here for at least four more hours."

David sat silently, trying to maneuver through the fog remaining in his head. "How about the boat dock? Please take me there."

"Ah, so you are from a cruise ship. Well, you missed curfew. De cruise ship dock is secured and dey cyah let you on your ship till later dis morning."

"No, I mean the fishing dock. Please—take me there and I'll hire a boat."

The cab lurched forward, "Foofoolday," the cabbie mumbled under his breath. "Okay, if you want to lime at de fishing docks, ah will take you there. It's probably a good place to sober up anyway. You won't find any fisherman dere at dis hour, so ah suggest you take a nap on de beach. When you wake, you will have a terrible headache, but you will be in much better shape dan you are now."

Within five minutes, the cab stopped in front of a long dock. David handed the cabbie a hundred-dollar bill from his stack and told him to keep the change.

"Well yes!" the driver said. "Ah come back and look for you later dis morning. Take you back to your cruise ship, no charge."

David simply waved as the cab moved off into the night. The cabbie had been right. No one was at the dock at this hour. David dropped his duffel near a bench on the dock and sat down, then lay down. He needed to clear his mind, decide on his next move.

David thought about his mistakes, his near misses… But most of all, he tried to think of a way to rescue Christie and Davy. He considered and discarded several plans, and the best one he could come up with—not that it satisfied him—was to get to Caracas, call the authorities, and try to negotiate an exchange for his wife. First, he would call the American embassy and see if they would act as mediator. If they refused, he would call the police directly. He would offer first himself—and if that wasn't enough, the money he had hidden—as the ransom. And if that failed, he could finger Carlos and his friends and tell the authorities where to find the true assassins, in exchange for the release of himself and his family.

Not a great plan, but the best he could come up with in his current state. Maybe he'd be able to think better in the morning.

Foofoolday he was indeed.

CHAPTER THIRTY-THREE

Stephen Eller woke again around five and lay restlessly in bed for the next half hour. At five-thirty, he picked up the phone and dialed. After it rang several times, a familiar croaking voice answered: "Hello."

"Art, sorry to bother you again so early, but there's been another complication."

"Eller! For ... Don't you ever sleep?"

"Not very well last night, thank you. I've been waiting for a couple of hours to call you."

"Well, you should have waited at least a couple more."

"Art, listen—the Venezuelan authorities have my sister-in-law and my four-year-old nephew in custody. They were on a small fishing vessel trying to escape to Grenada when they were intercepted by the Venezuelan Coast Guard. The report said they were seriously injured."

"Oh, man, Stephen—that's horrible. I'm sorry. What do you want me to do? Or let me put it another way. What do you really think I can do about it at this hour of the morning?"

"I was hoping you could call Dennis Vansant again and see if he could do something."

"You think that's a good way to motivate him? Call him at five-thirty in the morning?"

"Well, no, not right now... Hey, I'm sorry, Art. I wasn't thinking. It's just that I'm really worried."

"Stephen, look—I'll call Vansant later this morning and see if I can find out what's up. Maybe this will shake something loose."

"Be sure to ask him whether they can confirm the report of injuries to Christie and Davy," Stephen said.

"Anything else?"

"No. I really appreciate this, Art."

"Can I go back to sleep now?"

David awoke to a mechanical sound. He shook his head, tried to focus, and saw headlights rounding a corner. Carlos? The police? He grabbed his duffel and stumbled behind a small shack near the dock, then peeked out and watched as a rusty Toyota pickup drove up and parked. Two fishermen exited the truck and began to retrieve their gear.

It was clear who the boss was. Shorter and older, he nevertheless barked orders to the younger, taller man.

As they moved toward the dock, carrying their gear, David stepped from his hiding place. "Hello!"

The startled men stopped abruptly, the taller one dropping one of the poles he was carrying.

"I need to get to Caracas," David said.

"You makin' joke!" the boss man said. "Venezuela a hundred and forty kiloms dat way," he said, pointing to the west.

"And we headed *dat* way," the other man said, pointing to the south.

"Dere's no way we going to Venezuela, Mister," said the boss man.

"I'll make it worth your while," David said. 'I'll pay you five thousand dollars to take me there."

The men looked at each other, slowly setting down their buckets on the dock.

"Show me de money," the boss said.

David pulled the bundled wad from his back pocket and held it up.

"Bun Jay," the taller man said, stepping forward and whistling.

The boss man stuck out his arm, preventing the younger man from moving closer. Then the boss man smiled and stuck out his hand to shake David's hand.

"I think we change our plans for today," he said. "Robert, go check and see we have enough diesel on board."

Robert grabbed his bucket and scurried down the dock.

The boss man smiled at David. "I require half de money now, de other half when we dock in Venezuela. You have to find your own way to Caracas once we get to shore."

David counted out $2500 dollars into the man's hand.

Stuffing it into his coveralls, the boss man smiled and waved David forward. "My boat is down toward de end of de dock, on de left. It is de *Sea Eagle*."

Hawkeye woke first. Not bothering to check on any of the others, he began opening and slamming cupboard doors and drawers in the kitchen, looking for coffee filters.

"You could wake the dead with that racket," Zach moaned from the sofa.

"You want to do it yourself?" Hawkeye said. "And how come you slept with your gun?"

Zach sat up, rubbing his eyes. "What?"

"You heard me. Afraid of being attacked by a vicious missionary?"

"I didn't sleep with my gun, it's right there on the table."

"The holster's on the table. Not your gun."

Zach felt around the edges of the sofa, then on the floor nearby. "No, I left it on the table."

Zach and Hawkeye looked at each other, and the thought struck them at the same moment. They both moved quickly to Eller's bedroom door and pushed it open.

"Carlos!" Hawkeye hollered. "Your missionary's gone!"

"And he stole my pistol!" Zach yelled.

Carlos was up in an instant and joined them, peering foolishly into David's empty room. "Where were you guys?" he said, his throat thick with sleep. "Didn't you hear him? How could he get out without any of us hearing anything?"

294   The Missionary

"His duffel's gone," Zach said, "all his stuff —"

Carlos bolted back to his room, stopped in the doorway, and yelled in frustration. "He got the briefcase!"

"My gun, our briefcase full of money—I'll catch him and kill him!" Zach growled.

"Get your clothes on. He can't have gone far. We'll find him," Carlos said, rummaging around his bed for his clothes.

"I'll kill him," Zach mumbled.

Spilling out the front door, they fanned out, Hawkeye and Zach to the right, Carlos to the left. Five minutes later, Carlos was pounding on the upstairs door above the Mourne Rouge Beach Bar, where the owner and bartender lived.

The door opened a crack. "No Coronas this early, Carlos. Why are you pounding down my door at this hour?"

"Did you see a guy come by here early this morning? Probably *very* early. An American, maybe five-ten?"

"Well, there was a cabre who wandered in here about four-thirty or so, when I was mopping up. He was so tight he could barely stand. I called him a cab."

"That's him. He wasn't drunk, he was drugged. What cab did you call?"

"Bucky."

"Bucky?"

"Yes. Bucky's always the first guy I call."

"Where can I find Bucky-the-cabdriver's number?"

"I know it by heart." He gave Carlos the number.

Carlos dialed it and asked for a pick-up. Waiting for the cab to show, he dialed Hawkeye, letting him and Zach know he was on Eller's trail. They joined him at the bar just before the cab arrived.

Bucky nodded and grinned. Yes, he remembered the fare. "At first he wanted me to take him to de airport. When I told him dere would be no flights for hours, he wanted to go to de fisherman's dock. Said he wanted to find someone to take him to Caracas. He was pretty drunk. A bit of a bol'face actually. I told him to find a place to sleep it off."

"Did he have some bags with him, some luggage?"

"Yes. He loaded it himself, so I didn't pay much attention."

Carlos jumped into the cab. "Take me to the dock where you left him," he said. "Hawkeye, you two go back and get one of the Donzis at the marina, fill it with gas, and bring it to the fishermen's dock."

Within twenty-five minutes, Carlos, Hawkeye, and Zach were headed out to sea toward Venezuela.

CHAPTER THIRTY-FOUR

Christie woke early. She heard the slow deep-sleep breaths of Davy in bed next to her. It was still dark.

After her interrogation by Dukai the day before, she was less worried about her own fate, and Davy's. She'd done nothing wrong, and eventually they would have to let her go—if not because Guzman wanted to, then because the U.S. government wouldn't stand still for having an innocent U.S. citizen detained indefinitely by a foreign power. They would put considerable pressure on Guzman. But she wasn't so sure about Felix's safety—and she was certain that, if David were caught, his life would be in grave danger. It was an inescapable fact that he had committed a crime against the Venezuelan government punishable by death.

If David somehow found a way to escape, what would she say to him when they were reunited? One thing she knew: Regardless of what he had done, regardless of whether she could ever trust him again or even whether she could remain married to him, she loved him, and it would be an emotional reunion.

But so many problems! So many betrayals!

And so much that they had shared, and still shared. Hearing Davy breathe next to her in the bed made her long to have another baby with David.

A tear slid down her cheek and onto the pillow. *Oh, God, let him be safe. Let us be together again.*

It was Zach, scanning the ocean ahead with high-powered binoculars, who spotted the fishing vessel first, off to starboard. Carlos guided the Donzi in that direction, and when they got closer, through their binoculars they could see two men who fit the description given to Carlos at the fishing docks: one short older man, one tall younger one. A little closer, and they could read the name *Sea Eagle* on the stern. Carlos pulled up beside the boat, within hailing distance, and Hawkeye ordered the boat to stop. The tall younger one, who was driving, started to slow, but the older one motioned for him to keep going.

That's when Zach pulled out his gun and fired it once into the air, then aimed it at the short older man.

"Stop," yelled Hawkeye again.

The fisherman cut the throttle; the boat slowed to a gentle drift.

Carlos pulled the Donzi closer until it was nearly touching the *Sea Eagle*. "We mean no harm to you!" Carlos yelled. "We want your passenger. Have him come out on deck."

The older man shrugged his shoulders and motioned for the younger man to go below.

He didn't need to. The cabin hatch immediately flew open, but the opening remained dark and empty. "I'm not going with you!" David shouted out. His arm appeared, waving Zach's pistol. "I'm going to Caracas to get my wife and son!"

"That's not how it works, David!" Carlos shouted. "Work with us, and maybe we can accomplish something. Go into Venezuela on your own, and you'll just be captured, imprisoned, tortured, and killed. And why would they agree to release your family once they have you, anyway? Think, David."

"I have thought!" David shouted back.

Carlos made eye contact with Zach, and Zach slipped to the rear of the boat and tossed his gun onto one of the Donzi's seat cushions. Carlos brought the Donzi close enough alongside that Zach was able to step across to the fishing boat and slip around the stern to the far side.

"I have thought, and the one thing I know is that I can't trust you!" David said. "You led me to believe you were working for the CIA, but the CIA says they've never heard of you! And as far as I'm concerned, that means you're working with the drug cartel."

Zach's head appeared above the cabin's roof on the far side, and he slipped slowly and carefully across the roof until he was directly over the hatch through which David was shouting.

"I believed you, and because of that I'm wanted for attempted murder and my family, including my four-year-old son, is in some prison somewhere—"

Zach lunged downward, reached through the hatch, and tumbled off the roof, all in one motion. David emerged through the hatchway, his gunhand wrist held tight by Zach, with all the dignity of a rag doll being shaken by a rottweiler. The gun went off, and wood chips flew from the gunwale of the fishing boat.

Zach stood and yanked David to his feet, David's wrist still clamped in Zach's massive fist. But David wasn't out of the fight yet, even though Zach was a trained mercenary who outweighed him by fifty pounds. David did something that took Zach totally by surprise—he head-butted Zach squarely in the mouth. Anger flashed in Zach's eyes, and in an instant the two were down on the deck with Zach on top, one hand maintaining a choke hold on David and the other punching the smaller man in the face. The pistol clattered across the deck.

By the time Carlos had pulled the Donzi alongside, turned the wheel over to Hawkeye, and jumped onto the fishing boat, David lay motionless on the deck, his nose bleeding, and Zach had stood to retrieve his pistol.

Carlos lifted the stunned David to a sitting position. "Go down and get his things and the briefcase," Carlos told Zach.

David shook his head. "You're a lying drug runner, Carlos," he said, his voice thick. "I'm not going anywhere with you." He spat saliva and blood.

300 The Missionary

Zach emerged from hatch. "Here's the duffel, but there's no brief-case down there."

Carlos looked at David. 'Where's the briefcase?"

"You're the last person I would tell."

Zach moved closer, pointing his pistol at David's leg. 'Tell us where you put the briefcase, you miserable little thief, or I'll blow your knee-caps off!"

"Nobody is going to shoot anyone,' Carlos said, waving off Zach.

Zach turned to the two fisherman. "Did he come aboard with a briefcase, besides this duffel?"

They answered together. "No, no."

"Just that bag there," the boss man said, pointing at the duffel.

Zach pointed the pistol at the boss man's head. "Tell me the truth!"

"I swear, that was his only bag!" said the boss man, while the tall man vigorously nodded.

"Search the boat!" Hawkeye yelled from the Donzi.

A few minutes later, David was on his feet and Carlos was holding tight to his right arm, transferring him to the Donzi. It appeared to Carlos that David had realized the futility of fighting.

"Let these guys go," David said. "The briefcase isn't on their boat."

Zach tossed David's duffel onto the Donzi. Then he pulled out a nylon wrist cuff. "This is to make sure you don't attack anybody else. It could get you killed." He pulled David's arms behind his back and fas-tened the cuffs. David winced as his left arm was pulled backward. Then Zach frisked him, pulled a wad of money out of David's pocket, and held it up for Hawkeye and Carlos to see. He stuffed it in his own pocket.

The fishermen were standing on the deck of the *Sea Eagle*, bewil-dered and watching, as Hawkeye turned the Donzi back toward Gre-nada and accelerated, Carlos turned to David. "We need to talk."

David shook his head. "Forget it, Carlos. All you've done is lie to me since day one."

Carlos shrugged. "It's true that things are not what they appear to be. I can explain that. Don't make this a bigger problem than it already is."

David adjusted his position, looking uncomfortable with cuffed hands behind his back. "How could it be any bigger? You drug me, you handcuff me, and I know you plan to kill me. That's a big problem for me—probably all in a day's work for you."

"No one is going to kill you."

"Why should I believe you? You told me it would be a peaceful coup. You let me believe you were CIA."

"Listen to me, David. I—"

"I've listened to you too much already, and look where it got me. Lots of people would like to see me dead! Including you, according to my brother."

"Just listen to one question, David. How do you think we found you on Isla Margarita?"

David thought briefly, then shrugged and said, "Probably tortured and killed the people who helped me."

"No, David, we found you because you emailed your location to your brother. That information was relayed to me."

"You spoke with my brother?"

"I didn't say that. I said the information you emailed your brother was relayed to me. That's how we knew where to rescue you."

David looked out toward the horizon, his expression troubled. "Rescue me? I'd say you captured me! Why else would you feel it necessary to drug me last night?'"

"Believe it or not, David, but that was for your own safety. We knew you were being hunted by Guzman. We assumed that your brother had told you that some bad guys from the drug cartel were chasing you—which is true. I knew you thought I was one of the bad guys. So we felt it was best to treat your rescue as an abduction to avoid injury to you or to us."

David leaned forward and spat more blood onto the floor of the boat. "I still think you're the bad guys." Nodding toward Zach and Hawkeye, he continued, "You and these two macho idiots you recruited."

Zach turned to stare at David. "Why don't we just shoot him and feed him to the sharks."

"Shut up, Zach," Carlos said. "David, if we're the bad guys, why did we just take you off that boat headed for Venezuela, where both Guzman and the drug lords want you, and put you on a fast boat back to Grenada?"

By the time they reached the marina in St. Georges, David had calmed enough that Carlos had removed the wrist cuffs.

At the condo, David was escorted to his room by Carlos. "Take a shower and put on some clean clothes. Then we'll re-dress your wound and talk about how we can negotiate your wife and kid out of Venezuela."

Zach was stationed in the kitchen to watch David's room.

CHAPTER THIRTY-FIVE

It was 7:45 a.m. when Carlos dialed a number that connected him to a secure line and said, "Leprechaun."

"What's the latest?"

Carlos gave his account of their rescue of David, and David's temporary escape and recapture. "He's taking a shower right now."

"I still can't believe you recruited Eller in the first place. This whole mess could have been avoided if you'd picked some Venezuelan schmuck nobody cared about."

Carlos didn't answer.

"Any other collateral damage or problems I need to know about?" Leprechaun asked.

"No, everything's under control here. At least for now."

"Tell Eller as little as possible. He could be a loose cannon when he returns to the States. His brother's been sworn to absolute silence, but David's a zealot. I don't trust him."

"Any news about his wife and child? Are the injuries real?"

"Funny you should ask. I just hung up from a conversation with a friend of Stephen's who was asking the same thing. I'll tell you what I told him. We're pretty sure she's okay. Our people on the ground there have checked and rechecked both University Hospital and the other hospitals. She's not there, under her own name or any other."

"I think it's a ploy by Dukai to get Eller to turn himself in," Carlos said. "Dukai has no way of knowing I have him. He probably thinks he's still in Venezuela." He paused. "I'd like to get her out of there."

304 The Missionary

"At this point, there's nothing we can do except play the waiting game. I doubt they'll harm her. The Embassy has already filed a petition seeking her release."

"That could take weeks. Months."

"True. But there's nothing else we can do."

"Not good enough. There are dangers for us in leaving her there."

Carlos could almost hear the sound of Leprechaun gritting his teeth over the phone. "*What* dangers?"

"I met her. We talked. She can connect the name of Carlos Edwards to the assassination attempt. She'll give them that name eventually, and in time they might—"

"That's it?" Leprechaun asked, his voice more relaxed. "That's the danger? Forget Carlos Edwards. You've got enough aliases you never need to use that one again, and if you need more, we'll get you more. *So what* if she gives them Carlos Edwards? They'll never prove a connection to us. Listen, I'd like to get Mrs. Eller out soon too, but we'll just have to go through channels."

"There is one way."

"Hold it. I am *not* interested in another hare-brained rescue scheme."

"Hear me out. This idea comes from last night's newscast. I take it you've seen the Dukai clip that played on Venevision News last night?"

"I reviewed the tape this morning. What do you make of it?"

"Dukai's beginning to feel the heat. He's sending a message," Carlos said. "Guzman is breathing down his neck wanting a quick and satisfying resolution to the investigation—a resolution that gives him someone big to burn. Maybe we can provide that. I have, of course, in my possession, all the tapes and photos showing La Fraternidad conspiring in the assassination attempt. The most recent tapes reveal much about the cartel's organization. It's iron-clad evidence, Leprechaun, and Guzman would love to have it."

"*He* would love to have it? So would we! And we've invested a lot in getting it. What are you suggesting?"

"Think about this. The drug lords are much bigger fish for Guzman to fry than Eller. Remember: Operation Two-Bird was designed to get double benefit. Well, we missed getting bird one—Guzman. But if we turn this information over to Dukai, I guarantee you Guzman will go after the drug lords—bird two—and we also rescue Eller's family. Plus one other benefit. Dukai let slip that one of the commandos is still alive. I think he did it on purpose. For just this reason."

There was a pause.

"I don't like where this conversation is headed. Operation Two-Bird is over. Face it. We failed. I'm not willing to keep freehanding this operation—make decisions on the fly, eventually you have disaster. The operation was a bust. But at least we have Eller out and alive—that's decent damage control. Let's not push our luck."

"What about bird two? We can still nail the drug lords. And maybe rescue the—"

"The answer's no. We *will* use the tapes and photos, and we *will* nab the drug cartel. Eventually. We just haven't decided how to do it yet. Bring Eller back and tell Hawkeye his job is done."

Carlos heard the phone click off.

"Okay, assuming you don't work for drug lords," David said, "and frankly I no longer care who you work for—why did you recruit me for this thing? I told you I was a novice."

David was feeling much better after his shower—despite the added pains from the beating he'd taken from Zach—but he was still angry. Now he and Carlos were sitting on the edge of the bed in the room David had sneaked out of a few hours earlier.

"I recruited you to help your work," Carlos said, taping in place the gauze wrapping he'd just applied to David's shoulder. "I felt confident the coup would succeed. Little risk to you, lots of money for your mission."

306   The Missionary

David snorted. "Well, it *didn't* succeed. Carlos—or whatever your name is—you lied to me and manipulated me. And right now you're safe, but my family's in danger." David could feel the heat in his face. He stood and leaned over Carlos, almost spitting the words in his face. "When everything went wrong, you guys fled to save your own butts. Not a word to me, or the offer of a helping hand, no explanation, nothing! I became the front man, the guy who could be identified. I stuck my neck out for you. And you couldn't care less if I was killed. Not to mention my family."

Now Carlos was angry. He stood, poking his finger in David's chest. "Don't put this on me. You made the choice. I gave you the option to get out more than once. I told you the night we had dinner in the hotel there was some risk. I told you I wasn't sure it was wise to involve you. I thought about the potential danger if something were to go wrong. I debated whether this would compromise your work. But I thought we would succeed. I was wrong."

Carlos turned his back toward David. "Blame me if it makes you feel better, but you need to ask yourself why *you* said yes. I know what my motive was for recruiting you." He turned and looked into David's eyes again. "I took a chance on you because I wanted to help Hope Village. What was your motive?"

David stood silent, glaring at Carlos, then finally said, "You have a lot of gall standing there and saying your motive was to help Hope Village, and suggesting mine was otherwise. I gave that mission years of my life, night and day. Christie and I both. Now we can never go back, and the mission may not survive." The two men stared into each other's faces for a several seconds. David broke first. He sat again. "You said you spoke to someone who had spoken to my brother. I want to call my brother and see if what you said is true."

Carlos seemed to consider this, then retrieved his phone from the kitchen and handed it to David, who dialed quickly.

"Stephen, it's me, David!" He was grinning.

"Where are you?"

"In Grenada. Carlos Edwards says you told him where to find me."

"I don't know Carlos Edwards. I told Vansant where to find you."

"Who's Vansant?"

Stephen paused. "I got a call from Art Snell an hour ago. One of my contacts here. He told me, 'Our people have your brother.' 'Our people,' he said. So I think you're okay with whoever has you."

David looked at Carlos. "Wish I could be as sure of that as you are. But I'm finding out that's half the battle. Stay skeptical, ask lots of questions."

Then Stephen laughed. "Forget it. If you're in Grenada, you can always just take a cab to the airport and get a flight home. I'm just glad you're safe."

"Christie and Davy are still in Venezuela. I need to try to get them."

He heard a familiar sigh. "David, you're not James Bond, okay? You're a great youth worker, a great missionary, but when it comes to espionage, you have absolutely no idea what you're doing. I'm still trying to get our government to pressure Venezuela to release your family. Let us work it out from this end."

"And how will they treat Christie during her imprisonment? You have no idea what Guzman is capable of."

"David, come home! Be reasonable."

"Reasonable? My wife and child are being held by a maniac. I'm beyond the point of being reasonable, Stephen."

"Look, promise me you won't do anything stupid, okay? Tell me you'll come home as soon as you can get a flight out."

"I promise I won't do anything stupid—I've done enough stupid things. But I can't promise I won't explore other options. And I want to stay here in Grenada where I'm closer to Christie and Davy, at least for now."

"David, I think you should—"

"Stephen, I love you, but I have to get off this phone now. I'll call you later, okay?"

"David, listen—"

308   The Missionary

David handed the phone back to Carlos. Carlos listened for a few seconds, then clicked the phone off. "Your brother is not very happy with you right now."

"My brother's wife and child are not the ones being held by Guzman." David took a deep breath. Then he spoke in a soft voice. "If I decided to go to the airport and catch a flight back to the states right now, would you stop me?"

Carlos said, "I think that's exactly what you should do." He grinned. "After you tell us where the briefcase is."

David exhaled. "Okay, Carlos, I believe you. I'm not sure why. And I still wish you'd never entered my life. But I believe you."

"Good," said Carlos. "Because I've got a plan that just might work."

CHAPTER THIRTY-SIX

David ran his tongue along the inside of his swollen lips as he and Zach trudged up the Grenadan street. The skin was broken in several places, although the bleeding had stopped. David didn't think it was his imagination that a couple of his front teeth felt loose.

"Tell me, Zach, is there any problem, however simple and minor, that you don't try to solve through violence?"

"When your toilet is leaking," Zach said, "do you call a piano player? Do you call a missionary?"

Carlos did, David thought.

"You call a plumber. That's what he does. He does that one thing, all day long. I'm a soldier. When your government needs a rough man who's not afraid to blow a hole in someone, they call me. It's what I do."

The mid-morning sun was already almost too warm, but David closed his eyes and basked in it. He felt as if he'd been miserably cold for days. He didn't think he'd ever get enough warmth to chase the chill away. Besides, he didn't like looking at Zach. "You're not a soldier. You're a mercenary."

"Same thing. Violence for pay."

No, David thought, violence for pay sounded more like a hit man. But there was no point in arguing. He pointed off the road down toward the beach, and Zach stayed by his side through the soft sand down to the surf, where David kicked off his sandals and let the waves wash up around his ankles as they walked.

Zach watched him. "You buried it in the ocean?"

310   The Missionary

"No."

"Then why are we walking down here?"

David stopped and picked up a shell, then another, then another. Perfect specimens—he had no idea of their names, but he was sure American tourists poking into little shops along the marinas in San Diego or Biloxi paid money for shells not as nice as these. He put them in his pocket. Davy would like them. "We'll get to the money. Relax. Stop talking for a while. Listen to the seagulls. Listen to the waves. Listen—"

Zach grabbed David's upper arm in a vice-like grip and yanked him nearly off his feet. A sharp pain shot through David's shoulder. He could smell the stale breakfast on Zach's breath as the taller man hissed into his ear, "Don't be jerking me around, missionary boy. I want my money and I want it now."

"Lighten up, Zach. We're almost there." David led Zach across the loose sand again, sand sticking pleasantly to his wet feet, and stopped next to the shed near the Mourne Rouge Bar. He poked a sandy foot toward the loose soil beneath the pilings. "There 'tis."

Zach sat in the shade and leaned against one of the pilings. "Dig it up."

David sat against one of the pilings opposite Zach. "Dig it up yourself."

"You buried it."

"I've only got one arm. It'll take longer."

"Dig it up!" Zach growled. "I've had it with you!"

"Listen—it's your money. Dig it up or not. Your choice." David stood, ready to walk away.

Zach swept the soil away with one arm in two deep swipes that uncovered the edge of the briefcase, then dragged it out. "You only buried it a foot deep! The wind could have uncovered it! Island boys looking for lost coins could have found it." He pulled off the tape and opened the case. "Some is missing."

"My commission."

Zach stood, briefcase in hand. "Commission for what? For the privilege of saving your scrawny neck? If I had my way, you'd pay us a commission."

David sighed. "Sad to say, Zach, in this story neither one of us gets our way. Now let's get to the airplane. We have some people to rescue. You're right. This is when missionaries like me need brutes like you."

Zach didn't seem displeased by the thought. "You're the saint and I'm the sinner?" He even offered a hint of a smile.

"In that ledger, Zach, we're both far in the red."

Christie waited all morning in the hotel room for something to happen. At around nine a guard brought breakfast to her and Davy. Shortly after eleven, she heard a knock at the door and opened it to a guard who said, "Por favor, señora—get your things together. We are leaving the hotel."

Was this good news or bad? Christie didn't know. But she did know she had no choice.

Davy was sitting on the floor, drawing a picture.

"Come on, honey. We have to leave now," she said.

"Are we going to find Daddy?" Davy asked.

"I hope so. I can't say for sure." Seeing the confusion on his face, she said, "Let's pretend we're on an adventure."

This prompted a smile from Davy, followed by a run of questions about going on a boat again for their adventure, or maybe a plane, or a train…

Christie repeatedly mumbled, "Maybe," and "we'll see," while she quickly stuffed their things into her duffel. That was as much as she could tell him—she had no idea where they were going, or how. She prayed it was not back to the interrogation room, separated once more from her son. She opened the door to find three guards waiting. They took the fire exit down three flights of stairs and out a rear door to a waiting government van.

She didn't bother asking where they were going. These were soldiers under orders, and she was sure their orders did not include a conversation with her.

She turned her attention to a conversation in English with Davy. "Look, the sun is out. It's a beautiful day. That mountain over there is the same one you see every morning when you look out our kitchen window."

"Are we close to Hope Village? Are they taking us home to Daddy and Papa Cecil and Martha?" Davy asked.

"We don't know yet. Remember, I said this was an adventure."

Christie watched as they traveled through the busy streets of Caracas. *Are they releasing us? Turning us over to the U.S. Embassy?*

Her hopes swelled when they turned onto the large boulevard leading to the Radisson Hotel. Then the van slowed as it approached a small avenue to the left. A man standing at a gate in a cyclone fence swung it open for their van. Christie realized they were headed for the downtown airstrip known as La Carlota, used by private and military aircraft. Three small planes stood parked on a side tarmac two hundred yards in front of them.

The van slowed in front of one of the three: a smaller, boxy-looking prop plane. Another government car sat there, and standing at the rear of the car she recognized General Raldo Dukai. Smoking his cigarette.

Commander Torres hung up the phone thoughtfully. Like most senior officers in the Venezuelan army, he maintained a loose cadre of soldiers and officers loyal to him scattered throughout the military and the government. Torres's were more loyal and diligent than most, because they knew they had better be. And one of them had just come up with something very interesting.

Dukai had been busy. A rushed emergency meeting with *el presidente*, followed by a flurry of activity to round up the prisoners associated with the assassination attempt. And—this was most interesting—the commandeering of a Twin Otter aircraft capable of carrying several passengers.

What was Dukai up to?

Had Guzman authorized this flight with the prisoners? Or was Dukai's action an act of treason because he did not hear what he wanted to hear from the president? Torres wasn't sure. But he wanted to find out. And if there was anything improper about what Dukai was doing, or anything that could be made to appear so...

He picked up the phone. "Lieutenant Vasquez. This is Commander Torres. In a short time, several military aircraft will leave from the base, under orders to accompany a DeHavilland Twin Otter on which General Raldo Dukai will be traveling. You know of this? Yes. Good. I want to be on one of those aircraft. And I want as many of our team mobilized and on those aircraft as possible. Do you hear? Do not fail me in this. I suspect that treachery is afoot, and I must be in position to stop it, using the combat capabilities of those aircraft if need be. I am leaving for the airfield now. Have everything in place by the time I arrive."

A guard opened the sliding side door of the van and motioned for Christie and Davy to get out. General Dukai came toward them. "Buenas dias, Senora Eller. I trust that your accommodations were acceptable and you were able to get a good night's sleep."

"Please tell me what's going on," Christie asked.

"It's a beautiful morning for flying, so I thought we would take a little trip."

"Where to?"

"I am afraid our destination is something I am not at liberty to disclose, but I think you will be pleased." His thin lips pursed into a slight smile.

Another van came to a stop next to the van they'd just exited. A guard hurried to open the van's door. Christie stared in disbelief as Felix, Isabel, and Blanca emerged from the second van. She ran to embrace

314 The Missionary

them. "Oh, I'm so glad to see you!" she said. Turning to Felix, she asked, "Do you know what's happening?"

"No," he said. "I was locked in a cell all last night.

Christie looked around; Dukai was speaking to another government official and several guards standing nearby. "Do you have any idea where they are taking us?" she asked Felix.

He shook his head.

"We weren't even asked to bring any other clothing or supplies," Isabel said.

Christie didn't say what she was thinking, with a growing sense of panic: *Did David find out we were in custody and negotiate our release in exchange for turning himself in?* And then an even more frightening thought: Was it possible that the soldiers had not asked Isabel to pack for this trip because it was a trip none of them would ever return from?

Another vehicle pulled up: a Humvee painted in military camouflage.

Dukai turned to Christie and the others and said, "It is time for us to board. Please come." He motioned toward the steps of the plane.

"General," Christie said, "if we are being exchanged for my husband's surrender, I do not want to go. Please take Felix and his family and arrange for my son to go to his grandparents. I will stay here to be with my husband," she said.

His gaze hardened. "Senora Eller, I admire your courage. But if you want to see your husband alive and well, then please board the plane."

Isabel and Blanca climbed into the back two seats, Christie and Davy into the next two, and Dukai seated himself across from Felix. The door to the Humvee opened and a young man on crutches emerged, accompanied by two guards carrying AK-47's. His leg was bandaged and his face swollen. The two guards helped the young man climb into the seat in front of Dukai, then one guard buckled himself in by the door; the other seated himself in front of the wounded man—clearly, still guarding him, although the man on crutches didn't look as if he were in any condition to attempt an escape.

In the seat behind her, Christie heard Isabel begin to softly hum the hymn *Great Is Thy Faithfulness* again, as they had on the Coast Guard cutter. Christie turned in her seat and reached out to grip Isabel's hand. Together, they softly hummed the tune, neither of them knowing what was about to happen.

It was 12:45 p.m. when the plane started its engines.

The plane—an older DeHavilland DHC-6 Twin Otter with seating for twelve plus cargo that Dukai had managed to commandeer from an oil exploration company—taxied out to the west, circled at the end of the runway, and stopped.

The truth was, Dukai wasn't sure where they were headed either.

He took out his cell phone and dialed the number he'd been given. The voice on the other end said, "What is the call sign of your plane?"

Dukai asked the pilot, then relayed the information: "November four zero eight lima tango."

"Okay," came the voice again, "once the pilot has taken off, have him set his course heading at 135 degrees and tune his radio to 122.750. Once you're in the air, I will call your plane on that frequency with further instructions. Our call sign is Rendezvous One. Stay on a heading of 135 degrees until I call."

Dukai hung up and gave the information to the pilot. Then he sat thinking about what might happen next. The voice he had just heard on his cell phone was the same voice he had heard earlier that morning over the phone in his office.

The pilot, cleared by the tower, advanced the throttle of his turboprop engine, picking up speed down the runway toward the east. The plane ascended over the city of Caracas, then headed southeast over the Avila mountains. As the plane neared the Caribbean, Dukai heard the young boy say, "Look, Mommy, water! We're on our adventure!"

CHAPTER THIRTY-SEVEN

Hawkeye was piloting the plane, with Carlos as co-pilot. Both were trained to fly many different aircraft, but neither had ever before flown a BN Trislander, the triple-prop model they were in now. Hawkeye, however, had been able to convince the lease company that he was experienced with the craft. Manufactured in Britain, it was a workhorse of a plane, holding up to sixteen passengers and capable of landing on short runways. Before taxiing, Hawkeye had memorized its takeoff and stall speeds, gone through the checklist twice, and familiarized himself with all of the instrument readouts and controls.

The plans for this flight had been made earlier that morning when, after discussing his scheme with Hawkeye, Zach, and David, Carlos had phoned Venezuela to be patched into Dukai. Knowing that the conversation would be taped—and that Dukai's people would attempt to trace it with whatever level of telecommunications technology was at their disposal—Carlos got straight to the point when Dukai picked up the phone: "General Dukai, I have some information that I think will interest you about the recent assassination attempt on President Guzman," he said.

"Who is calling?" Dukai inquired.

"Who I am is not important. But what I have in my possession is extremely important to your investigation."

"I'm listening."

"I have concrete proof of who was behind the assassination attempt. I have tape recordings, videos, photos, and other conclusive evidence."

318   The Missionary

"And how did you acquire this evidence?"

"Again, General Dukai, this is not important. What is important is that I am willing to turn this evidence over to you for a specific exchange."

"Ah, so you are not just a concerned citizen of Venezuela who happens to have information, but we are negotiating for something, eh? I take it you want money," Dukai said.

"No, no money. I want the release of Senora Eller and her son, along with the wounded commando in your custody. I also want Felix Suturos and his family."

Dukai gave a scoffing laugh. "Why would I even consider releasing the commando? He tried to kill our president."

"The wounded commando is part of the deal."

"Senora Eller and her child are injured. They cannot be moved now."

"That is untrue," Carlos said. "You thought this trap would lure David Eller to turn himself in. In that you are mistaken. I have David Eller with me, and you will never see him. He is no longer in Venezuela."

Carlos heard what he thought was a sigh of relief from Dukai. "Then he is an international fugitive who will be hunted down and extradited."

Carlos was enjoying the conversational volley. "General, David Eller was a waterboy. A pigeon. He knows nothing. He was an overzealous and naive underling over his head in something he didn't understand. What I'm offering in exchange is solid information that takes you right to the top of this coup attempt—to those who made the decisions and held the purse strings. Certainly, General Dukai, you understand that if my evidence is solid, you can crack this case wide open for your government."

"What, exactly, do you have?" Dukai sounded more subdued.

"Video and tape recordings on which three key people on several occasions discuss the details of the assassination. I also have photographs of them meeting together. These are people whose names you will recognize immediately. Two of those names possess influence in your current government. Trust me—these three individuals will be of utmost interest to you and President Guzman."

"So—I take it that you were somehow involved in this plot as well?" Dukai asked.

"My involvement is not important. The men featured in the evidence I can give you will be prize enough."

"How do I know this is not a smoke screen…that Eller was not the brains behind this coup?"

"General Dukai, by now you have researched every aspect of Eller's life, and you know that he was a very small player. Does your government want this information in exchange for Senora Eller and the others, or not?"

"That is a decision for our President and his advisors. And you will have to give me something that will verify the authenticity of your offer so that I do not waste our President's time."

Carlos had been prepared for this. "I am willing to give you one of the names of the three principal people on whom I have concrete evidence. And I will tell you the motive for the assassination attempt," Carlos said.

There was a pause. "If you can provide one name capable of carrying out such an elaborate and complicated plot to assassinate the president, and a specific motive that makes sense, I will take your request to higher authorities," Dukai said.

This was the most crucial moment of the negotiation. Carlos paused, considered tone of voice, and then said, "The name is Tecero. Emilio Antonio Tecero. Do you recognize that name, General Dukai?"

Carlos could hear the pace of Dukai's breathing increase over the phone. "Of course I recognize that name."

"I think you can guess the motive. Guzman has been very hard on the drug cartel. It should be no secret that Tecero hates Guzman and has more than enough resources to pull this off."

"Tecero is Colombian. He is probably not in Venezuela. And if indeed it was Tecero's drug cartel behind the assassination attempt, then we could probably guess who the other conspirators were. His associates are well-known to us. Perhaps you do not have anything worth trading after all."

320   The Missionary

"Yes, General," Carlos said. "You could guess. But the other two persons whose names I will give you are Venezuelan citizens who have powerful influence and inside connections to your government. Guessing would not be enough. Their trials will be highly visible internationally. They will be able to afford the best lawyers and pay the highest bribes. You will need ironclad proof. And that is what I can provide. By convicting them, you will not only bring many to justice who were involved in the assassination plot, you will also deal a very serious blow to the drug cartel. Oh, yes. I have something worth trading."

"Your evidence is irrefutable?" Dukai asked.

"Absolutely irrefutable," Carlos replied.

"And why do you want the Suturos family as part of the exchange?"

"Because we know from news reports that you were detaining them for helping transport Senora Eller to Grenada. They are close friends of the Ellers who had nothing to do with the coup. We are concerned for their safety. It is part of the deal if you want this evidence," Carlos said.

The demand for the Suturos family's release had come from David, part of his negotiation for revealing where the briefcase full of money was hidden.

"How and when would we make this exchange?" Dukai asked.

"Today. You will need an airplane that can land and take off on short runways."

"I cannot find a plane for this purpose that quickly."

"Yes, you can. There are short-runway transports in your military as well as in private service. You have the power to commandeer anything you need. This exchange cannot wait. We must do it today," Carlos said. "I need to hear from you within ninety minutes if this is a go. Call me at 58-416-555-8457. If you do not call within ninety minutes to confirm, the deal is off."

"How do I know this is not a trap?"

"You don't. You may bring your own armed guards—only two. Believe me, if you try to set a trap of your own by bringing your military, the documents I have will be destroyed before you can recover them, and you will have nothing. Bring only one plane and land it where we tell you. One plane only, or there will be no exchange. And it must be you who comes, no one else."

"And you too will have armed guards where we meet?" Dukai asked.

"Of course," Carlos said. "A balance of power. But you and I will meet alone between our two camps when you land. You can examine a sample of the documents I have and decide. If you do not think they are worthy of the exchange, then get back on your plane and leave. I expect you to be ready to take off by one p.m. today. That gives you four hours to find the plane and gather the passengers."

"But there are formalities that must be—"

"General, this offer is good for today only. If I do not hear from you in ninety minutes, the deal is off. You know that eventually you must release Senora Eller anyway. Her embassy is watching closely."

"But we do not have to ever release the prisoner who tried to kill our president."

"Then that lowly prisoner, a foot soldier nowhere near the top of this operation, will be all you have to prosecute."

Now, Dukai was seated on the Twin Otter next to Christie Eller, his ticket to becoming a hero in the eyes of his country. The call with further directions should be coming any minute. Actually, Dukai felt that his breathing had barely returned to normal after the madhouse of activity this morning that had followed the fateful call.

After Dukai had hung up, he'd telephoned Guzman's office, and twenty minutes later, he was sitting with the still-bandaged president.

Holding his breath, Dukai had played back for Guzman the tape of his conversation with the dealmaker. Guzman's face flushed with anger as he listened to the voice describe Tecero's culpability. Before the tape was finished, Dukai could see from the expression on Guzman's face that he would agree to the deal. As paranoid as he had become, Guzman desperately wanted the information about who *in his own government* would have been so disloyal as to cooperate with the drug lords against him.

Without hesitation, Guzman agreed. Dukai was elated. This would salvage everything. Only seventy minutes had elapsed when he dialed the number he had been given to confirm that Guzman had approved the deal.

Dukai not only made arrangements for the plane in short order, he also made, per Guzman's instructions, a number of quick precautions against a double-cross. Dukai and his guests would be accompanied by military surveillance aircraft and followed not far behind by military transport and attack helicopters. But Dukai was confident that he would not need them.

While Dukai still did not know where they would be landing, he was certain they would not be landing in Venezuela. He would wait and see—keep playing the cards as they were dealt. So far, the plan was evolving perfectly.

The plane's radio crackled, and the pilot picked up his mike.

"November four zero eight lima tango," Carlos said, "this is Rendezvous One, do you read me? Over." He was sitting in the co-pilot's seat of the BN Trislander at an altitude of thirteen thousand feet.

"Rendezvous one, november four zero eight lima tango. We read you loud and clear. Over."

"When you are within twenty-five miles of Trinidad-Tobago, take a heading of 155 degrees and maintain heading until we call you again, over."

"Roger, 155 degrees. Rendezvous one, we have a maximum range of eleven hundred eighty-seven nautical miles, over."

"Roger, range of eleven hundred eighty-seven. We have noted that. You will be landing inside your limit. Rendezvous one out."

Carlos had made sure that they left Grenada early enough to land at the rendezvous airstrip well in advance of Dukai, but they were still some distance from there. The plan was to have Zach and Hawkeye stationed in the jungle vegetation, well hidden from view, on opposite sides of the runway with enough fire power to destroy a small army and provide cover for escape into the jungle should anything go wrong.

When the return call from Dukai had come in that morning, confirming that the exchange was on, Carlos had turned to David, Hawkeye, and Zach sitting in the kitchen and said, "We have a deal."

David had sagged with relief. His eyes had misted, and Carlos had looked away.

"Hawkeye," he'd said, "do you remember that remote landing strip in Guyana we used in a Peruvian drug bust several years ago, not far from the Venezuelan border?"

"How could I forget?" Hawkeye said.

David, now sitting midway back in the BN Trislander, had insisted on coming along. Carlos had tried to persuade him to stay in Grenada, but David had said, "This is my family. I'm going with you," in a tone that even Carlos had been able to see was not open to further discussion.

At 2:40 p.m., fifteen minutes before they expected to land, Carlos radioed Dukai's plane again. "November four zero eight lima tango, this is Rendezvous One. The landing site coordinates are north seven four six decimal zero, west five nine five zero decimal zero. Approach the airstrip from the west, landing to the east. You have a thirty-five-hundred-foot dirt runway."

"Roger, Rendezvous One, landing site north seven four six decimal zero, west five nine five zero decimal zero. Thirty-five-hundred-foot runway."

"Roger. Call us again when you are fifteen minutes out. Rendezvous One out."

Hawkeye buzzed the airstrip once, making sure it looked okay to land. Then in a series of three slow, expanding circles, they surveyed the surrounding jungle for signs of people or activity. About five miles out was a small village, but there was no activity near the airstrip.

After landing—about forty-five minutes ahead of Dukai, they figured—they taxied the plane back to the west end of the runway so that when Dukai landed, his plane would be at the opposite end. As they deplaned, Hawkeye pointed toward the edge of the runway and said, "Look—the leftovers of that drug plane we torched." Some parts had been dragged away, but there was the rusted engine and some of the frame, with jungle fauna growing up around it. The runway was still reasonably intact, some weeds having crept through the well-hardened dirt airstrip.

After doing a ground check of the area to make sure there were no surprises, Zach hunkered down, well camouflaged, in a thick part of the jungle not fifty yards off the runway, down near the far end where Dukai's pilots would be told to stop. His weaponry included an M249 SAW (squad automatic weapon), a massive machine gun with a 200-round capacity that could mow down an entire platoon in seconds, an M-4 carbine light assault rifle with an attached M203 grenade launcher, and a 9mm Glock and Heckler pistol. They also had their earplug radios so they could talk to each other and Carlos.

Hawkeye positioned himself midway between the two ends of the airstrip, hidden about seventy-five yards off the opposite side of the runway from Zach. Lying on his belly, under deep cover, he could not be seen, but had a clear view of this portion of the runway. He was armed with the same weapons as Zach.

"Do not cross the border into Guyanan airspace," came Dukai's voice over the aircraft's radio. "Circle and hold just inside the Venezuelan border until and unless you hear otherwise from me."

Torres felt the rage building within him to the bursting point. They were still within sight of the slow-moving Twin Otter carrying Dukai and the young commando, Torres's prize prisoner, along with the others whom Torres was itching to interrogate. He had been forced to sit for far too long while Dukai's mindless soldiers in this and three other aircraft shadowed the Otter; he was not about to lose sight of Dukai's plane now. It was his duty to bring the assassins to justice. And surely—surely!—by following Dukai's plane, he would find even more of those who had been involved in the plot to assassinate his beloved president. Every instinct Torres possessed told him so.

"Continue to follow that plane!" Torres shouted.

The pilot turned to look at Torres, confused. "But General Dukai just gave us orders not to—"

"I am overriding Dukai's orders! Follow that plane!" he shouted again.

Torres felt someone grasp him from behind. He lashed out, landing a blow or two, but Dukai's soldiers were strong and well trained, and within seconds a restraining belt had been thrown around Torres's waist and he was jerked back into his seat. Despite Torres's spirited resistance, shackles were soon in place on his ankles and he was handcuffed to his seat.

"I command you to remove these restraints!" he screamed.

One of the soldiers who had wrestled him back into his seat stood at attention, a trickle of blood escaping from a split lip, and said, "By order of General Dukai, I am placing you under military arrest for your attempt to disobey a direct order from your commanding officer, and to incite mutiny by inducing others to disobey that order."

Torres screamed in frustration and fought the restraints. Dukai was getting away! He twisted in his seat to see out the nearest window; the Twin Otter, now just a tiny image, was rapidly disappearing over the jungle.

Where were his men? He had specifically commanded Vasquez to make sure troops loyal to him were on each of the planes. Why were they not here, on this one? And why were his men not taking over the other planes to follow Dukai into Guyana? Torres watched in growing despair as the other three planes fell into formation with the one on which he rode and began to circle short of the border.

Torres was not used to failure, but he had surely failed this time.

In an hour or two, this aircraft would land. Torres was under arrest, and Dukai would use this opportunity to get rid of the thorn in his side that Torres had insisted on becoming. Torres could fight the charges, of course, but because he had failed to follow Dukai's plane to its destination, he had no proof of what he suspected—only his gut feeling. It would be Dukai against Torres—and the advantage now was definitely with Dukai. If Dukai won, Torres would face, at best, a year or two behind bars and then a dishonorable discharge and a life apart from the military—in Torres's view, not a life worth living.

And at worst...

For the first time in memory, Torres felt not just anger but real fear.

CHAPTER THIRTY-EIGHT

It took twenty minutes to set everything up. By the time they were finished, it was hot and muggy in the BN Trislander, even with the doors cracked open. Carlos was seated in the pilot's seat, with David still buckled down three rows behind him.

Carlos felt they had covered the bases as best they could, especially since the guards with Dukai would have no idea how many men Carlos would have hiding in the jungle surrounding the airstrip.

They'd been sitting for no longer than five minutes when the radio came alive. "Rendezvous one, this is four zero eight lima tango. Our ETA is approximately twelve minutes. Over."

"Four zero eight lima tango, call when you have the airstrip in sight. Out."

Carlos clicked on his handheld radio to communicate with Zach and Hawkeye. "We have contact. ETA is about twelve minutes," he said. "Remember, no hostile action unless something goes bad."

"Affirmative," Hawkeye said.

"Aw, shucks," Zach said.

Five minutes later. "Rendezvous one, this is four zero eight lima tango. We have the airstrip in sight."

"Okay, four zero eight lima tango. Remember to land west to east. When you land, taxi to the east end of the runway and stop there. Out."

Within a minute, they could hear the plane approaching. It flew once low over the airstrip, Pratt & Whitney turboprop engines growling like a dozen Mack trucks, then banked out to the west to make its approach. The Twin Otter swooped over the jungle and descended

328 The Missionary

sharply. Dust flew everywhere as the plane touched the dirt airstrip with full flaps down. Turning at the far end of the runway opposite Carlos's plane, General Dukai's plane stopped and powered down.

"Four zero eight lima tango, your instructions are as follows. General Dukai is to exit the plane alone and slowly walk about four hundred meters toward us to a mid-point in the runway, equidistant between the two planes. General Dukai, you will need to bring your handheld radio to communicate with your guards. I will meet you in the middle of the runway, alone, with the materials I have. Again, I repeat: come alone. Please have Senora Eller, her son, the Suturos family, and the wounded commando exit the plane and stand in front of it where I can see them, to verify that they are all on board."

Carlos watched through his field glasses as, some twenty-five hundred feet away, General Dukai exited his plane. The others followed, with one of the guards assisting Danny. The guard stayed by the plane as Dukai began walking down the center of the airstrip alone.

Carlos turned; David was straining to see the people at the other end of the runway. "David, don't get out. Stay in your seat. We don't want Dukai to see you. Our goal is to get your family back, but a foolish action on your part now could jeopardize all of that—and their lives. So play this just like we discussed. Are we agreed?"

David nodded.

Carlos stood, picked up an envelope containing a sample of the evidence implicating the drug cartel, and stepped out of the plane. He walked toward the center of the airstrip, careful not to look directly at the areas where Zach and Hawkeye were hidden, but scanning the entire area nevertheless, always alert for something out of place, something not right, and watching particularly the area around Dukai's plane.

When he was within about one hundred feet of where Dukai stood, he clicked off his radio mike.

Dukai's guards were no doubt watching the transaction carefully with high-powered lenses, so Carlos was careful to keep a poker face. When he was within ten feet, he said, "General, turn off your radio."

Dukai complied.

Carlos stopped when he and Dukai were three feet apart.

David couldn't stand it; he felt as if his skin was crawling with lice. His mind tortured him with thoughts of all that could go wrong still: one overanxious Venezuelan soldier could misinterpret some minor gesture of Carlos's and open fire, and Zach would spray the entire runway, including the area where Christie and Davy and the Suturoses stood, with machine-gun fire. Venezuelan military helicopters could suddenly descend. Carlos—or Hawkeye—or Zach—could turn out to be a traitor.

So many things could go wrong. And there was only one right outcome: David's wife and child and their friends the Suturoses could get on this plane and they could all go back to Grenada. One right outcome, so many wrong and deadly ones. Did that mean that the odds were against them?

He couldn't sit still. He'd unbuckled his seatbelt as soon as Carlos had left the plane, unable to stand being constrained when so much was at stake. He had carefully and slowly maneuvered himself into a good view of the runway and had watched as Christie and Davy had exited the plane a half-mile away and stood in front of it. There they were. So close. *So close* to having his heart's desire back again.

And what would he do with them if he got them back?

The list of resolutions and good intentions swirled through his brain. He meant them all. And he knew that he'd be lucky to adhere to ten percent of them. He felt like someone in need of a twelve-step program. He was powerless against his own stupidity.

How would he put things back together with Christie again? They would need help. He'd be willing to go to a marriage counselor. Willing? No, he'd insist on it. There was no way he'd be able to—

Listen to him. He'd insist on it? No. He'd insist on nothing in their marriage ever again. He'd suggest it to Christie, and they would discuss it, and he would *listen* to her, and together they would decide.

Yes. That's how it would go.

Or not.

His head sank into his hands. Why was he always only able to see how foolish and insensitive he was being *after* the fact?

"General, it is good to see you again," Carlos said. "Very creative of you to think of doing the TV broadcast, sending me the signal."

With his back to his plane, Dukai smiled. "Well, if Eller wasn't watching the broadcast, I supposed you would be, Carlos. And your plan of meeting here on a remote airstrip in Guyana is brilliant. I'll now have a way to prosecute the drug lords, and I'll be off the hook with regard to the investigation."

Carlos offered the envelope. "Here, General, open it and begin to examine the contents. These are all things you've seen before, of course."

Dukai opened the envelope, slowing removing and examining the documents.

"You should have seen Guzman's face when I played the tape of our phone conversation," Dukai said. "Without hesitation, he bought into your proposal. He was nearly salivating at the thought of concrete evidence against Tecero, as well as others inside Venezuela. He insisted that some Air Force assets follow us here, but I have ordered them not to cross the border into Guyana unless I call for them, so no need to worry."

"I must offer my apologies that we botched the assassination attempt," Carlos said. "We thought the plan was perfect. Who could have predicted that Guzman's granddaughter would mess it up."

Dukai continued to sift through the evidence. "And I am sorry that your team of commandos lost a man. Achieving agreement to release the young commando who survived was the most difficult part of this exchange. I thought I would have to phone you back to say he could not be part of the deal. But Guzman relented when I convinced him that the men we would be able to prosecute would be much more important than the young commando. Our official story will be that he died. Tell the commando leader that, unfortunately, and against my wishes, his man has been badly tortured by General Torres and may need rehabilitation. It's a miracle, frankly, that the torture didn't kill him."

Carlos nodded. "Torres is a dangerous man. A maniac."

"He is on one of the military aircraft in my escort now," Dukai said.

Carlos felt his blood chill. "He is what?"

"Do not worry. He was under the impression that each of the military aircraft in our covert escort had some of his handpicked men on it, but in actuality the rest of his men were detained at the base and are being held under guard. Except for Torres himself, all of the men on those planes are loyal to me. As expected, Torres attempted to supersede my orders and force the planes to land here, but in the first place, those jets require a longer runway. And in the second, those flights are under not just my orders but Guzman's. Torres will face charges when he lands."

Dukai returned the material to the envelope and looked up at Carlos. "My greatest regret in all of this is, I am sure, the same as yours: that Guzman was not removed. My country will continue to suffer under his rule. It was a well-thought-out plan. I doubt there will be another opportunity like it. But at least we can get half the job done by prosecuting Rafael Lopez and Julio DiMartino. And if Tecero ever enters my country again, I will try to take him down too." He smiled again. "Guzman is even considering a military incursion into Colombia to try to extract Tecero. That would be…interesting."

"Tell me, General. What would you have done with Eller if he had turned himself in after your evening news TV plea?"

"Eller was the only lead I could publicly track without blowing my cover. Had I tried to implicate Lopez and DiMartino, it would have raised suspicion about how I got this information and why I waited to divulge it. I was under extreme pressure to arrest someone. The young commando identified Eller, and I was obligated to act."

Dukai paused, looking off into the jungle, then added, "Frankly, if I'd found him, he would have been tried and convicted. But he would

332   The Missionary

have given me the opportunity to indict Lopez and DiMartino as well. I would have said that, in addition to the money, Eller was carrying the evidence against them in his briefcase. He would have been the sacrificial lamb."

Carlos nodded. "Thank God it didn't come to that."

"Yes. Thank God."

"How will this affect your position in the military?"

"Guzman will see this as a satisfactory resolution. He'll probably give me a promotion. The rest of the evidence is nearby?"

"In the notorious briefcase, hidden in the undergrowth beside the runway about twenty yards behind me. I'll hand it over when the hostages reach us. The photos and video recordings of the last meeting are most damning," Carlos said.

Dukai closed the envelope and placed it under his arm. "And you, Carlos?" Dukai asked. "Where will you go now?"

"This is my last assignment, General."

Dukai smiled again. "I have heard this before from people in our profession. Carlos, I have known you now for five years and have seen how effective you are. The people of the world who love democracy and freedom need men like you to help in secret ways."

"Thank you for the vote of confidence, General. But I have been responsible for the deaths of many people," Carlos said. "It's time to stop."

"I wish you luck in finding your next life."

"General, when you finally retire, look me up and we'll talk about this adventure again. I wish you every success in somehow bringing democracy back to Venezuela."

"I am assuming none of the others with you here know anything about my involvement?" Dukai asked.

"As it has been for five years, your secret stays with me and Leprechaun, General."

"It's time to make the exchange," he said. "Please let your guards know that one of my men will emerge from the jungle to escort Senora Eller and the others."

Dukai clicked his radio back on. "Instruct the prisoners to prepare to move," he said. "Someone will appear from the jungle near you to accompany the prisoners. Hold your fire."

Zach emerged from his hiding place with his M4 held at the ready across his chest and his M249 strapped to his back. Eyeing the Venezuelan guards warily—they had fanned out between him and the plane, and regarded him with suspicion and hostility—he slowly walked toward the six hostages standing on the runway.

Danny was leaning on his crutches as Zach approached. "Never thought I'd see you again, buddy," Zach said.

"Me either," Danny said, trying to smile, but the smile didn't make it past the corners of his lips. His pain was evident everywhere else on his face. He appeared to have aged ten years.

"Walk toward the middle of the runway, Mrs. Eller," Zach said. Her son clung to her leg and peered fearfully around her at Zach. "Go slowly so we can keep together." He didn't have to tell her twice; she picked up her son and began to move at once. The Suturos family followed closely, the little girl in her father's arms. Danny hobbled behind, keeping up as best he could with his crutches. Zach, at the back of the pack, walked backward behind the group, watching the guards around the Venezuelan plane.

Somewhere behind him, Zach knew, Hawkeye had his scoped assault weapon trained on Dukai.

Strangely enough, it was not David on whom Christie's thoughts were fixed as she started down the weedy runway, or even the armed Venezuelan soldiers behind her, or General Dukai.

It was her parents.

334   The Missionary

She imagined them walking beside her in the hot South American afternoon, in this place they would in all likelihood never have come to if they'd lived, would never have dreamed of. She imagined their hands on her shoulders, one on each side; she imagined their gazes of love at her son, their only grandchild; she imagined their quiet confidence, the self-confidence of self-reliant people who believed they had the ability to handle whatever surprises life threw at them.

And David—could he, too, handle whatever life threw at him?

One thing she knew: Like her father, David would throw himself into the fire, into the path of the lion that threatened his wife and child.

No, lack of courage was not David's problem. His problem was that he offered himself wholesale for anyone who had needs, and as often as not, without counting the cost first.

But he was David. He was the man she'd married, the man she loved.

Davy clung to her neck; she shifted his weight in her tired arms. She heard him sucking his thumb, something he'd given up many months ago.

The question was: Where now? As her parents' daughter. As God's child. As Davy's mother. Could she allow her destiny, and the welfare of her son, to be decided by a man as impetuous as David? True—the fight he fought was the good fight. But he threw himself into it like a kamikaze pilot. Like Don Quixote. Like…

Like…

Like Christie herself had at the riot a few days before, jumping out of the van just when David was trying to protect her, because she heard the sound of people in need. Just as David heard the sounds of people in need every night he drove the streets of Caracas.

Yes. In ways, they were two of a kind. If David's blunder seemed bigger, perhaps it was only because Christie hadn't gotten either of them killed with her heroics during the riot that day.

Perhaps this was where trust in God came in. Life, after all, was bigger than any of us except him. In the end, life had thrown even Christie's parents a complication they hadn't been able to handle.

Or had it? She thought again, as she had so many times, of her father carrying her to safety, of the handprint of wholeness he'd left on her thigh. She was marked for life by his love for her. He had not hesitated in offering his life for hers. Or she would not be in this place on this strange day.

A sudden jolt of realization, so profound and powerful she stopped in her tracks on the packed-dirt runway.

She replayed the scene in her mind: the man carrying Christie the little girl to safety, Christie with clothes in flames, Christie with her mouth open in pain so all-consuming that no sound came from her damaged throat, Christie with skin exposed, red, blistered.

And the man carrying her, the man giving his life for hers, in her mind's eye bore not the face of the laughing man in the photograph—but David's face.

She heard a sound, and the sound was her own groaning. She glanced back at Isabel, who was looking at her in concern. Christie smiled weakly to reassure her friend, the expression feeling unnatural and tight on her face, then looked forward again.

When the group had moved halfway to Carlos and Dukai, Carlos retrieved the briefcase, handed it to Dukai, and said, with his radio on, "You can start walking back to your plane now, General Dukai. Wait for my instructions before moving your aircraft."

Dukai stared into the eyes of Carlos for a few more seconds, then gave a brief nod, turned, and headed back toward his plane. He saw Hawkeye stand, still partially concealed in jungle cover, and watch.

As he approached the small group of prisoners moving slowly down the runway, Dukai made eye contact with Christie, and he remembered her anxiety in the interrogation room the night before. He wished he could erase that from her memory, and that of her son, but it could not have been helped.

Her eyes did not hold that same anxiety now. They seemed tired but resolute.

He smiled. "Senora Eller, I am glad things have worked out for you to be reunited with your husband. Goodbye," he said, and fingered the bill of his cap.

"Goodbye, General Dukai," she said, her voice quiet but unafraid. The others said nothing and avoided eye contact with him. Even the young commando looked at the ground and seemed to shrink as he hobbled past on his crutches.

Perhaps Carlos had the right idea. Perhaps it was time to think of getting out of the game.

Hawkeye waited until Zach and the group of hostages pulled even with him, then, keeping his eyes on the Venezuelan soldiers at the far end of the runway, he moved onto the runway and joined Zach. At first he walked backwards, as Zach was, but when they reached Carlos, he turned and said, "Quickly—everyone hurry to the plane!" He scooped an arm around Danny's waist and took one of the crutches as Danny reached his arm over Hawkeye's shoulder. "Great to see you again, kid," Hawkeye said, surprised at the catch in his own voice.

Danny looked at him and nodded but didn't speak, and Hawkeye noticed his rapid breathing, the wince on his face with every step, and knew that Danny was in great pain. *What had they done to him? Those ...* Hawkeye fought the urge to turn around right now and make them pay, but this wasn't the time. A time for every purpose under heaven, and right now was a time for rescue and rehabilitation.

Maybe later, a time for revenge.

"We aren't home free till we reach Grenada," Carlos said. "Move as quickly as you can, before they change their minds."

David tried unsuccessfully to still his own trembling—and to decide what to say, how to act. Apologize? Ask for forgiveness? But how do you ask forgiveness for something so unforgivable? Promise to do better in the future? Yes, maybe—that was one promise he would rather kill himself than break. He *had* to do better.

If David had any reason for hope, it was this: Somehow, by the grace of God, he was still alive. He tried to ignore the pain in his wounded shoulder. He couldn't. It was sharp and insistent and a constant reminder that he was indeed still living. The realization had come to him on the plane: *This pain is from a bullet. I've been shot. I, David Eller, missionary, have been shot with a gun. By a policeman. As I was stealing his car. I've been abducted in the middle of the night, drugged, and pounded in the face by a paid assassin. I've been the most hunted man in Venezuela for participating in a plot to murder the president. And somehow, in God's providence, I have cheated death.*

After this, how could life possibly return to normal even if I wanted it to?

And he didn't want it to. The old David Eller had been wrong about so many things. He didn't want to be wrong about those things ever again. No one should go through something this painful without learning all there is to learn from it.

He stood and moved to the door.

Christie, with Davy in her arms, was in the lead. The expression on her face was an odd combination of joy, fear, and determination, and to David she'd never looked more beautiful. Even her scars added character and grace.

She looked up and saw him, and her expression softened into something David had feared he'd never again see—relief and love. She ran the last few steps, and David, despite Carlos's repeated cautions, stepped out of the plane to meet her. As she threw herself into his arms, Davy lifted his head from her shoulder, looked at David, and with the innocent and unmixed joy of a child, shouted, "Daddy, it's you!" David felt the little arm go around his neck.

And then the arms were pulled away. Christie pushed herself back from him, looked at him with wet eyes full of anger and hurt, and hit him in the chest with her small fist. Hard.

"Ow," David said, surprised.

She embraced him again, crushing her face against his good shoulder, and he felt the dampness as her tears flowed.

David pulled his wife and son closer, tighter.

He had his family in his arms again. His job now was to keep them there.

That might prove to be the hardest task of all.

Printed in the United States
by Baker & Taylor Publisher Services